RAPTOR

B. A. BOSTICK

ENCHANTED INDIE PRESS

by

b. a. bostick

Urban Fantasy Noir
Book One of the Raptor Trilogy

PUBLISHER'S NOTE

All rights reserved under International and American Copyright Conventions. Published in the United States of America by Enchanted Indie Press. No part of these pages, either text or image may be used for any purpose other than personal use. Therefore, reproduction, modification, storage in a retrieval system or retransmission, in any form or by any means, electronic, mechanical or otherwise, for reasons other than personal use, is strictly prohibited without prior written permission.

This is a work of fiction. Names, characters, places and incidents are either the product of the author's imagination, or are used fictitiously. Any resemblance to actual persons, living or dead, business establishments, events, or locales is entirely coincidental.

Copyright © 2017 B. A. Bostick
Claw Image: by permission granted from
The Ohio History Connection
eBook Cover Design: Carol Terry
**eBook Conversion, Print Edition
Formatting and Cover Design:**
Tosh McIntosh

Digital Edition (v1.9.1)
ISBN-13: 978-1-938749-35-3
ISBN-10: 1-938749-35-9

Paperback Edition (v1.9.1)
ISBN-13: 978-1-938749-34-6
ISBN-10: 1-938749-34-0

ENCHANTED INDIE PRESS

DEDICATION

I would like to dedicate this novel to Joss Whedon. We have never met but he taught me everything I needed to know about writing a fantasy novel. Thank you Joss.

P.S. If my mother hadn't thrown out all my hundreds of original Marvel comic books the minute I left home for college I would currently be rich, bored and useless and never have written this book. Thanks, Mom.

IMAGINATION IS THE ONLY WEAPON IN THE WAR AGAINST REALITY

— Lewis Carroll

RAPTOR

*Demons only tell the truth when it will
cause more trouble than lying.*

PART I

- 1 -

Ariel had no fear of heights, but she'd never developed a fondness for crumbling masonry, broken glass and pigeon poop. To top it off, a wicked night wind was trying its best to peel her off the decorative stones ledge of the old building's top floor and smash her to the pavement nine stories below.

Built over one hundred and forty years ago, the building was designated an historic landmark. That meant the façade could not be altered unless public safety was involved. The brick building's old fashioned, double hung windows were long and wide with low sills and unreinforced glass. Their size maximized the view of the lake, and at night, the lights of the surrounding buildings were spectacular.

The view wasn't why she was here.

A row of office windows were only ten feet from where she'd landed, but they seemed miles away. Another gust of wind whipped a tangled mass of dark hair into her face. An impatient toss of her head sent the errant strands back over her shoulder. She thought briefly about the elastic band she kept in her coat pocket for occasions like this but searching for it meant letting go of the wall and letting go of the wall was not the best choice under the circumstances.

Her target, Nikolai Tesslovich, had been in his office for several hours. Ariel had watched him enter the building at nine o'clock that evening, and three of the attorney's most infamous clients had come and gone between then and midnight. These were people who preferred to conduct their business late in the evening rather than be seen going into the building in the light of day. Ariel assumed the lawyer was now alone, sitting at his desk, finishing his notes and adding up the enormous fees he would bill for every ten minutes of his valuable time.

A direct assault was not the strategy Ariel wanted to use, but Tesslovich had proved a hard man to get to. He was never alone even in his own house, and she was tired of following him and his bodyguards around waiting for the ideal opportunity to present itself.

What she'd finally decided to do was high risk, savage and messy, and best accomplished without witnesses. She took a deep breath.

Time to suck it up and get it over with.

Ariel looked down at her feet. She'd left them bare for better balance on the shallow ledge and, just as she'd predicted, she was now standing in a mound of fresh pigeon poop. Disgusting.

She began to inch toward the nearest window. Unfortunately, decorative limestone wasn't meant to survive over a hundred years in the wind and weather of an industrial city. Small cracks were forming, and she could feel pieces of it chipping off as her toes gripped and released the front edge of the stone.

At last, her fingers slid around the trim surrounding the first window. She hoped, unlike the ledge, it hadn't become too fragile with age to support her grip.

A quick peek through the window showed Tesslovich sitting

behind a massive, antique, desk making notes on a yellow legal pad. No one else seemed to be in the room.

She knew the lawyer might be alone right now, but his driver and bodyguard were sure to be nearby. There would be no time for a protracted fight, or loud noises that would attract attention.

Speed and surprise were her best options.

Ariel dug her fingernails into the soft wood of the old window frame, took a deep breath, pivoted in a tight arc and burst through the glass.

Instantly on her feet, she threw her arms wide letting the gravity knives strapped to her forearms slide beyond the cuffs of her long black coat and click into place.

Tesslovich reacted faster than she expected. He was already struggling to his feet and reaching into his coat as she leapt over his desk and hit him square in the chest with both feet. The sharp talons on her toes dug effortlessly through his expensive silk jacket and linen shirt into the soft flesh beneath. Her weight pushed him back into his chair. The momentum tipped it over onto its back with her firmly on top.

Tesslovich's hand was still pulling at the grip of his gun seconds after she'd slashed a blade backhanded across his throat, neatly separating his head from his body. Gouts of arterial spray began to pulse steaming green liquid onto the walls and floor.

At a sound from behind her Ariel spun around. She raised the blade in her right hand just in time to deflect the flight of a black steel throwing knife, then bat away another with the blood encrusted blade in her left hand. She ducked a third which sailed harmlessly over her head and buried itself in the wall.

The small, muscular attacker, who seemed to have appeared from nowhere, paused to give her a stare of venomous hostility, all-the-more incongruous coming from someone barely five feet tall dressed in a garish yellow-and-black, pinstriped suit and purple shirt.

Behind the little man, watching wide-eyed from a corner of the room, was a bruised and bloody man in a rumpled sports coat and jeans, gagged and bound to a chair with duct tape.

"What do you think you're doing?" Ariel asked the pinstriped man. "Get your tiny ass out of my way, or I'll kick it into next week."

"You will die in great pain for what you've done," the little man hissed. He had a foreign accent she couldn't quite place. He smiled showing a mouthful of twisted, brown teeth. A metal wand slid out of one coat sleeve into his hand. He popped a brief crackle of blue light off the end.

Shit!

Going up against a Taser with a steel blade was suicide. Time for Plan B.

Ariel retracted one knife back up her sleeve; scooped up Tesslovich's half-drawn weapon and shot pin-stripe twice in the chest. The surprising force of the bullets blew the small man out the smashed window.

"Wow." She hefted the gun. "Demon loads." She dropped it into the pocket of her coat. A girl in her profession couldn't have too many weapons.

Outside the office door, a commotion had started; fists pounding, loud voices demanding information. It wouldn't be long before someone smashed the door in.

Ariel turned toward the duct taped man in the corner. "And what about you, sparky?"

The man had duct tape over his mouth so, duh, his answer was unintelligible.

The blood and bruises on the man's face were enough to predict what would happen once Tesslovich's bodyguards got into the office. It was a rule of her profession to never let bystanders see her doing what she'd just done, but in all conscience, she couldn't leave him behind.

Ariel vaulted the desk and slit the cocoon of tape around the prisoner's chest with two quick, strokes of her knife. Wrists and ankles were next. A flick of her wrist and the weapon disappeared up her sleeve. She grabbed the man under his arms, dragged him over to the sill of the broken window and heaved them both into the cold night air just as the office door crashed open.

- 2 -

Two hours ago, when Nicolai Tesslovich's mutant circus freak had duct taped him to a chair, Frank Bishop decided this might be the worst night of his life. As he was falling through the air, toward the street below, he decided it might be the last. His 'rescuer' held him from behind, her arms wrapped around his chest, legs locked firmly around his hips. He could feel her strained breathing against his neck, and the muscles of her chest flexing in and out as they plunged toward the ground.

Suddenly, as if some critical point had been reached, they started to rise instead of fall. The rhythm of their ascent had become a successful fight against gravity. As the screaming buzz in Bishop's head started to subside, he thought he could hear the swish of wings.

He opened his eyes which had been screwed tightly shut since he'd exited the window. Big mistake. There was still nothing under them, but air and it was a long way down.

"Don't struggle," a voice hissed in his ear. "I might drop you, and for God's sake, shut up!"

Bishop shut his eyes again and tried to bring the volume of his terror down to a whimper. Screaming through duct tape hadn't been very easy anyway. He concentrated instead on trying to hold onto his rescuer as best he could from his face-forward position. This mostly consisted of hugging her arms more tightly to his chest and willing himself into rigidity.

That proved to be a mistake. Within a few moments, the legs around his hips unlocked and he was dropped feet first onto a hard-uneven surface. He immediately fell over on his face like a ten pin. The surface smelled of dirt and tar and was imbedded with little pieces of stone that were poking sharp points into his already battered cheek and jaw.

Roof, he thought numbly, feeling around with his hands before opening his eyes. He rolled over, not sure what to expect. A young woman sat on her haunches next to him, arms balanced on her thighs, a black coat pooling around her bare feet. Her dark hair had fallen forward obscuring much of her face, but her eyes weren't exactly friendly. She reached out one sharply pointed finger nail and ripped the tape away from Bishop's lips. The cuts, caused by a few well-placed punches to the mouth in Tesslovich's office, opened up and began to bleed.

As the words blurted out of his mouth, Bishop knew that he was asking the three dumbest questions in the English language. He just couldn't stop himself.

"What?" He babbled. "Who? How?"

"Just what I was going to ask you," the woman said.

"We were flying!"

"I was flying," she corrected. "You were screaming."

Bishop sat up, still slightly dizzy. "I hate flying." He started pulling left over strips of sticky duct tape off his coat and pant legs, throwing them onto the roof. "The last time someone made me fly I ended up in Iraq."

"What were you were doing taped to a chair in Nicolai Tesslovich's office in the middle of the night?" Ariel asked. "Did you forget to pay your bill?"

"I'm a PI," Bishop fumbled in his jacket for his ID. He held it out.

"See? Frank Bishop. Licensed Private Detective. I have a client whose six-year-old daughter was abducted from a park three days ago. No ransom demand. The police haven't been much help. I said I'd look into it."

"At Tesslovich's office?"

"Rumor has it he's been involved in supplying kids from unknown sources for illegal adoptions. I thought I'd push him a bit. When he got out of his limo in the parking garage I asked if I could speak to him about my client. The mutant hit me with a Taser and they dragged me upstairs in the freight elevator. I think you saw where that got me."

Bishop held up a hand. "Not that I'm not grateful for the rescue," he said, "but now that Tesslovich is dead, I've lost my only lead. Plus, I seem to be stuck on a roof with a homicidal super-pigeon. What the hell are you, lady?"

Ariel got to her feet. "I'm a Raptor."

"A what?"

"A Raptor," Mr. Detective. "It's a bird of prey."

"So, you mean you're some kind of superhero?"

"No," she lied. "I'm special ops. If I tell you more, I'll have to kill you. Etcetera." She flexed a hand, extending wicked looking talons from the ends of her fingers, then she folded them back in. "I took a really big chance saving your life Mr. Bishop and I'd hate to see that come back on you."

"Yeah, right." Bishop wasn't totally unfamiliar with federal spooks and their threats. "I still don't understand why you killed Tesslovich."

"Orders."

"Seriously?"

Ariel sighed. "Maybe you noticed he wasn't exactly human?"

"I noticed he was a total asshole, but I guess that would explain the green blood."

"Demons don't bleed red, Ariel explained. "Cut them it's all green, blue or yellow, sometimes black, but never red."

"Well, my blood's red," Bishop wiped his bleeding lip with the back of his hand. "What color's yours?"

Ariel drew a talon across the palm of one hand and held it up for Bishop's inspection. A thin line of red welled up. She wiped it off on her jeans.

"Strangely," Bishop doesn't make me feel the least bit better."

- 3 -

Ariel paced while Bishop pulled himself together. Now that her adrenaline had dropped to near normal, she needed to take a serious look at her situation. She'd impulsively saved a quasi-innocent bystander from being tortured and killed by a demon. She'd lied about the whole special ops/technology thing, but the guy still knew a whole lot more about her business than he should. Although really, who would believe him? It was a long fall from the roof. Neat, clean, problem solved. Except the detective wasn't a demon, he was human, and she had issues with killing people just because they were in the wrong place, at the wrong time. *This will definitely come back to bite me in the ass,* she thought.

"I think I know somebody who might be able to help you get information on missing kids." Ariel said.

Are they in Special Ops?

In a way," Ariel said. "Hungry?"

Bishop looked at her like she was crazy…. well, crazier.

"A good kill always gives me a craving for pizza," she said. "With anchovies. I know an all-night place, not too far from here. The ambience sucks and the food is terrible, but there's someone there I'd like you to meet."

"Sounds like my kind of place." Bishop managed to get to his feet, avoiding the hand she held out to him. "My car's parked down on the street. Maybe we could take the elevator?"

"Wuss." Wings unfolded from beneath the Raptor's coat. They were feathered, dark, glossy brown and matched the color of her hair. She flexed her shoulders and spread them wide like an athlete a stretch before attempting something strenuous, then settled them against her back.

Bishop's face paled.

"H . . . How . . .," he stammered.

"Trick coat." Ariel showed him that the side seams of her long coat were open from the shoulder down to the hem, allowing the wings free movement.

"But . . ." he began. His feet lifted off the roof.

"No screaming," the Raptor said.

- 4 -

Back on the sidewalk, Bishop fought the impulse to throw himself to his knees and kiss the ground. The Raptor had folded her wings away and was impatiently waiting for him to lead the way to his car.

Once in the vehicle, her directions were terse. Their destination turned out to be a semi-subterranean coffee house, bar and internet café with a wonky, half lit neon sign whose remaining three letters spelled the word Caf in faded red script. Inside, the walls were a patchwork of exposed brick, plaster and graffiti covered wallboard. The floor was dirty, the ceiling a low collection of exposed pipes, cracked beams and drifts of dust so old they'd solidified into part of the building.

A bar, with a beer pump and an ancient espresso machine ran down one side of the room. A few mismatching computer stations had been set up along the walls and a collection of thrift store tables, couches and chairs huddled in between. A gnarled and scary looking barista was busy picking his nose and wiping it under the bar.

Bishop had expected dimness, and that had been achieved by

several old florescent fixtures whose ancient tubes gave off a sickly blue-white glare.

The Raptor led him through the clutter of tables and their occasional occupants toward an old chrome and Formica dinette set at the back of the room. A seated figure was hunched over a battered laptop decorated with an impressive collection of decals and stickers. Despite the buzz of the fluorescents and the tapping of keys, Bishop could hear her toenails clicking on the worn linoleum floor.

Uninvited, the Raptor pulled out a chair, flipped it around and straddled it, resting her chin on her hands on the top of the backrest. The boy at the table barely looked up. His pale, long-fingered hands were flying over the keyboard. The strange blue light of the fluorescents, plus the glare from his computer screen, washed out any color he might have had in his face. His skin looked dead white under lank, mouse colored hair that stuck up in random tufts all over his head.

Holding up one finger to indicate that he was almost done, the boy finished his last key stroke.

"El!" He grinned. "Something told me I'd see you tonight. Hungry?"

The Raptor smiled. "The gentleman's buying, Mouser. Knock yourself out."

"Garcon," the boy called to the ancient barista. "One of your finest extra-large bacon, pineapple and anchovy pizzas. Double cheese."

The boy gave Bishop the once-over. "Who's the wallet?" He asked.

"His name's Bishop," El said as Bishop pulled an empty chair over to the table. "He needs you to find some information for us."

"Are you on the internet?" Bishop asked. There were no wires connected to Mouser's laptop.

"Satellite," Mouser explained. "Super-fast; awesome firewall; untraceable IP address. Combine that with caffeine, pizza and beer and what more could a guy ask for?"

"A reasonable degree of sanitation?" Bishop's shoes made a sucking sound as he tried to slide them under the table.

"Dude. A few germs just bolster the immune system. You want to survive the coming plague, don't you?"

"Coming plague?" Bishop was sorry he'd asked. "I guess I didn't get the memo."

Mouser hunched forward. "It's the drug companies, y'know. Think about how much money they'll make if they already have the cure to their own bio-engineered disease?"

"Mouser," El interjected. "Can you put the multi-national corporate conspiracy theories on hold for a few minutes and help us out? There's money in it for you." She raised an eyebrow at Bishop.

"Oh, yeah," Bishop said. "Money. My client will pay for information."

"Cool. What's the deal?"

The pizza arrived. It was the size of a small satellite dish and smelled like the beach at low tide.

"Whoa, my complements to the chef." Mouser waved a hand at Bishop. "He's paying, so bring us some beers, my man."

Bishop started to ask Mouser if he was old enough to drink but decided to shut up. For all he knew the kid was a 300-year-old extraterrestrial with an anchovy addiction. He was here for information, and if it took beer and pizza to get it, he was okay with that.

The pizza was surprisingly good.

Once the food was dealt with, Mouser was more than willing to hear what Bishop wanted. El had pulled over an empty chair and put her feet up, crossing her legs at the ankles. The better, Bishop thought, to show off her high insteps, long toes, and black, viciously pointed toe nails. Watching her flex her feet was an exercise in queasy anticipation. He still didn't know exactly what she had in mind where he was concerned.

"Dude," Mouser said after listening to Bishop's questions about Tesslovich. "This town is lousy with demons. They got their fingers in everything, especially the tech industry. Whatever you do on-line, they know about it. You pay your bills electronically, they know who you owe, and how much. You order used panties on eBay, it goes in their data-base. You gamble, cheat the IRS, are into porn, or guns, little dudes or underage babes, they got your number."

"So, aren't you afraid anything you search for on-line can be traced back to you?" Bishop asked.

"Me? Naw. Not if I do it here. This place is shielded. It's your basic demon-free zone. We're the good guys."

Bishop took a skeptical look around. Most of their fellow customers were either deep into their computers, or practically comatose like the bartender.

"Ah, don't let appearances fool you, Bish, these guys are tougher than they look. Who do you want me to find?"

"It's something bigger than just one guy," Bishop said. "A lot bigger. Maybe a whole bunch of people or an organization that kidnaps and sells kids for adoption. What could you do with that?"

"A criminal conspiracy?" Mouser's eyes took on a luminous shine. "Dude, you have just wandered right up my alley. Start at the beginning, hang left at the Milky Way and don't stop talking 'til you've told me everything." The young hacker laced his fingers and pressed his palms outward until the joints cracked. "You mind if I take notes?"

Mouser switched from beer to caffeine somewhere around three in the morning. Four double espressos and he was flying. His fingers were little more than a blur on the keys and he'd begun talking to himself.

When the show tunes started, Ariel called it a night. She and Bishop stumbled out into the quiet, pre-dawn mistiness of a city holding its last peaceful breath before the chaos of a new day began.

"Can I drop you somewhere?" Bishop asked. "You probably have a nest full of little Raptors waiting for Mom to bring home the worms for breakfast."

"Amusing," Ariel said. "Don't you know we eat our young? Anyway, I live alone. Where, is none of your business."

"Isn't flying around during commute time going to be a bit obvious?"

"I'll take the subway. It's still early, I'll miss the rush."

Bishop looked at her feet. "I bet you never have any trouble getting a seat," he said.

"Piss off," Ariel reached into her pocket and pulled out a tightly rolled pair of ankle high moccasins with thin rubber soles. When she raised her leg to slip one on, Bishop was amazed to see a normal foot slide into the leather boot.

"Mouser should have what you want by tonight. He'll crash until midnight, then be back at the Caf' by one. See you then." She turned toward the subway entrance at the end of the block. With a swirl of coat-tails, she was down the sidewalk to the stairs and out of sight.

Bishop stood alone on the street, wondering if he might be waking up from a strange ambulatory dream. Worse, was the thought that it had all been true. True, and not even half as weird as it would probably get. He climbed into his car and drove home to get some real sleep.

Bishop startled awake from a nightmare that seemed to have something to do with going down with the ship. His t-shirt was wet, and the bed totally damp. He felt around under the covers--the ice pack he'd been holding to his face as he'd fallen asleep had melted all over the mattress.

Crap! He swung his feet onto the floor and stripped the t-shirt off over his head.

What time was it? He felt clammy and hot at the same time, and not very rested. He hoped none of his cuts and scrapes from the night before were infected. He headed for the bathroom mirror. Who knew what strange crud a demon might carry? He was almost afraid to look.

The battered face that stared back at him wasn't as bad as he expected. Most of the swelling had gone down, and the black eye and puffy lip lent him a kind of piratical air. Maybe a hot shower would relax his muscles enough to allow him to stand completely upright so he could look a little less beaten-to-a-pulp and more hero-at-large.

Bishop fumbled open his medicine cabinet, poured four

aspirin into his palm and washed them down with a handful of tap water. The digital clock on the bathroom wall said two p.m. Actually, what it really said was; 2:00:03-2:00:04-2:00:05-2:00:06.

The blinking was making him nauseous. He turned the shower on and stood under the hot water until it started to get cold.

Two strong cups of coffee later, he opened the morning newspaper. No mention of Tesslovich, his death, a headless body or anything like it. T.V. news was the same. Either no one had reported it yet or the police had somehow managed to keep it quiet while they looked into it.

By the same token, no progress had been made in the investigation into the disappearance of little Susan Elizabeth Morgan, age five. She was simply gone. A phone call to her father confirmed there was still no ransom demand. Mom was still sedated, and Dad sounded like he hadn't slept since they'd discovered the girl was missing.

Bishop told him he was following some leads and would be by to see them when he had more information. He knew that wasn't much comfort, but it was all he had to give.

Susan's nanny seemed to have evaporated into thin air. Bishop was still trying to build some background on her. She'd been recruited from an international nanny placement agency and had moved immediately into the Morgan's home. Susan seemed to like her and the Morgans' had no idea who the nanny's friends might be, or even if she had any.

Bishop had suspected the nanny the minute she disappeared, but since she was a foreign national he was having a hard time confirming her identity, let alone her history. Aliah Cherzen had been in the US on a work visa and had glowing letters of recommendations from families in Germany, France and the

Czech Republic. The agency said the references had checked out, but all Bishop had gotten was disconnected phone numbers and bounced-back emails. He'd given that information and the names of two other missing children cases he'd found in back issues of the local paper to Mouser, hoping for similarities, connections, people and places in common—anything.

Bishop was tempted to try searching for information on his own desktop, but Mouser had started him thinking about just how much privacy actually existed on-line. He looked at his watch again. 3:10. The public library was open until six. He still had time to poke around on their computers in relative anonymity.

An hour and a half later, Bishop had a pretty good over-view of Tesslovich's long and profitable career. Counsel had made himself rich, cutting deals, lying to judges, coming up with surprise defense witnesses, intimidating jurors, bribing police or anyone else who might need some incentive to see things his way. He'd gotten a lot of important people out of serious scrapes and had ended up on some of the most exclusive invitation lists in the city. He had, however, never been connected to sale of pornography or pedophilia, except in his professional capacity as a defense attorney. He owned a Jag and a Hummer, but almost always used a limo. Both he and his driver had a license to carry a concealed weapon. He'd been accused of being less-than-human by the families of his client's victims, but never of being a demon.

Bishop hoped Mouser was having better luck.

It was time to call in a marker. Bishop's brief career in the police department had netted him some good experience on the street, a lot of animosity from both his peers and the higher ups for not being a go-along kind of cop, and eventually the loss of his job and a damn good partner, courtesy of internal affairs.

His ex-partner Ray Mann, better known as 'Rain', possessed

an uncanny ability with numbers and a talent for working the street. Bishop and he had had a long, wild ride in Vice. Rain Mann was still a cop, and at five o'clock his tour would just be getting started.

- 6 -

The 17th Precinct was a time warp. Everything was battered-- desks, walls, floors, perps and cops. There were still bullet holes in the ceiling of the lobby from one of the more exciting free-for-alls that sometimes happened when multiple arrestees with competing interests ended up in the same place at the same time. The glass in the old chicken-wire windows was cracked and dirty. Rumor had it they hadn't been washed since 1932. Nobody cared because there was no view.

Vice was on the second floor along with Homicide. In a modern precinct, there'd be bullet proof glass and buzzers between visitors and their destination. If you worked at the 17th you took your chances on getting a nasty surprise just like everybody else in the neighborhood.

The desk sergeant knew Bishop and only gave him an eyebrow tilt as he started up the stairs. The Sarge was aware of his pariah-like status, but he didn't like the Captain any more than anybody else and was probably hoping for a few fireworks from above to relieve the boredom of his day.

Rain was at his old desk in a corner of the bullpen, shuffling papers. When he spotted Bishop, his eyes flicked sideways to one of the partitioned offices along the side wall. The offices had windows that looked out into the room, so the Captain and his weasel assistant could watch the activities in the pen. When the furniture started flying though, the blinds came down and the doors stayed shut. Two Homicide detectives, whose desks faced each other, had been in the middle of a friendly argument about something that hadn't sounded work related. Bishop's appearance stopped the conversation cold. He felt their eyes track him all the way to Rain Mann's desk.

As Bishop approached, Rain shoved his chair back. Instead of getting up, he did a slow lean back, put his feet up on one corner of the desk and laced his fingers over his flat stomach.

"Hey, Rain," Bishop said.

Rain nodded. "Frank. Surprised you had the balls to come back up here."

"All nerve and no brains, remember? I was hoping you could help me out on something. Old time's sake, and all that shit."

Rain didn't say anything, just gave Bishop the perp-crusher stare that all cops eventually developed. But Bishop wasn't watching his old partner's eyes, he was watching his hands.

Rain was clicking the first and second fingers of one hand together, almost like scissors, but with one finger on top of the other. Then there was a flash of two fingers and a quick 'o' of thumb and first finger.

"Not interested," Rain said.

Bishop gave a quick jerk of his head toward the stairs like the reply had stung him.

"Sorry you feel that way," he shrugged.

He turned to leave when one of the office doors flew open. Rain had already done the dirty work; this was the coup de grace.

"Get the hell out of here, Bishop!" the Captain yelled from the doorway, cheeks flushed with rage. "You burned your bridges.

I don't want to see your face anywhere near this precinct again, or I'll bust your ass for vagrancy."

Bishop took a step in the Captain's direction. The color drained from the man's face. His eyes darted around the room looking for help. Nobody was moving except Bishop, who took another step forward. Fully alarmed now, the Captain jumped back into his office, and slammed the door shut with such force the blinds danced against its window.

"Dick." Bishop muttered, turning back to the stairs. Out of the corner of his eye he could see Rain was trying very hard not to smile.

Twenty minutes later, Rain and Bishop were eating Mu Shu Pork and Imperial Chicken in an old, back-alley Chinese restaurant called The Hidden City. He and Rain had favored it when they were working together. It wasn't a cop place, and the booths had high backs and curtains across the front for privacy. Bishop ordered a beer, reasoning it would help keep his muscles loose; an after-dinner coffee he could get at the underground café. If you measured the quality of your caffeine in sheer strength, an espresso from Hacker Haven was a four-star buzz.

"That was frickin' hilarious," Rain was saying, his dark eyes dancing with delight. "I bet you made him crap his pants."

"Didn't mean to mess with your pension. I was just in the neighborhood."

"Yeah, yeah. Don't bother to apologize, I wouldn't have missed that for the world. Besides, I probably got some points for kicking your ass back down the stairs."

Rain took a bite of pancake stuffed with Mu Shu Pork and plum sauce. "You're buying, by the way. Put it on your client's expense report."

"Yeah, the way things are going the guy's going to think I spend all my time eating instead of looking for his daughter."

"Is that what this is about, a missing kid? I'm Vice, remember?"

"You're also somebody who knows something about everything that's going down in this city. Besides, it's three kids, not one. I've been thinking about the vice angle. You think these kids are being abducted for who knows what, or you think this could be some kind of child porn or prostitution thing?"

Rain wiped his mouth. Child sex crimes really got to his old partner.

"I know the cases. Downtown is keeping a tight lid on them, but word gets around, you know. None of the kiddie porn we've turned up in the last year has any of these kids in it. Sex Crimes has pulled in every known perv and procurer in the area. Nobody knows nothin' and some of 'em would be glad to rat out a pal if it would get them a pass. But, here's something you don't know—-a lot of street kids are coming up missing too. This goes back two, maybe three years. Nobody paid much attention because these kids come and go. They got nobody to report 'em gone and, mostly, nobody who cares, except maybe that babe who runs the runaway program over on third. Catherine?"

"She's a nun, Rain, not a babe," Bishop interjected. "Sister Catherine."

"Yeah, well we didn't have any nuns looked like that when I was a kid. Anyway, she's been harassing Missing Persons about disappearing kids. Ones from the shelter. She claims they wouldn't have just disappeared like that. Claims they were kidnapped just like the kids you're looking for. Only these kids are older. Fourteen, fifteen, even a couple older than that. She says the older ones wouldn't have gone quietly."

"I guess it's possible they were drugged," Bishop said.

"Yeah, but then you've still got what? A hundred and thirty, hundred and forty, pounds of unconscious kid to deal with. Got to be more than one person involved."

"Were all these kids' boys?"

"Most, not all. Both sexes is unusual for a serial killer or a pedophile. If they're leaving the country though, it might be some kind of kid-by-mail-order thing, but seventeen-year-old boys? Naw."

Bishop decided he'd try the Tesslovich angle. He pushed the call button for another beer. Rain didn't drink. He said it slowed his brain down, kept him from computing the odds and he didn't like that. Rain was a guy that needed to calculate the odds, whether it was a long shot on the ponies or the odds of solving a case, so he could kick the shit out of them. Rain needed to win.

"You know this lawyer, Tesslovich?"

Rain gave him a squint. "Everybody knows that scum sucker. Come up against him in court and you can kiss your bust good bye. Why?"

Bishop hesitated. Rain had been his friend as well as his partner. He'd trusted him then, but the man also had his own skin to look out for. The department was full of corruption and just keeping your job meant you compromised something.

As if sensing Bishop's hesitation, Rain said, "Hey. It's me man. I know what you're thinkin', but we're solid. You gotta believe that."

Bishop nodded. "It's just that this case is beginning to take on a whole load of strange."

Rain waited.

"I was tracking down some rumors about Tesslovich and he seems to have, um, disappeared."

"How long ago?"

"Not very."

"Hmmm." Bishop knew that Rain was hating not being able to say: Yeah, I knew that.

"Not on the radar, huh?"

Rain shook his head. "I'll ask around."

"Carefully." Bishop warned. "Like I said, we may be into the weird and dangerous here." He picked up the check the waiter had just discreetly inserted between the closed curtains, counted out some bills and added a generous tip--discretion wasn't free at The Hidden City. Then he handed Rain one of his cards.

"Bishop Investigations," Rain read out-loud. "Classy. Goes nicely with that mouse under your eye."

"It has my cell phone number on it," Bishop said. "Keep in touch. And I mean it about being careful."

"Hey," Rain said. "I'm the Rain Mann, remember? Careful is my middle name."

- 7 -

The Raptor told Bishop that Mouser wouldn't be at the café until after midnight. Bishop couldn't imagine where the young hacker might hang out when he wasn't doing a deep dive into the free-fire zone. Where did a kid like that live? Did he have the kind of parents who just didn't care whether their kid's bed was empty at three a.m.? Or maybe he was on his own. A runaway who'd managed to score a computer and use it to earn a few bucks.

He and Rain had left the restaurant separately and Bishop took the opportunity to stretch his legs, work out the kinks the beating had left in his muscles, hoping the bustle on the sidewalk would distract him for an hour or so. He began to wander, looking in shop windows at displays of tourist junk, Chinese patent medicines and weird roots and even snakes, pickled in jars of sweet rice wine. He moved past produce stands with bins full of unknown vegetables, held his breath as he passed butcher shops that displayed hanging duck and pig carcasses, and crates of live fowl stacked on top of each other outside the stores.

Chinatown never slept, the stores were open at all hours. The streets always had at least a few pedestrians scurrying from place to place. Tonight, the traffic seemed mostly made up of dinner goers; couples and student types eating on the cheap, tourists, and a mix of Chinese going about their evening activities. It looked like a normal evening, but Bishop had noticed ever since he'd met the mysterious El and found out about her belief in demons, he'd started looking at the people around him in a different way. The scuttle and stride of fellow pedestrians now seemed ripe with possibilities.

Who would know human from demon? And what was the threat, really? Too much for his tired brain to contemplate: It was time for that coffee.

Although it was still before midnight when Bishop walked through the door, Mouser was already sitting at the bar drinking coffee with his laptop open in front of him. The young hacker wore a faded, over-size red t-shirt with a flaking logo for some Goth band called 'Death Knell'. His faded, ripped jeans were baggy and puddled over his sneakers like a set of casino drapes. Both wrists sported black elastic braces.

Mouser looked up, spotting Bishop. "Dude!" He grinned. "What a night! Well, a day, then night, but who's tracking. I've been surfing the minefields of the information highway. It's been wild. The off-route blog-o-sphere is rife with rumor if you can mole your way into it without getting nuked. Plus, I found a guy, who knows a guy, who knew a guy that got snatched just like one of your kids, and he wasn't the first. We can get face time with him later. When will El get here?"

"How much coffee have you had?" Bishop asked him.

"Lost track."

Bishop sighed. "Beer," he said to the old bartender who was sitting on a stool on the other side of the counter reading a tattered paperback. "Actually; a beer, a shot of Jack and a double espresso."

He steered Mouser over to a table.

"Whoa, JD." Mouser looked impressed.

"This is a onesie, kid. To stop your head from taking off and flying around the room like an escaped balloon. The beer and coffee are for me."

He'd just gotten the liquor into the kid when El walked in the door. She looked surprised to see him. It only confirmed Bishop's suspicion that each one of them had been trying to get to Mouser first.

"What are you doing?" Ariel asked. "How much do you expect to get out of him if he's drunk?"

"Drunk? He has enough caffeine in his system to run a small city for a week. I'm attempting to apply an antidote."

"How did he afford that many espressos?"

"They seem to be on my tab, along with another disgusting pizza combo." Bishop examined the grubby check that had arrived with the drinks. "Forty-eight bucks worth."

He looked over his shoulder at the bartender. "I'm cutting him off," he said loudly.

The bartender didn't bother to look up.

Mouser was paging through his files. "I looked up the missing kids," he said. "Getting into the CPD is insultingly easy for a man of my talents. The three you gave me are just the tip of the iceberg. I got eight over the last three years, all under the age of twelve when they were snatched. This is not including street kids, which we'll get back to in a minute.

"The M.O.'s similar. They were all taken from public places. Two from the park, one from a school yard, three from a shopping mall. One from a video arcade at the movies while mom and dad were buying popcorn. No trace. The cops are trying to keep the lid on a serial killer panic, but that lid's about to blow. I did a comparison of victims: age, sex, where they lived, family income, credit history, parent's professions, schools, childcare, after school activities, domestic help, nannies. This is where it gets interesting. Although only three of the kids were young enough for nannies, all their nannies were foreign--two Russians, one Serb. Different agencies, but the same general circumstances. Only one nanny actually 'disappeared'. The other two were 'dismissed' when the child wasn't found. No kids, no work. Plus, they were supposed to be keeping an eye on the young 'uns when the abductions took place. That's gotta go against you when it comes to job performance. Those two are also nowhere to be found. Never went back to their agencies, never left the country by any traceable route. That probably means forged identities, fake passports, bogus letters of recommendation. The usual illegal alien stuff."

"Take a breath, kid." Bishop pushed the remains of his beer in Mouser's direction. "What about Tesslovich?"

"Patience, Bish. I ran your Nicolai Tesslovich, Esq. through the sieve, and guess what? Russian immigrant. Supposedly came here with his mom from Soviet Georgia when he was seventeen. High School GED, college, then law school. He has transcripts but no history in the places he went to school. He's not in dorm records, didn't have a cafeteria card, no driver's licenses, checking account or earnings tied to his social security number until twelve years ago, when he turned up as a full-fledged member of the bar, and soon to be practicing attorney.

"So Tesslovich and the nannies all had fake identities?"

"Right. Also, no word on Tesslovich being missing. Although, how long can that last? He's on the court calendar for Thursday. Tongues will wag if he doesn't show up."

Ariel had signaled the bartender for her own coffee and was lacing it with packets of sugar as Mouser wound down.

"Makes sense," she said. "Set yourself up as a refugee from hard times in another country. Easier to get away with 'lost' records, and an un-documentable past. If you look a little strange, you're just a foreigner who's come to the U.S seeking a better life."

"What about the blogs you were talking about?" Bishop asked. His double espresso was circling his brain like a runaway jet ski. He had a new respect for Mouser's metabolism.

Mouser grinned. "Last night I managed to peel my way through a few layers of heavy security and get down to some way underground blog sites in the dark web. These people are into some heavy conspiracy stuff and they've caught on to the demon-thing. Not only that, they're trying to map them."

"Map them?"

"Yeah, like identify who/where/what. Names, places, connections, species. It was gold, dude. I got some links for Tesslovich. Not just clients who're probably demons, but some heavy hitters around town."

Bishop pulled a small notebook out of his jacket. "Now we're talking. You have some names?"

Mouser grinned. "How about Chief of Police E. Wayne Frankle (the "E" is for Elmore, by the way), and Yamazaki Kiriyenko?"

"Who?"

"Yamazaki Kiriyenko. Better known as Zaki. Japanese mother, Russian father. Currently reviled as the Anti-Christ of the tech industry."

"I thought that was Bill Gates," Bishop said.

"Dude, Bill Gates is an Eagle Scout compared to this guy. Zaki doesn't just crush his competitors, he folds, spindles and mutilates them."

"Then why don't we hear about him, like we do Gates? As far as that goes, if he's a competition killer why hasn't he gone after Microsoft or Apple?"

"Zaki's ruthless, but he's also low-profile. Stealth competition. Cutting edge development. Niche marketing. The Blogs say he's into nano-technology now. A bot in every brain or something. He lives here, just outside the city."

"And he has something to do with missing kids?"

"No, man," Mouser gave a long-suffering sigh. "He's a link to Tesslovich. Apparently, they very pally. And he's probably a demon, per the blogs. He's a big sports nut; owns a soccer team, likes ice-hockey, horse racing, and—-get this—-pro-wrestling. That steroid case on TV that's always tossing his opponents out of the ring, Dimitri 'The Demon' Diminovich? Guy's under contract to Zaki."

It was Bishop's turn to sigh.

"Do you have his address Mouser?" Ariel asked.

"Do girls have feathers?" Mouser copied an address from his screen onto a napkin, then stabbed a button on his keyboard. Pages started to slide into the tray on a nearby printer.

"Just what do you have in mind?" Bishop asked Ariel.

"I thought I'd do a fly-over," she told him, folding the napkin into her pocket before Bishop could see it.

"You're not going without me," Bishop grabbed the pages out of the printer and shoved them into the inside pocket of his jacket. "It's going to be a drive-by, and I'm doing the driving."

Mouser yawned. Closed the lid of his laptop and kept on yawning, like once started, he couldn't stop. Ariel patted him on the shoulder and motioned to Bishop that they should get going.

As they left the Caf' Bishop asked, "Is the kid going to be all right? Maybe we should drop him off somewhere." He looked over his shoulder. Mouser's head was already on the table.

"Don't worry," Ariel told him. "Ez will look after him."

"Is that a good thing?" Bishop couldn't imagine the stolid bartender taking an interest in much of anything, let alone Mouser.

"Ez has hidden talents. Mouser will be fine."

"Do I want to know what hidden talents?"

"Probably not."

Bishop nodded. "Ignorance is bliss."

8

Ariel had reluctantly agreed to let Bishop drive to the expensive lakeside community where Zaki's compound was located. She could have flown there and been back in half the time, but it was either go along, or let him galump around on his own, calling attention to himself and messing up any element of surprise they might need in the future.

If Zaki was a demon, he'd have more than normal security, some of it undetectable to human senses. He might already know about Bishop and Tesslovich. Hell, he might even know about her and Tesslovich, although she hadn't exactly taken the stairs or left any witnesses.

She kept her eyes fixed on the window as the highway slid by, illuminated only by their headlights and a wan quarter moon. She was mad at herself. She'd been late getting to Mouser and now Bishop had all the information she did. This whole breach of secrecy wasn't her fault, exactly, but there weren't any excuses either. And Bishop wasn't the only problem. She was exceeding the instructions she'd been given on this job. There would be consequences.

". . . Zaki guy on your radar?"

"What?"

"Zaki. Is he a demon?"

"Never heard of him," Ariel confessed. "But anything is possible. Today's demons have moved beyond human possession and bubbling vats of body parts into the mainstream. These days, most of them look just like you and me."

Bishop raised an eyebrow.

"Okay," Ariel conceded. "Like you. I doubt we'll be able to get anywhere near him anyway. Guys like that have heavy security, dogs, guns, spells.

"Spells?"

"If he's a demon, I mean. There'll be wards to protect him. They're kind of like silent alarms connected to booby traps. Hopefully they don't extend beyond his property line. Anyway, they're better at protecting the inside of buildings because they tend to deteriorate after too much time out in the open."

"Like how much time?" Bishop sounded hopeful.

"Oh, in this climate," Ariel estimated. "They'd only last about five years or so without being recharged."

Bishop took the exit ramp to Lakeshore Dunes Estates. "Swell," he said. "Somebody else who's just dying to tell me the odds."

At the top of the ramp, a yellow, hyphenated line divided a narrow blacktop into two lanes that disappeared into the darkness in both directions.

"Which way?" Bishop asked.

Ariel dug the napkin out of her coat pocket.

"Right," she said. "Then first left. About three miles down that road we start looking for addresses, or names. His property is called Gates of Eden."

"Not too pretentious. Seems a little out-in-the-middle-of-nowhere though."

Ariel shrugged. "The ultra-rich don't need to run to out to the

7-Eleven for a quart of milk and a box of pampers, they have people to do that. What they want is distance from the herd. I bet Zaki has a helicopter pad and pilot just so his limo doesn't have to fight the traffic on the way to his office."

Once they'd made the second turn the woods seemed to be the only thing on either side of the road. No driveways, mailboxes or visible lights from dwellings of any sort.

Then the wall started. Set back about twenty feet from the shoulder, it had been built on a low berm, which made it seem even taller than its regulation ten feet. It appeared to be made of solid concrete covered in a layer of decorative stone. Topped with a discrete spiral of razor wire set at an outward angle, its square cap was designed to further discourage the ambitious trespasser. Small metal plaques set every thirty feet warned that the wire was electrified.

"Jesus," Bishop said. "What happened to a simple 'Beware of the Dog'? Is this property all Zaki's?"

Ariel shrugged. "You should have just let me . . ."

"Yeah, yeah. Fly over. He probably would have shot you down with his handy, home-laser defense system. The gate's coming up."

"Just drive by," she warned. "Don't slow down."

"I was a cop, Bird-Girl. I know how to do surveil . . . Wow!"

Spotlights on either side of a wide driveway illuminated the huge gate. Two massive wings of bright steel, twelve feet tall at their highest point, had been covered in finely-wrought metalwork. Leafy vines weighted with fruit sprouted from a massive metal tree trunk that split in half when the gate was opened. A serpent wound its way around the tree holding a bright golden apple in its mouth. Bishop caught a glimpse of naked human figures to either side. The pillars that supported the gate were topped with giant . . .

"Gargoyles!" Ariel said as they sped past. "This is not good."

"What part of 'not-good' are we talking about here?" Bishop asked. "Did you see a gate house, were there cameras? Do you think anyone saw us?"

"Oh, yeah."

"Was there a guard? I didn't see anybody."

"I think the night shift is on duty."

Bishop slowed the car. They were coming to the far edge of the estate's wall, with any luck, out of sight of gate security. He planned to pull over in a mile or two and sit there until Ariel explained what the hell she was talking about.

"Let's get off the road," Ariel suggested. "I think there's a place right up there."

It was the faint remnant of an over-grown track that looked like it led nowhere except into the woods.

Probably an old lover's lane or unpaved road leading to an abandoned summer cottage. At least the woods would hide the car.

He pulled in, rolled the front windows down and shut off the ignition. The only sounds were the engine ticking as it cooled, a chorus of crickets and, after a minute or two, the muted scurry of ground scavengers going about their business in the dark.

"You know," Bishop said. "Before I met you my life was pretty simple. All I had to do was stay on the good side of a few people who could toss business my way. I spent my time finding runaway kids, doing the occasional skip trace, and investigating a nice, steady stream of insurance fraud. Now, suddenly, I'm in the Twilight Zone with flying avengers, demon billionaires, and dead lawyers who are a lot scarier than the mob bosses they get off on technicalities. What else is out there? Vampires? Werewolves? Brain eating Zombies?"

"I'd really rather not get into that right now," Ariel said primly.

"Great!" Bishop threw his hands in the air. "I'm telling you, if one of them sneaks up on this car and tries to bite me, I'm taking you with me."

"I don't think that's our immediate problem."

"Well, we're obviously not getting any closer to Zaki than that front gate. Electrified razor wire! The grounds are probably patrolled by packs of wild dogs. I guess he doesn't think he needs a guard at the gate on top of all that."

"The gate is guarded," Ariel said. "He's got Gargoyles."

Bishop slapped one hand on the steering wheel. "Well, of course. Why didn't I think of that? Cement statues make all the difference."

"They're not cement."

"El, there are Gargoyles on old buildings all over the city. They're decoration. They're even on Notre Dame for God's sake!"

"The ones on the gate are real. You don't notice it because they're like chameleons—-they can take on the color and texture of their surroundings, that's why they look like stone—-and they can stay immobile for hours, days, weeks at a time. They only blink about once every forty-five seconds and their respiration is extremely shallow. No one ever stares at them long enough to see them move, and if they do their brain just writes it off as a trick of the light, or fatigue. Gargoyles have been around as long as demons have. They're not too bright, but their eye sight is excellent, even in the dark. They're ideal for what they do, they watch."

"That doesn't sound very threatening."

"Unfortunately, they can also be pretty quick when they need to be. I once saw one eviscerate a whole cow in about twenty seconds. Zaki probably rewards their service with small livestock. Watching them feed is disgusting, by the way."

Right at that moment Bishop noticed a low buzzing noise in his ears. It sounded like a radio losing the channel. Was it lack sleep or the prelude to losing touch with reality? Someone poked him in the arm.

"Bishop!"

There was that poke again.

"This is no time to have a psychotic break," Ariel told him. "I'm going to fly over the estate. I'll get as high as I can and come in from the lakeside. If I'm not back in twenty-minutes, go home."

"We could both just go home right now and forget the whole thing." Bishop said. Gargoyles were beyond his pay grade.

"Can you really do that, Frank?" Ariel's eyes had a light in them he found disturbing.

Bishop took a minute. "Unfortunately, no," he admitted. He reached up and clicked off the inside light, so it wouldn't come on when the door opened. "Don't get caught, okay?"

Ariel pulled off her boots, dropped them on the floor mat, and slid from the car. She slipped out of her coat and tossed it on the seat before quietly closing the passenger door. Her naked back flashed white against the darkness as she made her way through the trees toward higher ground. Bishop could have sworn she'd been wearing a black turtleneck.

Now that Bishop was alone, the night noises outside the car seemed to take on a deeper and more sinister tone. Just in case he fell asleep, it would probably be a good idea to engage the automatic locks and roll the windows all the way to the top. For the next several minutes he tried to stop himself from thinking about what the word 'eviscerated' really meant.

A knock on his window brought Bishop straight up in his seat. He made a lunge for the other side of the car before he realized he still had his seat belt on. He was clawing at the buckle as El's voice hissed, "Bishop, open the damn door!"

Deeply embarrassed, he sat back and pushed 'unlock'. El slipped back into her coat and slid in beside him. Another glimpse of her back showed him that her shirt was backless from the collar to just below her shoulder blades. A dark line followed the inside curve of each scapula, but there was no evidence of wings.

"Everything go okay?"

"I should be asking you the same question. I got a pretty good look at the layout. Zaki must have about 120 acres of prime lakefront property, completely fenced. The house is set back on a rise overlooking the lake, but there are also a lot of other buildings. Two look like they might be labs or office buildings. They have a good-sized parking area and connect to each other by a second-floor walkway."

She felt around on the floor for her boots.

"Then there's a really big building with a glass dome roof. It looks like a stadium, but I have no idea that's what it's for unless Zaki brings in sport teams to play private games for him and his friends. Again, it's got a good-sized parking lot that might hold fifty or sixty cars. The wall encloses the property all the way down to the beach and ends at a bunch of rocks on both sides. Zaki may have people working for him in there but he obviously has no intention of letting the neighbors wander over for tea and a swim."

She peeled a couple of damp leaves off the bottom of one naked foot and pulled on the boots.

"Except for the stadium, the architecture has a neo-gothic feel to it like those robber-baron estates built before rich people paid income tax. That implies that the Gargoyles we saw at the gate aren't the only ones on the estate."

Bishop rubbed the space between his eyebrows. The lack of

sleep was getting to him. "So, whether he has anything to do with missing kids or not, he's probably a demon?"

"Not necessarily," Ariel said. "He's obviously very security conscious. The Gargoyles could just be a gift from a grateful friend."

"Some friend." Bishop started the car. "Can we get out of here without going past the gate again?"

"Nope. This road ends at a dead end 'T' about three miles further on. There are two big houses down there, but the people in them all have to come back this way to get to the highway."

"Okay. Here's the plan. I turn around and go back the way we came. I don't know how discriminating Gargoyles are about cars, but this one doesn't look like it would end up parked at the front door of those houses. You get in the trunk. If I'm alone maybe they'll think I'm just the maid-from-down-the-road's boyfriend dropping her off after a date."

Ariel gave him a slit-eyed 'I'm-not-getting-in-any-car-trunk' look.

"Or," Bishop back-tracked. "You could sit a little closer to me, I could put my arm around you and maybe they'll think we're just a couple who needed a dark, deserted road for about an hour."

"Or," El said, getting out of the car again but leaning back in to take her parting shot. "I'll be the angry date who had a fight with her grabby boyfriend and decided to fly home on her own." She turned and disappeared into the woods, leaving Bishop to reach across the seat and pull her door shut.

Bishop managed a tight U-turn and drove out of the woods hoping he could make it home before he fell asleep at the wheel. As he sped past the Eden gate, he could have sworn that one of the Gargoyles turned his head ever so slightly to watch the car until it drove out of sight.

9

Bishop's cell phone woke him what seemed like minutes after he'd fallen asleep. The phone had an obnoxious ring the know-it-all sales punk had programmed into it while he sneeringly tried to teach Bishop how to access all its 300 hundred features. So far Bishop had mastered "on", "off", "dial", "answer" and "retrieve messages"

"What?" he said, hoping it wasn't a client.

"Yo, man. Bishop? Did I wake you?"

"Rain?"

"Yeah, man, wake up. It's after eleven and I've got news."

Bishop lifted his head to squint at the clock then threw himself back against his pillow. "Okay. I'm conscious. Try to keep it to words of two syllables, I had a long night."

Rain laughed. "Hope it was worth it. Anyway, I had to be in court this morning for a case. And guess who was there? Tesslovich."

"What?!" Bishop sat up.

"Tesslovich. Your missing lawyer. He had a bail hearing for one of his clients. Some greasy little . . ."

"Rain, you sure it was him?"

"Man, everybody knows Tesslovich. It was him in living color. Though I must admit, he wasn't lookin' too good."

"What do you mean?"

"He had one of those neck brace things on. You know, a big white collar that holds your head straight, and he was moving pretty slow, like it was an effort to get everything going in the same direction. His voice was also pretty messed up. The judge kept asking him to speak up, but he couldn't do it. He and the prosecuting attorney finally had to go up to the bench to get their business done. I heard later he told the judge his limo had been rear-ended by a drunk driver, which is bullshit because I saw him being helped out of his limo on my way into court. It's the same one he's had for two years and there wasn't a scratch on it. You want me to ask around about the 'accident'?"

"No!" Bishop took a breath. "I mean, no. Thanks. I just heard about his disappearance from somebody involved in another investigation I've been working on. He's obviously not dead, so there's nothing else I need to know. Thanks, man."

"Anytime. Hey, they're calling me back into court—gotta run. Keep in touch, Frank, I might hear something more about the kids."

Bishop thumbed the off button. He was wide awake now. He'd seen Tesslovich's head leave his body. He was sure of that. There had been green blood everywhere. Then an armed and dangerous bird-lady had shot a gypsy, dragged him out a ten-story window and flown him to the top of a nearby building.

If that was an elaborate series of special effects, somebody was really, really good at it. And if it was faked, why do it for him? It had to be real.

But had he ever seen El fly again? No. In fact he hadn't seen much the first time either since he'd spent most of it with his eyes shut. Maybe she was on wires.

And the Gargoyles? They looked like statues to him—ugly

half-human faces, wings, pointy tails, just like the ones on historically preserved buildings all over town. It was her story that they were guarding Zaki. That is when they weren't flying around the countryside eviscerating cows.

What a chump! But he still had to figure out why Tesslovich would appear in court in a neck brace? Because Rain would be there to see him and tell Bishop? Naw. Coincidence? Maybe. Or an impressive performance by the lawyer's 'enemy', Ariel.

Bishop swung his feet over the side of the bed. Dead tired, he'd thrown his jacket over a chair as he shed clothing on the way to his mattress early that a.m. One sleeve trailed the floor and the left side had flipped open showing the lining.

Mouser's printouts were sticking out of the inner pocket. Back at the Caf', when he'd been more interested in keeping up with El than looking at Mouser's Blog gossip, he'd given the pages a quick length ways crease, and shoved them away. There must be at least ten pages there that Mouser had either made up or doctored-up from other sources. He was tempted to toss them, but maybe they would at least give him a clue of what the intention of this whole con might be.

Taking them with him, Bishop staggered into the kitchen and put on a full pot of coffee. It was going to be another long day.

～

Bishop started with the missing persons reports. To his surprise, they seemed perfectly legitimate, if illegally obtained. The PD had become a lot more automated since his stint there, although he suspected the 17th was still using the same ancient PCs he'd prepared his reports on.

Mouser had been right. Over the last three years, a parent, or parents had filed eight reports on missing children. The responding officer's notes had been transcribed into the report, and further notations added as the investigation proceeded. The children were uniformly bright, well fed, upper middle-class kids with no history of abuse, truancy, medical or mental problems. Investigation of the parents, neighbors, teachers, etc. had all proved negative. Investigation of the nannies, for those children who had one, had come to a dead end. They were suspect, but also missing and therefore un-chargeable, except in absentia.

Bishop was surprised that that many missing kids hadn't created a firestorm of publicity and demand for action from the parents and local, even national, advocacy groups. It was as if the whole thing had just been hushed up and put away as an unsolved disappearance. That often happened for adults, but rarely for kids and certainly not so soon after they went missing.

Bishop got out his notebook and copied names, addresses, precincts and the names of investigating officers into it. His own client wasn't even the last family that had lost a child. There was a nine-year-old boy who had disappeared less than two months after little Susan Elizabeth with hardly a peep from the media.

The next few pages contained missing persons' reports, all filed by the same person, Sister Mary Catherine from the Children's Shelter Project. These kids were older as Mouser had pointed out, and both girls and boys like the other missing children. Many of them, however, did have a history with the police as runaways often did; battery, drugs, theft, solicitation, even arson. Sister Catherine had insisted that every one of them had been coming to the shelter, getting their lives together, even getting jobs, before suddenly disappearing. She was sure something bad had happened to them. The investigations were all perfunctory or non-existent. The police didn't care about one more teenage street punk who'd decided to move on. After all, that was the 'away' part of being a runaway.

Bishop wrote those names down as well under the heading

"Sis. Catherine." He knew where to find her and he wanted to know what she had to say.

The last few pages had been printed from the blogs, where a myriad of faceless conspiracy theorists traded rumors and gave their opinions on the validity of the rumors in other theorist's posts. Some user names turned up in more than one chat room, or even in all of the sites Mouser had copied. Although disputes ran rampant, and some posters were vituperative to the point that their access had either been revoked, or they'd been frozen out by no one replying to anything they posted. The commonly held belief seemed to be that demons were real, they walked among us and their goal was, (surprise!), world domination. High profile politicians, corporate moguls, businessmen, lawyers, famous criminals, rock stars and other celebrities were outed as demons, or accused of being their minions.

Bishop could feel his level of frustration climbing. Even as a cop he hadn't run into this level of supernatural paranoia. It sounded like group fantasy taken to weird and twisted heights.

The list of U.S. based "demons" on the back page of the report included, the President of the United States, Mike Pence, Carl Rove, Paul Ryan, the Koch brothers, Mitch McConnell, Ted Cruz, Sarah Palin, Mark Zuckerberg, Bill Gates, Michael Jackson, Vladimir Putin, Nicolai Tesslovich, Yamazaki Kiriyenko, and, interestingly enough, the entire executive hierarchy of Walmart, their wives, children and dogs---along with the reasons each listee was suspect. The Bloggers made some good points, but Bishop really doubted than anyone had solid proof that Vladimir Putin and Mitch McConnell cast no shadows. He tossed the blogs aside.

The last three pages were profiles of Tessolovich and Yamazaki Kiriyenko. Mouser had even found a classified military satellite photo of Yaki's estate. It was much as Ariel had described, but a picture was truly worth a thousand words.

According to his profile, Yaki had started at MIT at fourteen and finished his post graduate work at a bio-tech think tank in New Mexico---all very secret and privately funded—at twenty. By twenty-three he owned his own company that, among other things, was working on developing an organic computer system run by a self-perpetuating culture of designer bacteria. The Environmental Protection Agency, in collaboration with the Center for Disease Control in Atlanta, shut down the project over fear that the culture could escape and start a worldwide plague.

Zaki's company then moved into more conventional bio-technology research where he amassed a huge fortune, built over the ground-up bones of other companies and associates foolish enough to challenge his products. However, rumors in the intelligence community implied that his first project had never gone completely away. Government collusion was mentioned.

Although still very much involved in business decisions, five years ago Zaki had turned over the day-to-day running of his empire to his long-term second-in-command. His press release explained he had become bored with business and wanted to go back to his first love—development. Workers, who had been involved in construction projects on his estate, revealed that the new buildings were private research laboratories.

In an exclusive interview, Zaki conceded he had built a facility where he could 'dabble' in experimental technology projects for his own amusement. He even provided the television crew with a tour. The buildings were crammed with the latest electronic equipment, but not a Petri dish or electronic microscope was in sight. The government and the media decided to leave the eccentric billionaire alone.

Bishop was having a hard time making the connection between Tesslovich and Yamazaki Kiriyenko except that Zaki gave lavish parties to which many local movers and shakers, including Tesslovich, were invited. The soccer team, which Bishop hadn't even been aware Zaki owned, had been on a major winning streak. Bishop didn't follow Pro Wrestling, since it was just so much bullshit, but he assumed if Zaki owned a high-profile wrestler, the guy was probably kicking ass. A recent picture of Zaki showed him next to a race horse draped in flowers. If the horse belonged to Zaki, it was probably a winner as well.

Putting Mouser's printouts back in order, Bishop tidied them into a neat pile on the table next to his notebook. He pinched the bridge of his nose for a few seconds hoping to relieve what was shaping up to be a doozie of a headache. The glass coffee pot he'd set on the table next to his cup was empty, and he barely remembered pouring the first cup. Leaning his chair back until the front legs left the floor, he reached over his head and fumbled the receiver off the old fashioned, jaundice-yellow wall phone next to the stove. He liked it because the receiver was attached to the phone by a long cord, so he couldn't lose it somewhere in the house like he did his portable phones, and the buttons were on the handset. Letting the chair back down, he pulled his notebook over in front of him and started to dial.

10

Bishop pulled up in front of Susan Elizabeth Morgan's house. He always thought of the homes of the people who had hired him as belonging to the most important person in the investigation—the potential victim. So, he had called Susan Elizabeth's house and asked if he could come by and ask a few more questions. Her mother, who had obviously come out of her bout with sedation, seemed both eager for news and reluctant to talk to him. It wasn't an uncommon mix of reactions when it came to the parent of a missing child. There was always the fear that the investigator was bringing bad news.

Mrs. Morgan had faded visibly from the last time Bishop had seen her. Everything about her was a little more pale and lifeless, like an old photograph bleached by time. In normal circumstances she would be a very attractive, vibrant woman, but loss and worry had taken its toll.

"Do you have any news?" The front door had opened before Bishop made it half way up the walk. He shook his head. There was both resignation and relief in the way she slumped her shoulders at his answer. No bad news at least meant that Susan Elizabeth was still out there to be found, alive and well.

"We can sit in the family room. My husband will be home in a few minutes. Can I get you a cup of coffee or ice tea?"

Bishop accepted the tea; additional coffee was more than he could handle.

"I found another photograph of Susan Elizabeth. It's a recent one. I think it looks more like her than the other two."

Bishop accepted the photo gravely, with all the importance it deserved. "Thank you," he said. "I'm sure this will help. Mrs. Morgan some other facts have come to light since Susan Elizabeth disappeared. I wonder if I could share them with you and ask you what you think they mean."

"I think you should call me Barbara, Mr. Bishop. Mrs. Morgan always makes me worry that bad news is coming, as in: Mrs. Morgan, I'm so terribly sorry." Barbara was holding her entwined hands together so tightly that her fingers had gone white. "It just seems more neutral."

Bishop smiled. It was his reassuring one. He often meant it, like now. "Barbara," he said gently. "It's come to my attention that Susan Elizabeth isn't the only child whose gone missing lately."

Barbara looked down at her hands, but she was listening.

"The other disappearances were very similar to your daughter's. And just like in her case, there was little or no mention in the media, no posters, no searches of the woods or neighborhood around the houses. Can you tell me why that is?"

"No." He could barely hear her.

"No, you don't know. Or, no you won't tell me?"

She shook her head.

"Barbara," Bishop said again. He could barely stop himself from reaching out to untwist the woman's hands, so the blood could come back into them. "Why did you hire me, when you won't tell me what you know? If you have a secret that will help me get your daughter back, I promise you, unless it's a crime, I will keep your confidence rather than make the situation worse."

"My. . . my husband wouldn't believe it. He wanted . . . he wanted to tell everybody, anybody who could help. He hired you without talking to me about it, but I made him promise not to, not to tell. The police said that was best. They didn't want you involved. The detective said it was probably okay though, because you couldn't find your ass with both hands." A hysterical little giggle escaped her lips. She unwound her fingers long enough to press one hand to her mouth in case another one tried to follow.

"Why did the police want to keep this quiet?"

"Because . . . because they knew what had happened to her."

"What?" Bishop was startled by the loudness of his own voice. More quietly he said, "Barbara, what are you telling me? Do you know where Susan Elizabeth is?"

"No, but they said she had probably been kidnapped by this religious cult that takes children away to protect them from the evils of the world. They keep them for a while and bless them and then return them to their parents as long as the parents haven't told. They brought a woman here who had the same thing happen to her child. She said it was true and that her daughter had come back, and she was okay. She also warned us not to tell."

"Do you remember the name of this woman?"

Barbara sighed. "It was all . . . I was very distraught. I'm not . . . I think it was a C--Corrin? Corvin? Corbin? Yes, Corbin. Mrs. Corbin." She clutched at his sleeve, "Please don't tell. Please. They'll never let her come back if you tell. If Suzee doesn't come back to us I don't know what I'll do." She burst into tears.

Bishop pulled tissues out of a box on the coffee table, a place it probably had never been kept when Susan Elizabeth was at home.

"I'm very glad you told me, Barbara," he said patting her hand. "I know it was very hard to do it. I promise you I won't betray you. I just want what you want—to have Suzee come back home."

Back in his car he opened his notebook to the list of missing children. Jennifer Corbin, age nine and a half, was the third entry. As he was pulling away, Susan Elizabeth's father pull his car into the driveway and hurried into the house. He and his wife were about to have a lot to talk about.

- 11 -

The Children's Shelter Project was open twenty-four hours a day, seven days a week. Sister Mary Catherine preferred the hours between seven p.m. and three a.m. She cared most about the homeless kids that came out at night because they had nowhere to go. The wannabes, the kids who came in from the suburbs, or skipped school to hang out on the streets because it was cool didn't interest her. She wanted the hardcore street kids, the ones who stole and lied and sold their bodies to survive.

Bishop had known the Sister for a long time. Even when he was a street cop he'd bring her kids, the ones who'd never survive in juvie, the thirteen-year-old baby hookers who might still be saved, the hard cases for whom jail would just be a graduate course in crime. She took them all, and gave them as good as she got, but always with an underlying compassion. She was impervious to being played.

If God was keeping score Sister Catherine was probably on the losing team, but she considered every small victory a solid win.

Bishop found her in the shelter lobby in the middle of what his politically incorrect self would have called a Mexican Standoff. Toe to toe with a teenage gang banger, she was arguing for possession of a thin, very pregnant girl of about sixteen. The girl's arms were covered with scabs and she was shivering with need. He boyfriend wanted her back on the street, so he could fix them both up.

Sister Mary Catherine was a nun, but she was also a gangly six-foot blond with the build of a natural athlete. Dressed as usual, in sneakers, jeans and a Loyola sweatshirt, she and her tattooed opponent were screaming into each other's faces, neither of them giving an inch.

Bishop had no gentlemanly impulse to step in and save the Sister. He'd seen her deck a pimp who'd pulled a knife on one of her kids with a straight right to the chin, then toss him unconscious into the gutter. He wouldn't have bet on the banger's chances once Cate became really pissed off. He waited quietly until the banger just gave up and left.

Catherine gave him a nod and motion of her head to follow her into the shelter as she herded the girl through the locked doors and into the care of the volunteer doctor on duty.

"Frank," Catherine said. "Long time no see."

"Yeah, the PD and I kind of parted company. I'm private now. I don't get down here so much anymore."

"You were one of my best herders, Frank. You had a real feel for these kids. You could always volunteer."

"Umph. Straight shot into the old guilt basket, Cate."

"Just trying to save your soul, Frank."

"Yeah, I'm still working on that 'road to hell' thing."

"I'm pretty busy here tonight, Frank. If you just stopped in to say 'Hi', I appreciate seeing you, but I have to get back to work." She started to move away from him toward the large room that served as a meeting room, lounge, holding tank and over-flow crash pad.

"I came about your missing kids, Catie." Catherine turned on her heel. He had her attention.

"Do you have some word on them? Do you know where they are? The cops won't even return my phone calls anymore. Bastards!"

"Sister!" Bishop was only feigning shock; he'd heard Sister Catherine's complete vocabulary on more than one occasion. She shrugged and looked at her watch.

"I'll give you ten minutes, Frank. Let's go into my office."

Sister Catherine's office was more like a broom closet. Bishop always thought of nuns as neat and organized—one plate, one cup, one pair of shoes type of thing. Sister Mary Catherine not only defied that stereotype, she exploded it. Her tiny cubicle was jammed with books, papers, half-drunk cups of coffee and articles of clothing. The visitor's chair contained a hooded, winter parka and two pairs of shoes which she scooped up and literally stuffed into an already bulging closet. "Donations," she explained.

Indicating that Bishop should take a seat, Sister Catherine dropped her lanky frame into her own rump sprung office chair and fixed him with her Mother Superior stare. It always made Bishop sit up a little straighter, even though he and Catie were about the same age.

"I'm working on a disappearance," he began. "A six-year-old girl kidnapped out of a park while she was supposedly being watched by her nanny." He could see Sister Catherine was about to interrupt him with a response. He raised a hand. "Hear me out," he said. "This comes around to your missing kids.

"It turns out that this isn't the only kid that's been snatched right out from under the noses of their loving family, but the weird thing is there's no media coverage of any of the disappearances. Your kids, even though they fit another profile because they're a bit older and homeless, fit into the same time frame. I think the two might be connected."

Sister Catherine sat forward. "Why?" she asked.

"Call it a hunch. But I really think it's too much of a coincidence to ignore. What I need you to help me figure out is what all these kids had in common. We've got eight kids under twelve from middle class families, and then we have I-don't-know-how-many, street kids all in the same time frame."

"Twenty-two," Sister Catherine said.

"What?"

"Twenty-two street kids I know of over the last five years, who either came to the Shelter Project or had a friend come here looking for them after they disappeared. At least that many. I'm afraid there's more."

"Do you have any idea why somebody would want to snatch homeless kids off the street?"

"Well, unfortunately there's a lot of reasons. Although they think they're pretty smart about surviving, runaways are really pretty vulnerable to adult predators, especially if they're hooking. We also have the occasional OD, stabbing, like that. Sometimes I don't see them for a while because they're in jail. That's why I went to the cops—to see if any of them had been arrested."

"Do you think they might have just moved on? Headed off to another city, greener pastures?"

"My gut feeling is no. One of the older ones even worked at the shelter. Jamal Perry. He also slept here in case there was a problem, or somebody rang the night bell. He was eighteen which is pretty much our age limit, but he was six months clean and sober and didn't want to be out on his own where he might slip. He was a really great kid. He spent his off time canvassing the squats and alleys for the first few of our missing kids. He always came back with two or three new runaways in tow, but never the ones we were looking for. He disappeared not too long after we started to be really concerned about what might be going on."

"Do you have any information on the kids, pictures, anything?" Bishop already knew the answer to this question.

Sister Catherine gave him a long look, then reached into a desk drawer and pulled out a folder. Inside were sixteen photographs with information written in pen on the back. "We try to photograph each kid that stays here even one night," she said. "Sometimes we need it to identify a body." She fanned the pictures out for Bishop. Sixteen young faces stared back at him with expressions that ranged from scared to solemn to defiant. One kid just looked blank, as if the experiences in his young life had rendered him numb and hollow.

"Can I take these?"

She shook her head, scooping the photo back into a pile. "These are mine, but I made some copies for the cops. I'll give you those. Are we done?"

"Two more questions: Do you know the name Nicolai Tesslovich?"

Cate surprised him. "Sure."

"I mean personally, not from newspaper coverage of a trial or something."

"Yes." Sister Catherine made a point of checking her watch. "He does some volunteer work for us. He renegotiated our lease and he helps us with emancipation applications and the occasional foster placement. Some of the foster homes these kids have been put in are worse than being on the street—sexual abuse, physical violence, bullying by older kids—some kids have even been pimped out by their foster parents. The only way we can keep them out of the system is to get them declared an emancipated minor. I was thinking of asking Nicolai to be on our board of directors."

Bishop bit his tongue. He wasn't going to tell Sister Catherine that Tesslovich was either a demon or involved in some strange set up that made it seem like he was one. That could come later. "How about Yamazaki Kiriyenko?"

"Nicolai introduced me to Mr. Kiriyenko at a big fund raiser we had for the Shelter. He gave us a very generous contribution and even some free computers and software to replace the dinosaurs we were working on. He seemed very nice."

"Has he ever been to the shelter?"

"No, and I can't quite imagine that happening. A guy who wears $10,000 suits isn't about to rub elbows with filthy street kids who've been sleeping in dumpsters. I hope he'll keep us in mind as far as the money goes though."

"What about Tesslovich?"

"Oh, yeah, he's been here. He'd rather come here than have our kids in his waiting room." She smiled. "We always try to give him the cleanest office and a decent chair."

Bishop stared at his notebook. He was going to have to think about this. He flipped it shut. Sister Catherine slid an envelope across the desk to him. Several papers followed in its wake, floating to the floor. As he started to lean over to pick them up she said, "Don't bother. It's a losing battle, I'll get them later." She stood up to see him out.

"Are you really going to look for my kids, Frank?"

Bishop nodded. "I think it's all connected. I'll do my best."

"We can't pay you anything, you know."

Bishop looked around at the well-worn lobby and shabby, second- or third-hand furniture. Stuffing was coming out of more than one couch and the tables had seen generations of shoes, cups, plates, knife points, ball point pen tips---whatever kids could manage to put on them or carve in them.

"Never expected you to, Catie. If I turn up anything, it's on the house."

As he headed for the front door Sister Catherine put a hand on his arm. "Thanks, Frank," she said, and let him go.

Now what? Every time Bishop turned around there was another weird twist in the case. If he was being conned he should stay away from Ariel and Mouser. If he wasn't, and the universe really had just been turned on its ear. Ariel could be in a lot of trouble that she had no idea was coming her way. At the very least, Mouser's info had panned out, and he'd also promised Bishop a witness to one of the disappearances. Bishop unlocked his, car, got in and started the engine. It was too late to do anything else, so he headed for the Caf'.

As he started down the steps to the Caf', the dim blue glow of cheap neon lighting coming through the single window at the bottom made Bishop think of the aquarium his uncle had given him as a kid. The floor of the rectangular glass tank had been covered in bright blue gravel into which he and his uncle had stuck some limp plastic fronds, a plastic diver and a cheesy miniature pirate's chest. The combination of the blue gravel and the dim light illuminating the tank made the few varieties of fish Bishop could afford look even more anemic and colorless than they had at the fish store.

He'd quickly discovered that since they did nothing but swim around, fish were really boring, except that everyday there seemed to be fewer in the tank. His uncle finally told him that was probably because they were eating each other. Alarmed, Bishop started to feed the fish more often, only to find his former cannibals floating belly-up on the surface of the water, ready to be recycled by the great cosmic flush.

Except for the cannibalism, the occupants of the Caf' reminded him of his fish, only instead of guppies they were geeks, vagrants and losers, swimming around in the same place, with no obvious interaction with anyone else, including each other. When he opened the door, no one even bothered to look up.

Before Bishop could ask, Ez jerked a thumb in the direction of the swinging doorway behind the bar.

Jesus, I've become a regular at 'Loser Central'. He flipped up the hatch that allowed entry behind the bar and pushed against the grimy hand plate on the swinging door that led into the café's kitchen. An old Chinese man in a filthy, food spotted cook's jacket was leaning against a counter smoking an unfiltered cigarette, letting the ashes drift onto the floor.

Mouser's back was to both of them. The young hacker was wearing headphones connected to a small box at his waist, his body bopping and swaying to music only he could hear as he transferred dishes covered with suds out of one side of the sink, into water in the other before setting them in a wooden rack to dry. Bishop had to touch the boy on the arm to get his attention.

Mouser looked over his shoulder, then pulled the head phones down around his neck. "Hey, Bishop," he said cheerfully, shaking the suds off his hands. "How's it goin'? I'll be with you in a minute, I'm just workin' off a couple of pizzas here. You want something to eat? Chen makes a mean bacon chili-cheeseburger with everything."

Bishop eyed the cook who narrowed his eyes as if daring him to interrupt his smoke.

"Uh, no thanks. I don't think I'm up to date on all of my shots."

The cook snorted and started waving his cigarette around, muttering to himself in Chinese.

"Aw, Dude, I think you hurt his feelings."

The large cleaver sunk tip first into an old butcher's block not too far from the cook hadn't totally escaped Bishop's notice. "Sorry," he called and beat a hasty retreat back into the café.

A beer and a double espresso were waiting for him on the counter. Scooping them up, he took them over to the nearest table. Mouser joined him a few minutes later, after stopping to retrieve his laptop from under the bar.

"Is El with you?"

Bishop shook his head. "I was hoping she was here, or if not, that you'd know where she is."

"Has something happened?"

"In a way," Bishop said. "El could be in trouble, hell both of us could be in trouble. I need to find her."

Mouser spread his hands. "I don't know where she is. She always comes here to see me."

"You don't have a phone number, email, something?"

Mouser shook his head. "Is she in danger?"

"If a mutual acquaintance finds her, I'd say yes."

Mouser tugged at his ear. "You're putting me on the spot here Bish."

"Do you know how weird all this shit is for me, kid? Either I'm being conned by a pro, for reasons I can't begin to imagine, or your feathered friend saved my life. Maybe she's perfectly safe, but I feel like I owe it to her to warn her."

Mouser stopped tugging his ear and scratched nervously at the back of one hand.

"I could give her a message."

Bishop shook his head.

Mouser sat.

Bishop drummed his fingers. "Okay," he finally said. "Tell her a mutual friend of ours showed up in court this morning."

Mouser stood up with a suddenness that made Bishop lean back. Picking up his computer in both hands, he ducked behind the bar and leaned over to say something to Ez. As Mouser whispered urgently in his ear, Ez raised his eyes and gave Bishop a penetrating stare. Bishop stared back. Without looking away, the barman gave the boy a barely perceptible nod, then took Mouser's computer and stuck it back under the bar. Mouser slipped through the kitchen door and disappeared.

Bishop sighed and turned back to his beer. He had no idea whether he'd done the right thing, or just worked himself deeper into the trap.

- 12 -

Ariel had just poured hot water on the tea leaves in her cup when the tapping on her window began. She cocked her head wondering if there was a wire loose outside, or if the wind had finally managed to start taking the building apart, one piece at a time.

She had become very philosophical about the old building's eccentricities. Alternating current meant 'sometimes I have electricity' and hot water was often accompanied by loud banging in the walls and strange burping noises from the drains. Nevertheless, she found her roof top apartment a comforting sanctuary. It was funky and basic, with a big open living space, large windows and few amenities. The rent was cheap, and the building was built like a fort. She felt both safe and protected and the bikers who ran the motorcycle repair shop in the attached garage on the ground floor seemed to look out for her. She'd decided it was probably the weird hours she kept and her cool leather coat.

The tapping started again. She leaned toward the window over the sink. A rusty brown hawk was flapping its white striped wings against the glass.

Ariel cranked the window open and the hawk streaked through. It landed on the wooden floor and quickly morphed into a naked Mouser. Ariel grabbed her coat from the back of a kitchen chair and tossed it to the young hacker who dove into it lapping the front.

"Sorry."

"No problem," Ariel said dryly. "Where did you leave your clothes?"

"On the roof, back at the Caf'. Can I have something hot to drink?"

Ariel handed him the cup of tea she had in her hand and pulled another mug off the shelf and made another cup for herself.

"This place is so cool. You could skate board in here."

"It's changed a bit since you were here last."

"More paintings." Mouser walked over to take a better look. "I like the blue one."

Ariel smiled. Blue was Mouser's favorite color. "Be careful, it's still wet. What are you doing here, Mouser?"

"Bishop is at the Caf'."

"So?"

"He came looking for you. He says you might be in danger."

Ariel's brow wrinkled. "Why?"

"He wouldn't tell me, but I could tell he was worried. He said something about a mutual friend showing up in court this morning. Ez's keeping an eye on him 'til we get back."

The wrinkle turned into a frown. "Did he give you a name?"

Mouser shook his head. "I don't think he wanted me to know. But I got the idea it was one of the names he gave me to research."

Ariel ran a hand through her hair. Bishop had to have meant Zaki. Tesslovich was dead. Why would he care if Zaki ended up in court?

"Okay," she said, indicating the metal French doors that opened onto her black tar front yard. "I need to change my shirt then I'll follow you back. You can wear that coat until we get out on the roof." Mouser was a dot in the air before she finished her sentence.

≈

A fully dressed Mouser was waiting for Ariel when she landed on the roof of the building that housed the Caf'. "Speed demon," she told him.

"It's a nice night for flying. I gave those falcons that roost on the Kastle Building a run for their money."

"You need to be careful, Mouser. There's more predators out there than you think."

Mouser just grinned at her and headed for the stairs.

Bishop had just started his second beer when Ariel pushed her way through the kitchen door, Mouser in her wake. A flood of unexpected relief hit Bishop. He'd told himself that he needed to see Ariel again to hear her explanation for a resurrected Tesslovich, but he also wanted to see that she was okay, especially after her refusal to ride home with him from Zaki's.

Ariel flipped open the hatch in the bar and threw herself into a chair at Bishop's table, long legs out in front of her, hands thrust deep into her coat pockets.

"Well?" She said.

Bishop checked out the rest of the room. Just because he saw most of the same faces didn't mean he should be sharing Ariel's business with them.

He hunched toward her. "Is there someplace more private we can talk?"

Ariel got up and headed for the far corner of the room where three over-stuffed chairs were pulled close together around a battered coffee table. Two were occupied by sallow teens with laptops.

"You mind?" Ariel asked. "Thanks."

The lapsters headed for an unoccupied table out of earshot. Bishop sat, sinking deep into the tired springs of his chair. Ariel sat a bit more carefully, having experienced the quality of the Caf"s furniture. Mouser perched on the arm of an empty chair.

Bishop cocked an eyebrow at Mouser. "He can stay," Ariel said. "We might need him."

"A guy I know, had to be in court this morning," Bishop began. "He told me a client of Tesslovich's was on the docket for a bail hearing——the counselor showed up with his client, 'big as life' you might say."

Ariel looked at Bishop as if he'd just said, 'pigs fly'.

"I mean it. He was there. My friend said he didn't look too good. Had on one of those cervical collars that hold your head up straight, but he was alive and talking—well whispering."

"That's impossible."

"Maybe he's some kind of regenerating demon? Pop his head back on and he's good to go?"

"He's not that type of demon. Plus, even that kind of demon doesn't regenerate after being decapitated."

"Cool," Mouser said.

"You're absolutely sure it was him?"

"I didn't see him, but my friend said there was no mistake. Everybody knows Tesslovich and everybody thought it was him."

"Maybe it was some kind of Zombie animation spell?" Mouser offered.

"See, I knew there had to be Zombies," Bishop said.

"Shut up Mouser," Ariel said. Then to Bishop, "He's not a Zombie."

"Maybe it was a glamor?" Mouser continued.

"Then why put him in a collar? Why not just make him look normal?"

"You're sure you actually . . .?" Bishop asked.

"Right off his shoulders in one clean stroke."

"He's seen us both, you know. He knows my name and address. I showed him my license."

"And if he finds you, he'll be one step closer to finding me," Ariel pointed out.

"Hey, I didn't tell him anything when he was having circus boy slap me around."

"That's because you didn't know anything, Frank. Now you do. And that beating you were getting? That was foreplay. The fun part was yet to come."

Bishop rolled that thought around in his head for a few seconds. He didn't like where this was going. "So, what do you suggest?"

Ariel shrugged. "He doesn't know what happened to you, and his witness went out a ten-story window and didn't get up and walk away, I can guarantee that. Maybe he'll leave you out of this."

"Yeah, I'm lucky like that," Bishop said. "C'mon. You know I'm right in the middle of this, whatever this is, and Tesslovich isn't going to forget about me, because I'm not going to forget about him. I went to the Runaway shelter tonight. The nun who runs it is an old acquaintance of mine. She's filed missing persons reports on twenty-two kids over the last five years. The police paid no attention, and none of the kids have ever shown up again."

Bishop reached into his coat and spread the pictures out on the coffee table. "She gave me photos of some of them. This one was a bit older than the rest." He pushed the photo forward. It showed a tallish, nice looking African American kid in his late teens with smooth mahogany skin, a short cap of copper dreads and an open smile. "He worked at the shelter. I got the impression he was a pretty responsible kid."

"Yeah?" Ariel scooped up the photos, shuffling each one to the top of the pile for a few seconds of scrutiny, then handed them to Mouser. "You know anybody here, Mouse?"

"A couple look sorta familiar. I can show the photos around."

Bishop nodded at Mouser. "I also want to meet that friend-of-a-friend you mentioned," he told him. "But I'm not finished. The most interesting thing I found out, is that Tesslovich was, is, a volunteer lawyer for the Shelter. He helped with petitions for Emancipated Minor status for some of the kids, negotiated some foster placements. Met with his clients at the shelter--alone. And he introduced Sister Mary Catherine to Yamazaki Kiriyenko at a fund raiser. Zaki gave them a donation."

"Could just be coincidence," Ariel said.

"Like Tesslovich's resurrection---pure chance in a random universe? You believe that, huh?"

"No," Ariel said, taking the photos back. "I believe something really nasty is happening, I just don't know why or how. But I do know that when I kill a demon, I expect the damn thing to stay dead! Can I keep this one?" She held up the photo of Jamal. "I think I might've seen him somewhere?"

"Keep them all, I have copies." Bishop took two business cards out of his pocket and handed them to Mouser and Ariel. "Call my cell if you come up with anything."

"You want us to talk about this on a cell phone?" Mouser seemed appalled. "Dude, does it have a scrambler?"

Bishop sighed. "I'm a private investigator, kid, not James Bond. The best deal I've got on my cell phone is unlimited long distance on weekends."

Mouser's disappointment in Bishop's judgment was palpable.

"Look. If you must call just pretend you're talking about something else, okay? I'm sure I'll figure it out. In the meantime,

I need to stop by M's workshop and pick up my new Demon Detect-o Ray 5000. Then I might try to actually get some sleep before the next Bat-Signal goes up." Bishop stood up and headed for the door. As he disappeared up the steps Mouser turned to Ariel. "We have a Demon Detect-o Ray? When did that happen?"

Ariel shook her head and leaned back against the grimy leather of the chair. She closed her eyes, fingering the photograph she'd slipped into her coat pocket. She didn't know what to think about the young man in the picture, let alone the fact that the demon she'd been instructed kill was still very much alive. It was only a matter of time before someone higher up noticed she'd blown her assignment and demanded to know the reason why. She didn't have a very good explanation for that yet.

And then there was Bishop. The Guardian's reaction to bringing a civilian into this mess was going to be ugly. She needed to pay somebody a visit before the whole thing blew up in her face, and she preferred the Raven to the Guardian any day of the week.

Besides, she had his picture in her pocket.

Ariel left the Caf' through the door to the alley behind the kitchen. She startled a cat foraging for food in the garbage cans next to the door. The thump and rattle it made lunging for safety behind the dumpster made her jump. That pissed her off, she was usually the one that made people look over their shoulder as they scuttled down alleys trying to escape.

She'd made up her mind to go talk to the Raven, better known to her as Tomas. Tomas had trained her. Taught her how to fight, choose the best weapons, how to survive. The Guardian had taught her the mission. She'd argued and fought with and even loved Tomas. She obeyed the Guardian.

When it was time, she'd been sent to the city. She had been here two years and in all that time no other Raptor had visited her even once. She liked to think that was because they had their own responsibilities, but it was also lonely.

She assumed Tomas was still in the same place. He'd been given a Dojo in another city about six hours drive away. It was a good cover, and no one ever questioned why he had all those strange weapons and taught special students how to use them in ancient forms of combat.

Ariel didn't have a car. The night was still young, and she could fly the whole distance, but it would take her longer than other forms of transportation, and she preferred to get there before first light. That meant the train. There was a freight that left the city yard at midnight. It always moved at a much slower speed until it reached the outskirts of the city where it could pick up the pace. Ariel knew which trestles and bridges it passed under as it headed out of town.

She didn't quite know where this skill at train jumping had come from, but it had helped her out more than once. If she hustled she could make the Third Street crossing with time to spare.

The trestle over Third Street was ancient, flaking black iron. It carried a single track and you could look straight through the ties to the rails of another track passing directly beneath it. It had its share of graffiti, but mostly its only visitors were Ariel and the trains. Ariel had been perched on the parapet of the trestle for five minutes.

Damn trains. Nothing runs on time anymore. But then the vibration started. She could feel it through her feet which were currently bare, so she'd be able to get a good grip when she jumped. There were always empty or partially loaded cars these days and the railroad usually forgot to lock the roof hatches. She liked train travel, you just had to know when to bail. With all the Homeland Security stuff there were more guards in the train yards than there used to be. Better to get off before you got there.

Ariel looked over her shoulder. The bright Cyclops eye of the engine was bearing down her. The train was only going 20 miles an hour, but that was fast if you had jump on as it went by. Ariel let the engine and maybe twenty cars pass under her. She could see some open car carriers coming up with more wooden freight cars behind them. The first freight car behind the carrier was her target.

Springing from the trestle she hit the roof of the car on all fours. The talons on her fingers and toes dug into the old wood as the car began to sway around the curve that took the train behind a neighborhood of tenements and rundown buildings that made up part of the south side slums. This was always the worst part of the ride. It brought Ariel even with the third-floor windows in the back of some of the buildings. Sometimes a light would be on inside and she could see the shabby, hopeless rooms with their shabby, hopeless occupants. People shouldn't have to live like that.

Scrabbling forward she made her way across the top of the car. It had a hatch in the roof, she could ride inside if she wanted to, but she had a much better target in mind---a whole carrier full of expensive comfort on wheels. They were just sitting in their little racks, noses pointed slightly to the sky just like the upper-class people who would eventually buy them.

Ariel swung down the ladder at the front of the freight car and leaped the gap between it and the carrier. Climbing up the rack, she picked the biggest car. A silver Mercedes with a huge back seat and an awesome satellite radio and CD player. Pulling a flat strip of flexible steel out of her sleeve she easily popped the door lock, opened the back door and slid into the plush, all leather backseat. She found a station she liked on the radio, lowered the volume to a comfortable level, set her internal clock for the appropriate wake up time and let the cadence and sway of the train rock her off to sleep.

~

At five a.m. the sky was barely tinged with light, so Ariel risked a short flight from the edge of the train yard where she'd glided, unseen, off the top the carrier to the flat, tarred roof of the Dojo. She folded her wings and used a convenient steel ladder to climb down the fire escape to Tomas' bedroom window. She tapped on the glass. She could have popped the lock and slipped into the room without much trouble, but Tomas was a Raptor and she didn't want to lose her head before she'd had a chance to explain what she was doing there.

The bottom of the window rose slowly on its sash. No one was visible on the other side. It was an invitation, but if she were Tomas she'd be flat to the wall on one side of the window with something large and pointy in one hand and extended talons on the other.

"Tomas? It's me, Ariel. I need to talk to you."

"Ariel?" Tomas dropped from the edge of the roof onto the fire escape rail behind her. She spun around. What was she thinking? Tomas' first rule had always been 'surprise the enemy'.

He dropped into a crouch, perching on the rail. He was dressed in black, string-tied cotton pants and no shirt. She'd obviously gotten him out of bed. His bare chest was a lesson in musculature, each one lean, taut, and defined.

"Are you crazy?' He hissed. "What are you doing here?"

"Fine, thanks. And you?" Ariel hated being snuck up on.

Tomas cocked his head and gave her his best Boot Camp instructor stare.

"Okay, I have a problem."

"You sure do if the Guardian finds out about this. We're not supposed to cross territories unless we have orders." Tomas jumped lightly from the rail and motioned Ariel through the window. Following behind her he switched on a bedside lamp as he walked past it.

Tomas' room was a lot like Tomas himself, stripped down to the essentials. Clean, neat with none of the normal clutter Ariel associated with men living on their own. Not that she'd had much experience with that.

Tomas retrieved a black t-shirt from a hook behind the door and pulled it on. It wasn't modesty Ariel knew, it meant whatever it was she had brought to him it had better be business. "Coffee?" he asked. Ariel followed him into the small kitchen down the hall from his bedroom.

This apartment was Tomas private quarters. Students lived in a dormitory downstairs next to the practice room. When Ariel was there the students referred to the Dojo as "Boot Camp", which was what it was. Get up early, stay up late. Get strong, be fast, face the enemy and survive. And: practice, practice, practice.

"You have any students downstairs?" she asked as Tomas set out cups and poured coffee.

"Not at the moment. Things are pretty quiet out there. We haven't lost anyone for a while and there's not much local activity. I haven't gotten a new recruit or a letter in at least a month."

Ariel fiddled with her cup trying to decide where to start. "Do you remember 'before' Tomas?"

"Ariel, if this is about us, that's over. We're Raptors, we can't have that any more. It doesn't work."

"I wasn't talking about us, Tomas. I meant before all this. Before we became whatever, it is we are."

"I only remember being what I am, El. There is no 'before' for me. It doesn't help to imagine there was."

"I still have the dreams, but I can't see the faces. Not clearly, not well enough to know them. The other thing I remember is the darkness . . . and the pain."

"We all remember that, El. That's why the Guardian was there when you woke up. Someone has to tell the new ones what they are. Are you still painting?"

"Yes."

"Maybe that's not such a good idea. Maybe you should just let it go."

"I blew my last assignment, T."

"What?"

"That's one of the reasons I came here."

"You missed the target? Try again. You don't need me to tell you that."

"That's the thing, I didn't miss him. I cut his head off. Green blood everywhere. He was dead when I left. Two days later he's in court in a neck brace, big as life. I know I have to try again, but he's going to be really hard to get to now, and what if the same thing happens?"

"Does the Guardian know?"

"Nope. But it's only a matter of time."

"You need to tell him."

"I'd rather be plucked, battered and deep fried. There's also something else. Over the last five or six years a lot of kids have just disappeared. Some younger, some older, some of them runaways, some regular children from loving families. There's a trail straight back to Tesslovich. What if I kill him before we find out why this is happening and what connection Tesslovich has to do with it? Maybe he's the link."

"Maybe that's why the Guardian put out the hit on him? Did you think of that?"

"That doesn't feel right I think Tesslovich is just part of the picture. I think there are other demons involved. If I go after him again they might become impossible to get to." Ariel looked straight into Tomas' eyes. "They're snatching kids, Tomas. What if we could find them? Get them back to their parents, wouldn't that be worth the wait to kill one demon?"

"We do one thing in this world, Ariel. We kill demons. The rest isn't any of our business. It has nothing at all to do with us."

Ariel stood up. "Maybe it does. Maybe it has everything to do with us." She reached into her coat pocket. "Twenty-two kids living in the Runaway Shelter downtown have disappeared in the last five years. The nun who runs it has pictures of most of them. She really cares about those kids, T. Even me, I care about at least one of them." She set the picture down on the table in front of Tomas. "Because you see, I'm pretty sure that kid in the picture is you."

- 14 -

Bishop was standing in the order line at Starbucks. He'd run out of coffee at home but somehow managed to get dressed and stagger down the street until he found the nearest source of caffeine. It wasn't hard. He could have staggered in any of the four available directions and found a Starbucks located equidistant from any of the others.

He was just telling the barista, "Triple espresso, no milk, no sugar, no flavors, no straw," when cannons started to go off in his pants. He grabbed for his cell phone. He was seriously going to kill that smug little shit at the cell phone store for making his ring the opening to the 1812 Overture.

"Bishop," he said, both into the phone and to the barista so she could write his name on the cup. He threw a five at her and retreated to the line for picking up drinks.

"Hey man, it's Rain. You awake yet?"

"I will be as soon as Starbucks gives me my coffee. What's up?"

The clerk called "Triple espresso." Bishop took it over to a table where it was quieter. His first sip was vaguely unsatisfying after the espresso at the underground cafe.

"Feel like going to the track?"

"The race track? You know I couldn't pick a horse if my life depended on it."

"I got a winner for you this time, my man. Quantum Leap is racing in the fifth. That's Zaki Keriyenko's horse. This is his professional debut, but I hear he's going to be hard to beat. His owner has a star box, but I'm sure he'll be at the rail for this one. I thought you might like to check him out."

"Pick me up in twenty minutes," Bishop told him. "I've just become a horse race fan."

Rain was dressed for a day at the track. His version of casual was a lime green silk polo shirt and perfectly pressed black slacks. Bishop had gone home, taken a shower, put on clean underwear and climbed back into what he'd put on that morning when he rolled out of bed, jeans, a blue t-shirt and a brown suede sports coat. Rain didn't comment. Bishop knew his former partner had moved from despair over Bishop's wardrobe to resignation a long time ago.

The track was surprisingly crowded. Diehard fans had suffered through the first two races and were poised for the third which was set to go off any minute. Rain had insisted on tickets for the second tier. Bishop had to admit the view was better there and they could order drinks from their seats. Rain had just managed to place a bet before the bell and he slid back into his seat as the horses in the third race burst from the gates.

"I put your pissant two bucks on Darby Sue to win." He handed Bishop the ticket. "I was embarrassed. I had to tell the guy I was doing it for my grandmother who was on a limited income."

"I'm on a limited income," Bishop told him. "It's getting

more limited all the time. I don't get all the perks you vice cops get."

"Hey! The hookers get older every year and the pushers get uglier. They should give those guys a dental plan."

Darby Sue won by a length.

"Mmm, mm, mmm, mmm, mm!" Rain gloated over his ticket. He snatched Bishops out of his hand. "Allow me to collect your six dollars, big spender. You should have trusted the Rain Mann. You want me to roll it over into another bet?"

"I think I'll stop while I'm ahead. There's a Happy Meal with my name on it tonight and I'm going to spend my winnings on extra fries."

While Rain was off placing his bets, Bishop settled back in his chair and looked around. He'd been to the track a couple of times with Rain when he was in Vice. One time they were following a big-time drug dealer indulging his hobby, the other was so he could lose thirty bucks while Rain perfected his system. He knew horse racing was big business and that bettors were addicted to the adrenaline rush of watching their horse try to make it to the finish line ahead of a pack of other horses trying to do the same thing. Unfortunately, that was the best part. It was the long waits in between races that bored Bishop out of his skull. When the waitress came around he bought a beer for himself and a diet coke for Rain. He set the coke in the cup holder on Rain's chair. He was now ten dollars in the hole, not counting admission. No large fries tonight.

Rain lost the fourth race. He tore up his ticket up in disgust and suggested they walk down to the paddock and see if they could get a look at Quantum Leap and hopefully his owner before the fifth race. That's when things started to get interesting.

Rain and Bishop weren't the only ones at the fence. Other race fans had obviously heard about the new entry and wanted to get a look at him before risking a bet. Bishop didn't know much about horses, but he knew a beautiful animal when he saw one. Quantum Leap was more than beautiful, he was magnificent. His coat was a chestnut brown so dark it was almost black. Muscles rolled under his skin as he moved. He held his head high, tolerating the attention he was getting, disdaining to react to any of the other horses around him as he was prepared for the race. The horse and his jockey wore scarlet and silver. Bishop seemed to remember from his research those were Zaki's corporate colors. Kiriyenko Industries logo was a scarlet disk with a raised, silver infinity symbol in the middle. Zaki obviously had plans for eternity.

"Wow." Bishop said.

"Really something, huh? Whoops. The odds are starting to change. Gimme a twenty," Rain demanded, "You are placing a bet on this one."

Bishop absently handed Rain a bill out of his wallet. The horse deserved a bet from him he thought, even if he lost. Rain hurried off to place their bets, Bishop stayed at the fence. All of a sudden there was a flurry of activity at the entrance to the paddock. Zaki had arrived with his entourage.

Zaki Kiriyenko's facial features had been given to him by his Japanese mother. He had the eyes, high cheekbones and haughty demeanor of a Samurai. His Russian father had given him his height and breadth of shoulder. Zaki was at least six three and wore his straight black hair in an unruly Cossack knot at the back of his head. It was the sort of non-hairstyle actors and models affected to show they could be tousled but still beautiful. It didn't make Zaki look the least bit effeminate. Instead he looked like Genghis Khan in a custom made Italian suit.

Bodyguards, minions, track officials, and two exquisitely beautiful women trailed in his wake. Behind them, like pilot fish, came the people who'd been lucky enough to be invited to his private box to watch Quantum Leap run. Zaki ignored them all and so did Bishop. He watched as Zaki ran his hands over the horse's neck, shoulder and flank as if feeling for the power he was about to unleash. The horse turned his head at his owner's touch, and his eye met Zaki's for a long moment, broken only by the jockey's hurried approach to the mounting block. As the jockey settled into the saddle, Zaki leaned in and gave him a final instruction. The jockey nodded as the groom began to lead the horse toward the gate.

Bishop's attention wandered to Zaki's guests. He recognized two politicians, a couple of famous sports figures, an actor and his latest girlfriend, and a familiar stripped suit. He couldn't believe it! It was the bandy-legged circus freak, the one who'd taped him to the chair in Tesslovich's office and tried to rearrange his face and puncture a lung. He was standing beside Tesslovich himself. The lawyer had traded in his neck brace for a white bandage. Bishop could see it circling his neck above the collar of his shirt.

As if feeling Bishop's eyes, the circus freak looked straight at, then past him. No recognition at all. But Tesslovich turned his head at the same time, following the little creep's gaze to the fence. Bishop ducked back into the crowd. Unless the decapitation had done something to Tesslovich's memory, he was sure the counselor would have no trouble at all recognizing him. Still stunned and unsettled, Bishop hurried back to his seat to watch the race.

Quantum Leap was the third horse. When the bell went off he came through the gate like a steam locomotive, shouldering his way through the other horses with long, powerful strides that ate up the track. It seemed effortless. His jockey was neither holding him back to conserve his strength for a burst of speed at the end or using the whip to drive him forward. He was just letting him run.

"Whoa!" Rain yelled in Bishop's ear as they leaped to their feet with the rest of the crowd. "Look at him go! That jockey's just along for the ride."

Quantum Leap won by two and a half lengths, blowing past the finish line, slowing, then turning with a bit of a prance as he was urged toward the winner circle by his rider.

Rain was doing a little dance too next to Bishop when he suddenly remembered he was cool, then he lost it again.

"Calm down," Bishop told him. "You're going to throw a clot or something."

"Ha, ha, ha, ha, ha!" Rain yelled. "Daddy gets a new pair of shoes!"

"Jesus." Bishop gave him a light shove. "Go collect your money. I haven't seen you this happy since you caught Tony 'The Horse' Ciceroni in the mop closet of his neighborhood Sports Club with three kilos of coke and a transvestite hooker."

"Yeah, yeah. I remember. He claimed the coke and the hooker were for personal use until he found out he'd just gotten it on with a dude." Rain started laughing again. "I'll meet you at the winner's circle."

Bishop wasn't certain that was a good idea. He hoped he'd ducked away fast enough for Tesslovich not to see him. He didn't understand why the little freak hadn't said anything to his boss. The two of them had been fist to eyeball for at least ten minutes, he couldn't imagine why the guy hadn't recognized him. Maybe he'd gotten a new brain after the first one splattered all over the pavement.

Bishop hung back. The pack of toadies hadn't followed Zaki down to the circle. They were probably still in the Star Box, drinking Cristal and toasting their connection to the rich and famous. Bishop could see Zaki and the horse with its garland of flowers. Their photos had already been snapped and Zaki was ordering the groom to remove the garland from the horse's neck. A small man in a white coat was going over Quantum Leap with great concentration. He listened to the horse's heart, looked in his eyes, ears, and mouth then felt his legs, running his hands up and down each leg, flexing them at the knee, examining the hooves. He hovered over a back leg and then popped something into his pocket. Finally, he waved at the groom, indicating that he could lead Quantum Leap back to the stalls. Zaki and he had their heads together when Bishop felt a tap on the arm. He jumped and swung around expecting freak-boy had crept up on him when he wasn't paying attention.

"Hey," Rain said. "It's only me. Me and my roll of cash. Let's go catch some dinner, I don't want to start handing over twenty-dollar bills in front of this bunch of losers."

Bishop remembered he'd given Rain a twenty to bet for him. "What did I win?"

"Five-hundred and fifty little green soldiers, man. I told you the Rain Mann knows what he's doin'"

"Five-hundred and fifty dollars? Me? What were the odds?"

"Eleven to one."

"That's too much."

"Too much? You gave me a fifty, man. I put it all on the nose."

Bishop felt a moment of vertigo. He'd almost lost fifty bucks. What was he thinking? Then he reconsidered. Hey, I won Five-hundred and fifty bucks! What about that?!

"How much did you win?" he asked Rain.

Rain made a little humming sound. "Don't ask, man. Just don't ask."

≈

Rain picked up the tab for dinner, which was very unusual. Bishop figured he must have won a packet. Otherwise he'd be waiving the bills in Bishop's face and crowing about the amount. If it was too much to brag about, it was a lot.

"So," Bishop started. "That was a really fast horse."

"Fast? I've never seen a horse run like that in my life. If they didn't booster test before every race, I'd have said he'd been doped. I bet there's already been a complaint filed. But the track paid off so it's just sour grapes on somebody's part."

"I saw what looked like a vet going over the horse after the race. I think he took some blood. But I couldn't really see him doing it."

Rain shrugged. "A good race horse is worth a lot of money. They have docs hanging all over them making sure they're okay. That horse is going to be worth even more after this race, although he'll never have the odds he had today. I would've thought they'd hold him back for a few races until he qualified for a big one, then let him beat the pants off everybody else's winner for a high buck purse. Maybe Zaki's too rich to care about the money. Maybe he just likes to win."

Bishop finished his beer. "I don't know why, but that's what I'm afraid of."

Rain threw some bills on the table for a tip. "You know, just because I'm celebratin' doesn't mean I haven't noticed you're not telling me what's goin' on."

"Hey, I don't understand what's going on. It's complicated." The image of the little man in the stripped suit popped back into Bishop's brain. "And weird. Really, really weird."

- 15 -

So much for having the last word: You come to town in a Mercedes and go home on the bus.

Ariel hated the bus, but she didn't want to chance jumping a train in broad daylight. She walked to the bus station, bought a ticket on the first bus going in the right direction and claimed a window toward the back. The guy who took the aisle seat next to her smelled like rancid Cheetos and three-day old beer. He'd tried to start up a conversation, but one look from Ariel's angry bird-of-prey eyes and he shut up. When he got off he was replaced by a kid with an iPod implant that was leaking an angry Rapper rant through the multiple holes he'd pierced in his face. Perversely, it seemed the perfect background noise for bus travel.

Ariel wrapped herself tighter in her coat and shut her eyes. Tomas had been a bad call and a wasted visit. She'd gotten nothing, except she could tell that the photograph had caused the tiniest crack in the Raven's glacial cool. She left it on the kitchen table when she stomped out. It wasn't her problem now, it was his. Maybe. She made a mental note to check if Mouser had had any luck getting a lead on the other lost kids. If not, she was going to start turning over some rocks to see what crawled out. She hadn't done that in a while. It would be fun.

- 16 -

Bishop asked Rain to drop him off at the old office building where he rented a space for Bishop Investigations. The building wasn't far from his apartment and he needed to check his mail, send out a couple of invoices and throw out the latest in a long line of neglected potted plants before he called it a night. Bishop didn't know why he kept buying plants for the office since he never took care of them. At least they weren't puppies.

As he climbed the steps to the front door, the target zone between his shoulder blades began to itch. It was the place in Bishop's imagination where his own personal bull's eye was painted. To the left of it, and higher up on his shoulder, was a real scar. The shooter had missed the kill zone, but Bishop still spent three weeks in the hospital and two more on pain killers while internal affairs raked his ass over the coals for shooting back.

The office was a third-floor walkup. Bishop liked to think of it as very Sam Spade, but that was mostly because nothing in the building had been up-graded since 1942. He had one big room with an old wooden desk backed up to a set of large, double-hung windows. Two client chairs faced the desk even though clients usually came to Bishop in ones, wanting to hire him to follow the person who might normally be occupying the other chair. A red couch, old leather recliner and a Salvation Army coffee table sat in a loose group against the opposite wall on an old oriental rug left behind by the previous tenant. A small closet had coat hooks on the back of the door and a sink inside with a mirror over it. The toilet was down the hall.

The office was basic, it was cheap, and it had been totally trashed.

Bishop stood in the doorway, one hand on the knob, the other on the light switch, his mouth open in disbelief. All the drawers had been pulled out of his desk, file cabinets hung open, their contents scattered all over the floor. His furniture had been over-turned, gutted and smashed. Stuffing from the couch had been pulled out and tossed in all directions. His small television lay in a puddle of what he hoped was stale coffee from his broken coffee pot and his computer monitor had ended up in the wreckage of his recliner with a chair rail sticking out of the screen.

There was also a disgusting stench that made Bishop think of rotting Gyros. He moved reluctantly into the room and shut the door. Except for the missing drawers, his desk seemed to be remarkably intact, all the better to display what the vandals had left behind.

The reeking goat head on the desk top stared balefully at Bishop with dead, amber eyes. It had been a white goat with horns and a long, pointy tongue that now protruded obscenely from between its teeth. To make sure the tongue didn't creep back into the goat's mouth when no one was looking, a black handled knife had been jammed through the swollen organ to hold it to the surface of the desk. The goat's pristine white coat was embellished with red and black symbols; whorls, triangles, squares and wavy lines. None of it made any sense to Bishop except he knew a dead goat when he saw one.

Since his office phone had been ripped out of the wall, Bishop started to pull out his cell to call 911 when he heard the door open behind him. He whirled around, grabbing at his hip, only to remember his gun was still safely locked up in the metal box in his closet at home. He was about to grab a convenient chair leg off the floor when a familiar voice said,

"Jesus, Bishop. You need to do something about the janitorial services in this dump."

Rain shut the door behind him. "After I dropped you off I saw some little weasel in a striped suit come slinking out of the alley carrying what looked like a computer deck. He was behind me, so I only caught him in the mirror, but it gave me a bad feeling. I thought I'd come back and make sure you were okay."

"Just peachy," Bishop said, setting the only un-smashed chair back up on its feet. "I was so busy admiring the rest of the redecoration I didn't notice my computer was missing." He walked around the desk, glanced into the knee hole, then stuck his head out the open window behind him.

"Yup, gone. But there's my desk chair, telephone and a dead Fichus sitting in the alley. Man, I'm going to miss that plant."

"Bishop?"

"Mmmm?"

"I didn't want to say anything while you were taking your moment, but there's a goat head on your desk."

"Yeah, that wasn't there when I locked up the other day. What do you think it means?"

"You have a fan club that's into livestock?"

"Nope."

"Then I think it's some sort of warning. Maybe even a curse."

"Huh? Okay, a threat, sure. Divorce work's a risky business.

But a curse? What's it supposed to do, doom me to buy new office furniture? And what's all that red, squiggly stuff? And the knife? Somebody stuck a knife in my perfectly good, seventy-year-old desk. What am I supposed to do about that?"

"Calm down, man. How did the guy get in here in the first place? Was the door open?"

"Locked when I got here," Bishop told him. "The window was open."

"So, what you're sayin'," Rain pulled a pen out of his pocket and began to poke at the goat head. "Is somebody either had a key or he shimmied three stories up a brick wall with a goat head under his arm, trashed your office and stole your computer."

While Bishop pondered that concept, Rain worked on the goat head. He stuck his pen into the goat's mouth and wiggled it around. Then he reached into his pocket and pulled out a white handkerchief. Wrapping it carefully around his hand, he pulled the knife out of the goat tongue, leaving a deep, triangular shaped hole in the desk. The head fell over onto its back. Rain grabbed its snout and started prying at something inside the mouth.

"Are you dating a Gypsy with a jealous husband?" he asked, as he tried to make the jaws open a little wider around the swollen tongue

"Of course not," Bishop said. "That's disgusting!"

"You got something against Gypsies?"

A wadded-up ball of paper popped out of the goat's mouth like a cork out of a bottle. Rain caught it before it hit the desk. He used his gloved hand and the side of the pen to unwad it and smooth it flat on the wooden surface. It was covered in strange brown letters and symbols that appeared to have been made with an old-fashioned ink pen.

"I meant what you were doing to the goat." Bishop said. He peered over Rain's shoulder at the paper. If the writing was a series of words, it was in a language he'd never seen before.

"What is that?" he asked. "What does it say?"

"I don't read Romanian," Rain told him, holding the paper up to the light. "But that thing I said about having something against Gypsies? You can start that anytime. I think this is written in blood."

- 17 -

Bishop felt like an idiot. He'd let Rain drag him to a seedy part of downtown, so he could stand in front of Madame Zebella's Good Fortune Grotto, holding a plastic bag filled with ripe goat head like some lost shepherd of the damned. Rain had already rung the bell, only to be told in a heavily accented voice, Madame Zebella was currently with the spirits and would be with them in a moment. The electric lock clicked the door open and admitted them to an equally seedy waiting room containing four orange plastic chairs, a profusion of purple curtains and a collection of mystic trash.

All religions were equally represented in the decor. Bishop particularly liked the 3D plastic portrait of a Hindu goddess with six arms and a necklace of skulls. The arms moved, and the skulls smiled or frowned depending on how he tilted his head. Her eyes seemed to follow him around the room no matter what he did to avoid them.

"When did you start hanging out with Gypsies?" Bishop asked, turning his back on the goddess.

"Zebella and I go way back," Rain told him. "When I was a

beat cop I used to bust her on a regular basis for shop lifting and general grift. When she moved up in the world and I got my gold shield we came to an understanding."

"You mean she's one of your snitches?"

"I retain her services as a consultant," Rain said primly. "She knows every con artist in the city."

The curtains on the back wall suddenly parted, launching an ocean liner of a woman draped in layers of colored scarves, skirts and shawls. Her pudgy arms were loaded with gold and silver bracelets, rings sparkled from every finger. Her hair was a tangle of dyed black curls and despite the purple eye shadow; her eyes were bright and intelligent.

"Mr. Rain," she said in mock admonishment. "You tell your friend lies about Zebella. I am an honest woman. I only tell the truth!"

Rain took Zebella by the hands and surveyed her generous charms. "As gorgeous as ever, Bella, and not a day older than the last time I saw you."

"Pffft!" Madame Zebella gave him a small shove. "Who's liar now? You don't come to see me anymore. My feelings are hurt!" She looked over at Bishop.

"Your friend smells like a goat. What you want from Bella, Mr. Rain?"

"My friend needs a consultation. I think he may have acquired a bit of a curse."

Bella's eyes took in Bishop's plastic bag. "Come," she gestured. "We go in the back. I think I need my special equipment."

The back of Madame Zebella's Good Fortune Grotto was much more elaborate than the front. Behind the curtain was a steel reinforced door with several locks which Zebella shut behind them with a decisive thunk.

"Thieves," she explained. "You can't be too careful."

Rain grinned at Bishop as Bella led the way to a round, satin draped table with a crystal ball in the center. The room was lined with dark mirrors that reflected the muted light of numerous sconces shaped like angel wings. The air was heavy with the smell of incense, which was probably a blessing considering the goat.

"You sit." She instructed. "Tell Madame Zebella your troubles and she will advise what to do."

Bishop put the bag with the goat head on the table and peeled back the plastic. "Somebody left this in my office with a note. Unfortunately, I don't read dead goat. Rain thought you might be able to help."

Madame Zebella's ringed fingers flew to her mouth as if she was trying to catch the gasp she'd made before it got out into the room.

"So, it's a problem?" Bishop asked.

"This is bad, very bad!"

"You want bad? You should see my desk. I don't think it's going to be easy to get that blood stain out."

"You have note?"

Rain handed the note across the table and set the knife gently on the edge of the open plastic bag.

Madame Zebella produced a pair of very un-Gypsy like reading glasses and leaned over the note without touching it. Her lips moved silently as she read, then clamped tight as if even mouthing what was written carried a risk. When she was done she snapped the glasses off and tucked them into a fold of her voluminous skirt.

"This curse is in an ancient, pre-Christian dialect from the area we now call Romania."

Bishop goggled. Madame Zebella's accent had totally disappeared.

"It's still spoken in some form today, mostly by Travelers, which people like you call Gypsies. The curse, in this form, is referred to as "The Revenge of Three". It's a very unusual invocation. Like many curses, it involves a blood sacrifice. The goat is the vessel that carries it to its target. All those markings on the head make sure the curse doesn't get lost on the way."

Bishop frowned. Madame Zebella was even more of a surprise than he'd anticipated. "What is this curse supposed to do?"

"It's a death curse. Meaning that it's both revenge for a death, and a promise that blood will be spilled in return. This knife," Madame Zebella indicated the wedge-shaped blade, "is a traditional Romanian throwing knife. It's often used in carnival acts where one performer is strapped to a spinning board, and a partner throws a knife that barely miss hitting the body. A blessing is often done before the performance to protect the person on the board by making the blade fly true. This curse attracts the knife, rather than repels it. The triangular shape of the blade repeats the rule of three as well as making quite a wound if you're struck by it."

Bishop felt the bull's eye between his shoulder blades light up like a neon sign. "Can you cancel this curse thing? Put a counter-whammy on it or something?"

"Let me see your hand." Madame Bella's own fingers were remarkably warm, although Bishop imagined his own hand had gone stone cold because all his blood was in the process of rushing to his head.

"Your fate is unclear," Madame Bella intoned. "As long as the one who initiated the curse is still alive the curse will be active. Therefore, your death is in the hands of others. But I can see that you have strong and unexpected alliances. That means your life may also be attached to the will of more positive forces. There is hope, but I would be very, very careful."

Bishop took his hand back and examined the palm. "You saw all that in there? Before I start assuming any of this is true, let me ask you a question. Is this all an act? You don't sound much like a Gypsy anymore."

Madame Zebella pressed one ringed hand to her chest. "Dr. Bella Zalbeck," she said with a slight bow toward Bishop. "Professor of Eastern European Mythology and Ethnic Studies. I come from a long line of full-blooded Romany Travelers. I put myself through college working this neighborhood in a slightly different profession than I have now." She nodded in Rain's direction. "Madame Zebella funds my research, but it's not an act. You are in serious danger."

Bishop looked over at Rain, who gave him a grim little smile. He'd known what Madame Zebella was all along.

"What do I owe you?" Bishop asked, wanting to escape to fresh air.

"I cannot take money from you for this. It would bind me to your fate and I am not willing to risk that. I can, however, provide you with a small charm of protection."

She stood, her skirts swaying to the undulation of her generous hips as she made her way to a large wooden cabinet with many small drawers. After a moment's thought she pulled one out and removed a round piece of yellow metal about the size of a quarter tied to a red string.

"Carry this with you at all times," she said, placing it in Bishop's hand. "If it becomes warm to the touch, prepare to defend yourself."

Going back to the table, she placed the note and knife into the plastic bag with the goat head and knotted it shut. Waving her hand toward Bishop, she indicated that he was expected to remove it now that she was done with it.

"Burn it," she instructed.

As she saw them out Bishop watched her put a hand on Rain's arm and whisper something in his ear before she closed the door behind them. Locks clicked into place one, by one.

"What did she say to you?" Bishop asked, holding the bag with the goat head at arms-length.

Rain looked back over his shoulder at the door. "She told me I needed to be careful carrying so much money in my pocket in this neighborhood."

Bishop shook his head. "And I thought I had weird friends."

Rain insisted on taking the knife with him. It was evidence and there was the possibility of fingerprints on the handle. He made Bishop dig it out of the bag and drop it into one of the plastic evidence bags he carried in the trunk of his car.

"If there's prints I'll run them through the database. It may take a while. Un Uh!" he said as Bishop opened the passenger door. "You're not bringing that stinky goat head back into my car."

"She told me to burn it. I can't do that right in the middle of the street, I have to take it somewhere."

Rain sighed. "Okay. I know a place, but nobody better see us. I think it's against the law to burn ungulates inside the city limits."

The abandoned lot was next to an empty brick warehouse and a freeway bridge. A couple of oil drums on the property had already been used for fires, probably in the winter when the homeless gathered to camp in abandoned buildings and under bridges.

Rain pulled a gas can out of his trunk, leaving the bag to Bishop. "Throw it in there," he said.

Bishop dropped the bag into the drum and stepped aside to let Rain soak it with gasoline. Rain produced a book of matches, lit one and threw the rest of the book in after it. The can ignited with a loud whoosh.

"Done," Rain said, the light from the fire gave his face a demonic look. "Let's get the hell out of here."

From a decorative parapet high up on the old building, eyes watched their movements. As they accelerated down the street, leathery wings unfolded to follow the car.

The Seventh Circle was a bar down by the waterfront in a decidedly non-yuppie neighborhood. All the flickering red neon sign mounted on the outside wall said was: BAR. A drippy red circle with a slash through was painted on the door was over black letters that said 'Abandon All Hope'---it was either a real warning or a 21st century demon joke.

Tobacco-yellowed scenes from Hieronymus Bosch paintings covered the walls inside. Ugly, round little demons with bird heads prodded naked, potbellied humans into flaming holes in the earth.

No one who patronized this bar ever said to a friend, "I'll meet you at the Seventh Circle." They said, "See you in hell."

It was that kind of place.

Smoky was an understatement inside the Circle. The atmosphere was more like a fog bank. Smoke hung in the air like it was part of the building. Opening the door brought in unwelcome rushes of slightly cleaner air that soon gave up and joined the general sea of pollution. Nobody enforced non-smoking laws in this bar, and it wasn't all tobacco. Heads turned when Ariel walked in, but nobody stared. The Circle was a truce bar. It catered to a mixed crowd, supernaturally speaking, and if patrons had issues with each other, they took them outside.

It had been awhile since Ariel had gone out for a drink. She'd dressed for the occasion; black leather jacket over a bodega t-shirt with a picture of a shackled woman surrounded by a sea of flames, a mid-thigh black kilt with buckles and straps, ripped tights and battered engineer boots. She let the talons on her fingers slide out. They were cheaper than nail polish and probably more conservative than the accessories of some of the other patrons.

Ariel hooked a stool at one end of the bar with a booted foot and slid onto it. She could see most of the room in the mirror behind the liquor shelf. It was early yet, and she didn't see anyone she knew except for the bartender, who set a shot glass of tequila in front of her next to a bottle of beer. His knobby head was speckled with irregularly shaped yellow spots and there was just a bit too much peak to his ears and point to his teeth for human. As he set down her drinks he said, "No trouble, okay?"

"It's my day off," she told him. "People leave me alone, I leave them alone. It's as easy as that."

The bartender shook his head. Ariel had no days off where trouble was concerned. She ignored him. He worried too much. If somebody tried to start something with her, was that her fault? Any demon in here should know better, but some hotheads never learned.

"You seen Timmy Jon?" She asked the bartender. Timmy Jon was a polite, soft-spoken thief of southern extraction. He was also a demon, but basically harmless. He broke into empty apartments during the day, and shops at night after everyone had left. Timmy Jon didn't want any trouble; he just wanted to make a living off other people's stuff. He also sold information.

Timmy Jon was nosy. He listened to other people's conversations and he read other people's mail. When he broke into people's houses he raided their refrigerator and surfed porn sites on their computer. He also looked at their email and rifled through their underwear drawers. T' Jon knew a lot of things about a lot of people, and he could be persuaded to share what he knew with the right people, for the right price.

Ariel was just considering switching to white wine when T' Jon walk through the door. He'd either recently robbed a pimp or someone in the Vegas end of the entertainment industry. His jacket was an appallingly shade of chartreuse over an expensive maroon polo shirt and yellow slacks. If the demon-thief had a professional fault, it was a total lack of subtlety.

He nodded to Ariel and sauntered over to the bar. "El," he said, taking the seat next to her. "Long-time-no-see. I was starting to worry. How is my favorite feathered female avenger?"

"Same old, same old," El told him. "I imagine you want me to buy you a drink?"

"So, kind. Bartender, a Kettle One Greyhound in a large Martini glass, double eye balls."

"You do that just to gross me out, don't you?"

T' Jon gave an elaborate shrug. "I'm a dog lover, what can I say?"

The bartender delivered T' Jon's drink. "I need information," Ariel told him after the bartender had moved away.

"Quelle surprise." T' Jon took a sip of his drink. "Domestic grapefruit," he complained. "I really should change bars."

"What do you know about resurrection?" Ariel asked impatiently. T' Jon had the palate of a homeless Sterno addict.

"I assume we're not talking about 'The' Resurrection?" T 'Jon made quote marks in the air with his fingers. "I'm not willing to get involved in those politics."

"I'm talking about demon resurrection Timmy."

"Me too but be that as it may. What demon?"

"Nicolai Tesslovich."

"Tesslovich? Hmmm. He has been looking a mite peaky lately."

"I'm serious, T' Jon. I killed Tesslovich myself. Dead. Three days later he was back in court, head on his shoulders and slimy as ever."

"Curious." Timmy mused. "He's not that type of demon."

"Precisely my point. Something strange is going on and I need to know what it is."

Timmy Jon toyed with his glass, spinning it on the bar top by its stem. "I have heard . . . something. Just rumors. Some sort of regeneration technology. Not magic though. Science. I don't have any details, but there's buzz."

"Can you find out for me?" Ariel slid a small square of folded green across the bar. It disappeared like magic into T' Jon sleeve.

"If I can't, girlfriend, no one can."

"Be careful, T' Jon. There's something bigger going on than we know about." Ariel slid off her stool and threw a twenty on the bar. "Another double Greyhound for my friend," she called to the bartender. "Hold the eyeballs."

As she crossed the barroom to the door the bartender said with a certain amount of wonder, "No Trouble?"

Just before the door closed behind her she heard T' Jon say "It's all a matter of perspective, my friend. All a matter of perspective."

19

It was a great night for flying. The thermal currents created by the tall buildings and the updrafts from trapped ground heat made it a challenge. Mouser thought of it as air surfing; catch the lift, take the drop, ride the invisible wave until it was ripped out from under your wings by a change in geography or a wicked shift in the wind. It was the most alive he ever felt, except for a few hacks that had taken him places in the web he'd never expected to go. That was cool. But flying was better.

Still, he had to be careful. There was more than one kind of predator using the sky. Some of them roosted on the ledges of tall buildings waiting for unwary prey, others aggressively defended their territory like the falcons living on the Exchange Bank Building who chased him for blocks every chance they got.

Most, like the falcons, weren't shifters, although Mouser had met a few who'd gone totally feral, never changing back into their human form. They liked living high up. Mouser could understand the freedom it brought them, but he passed on their diet. He'd eaten one mouse too many in the early days, now he was strictly PBJ, pizza, burgers and coffee.

Ariel had made that possible for him. Two years ago, she'd

saved his feathered butt from a much bigger hawk that he couldn't seem to out-fly. Swooping in from nowhere she'd grabbed him right out of the sky. By the time they hit a roof he was a naked twelve-year-old, shaking with cold and fear at his narrow escape. Ariel had wrapped him in her coat, taken him home and put him to bed on her couch.

When he woke up the next morning he'd asked her why? How did she know he wasn't just another bird losing its battle for survival of the fittest?

"I've been watching you," she told him. "I couldn't let that happen."

She got him off the streets, out of the cold. He couldn't remember how long he'd been on his own, it seemed like years, and he couldn't remember anything before that. Nothing about parents, family, friends--- just the day he discovered he wasn't all human, and best of all, that he could fly.

Mouser had a crush on Ariel, but he knew he was just a fourteen-year-old kid. She treated him like a younger brother, but she'd also taught him things. Important things. Survival things. She taught him how to defend himself and how to watch his back. She found him his first computer then turned him over to Ez at the Caf' so he could hang with people like himself.

Ez had some interesting tricks of his own to share. Each kid at the Caf' had his or her own set of skills. Some, like Zoe who could open any lock in a matter of seconds, didn't invite too much scrutiny. They all gamed and surfed and hacked, but some of them had jobs too. They went out into the world, but they came back to where it was safe. Mouser sometimes imagined himself to be one of the Lost Boys, except Wendy killed demons and there was no Peter Pan.

Ez warned all the younger ones not to go out alone at night, but Mouser had promised Bishop he'd show the photos of the missing street kids around. He was part of the team and he had a job to do.

The only inconvenient thing about shifting from a hawk to human was you came back naked. Mouser had a shifter's usual lack of modesty, but you couldn't run around the streets naked for very long before somebody freaked out. Alleys were good for stashing your clothes, but roof tops were even better.

Mouser shrugged back into his clothes. They were his usual thrift store, poor box mish mash. He still looked like a street kid and he still knew where street kids hung. He'd scouted this neighborhood with care.

Before he hit the fire escape, Mouser made sure he still had the photographs of the missing kids in his jacket pocket. If he didn't get any hits from the usual places he'd go deep. If these kids weren't on the streets anymore they had a good reason not to be.

So, he was going to go where you went when you were running from the Big, Big Bad. He'd taken a friend there once, when she was trying to get away from a father Mouser would have sicced Ariel on in a minute, if he'd known her then.

The Deepers had wanted to keep him, but he wasn't running from anything except hunger and loneliness, so he'd slipped away before getting too far in. He hoped Sissy was okay now, that she'd made it to California like she always wanted. She told him she'd heard if you went deep enough there was a train to the other side of the world, where you'd be safe and warm, and nobody would try to hurt you just because you were a kid that nobody would ever miss.

He didn't believe that, but Sissy did. And Mouser thought everybody ought to be allowed a dream.

20

Trashed, smashed, tossed, wasted, torn up, obliterated and destroyed. Bishop had always been told that things looked better in the morning, but as far as his office went, things looked worse. He'd left the window open hoping to air out the smell. All it did was blow his paperwork around, creating even more of a mess. The goat head was gone but some enterprising pigeons had found their way in and used the top of his file cabinet as a latrine. He booted one off the window sill before slamming it shut. Now it was just him and the mess.

Ariel found him sitting in the last un-smashed chair, looking like Hamlet after he'd been told the bad news.

"This is your office?" she asked, shutting the door. "What happened?"

"It's part of a curse," Bishop told her. "You missed the flaming goat head and threatening note. That was last night. I'd offer you a chair, but I'm sitting in the only one that still has four legs and I'm not getting up."

"What were they looking for?"

"Beats me. They took my computer, I can't tell yet if there's any paper files missing, but off the top of my head I'd have to say it's the missing kids. How did you find me?"

"You gave me your card, remember?"

"I'll have to stop handing those out. It attracts the wrong element. What can I do for you?"

"I'm looking for Mouser. Ez says he hasn't seen him for almost 24 hours. I thought he might be with you."

Bishop sat up straighter. "I haven't seen him since the other night at the Caf'. Maybe he's visiting friends."

"Mouser doesn't stay out all night unless he crashes with me. It's too dangerous. Ez is really strict about it."

"Ez? The petrified man? He can barely make himself move from one end of the bar to the other."

"That's not . . . he keeps an eye on the kids who hang out in the Caf'. They crash in the back. He feeds them, tries to keep them out of trouble. He knows where they are most of the time. When Mouser didn't check in by this morning he gave me a call."

"He was going to check out the kids in those photographs, you don't think . . .?"

Ariel shrugged. "I'm worried, Bishop. He gets really into conspiracy theories, and flying saucer sightings and video game superheroes, he's amazing on the computer, but he's just a kid. I'm afraid he might get in over his head."

"Space aliens, superheroes?" Bishop cocked an eyebrow at Ariel. "Yeah, who'd believe in that?"

"I'm serious, Bishop. Will you help me find him, or not?"

"Look, I'm sure the kid's fine. But I'll be happy to help you look for him. The only problem is I need to go talk to this woman who said her kid came back months after disappearing, perfectly fine. She told my client that if she didn't tell anyone her daughter was missing she'd get her back too."

"Well, maybe it is a little early in the day to go looking for Mouser. If he's hanging out with a bunch of runaways he probably crashed in some squat last night and won't be up until mid-afternoon..."

"Tell you what," Bishop dropped a pile of wrinkled papers and mangled file covers on his desk. "It doesn't really matter if I clean this up now or later. My filing system was pretty lousy to begin with. Why don't you come with me to the Corbin's? Maybe you can get the kid to talk while I chat up the parents, then we'll look for Mouser. I bet he'll be back safe and sound at the Caf' by the time we're through. I'll buy him pizza while you get all scary and parental. It'll be just like a night with the Addam's Family."

"This won't take very long?"

"Twenty-minute drive, fifteen minutes with the family, in and out."

"Can I drive?"

"No."

21

The Corbin's neighborhood was more down scale than the Morgan's. The houses were smaller and the upkeep not as good. Lawn cutting had been ignored by some residents; others used their front yard for extra parking. The Corbin house was neater on the exterior, but it had a solemn, internal look to it as if the residents seldom came outside to enjoy the fresh air. Bishop knocked.

Behind him, Ariel was giving the neighborhood a once over, her eyes flitting from one house to another, taking in the cars parked at the curb, the toys and trash in the yards.

"Stop that," Bishop told her. "You're making me nervous. I don't want to spook these people."

The door opened a crack. Just above the doorknob Bishop could see one bright blue eye and a tangle of light brown hair.

"Is your mother home?" he asked. "She's expecting me." The door opened wider.

"She's in the kitchen with Jen'fer," the child informed him. "Jen'fer was hungry. She won't wait when she's hungry."

"Can we go back and talk to her?" The five-year-old led the

way, her dirty flip flops making sticky flop, flop, flop noises on the scuffed hardwood floor of the hall.

The kitchen was in the back of the house, a window over the sink looked out into a small backyard, and a door to the outside opened onto a chipped, cement driveway that ended at the fence.

Mrs. Corbin was a harried-looking woman in her late thirties. She was just putting a small plate with a sandwich on it in front of a girl of about ten or eleven sitting in one of the four chairs at the small kitchen table. The child's back was ramrod straight, feet firmly planted on the floor, hands folded in her lap. She was dressed in a red cotton skirt and a neat white blouse. Her mother looked up when Bishop and Ariel entered the room, but the girl ignored them.

"Milk, please." The girl said, in a flat voice that made it sounded more like an order than a request

"Of course, of course." Her mother hurried to the refrigerator.

"Mrs. Corbin?" Bishop started.

Mrs. Corbin waved an arm in their general direction. "Millie, take these people back into the living room. I'll be right there." Ariel and Bishop followed the flip flops back down the hall.

The living room furniture, like the house, had seen better days, but the room was neat and clean although rather stuffy. The little girl turned on the television. It was tuned to the cartoon network. "Do you like cartoons?" she asked Ariel.

"I like to play outside," Ariel told her. "It's more fun than cartoons."

"I can't go outside without Momma," the girl told her. "The bad people might come and take me away."

"What people?"

"The people that took Jen'fer. They might come back an' take me."

"Where did they take Jennifer, Millie?"

"Church." Millie nodded. "Jen'fer had to go to church for a long time."

"Millie!" Mrs. Corbin bustled into the room. "Turn off the television and go back into the kitchen. I put a sandwich for you on the table."

"I don't want to go back there. Jen'fer doesn't like me to bother her."

"Jennifer's your sister, she loves you. Go on now."

Millie plodded off down the hall. Flop, flop, flop, flop, flop.

Mrs. Corbin looked tired, but tightly wound. Her slacks were wrinkled and her shirt only partially tucked in. She pushed a stringy hank of hair behind her ear with impatient fingers. Her eyes looked like she expected trouble but was too harried and beaten down to fight it. "What's this about? My husbands at work and I don't remember why you had to come talk to me right away."

Bishop and Ariel took seats on the edge of the couch, while Mrs. Corbin took the matching chair. Her hands gripped her knees.

"If you're from the school or Child Protective Services you can see Jennifer is just fine. I don't know why that happened, that boy must have been bothering her. She was just defending herself. He probably fell. It's only a broken arm. She's just a girl."

"Whoa, Mrs. Corbin," Bishop said. "I just came to ask a few questions about how Jennifer is doing. She's been through a traumatic event and we'd just like to wrap this up." Bishop was carefully vague about who the 'we' were.

"She's fine, just fine. You saw her in the kitchen, she's better than fine, she's perfect. She makes her bed and picks up after herself. She's quiet and polite. Doesn't have the mouth on her she used to. Maybe being away did her some good."

"How long was Jennifer away, Mrs. Corbin?" Ariel asked.

"Don't you have that in her file? Why are you asking me these questions all over again? You're not the police officers I talked to when she went missing."

"My associate is new to the case, Mrs. Corbin," Bishop said, smoothly. "You'll have to forgive her if she's missed some of the details."

"Five months and three days," Mrs. Corbin said. "I was so worried, but . . ."

"But you were told they'd bring her back?" Ariel asked.

"Yes, yes. They told me they would if I'd just be patient."

"And not go public with her disappearance?"

Mrs. Corbin looked down at her hands, they were twisting in her lap much like Sarah Elizabeth Morgan's mother's hands when she talked about her missing daughter.

"They brought her back," she whispered. "They did, just like they said they would, even though I told. But they said you'd soon get tired of looking and that was true."

"Did you inform the local precinct that she'd come back?"

"Them!" Mrs. Corbin's voice was full of contempt. "No, why should I? They didn't care what happened to her. I put her back in school, that should have been good enough."

"Is she adjusting well to being back?"

Mrs. Corbin fidgeted in her chair, looking at the floor rather than at Bishop. "I've decided to home school her. Her teachers just don't understand what she's been through." She looked up defying him to disagree. "I can teach her everything she needs to learn right here."

"May I talk to Jennifer," Ariel asked her. "Just for a minute?"

"I, I don't know. She's not in trouble, is she? Is that why you're here? The school . . ."

"She's not in trouble with us, Mrs. Corbin," Bishop said. "We just wanted to be sure she was okay."

"I guess it's okay. I don't think she'll mind."

Ariel and Bishop exchanged a look. "I'll stay here with you, Mrs. Corbin, Bishop said. "My partner will just say hello to her."

Ariel went down the hall into the kitchen. Millie was at the table eating her sandwich. Jennifer was standing at the sink looking out the window at the yard but without much interest.

"Jennifer?" The child turned and looked at Ariel with flat, distant eyes. "My name is Ariel, I just wanted to ask you some questions."

"He pushed me," Jennifer said.

"The boy at school?"

"He pushed me, so I pushed him back. He got what he deserved. Everybody gets what they deserve."

"Do they? Who told you that?"

"They did."

"The people who took you?"

"They helped me. I'm fine. Everything is fine now."

"Where did they take you Jennifer? Where did you go?"

"Church," Jennifer said. "They took me to church, and now I'm back and I'm fine."

She turned back to the window, cocking her head to look at a bird scratching in the grass as if she'd never seen one before and didn't much care about seeing one now. "Go away," she told Ariel. "I know who you are."

"You better go," Millie whispered shifting her eyes quickly between Ariel, her sister's back and the rest of her sandwich. "Jen'fer doesn't like people in the house."

"No problem," Ariel told the child. "I was just going, anyway."

When she went back into the living room Mrs. Corbin leaped to her feet, rushing to open the front door and put a stop to any further conversation. "See Jennifer's a perfectly normal, happy child. But I'm going to have to ask you to go now. I have a lot of things to do today and my husband likes his dinner on the table at six thirty sharp."

"I'm very glad to hear that about Jennifer, Mrs. Corbin." Bishop took her reluctant hand in his own for a perfunctory shake. "We appreciate your time and hope everything works out for your family. Say good bye to Millie and Jennifer for me."

The door closed behind them with a soft, almost imperceptible thud.

They'd parked in front of the house, a short walk from the Corbin's front door. Bishop popped the locks with the remote as he stared absently over the roof of his car at the closed front door. Ariel got in on her side but followed the direction of Bishop's gaze as the detective slid into the driver's seat. She thought she saw a curtain twitch in the front window as they drove away. Jennifer Corbin's homecoming hadn't turned out to be the joyous occasions it was expected to be.

"That woman's so tightly wound up her head is about to spin off her shoulders," Bishop said.

Really? If anyone's head is going to start spinning I think it's Jen- 'fer's." Ariel looked over her shoulder, a little chill settling on the back of her neck.

"You think she's possessed?" Bishop asked, perking up. "Like the Exorcist."

"Something's going on. Her sister's afraid of her and I think the mom is too."

"Yeah. Sounds like something happened at school recently. It's too early for her to be home if she was still going. When does school get out?"

"I have no idea." Ariel said.

"You didn't go to school?"

"Not here." Ariel was dammed if she'd tell him she didn't remember going to school. Hell, she didn't remember Christmas or birthdays, a childhood or anything. Raptors didn't have that.

"With all these demons supposedly on the loose, why couldn't it be possession?"

Ariel sighed. She had to give Bishop points for trying to understand the strange mess he'd stepped into. Either that or he was pulling her chain. She knew he didn't quite believe any of it was real yet. He kept looking for the wires, and the man behind the curtain.

"Demons that possess humans are sly, but not very subtle. They take a body because it's cruel and destructive and they think it's fun to make the body perform disgusting acts of humiliation, but I don't think that's the situation here. A demon like that can't wait to show off. It wouldn't be able to resist an audience. But something has happened to that kid. She seems much older than eleven, bored, demanding and she seems to have the ability to hurt someone if she's provoked."

"Well, if she's come back home maybe some of the others will too, just like Mrs. Corbin said. We can see if they act the same way as Jennifer. In the meantime, we'll keep an eye on the Corbin's." Bishop turned right.

"Where are you going? I thought we were going to go back to the Caf' to check on Mouser."

"I saw a school down this block on the way in. It's almost three, I thought I'd ask if anyone knows about a kid who got his arm broken by a girl." Bishop jockeyed with soccer moms in cars for a place at the curb.

When the school doors burst open kids piled out like released hostages. He opened his door. "This'll just take a minute, you can wait in the car."

Ariel slouched in the passenger seat watching kids in jeans, shorts, t-shirts, and barely butt covering skirts mill around, teasing and laughing and flirting, the boys dropping their books and punching each other in the arm while mothers honked impatient horns, wanting to whisk their darlings off to various lessons' sports and other things that modern life used to fill up kid's lives. She saw Bishop catch a few kids that looked about the same age as Jennifer. He was back in the car in five minutes.

"Well?" she asked.

"Little Miss Muffet broke an eighth grader's arm."

"No shit?"

"He started hassling her about where she'd been and why she seemed so stuck up since she'd been back, showing off for his buddies. He got too close to her and she took him down. Twisted his arm until it popped. He's got a torn rotator cuff and a spiral fracture of the humerus. Sounds like the 'church' taught Jen'fer some moves."

"This is not good," Ariel said, wondering if this had something to do with the whole Tesslovich problem. She needed to find Mouser, then get Tesslovich taken care of before the Guardian found out he was still alive. Ariel had never blown an assignment before and she wasn't going to blow this one, especially now that Tomas knew about it.

Maybe too much time had passed already. Tesslovich was going to be looking out for her. He'd had time to build his defenses, get more body guards, put in alarms. There weren't going to be too many unguarded moments. Success was going to take, subtlety, finesse. Luck. Ariel hated to rely on luck, it always got you back in the end.

Bishop had barely bumped the curb when Ariel jumped out of the car, slammed the door and hurried down the steps to the Caf'. Bishop slowed to a stop and turned off the ignition. "It's okay," he said as he watched her retreating back. "Don't wait for me, I'll be right there."

He sat for a minute savoring the quiet. He really hoped Mouser was down there, otherwise it was going to be a very long night.

Bishop pushed the grimy door open. Ariel was deep in conversation with Ez who had just passed her a grey envelope the size of a party invitation from somewhere on the other side of the bar. Its shelves seemed to be the repository of all things. Just during his short visits to the Caf', he'd seen Ez hand out shoes, bicycle parts, tools, a computer keyboard and what was obviously a prized video game by the way its recipient clutched it protectively to his chest.

Ariel stuck the envelope in a coat pocket without looking at it, but she didn't seem happy about getting it. There was no Mouser in evidence.

Ariel looked up when Bishop joined them, Ez didn't. Bishop

suspected the bartender watched everything out of the corners of his eyes. He seemed to know what was going on in the Caf' at all times, even though he never looked directly at anything or anybody. Right then he was looking down at the bar top, nodding or shaking his head while Ariel asked him questions.

"He's not back," she said. "Apparently he sent all the regulars out yesterday with copies of the pictures you brought and some of the other kids who've disappeared over the last few months."

"Where'd he get those?"

"Google." Ez said. It was the first thing Bishop had ever heard him say. His voice was deep and growly.

"Is everybody back but Mouser?" Ariel turned to look around the room. Bishop followed her eyes. He'd never taken a really good look at the Caf's 'customers' before. He just knew they were young and scruffy. Fashion was a mixed bag: grunge, punk, geek and creature of the night. He thought that was called Goth. Normally they'd all be hunched over their computers, or deep into a comic or some kind of graphic novel. This afternoon they were all watching Ariel and Ez, poised for news or action. Bishop didn't know which.

A commotion in the kitchen turned heads. A few more kids pushed through its swinging door, to slip under the bar hatch and into the Caf' itself. This batch was older, all wore layered t-shirts, tight leggings or bicycle shorts with flames painted on the sides.

Bishop had seen kids like this all over downtown. He'd even used them to deliver contracts a few times. They were bike messengers, or, more accurately, maniacs with a death wish. Anybody who drove through the business district had seen them cut off buses, fly through red lights, slingshot off the back of trucks after hitching a ride to get up a little more speed. They had the souls of Kamikaze, but he had to admit, they got around. If you wanted to send a gang out on a hunt, they were the guys. And girls. He saw more than one female daredevil in the pack.

A kid of about seventeen with a bright red Mohawk, several earrings, and a collection of tattoos seemed to be the leader.

"Speed?" Ez asked him.

The Mohawk shook his head. "Couldn't find him. Zoe was the last one who had him on channel, then he dropped off and we haven't been able to raise him since." He patted the walkie-talkie strapped to his chest like a bandolier.

"When was that?"

Zoe turned out to be a ninety-eight-pound whippet of a girl with short black hair and a ring in one eyebrow. "Last night around eight o'clock. I was on channel two. The dispatchers never use that one, and we keep switching so they don't wise up and listen in. He said he was near Hauptmann's, that old abandoned department store on third. He thought he might be able to get into the building."

"Why would he want to get into Hauptmann's?" Ariel asked. "It's been closed for almost twenty years. Is it a squat?"

"Naw. Well . . . maybe, but everybody says the place is haunted, so I told him to steer clear. All I got back was static."

"We went back and took a look today," Speed indicated the rest of the bike messengers behind him. "They've sealed the building up pretty good with gates and bars an' stuff. I don't know how he'd get in. People stay away from that building, man. It's got weird noises and lights, and sometimes the ground vibrates. I don't ride near it and nobody, but nobody walks that side of the block at night."

"How did you decide who went where with the pictures?" Bishop asked.

"Mouser gave us maps. Not that we don't cover most of this burg everyday deliverin' packages, but he didn't want us wasting time overlapping." Speed pulled a sweaty piece of paper out of his sleeve. It showed a section of downtown with subway entrances circled in red. "We went into the stations to talk to the trolls who panhandle there, but not any deeper than that."

"Yeah," More than one of the bike messengers agreed. "The tunnels are bad news."

"I got a section near the vats." one said.

"Barkley squats," another piped up. "

"So, everybody got a map section?" Bishop asked.

Nods all around.

"Lay 'em out here on the bar." Pages were extracted, smoothed out. Everyone crowded Bishop as he moved the pieces of the puzzle around, fitting the pages together until they made a complete map, except for one section in the middle.

"What goes there?" He asked.

"Hauptmann's block," several voices said at once.

"That was Mouser's page," Zoe said in a worried voice. "I told him not to go there!"

"Chill, Zo," Mohawk massaged her shoulders for a few seconds -- bike messengers obviously weren't big huggers. "You couldn't have done anything to stop him."

"These maps are downloads, right?" Ariel recognized the web site logo on the pages. "So, where's Mouser's computer?"

Ez reached under the counter and set a laptop on the bar. It was where Mouser always left his computer when he went out. Ariel grabbed it, spun it toward herself, flipped it open and booted it up.

"How are you going to get in?" Bishop asked. "You need a password."

Ariel typed c0nSpirAc3y and the screen opened.

"Kid's losing his touch."

"I peeked over his shoulder." She saw with relief that Mouser had saved his maps.

"Damn!"

"What?" Bishop asked.

"I think he's gone into the tunnels."

"The subway tunnels? How do you know?"

She stepped away from the screen. Mouser had surface maps, but he'd also found plans for what was underground.

"What am I looking at?" Bishop was still confused.

"Schematics of what's under the sidewalk."

A small grunger from the gaming pool pushed his way between Ariel and Bishop. "We hacked into city records. This isn't everything, only what's been put on-line in the last few years. This city started building subway tunnels over a hundred and fifty years ago, but then there's maintenance tunnels, steam tunnels, electricity, pedestrian tunnels between buildings, private tunnels dug by rich people who wanted a way to get from place to place without having to mingle with the masses. And all the forgotten tunnels that somebody built for something but stopped using. There's tons of other drawings still on paper or microfiche, a lot of plans are in storage or just gone forever. Nobody really knows what all's down there anymore, except maybe the Deepers. An' you don't want to mess with them, they eat people."

"That's a rumor," somebody said, and the debate was off and running.

"I'm going to kill him," Ariel growled.

Bishop could barely hear her over the argument going on behind them.

Ariel raised her voice. "If he's gone into the Deeps, I'm going to have him for lunch."

"What are the Deeps?" Bishop asked, louder than he intended.

"Take it somewhere else!" Ez shouted. The crowd at the bar shifted to the other end of the room.

Ez shook his head, "Lowest tunnels. People go down there

when they really don't want to be found. Problem is there are other things down there as well."

Things that eat people? Bishop wondered.

"Mouser's not that dumb," Ariel said. "Anyway, the really dangerous ones are more south and not so deep."

"Sometimes, if they're really hungry they come out."

"Shut up, Ez!" Ariel said. "If you think the Deepers may have gotten him, I'm going down."

"Not alone," Bishop told her.

"You'd only get in my way," Ariel said. "You'd be blind most of the time and that's too dangerous."

"What about you and Mouser?"

"We have excellent night vision. It's part of the package."

"What package? Never mind. I've been in the army and I was a cop for six years. I'm not exactly helpless."

Ez reached under the counter and put a set of night goggles on the bar.

"See?" Bishop said. "Infa-red. I've used them before."

Ariel ignored him, typing something on Mouser's laptop. Pages began to eject from one of the printers against the back wall of the Caf'.

"Um, excuse me." It was Speed the Mohawk. "Nobody recognized anybody in the pictures Mouser gave us. We've hit pretty much everywhere people hang."

"Thanks for trying. I appreciate it." Bishop put the goggles back on the bar.

"Yeah, there's something else, though." Speed glanced around to see who might be listening. "They're not the only ones who are missing. There's more. Everyday there's somebody else just gone. It's getting really creepy. People are freaked. Nobody wants to be out after dark anymore. Last night, this old dude, you know, one of the drunks that crib in the alleys downtown? He was lying under a piece of cardboard on the sidewalk, he grabbed my foot.

I nearly shit myself, he scared me so bad. Especially after all the disappearance stuff I'd been listening to in the squats. Then the guy said---'Go home, boy and you go quick, before they get you.'"

"I said--Who's gonna get me, old man?"

"An' he said -- Them hunters, boy. They don't care about some old sot like me, but they'd like you. You still got some spunk to you. You go on now before they get *you*."

"Man, I booked. An' I made sure everybody else came in. I don't know what he was talkin' about, but I wasn't losin' any of my peeps over it. Maybe Mouser went into the tunnels cuz something was after him. Maybe it is safer down there. I thought you'd want to know."

"You keep everybody home tonight, okay?" Bishop told the messenger. "Don't go out on the street until we figure out what's going on."

"Strength in numbers, bro." Speed held out his fist. "We'll fight if we have to. You find out who took Mouser and we'll kick their ass."

"I appreciate the back-up." Bishop gave him a solemn fist bump.

Ariel laid out the new pages, taping them together in two rows of five pages each. The tunnels looked like a tray of worms, curling over and around each other in different colored layers. Bishop didn't see how they could find one fourteen-year-old boy in a maze like that.

"I'll be right back," he told Ez. "Don't leave without me."

Outside he opened the trunk of his car. He always kept a couple of changes of clothes in the car in case he had to follow somebody and didn't want to stand out in the crowd.

He dug around until he found a pair of ripped jeans, an old hooded sweat shirt in a faded green and a pair of scuffed boots: I did undercover vice, he muttered to himself. I can blend easier than a pissed off bird girl in a long black coat.

When he went back into the Caf' Ariel was rolling the computer map into a tight tube that she stuck it into one of her coat pockets. "Give him the gun," she told Ez.

A familiar looking pistol was lying next to the goggles. It was big and black, and Bishop looked at it with a certain amount of envy. He'd always wanted a Glock, but he was in the middle of a pissing contest.

"I already have a gun."

"It's the one I took away from Tesslovich." Ariel told him. "Demon loads remember?"

Bishop remembered how the bullets had blown the little freak in the striped suit right out a window. He shrugged and took the gun. "Be prepared, I always say."

EZ pulled a battered green army fatigue jacket out from under the bar. "I'm going too."

"I can handle this myself, Ez." Ariel was all business now.

"I'm standing right here, you know." Bishop muttered. He picked up the objects on the bar. "Goggles. Gun. Yeah it's me."

"You need a tracker," Ez shrugged into the jacket. "I'm it. Chin's here if there's a problem."

"I . . ."

"Don't argue."

"Five minutes," Ariel said and headed for the back room.

"Bathroom's that way." Ez jerked a thumb down the bar.

Bishop changed. He stuck the big pistol into the waistband of his jeans and pulled the sweatshirt over it. He'd have preferred a shoulder holster, but this would have to do. When he came out Ariel and Ez were waiting, ready to go.

The Deeps? Any place with a name like that can't be good.

PART II

Hauptmann's Department store was three stories high and covered an entire city block. Bishop remembered being taken there as a kid. The store had everything, clothes, furniture, toys, jewelry, perfume, a fancy gourmet food department and an elegant restaurant. At Christmas it was the most beautiful store in town, its windows decorated with things that sparkled and moved. People came in from the suburbs to see the windows and do their Christmas shopping.

Urban blight and big box stores put institutions like Hauptmann's out of business. That, and a huge family scandal that ended in bankruptcy and murder. Or maybe it was murder and bankruptcy? He couldn't remember.

No one wanted to buy a big white elephant, so the bank boarded up the building to wait for some developer with a brain storm about wealthy people returning to apartment living in an urban environment.

Don't hold your breath.

He stared up at the building. "Now what?" he asked.

"We find a way in." Ariel tested one of the metal gates that closed off the entrances. "Solid," she reported. "Let's go around back."

The back was an alley that cut between two halves of the building. Enclosed bridges linked second and fourth floors, wide enough for both foot traffic and display.

Bishop remembered the one that led to the second-floor toy department. It was always lined with wonderful things; life-sized dolls, a jungle of stuffed animal; racks of electric trains, and at the end, a Toyland big enough to make any child's dream come true.

Now, everything was dark and forbidding. Bishop kept waiting for something to jump out of the dark and yell "Boo!"

Rusty metal roll-up doors sealed the loading docks in the alley although Bishop noticed they had new looking wires at the top that disappeared back into the building.

"It's alarmed," Ariel frowned. "Somebody cares enough to try to keep people from breaking in."

Ez's nose was in the air, sniffing the damp air of the alley. "He came down here," he said. His nose twitched until he was under one of the bridges. "Scent ends here. He must have gone up."

"Where are his clothes?" Ariel kicked at some cardboard leaning up against the wall. There were no clothes, but a walkie-talkie had been carefully placed behind the cardboard.

"Up where?" Bishop asked.

Ariel looked at the bridge, then leaned back far enough to see the roof. Bishop followed her line of sight.

"Even shifted he was strong enough to carry his clothes to the roof, but he couldn't manage the walkie-talkie. Or maybe he figured it wouldn't do him any good where he was going."

Ariel stripped out of her coat and threw it to Bishop. She had on a tight, long-sleeved turtleneck, backless from just below the knob of her spine to the bottom of her shoulder blades. Down the middle of her back she wore a rig like a double shoulder holster that held a long sheath with a handle sticking out of it.

"Hang on, I'll take a look. If I see a way in from the roof, I'll drop the fire ladder."

She spread her arms and flexed her shoulders. Deep brown wings unfolded behind her, spreading sideways until they were fully extended. One beat and she was airborne, another and she disappeared over the edge of the roof.

Bishop didn't realize his mouth was hanging open until Ez reached one leathery finger out and shut it for him.

"She's a beauty, isn't she?" Ez said, watching the edge of the roof. "Wait 'til you see her fight."

"I have," Bishop told him. "I've been trying to figure out the trick."

"No tricks lad, it's just her nature. Might as well get used to it."

Ariel circled the roof in the air, then did it again on foot. She could see where Mouser had gotten in through an air duct with a bent grill. He was small and skinny, and she wasn't sure the opening would be large enough, or the ducting strong enough to hold three adults.

The other option was the elevator shack. Not too many thieves were willing to risk a five floor fall to break into an abandoned building. The cable housing probably wasn't alarmed. How far down they'd have to climb would depend on where the elevators were stopped and whether they could get access to one of the floors through the safety doors.

She went back over the edge of the roof and down the fire escape to unhook and drop the ladder from the first platform to where it locked about two feet off the ground.

Ez and Bishop scrambled up to meet her. Bishop handed over her coat.

"I'm pretty sure he got in from the roof. I think we can too, if we're careful. The elevator housing isn't alarmed."

A sound like sheets snapping on a clothesline startled all of them. Coming over the edge of the roof, back lit by the ambient glow of dying light were three creatures. They were about forty pounds each, squat, and vaguely human, with stubby wings and bony chests. Their arms and legs dangled, trailing hands and feet with pointed claws. Their misshapen heads protruded from their shoulders, swinging back and forth like short-necked vultures scanning for prey.

"Gargoyles!" Ariel yelled pushing Bishop toward the elevator shed as she moved to meet them. She hoped he'd remembered his gun.

El ripped the boots off her feet, then pulled the sword from the sheath on her back. She'd only ever fought one Gargoyle, but she'd heard the stories. They were fast and vicious and used to the element of surprise. But their prey rarely had wings of their own.

Ariel snarled and risked a backward glance. Two more 'goyles were in the air behind her heading for Ez and Bishop, but she had no time to think about that now. She rose into the air, wings beating double time, hoping to pull her three attackers away from the roof into open air. Two rose to the bait, the other scuttled under her, going straight for Bishop.

She heard two rapid shots. Bishop had remembered the gun.

Ariel made a slow figure eight in the air with her sword. The double-sided blade was shiny, reflecting what light was available. Gargoyles were attracted to shiny objects. The reflection distracted one of the little monsters, obviously the dumber of the two, but the other one came barreling at her screeching, clawed feet extended. Ariel flashed on the disemboweled cow she'd told Bishop about--but her reach was longer than the 'goyle's. She turned sideways, raised her left leg and planted her clawed foot in the Gargoyle's belly ripping it open. She swung her sword and took the creature's head off at the neck. Head and body thumped to the roof and the creature's ochre blood began to smoke and bubble the tar coating.

Acid for blood. Great.

"Stay away from their blood," she yelled as the other Gargoyle began to circle her from a safer distance.

"Come on." She curled and uncurled her fingers to show she had talons of her own. She rose higher in the air, moving over the street where there were no obstructions. Her ugly, grey satellite followed, snarling and spitting down at her from over her head. Flapping in a circle, he tried to spin her until she was disoriented, so he could get behind her and go for her back. She let him make one more circle, slowing her own rotation so that she would make an appealing target.

Hearing the frantic acceleration of the creature's wings she rolled into a tight somersault that brought her up under the Gargoyle. With one beat of her wings, she straightened and thrust her sword completely through him, catching him under the tail until it exited through the crown of his head.

Letting her wings hold her steady, she flipped the sword downward and used her feet to push the body off the blade. It fell in a boneless tangle of limbs and wings, hitting the pavement below with the sound of an exploding water balloon.

Take that you little rat from Hell!

She spun around just in time to see Ez rip a Gargoyle in half. The spatter made patches of hair on his arms and chest sizzle and smoke, but he shook it off. His hair was so thick it was likely he hardly felt it.

Bishop stood with his back against the elevator shed, the Glock extended in a two-handed grip. His arms moved back and forth, following the evasive movements of the last Gargoyle. Four already lay dead on the roof, or maybe five. Ez had a way with dismemberment that made it hard to tell.

As Ariel watched, Bishop's 'goyle took three bounding steps and sprang, fangs and talons outstretched, his wings beating rapidly to give him momentum. As he started to arc downward, Bishop calmly put two rounds in his chest and one in his head.

"Watch the spatter!" Ariel called just in time for Bishop to pull up the hood of his sweatshirt.

"Oww!"

Ariel flew over and dropped to the roof. "Yeah," she told him as he scrubbed the backs of his hands on his jeans. "Triple threat; wings, claws and acid blood. Ez, you okay?"

Ez padded over, teeth exposed in a wolfish grin. He was upright, but his knees had a backward bend to them that was visible through his jeans. He'd discarded his shirt and jacket to accommodate broad shoulders, a muscular, fur covered chest and longer arms. His ears drooped at the top, trailing tufts of hair and his forehead and jaw had elongated into a prominent ridge over his eyes, and a muzzle full of sharp, white canine teeth. He pulled his lips up in a mock snarl and his jaw pulled back into a more normal shape.

"You think there's more?" He scratched at a place on his arm where Gargoyle blood had taken out a patch of fur.

Ariel shrugged. "We need to either get into, or off this building before reinforcements arrive. If there are sentinels on the outside, I have no idea what might be waiting inside."

"Mouser," Ez growled.

Ariel nodded looking at Bishop. "That was rough. Maybe this isn't your game anymore, Frank. We understand if you'd like to call it a night. Ez and I can handle it from here."

"No way in hell." Bishop pulled the clip out of the Glock and checked the remaining bullets. "I just killed two flying monkeys with acid blood, saw a bird woman dog fight like the Red Baron and met my very first werewolf. Why stop now?"

Ez gave him a pat on the back that almost knocked him to his knees. "We go in."

The werewolf ripped a side panel off the elevator shed. A rusty iron ladder was bolted to the side of the shaft which disappeared into darkness a hundred feet below.

Bishop stuck the Glock back in his waist band and peered over the side. "Got any more demon loads?" He asked.

Ez handed him a clip. "Always keep a spare under the bar."

Bishop slipped the spare clip into his back pocket and pulled the night vision goggles over his head adjusting them until they fit snugly around his eyes. He swung one a leg over the lip of the shaft feeling for the first rung of the ladder with his foot.

"Got any room for me under that bar? I can sleep anywhere, ask my ex-partner." He started to descend.

The soft echo of Ez' growly chuckle followed him down into the darkness.

Bishop stopped next to the first set of elevator doors. The goggles lit the shaft with an eerie green light. He could see the elevator safety gate was pulled shut over tarnished brass doors with raised art deco designs. The doors were built in four panels meant to divide left and right as the elevator opened. Bishop tugged at the gate with one hand. Flakes of rust rained down the shaft, but the gate wouldn't budge. He decided to continue climbing down the ladder to a set that was more accessible.

Luckily the rungs of the maintenance ladder had been set into a shallow indent in the brick wall next to the doors and it seemed to run the entire length of the shaft. If a set of doors opened even part of the way it would be an easy jump into the interior of the building.

The gate on the second-floor elevator was open and the doors didn't quite come together. The opening was maybe six inches wide. The interior beyond the opening was a deep green meaning there was no ambient light. That also meant that nothing was prowling that floor. It was an encouraging thought until Bishop reminded himself he was the only one who needed goggles to see in the dark. He reached out and gave the door's interior handle a one-armed tug. It didn't move. There was twenty years of grit and dirt in the track and quite probably, no one had oiled the doors since the building closed.

Ariel motioned him to move lower, following him down the rungs to give Ez a chance to reach the doors. Bishop leaned out to avoid the swirling tent made by her coat and looked up. The goggles made everything look like a bad horror movie. A hairy arm reached out to hook a set of claws into the opening. One solid jerk and the two left panels telescoped together and slid into a slot in the wall. Their screech of protest caused Bishop to hunch his shoulders in silent dismay. Ez swung through the opening onto the floor, followed quickly by Ariel and Bishop.

"Where are we?" Ariel whispered.

Bishop scanned the expanse. It wasn't as empty as he thought it would be. Square plaster and walnut pillars held up a dusty, but ornately stamped tin ceiling. Display cases lined the interior, shrouded in dusty white drop cloths. A low wall in the middle of the floor confused him for a minute until he remembered the long, wood-runged escalators that swept up and down from the second floor, past the mezzanine, to the high ceilinged first level. On the other side of the second-floor bridge there was an escalator to the third floor and the toy department. The space between the up and down hand rails had always held towering displays of one thing or another.

"We're on the Third Street side of the building," Bishop pointed past the elevator. "That opening is the bridge to the Fourth Street side. There's an escalator there to the third floor, or we can take this one down to the front door."

Ez raised his snout and wrinkled his nose in a sniff. Then he took another. "Bridge," he said.

"Mouser?" Ariel asked in a tight whisper.

Ez shook his head. "No scent of him, plenty of mice though, that's why we take the bridge. We need to backtrack to where he came in."

Ariel let the gravity blade in her right sleeve drop into her hand. She nudged Bishop forward with a finger poke in the shoulder.

The windows in the bridge let in enough light that Bishop had to take off the goggles. The floor of the entire store seemed to be covered with the debris of a hasty, resentful exit. Cardboard boxes, clothing, pieces of display stands had been left in haphazard piles that had quickly turned into rat condos. The faint smell of urine and dust made him want to sneeze. When he hit the dark on the other side of the bridge, he pulled the goggles down over his eyes only to stifle a shriek of horror. Boxes of dismembered arms, legs and heads jumped into green relief in front of him. Oh my God, his brain shrieked, it's a demon massacre!

Ez snickered.

Bishop took a closer look. Mannequins. His heart was still pumping two hundred beats a minute.

Ariel suppressed a grin.

Ez tapped his nose. "You don't smell dead, it's not a body." He loped ahead of Bishop through the mannequin holocaust toward the escalators.

≈

"Hey," Bishop said in Ariel's ear. "Not that I don't appreciate being on team Survivor: Haunted Department Store, but do you think Mouser is really in here somewhere? I thought everybody avoids this place like the plague. . ."

Ez's head hunched forward. It was the werewolf equivalent of going on point.

"Ez has something," Ariel whispered. She followed the werewolf quietly down the old, frozen, wooden escalator.

The steps were alternating slats of dark wood and steel that rose at the top, only to flatten and slide into a slot at the bottom. When it was turned off for the last time some steps had frozen into stair-like treads, others had flattened out, ready to cycle into the continuous loop to the next floor. Some steps looked a little shaky like they might collapse if enough weight was put in the wrong place. It was a long escalator since the ceiling of the first floor was the highest in the building. The slow, mechanical ride down would have given shoppers a panoramic view of the merchandise below before they moved out onto the floor to start shopping.

Ariel hit a bad step. It had somehow become unhooked from the track and her weight made it slide forward, throwing her off balance. She grabbed for the wooded hand rail and at the same time shot her bare foot out to hook the front of the step with her claw-tipped toes, so it wouldn't go crashing down the rest of the escalator. No point in causing enough noise to alert anyone else who happened to be in the building.

Bishop leaped forward and grabbed her around the waist with one arm, letting her regain her balance without losing the step. When Bishop looked up, Ez had leapt over the hand rail that separated the up and down escalators from the long metal slide between them. Without a word, he began to slide toward the ground floor, leaping nimbly over the end to wait for Ariel and Bishop.

"Good idea," Bishop whispered, and lifted Ariel onto the slide before she could protest. Ez caught her easily, then steadied Bishop as he made a perfect two-point landing at the bottom.

"Did that as a kid a couple of times. My brother dared me. We got chased out of the store by one of the floor walkers. I forgot how much fun it was."

"I don't need your help." Ariel told him, stiffly.

"Buzz kill," Bishop said, but he grinned at the memory.

On the main floor, a shorter set of escalators headed in the opposite direction from the one they'd just come down, ready to take them even lower.

"What's down there?" Ez asked.

"Bargain Basement." Bishop tried to remember the details of the floor plan. "It's been years since I've been in here. There's also access to the store's private subway stop down there. Hauptmann's actually had their own set of train cars. You'd get off at a regular station, then board the Hauptmann cars for a free trip to the store platform. It was a big, continuous loop. They sealed up the access when the store went out of business. I don't know if we can still get to the platform from the store."

Ez said. "Maybe there's a way into the Deeps from the tunnel."

Ariel peered into the darkness below. "I've never been into the tunnels. Not my kind of place."

"We had to roust some cookers out of the tunnels when I was back in Vice, but they weren't that very far in. Most of them rabbited down the hole when we broke in. We only followed them so far. The tunnels are a great place for an ambush. They probably just set up somewhere else."

"I've been down there," Ez said. "People who take to the

tunnels want to be left alone. Some of 'em are just trying to survive. Others got a more lethal perspective on visitors."

"Then we need to find Mouser before something happens to him," Ariel said firmly. "Lead on."

The short escalators proved a bit more stable. When they reached the basement, a faded sign marked "Subway" directed them to a set of wide steps between the electric stairways. A metal gate covered in plywood blocked the entrance.

"Now what?" Bishop whispered.

"Shush," Ariel told him. "Listen."

There was a soft rumble coming from the other side of the gate. It was the sound of machinery performing a task. Motors thrumming, ventilation fans whirring, the vibration of potential activity. It was impossible to tell whether there were people over there, using whatever the machines, enabled or not.

The rumbling began to fill the foyer near the gate. The air was suddenly sucked forward. Anyone who had ever stood on a subway platform as the train pulled in would know that sensation: a train was arriving.

The breeze ruffled whatever was blocking the light on the other side of the plywood. Light appeared at the bottom and the edges of the blocked opening.

Blackout curtains, Ariel couldn't imagine what else it would be. The heavy, rubberized material was as good as a moonless night unless disturbed. She pressed her face against the bars of the gate, trying to get a glimpse of what was beyond. A sudden bright line created by the billowing curtain spotted her vision, but she could still hear voices, the sound of feet, the pneumatic wheeze of train doors opening. Then, with a final sway of material, it was dark again.

When she turned away, Ez had his nose in the air. She cautioned Bishop to silence with a finger to her lips.

Ez held up two, then five, then seven fingers. Seven people or creatures behind the barrier. There was a screech of metal and a muffled thud. Ez shrugged and pointed back up the stairs. When they were safely up and around the corner Ariel spread her hands in a 'what?' gesture.

"Five humans, two demons. One young female. Two of the humans are younger than the rest and they're afraid. Fear has its own special smell," he told Bishop. "The only smell that carries farther than fear is blood."

"No Mouser," he said to Ariel. "But I smell him. He's been down here, but the scent comes from that direction." Ez pointed to a back corner of the bargain basement. "I think he may have been in the air, because there's no scent on the ground."

Bishop cocked his head at the word 'air'. The night vision goggles obscured the expression on his face. He was more interested in looking down the stairs to the subway platform, because he was trying to remember something.

Ariel tugged at his arm and pulled him away, toward the direction Ez indicated.

When they'd put some distance between themselves and the subway stairs, Bishop said, "I'm trying to remember what the platform looked like in the old days. It was wide, with tile everywhere and big glass display cases set right into the walls. There were always fancy clothes, or the latest furniture, or holiday scenes with toys and stuff inside. For Easter they had a giant lavender bunny in a bow tie with eggs the size of footballs. I always wondered . . . well, never mind. As far as I know there really are five-foot-tall, egg laying lavender bunnies. I just hope I never meet one."

Bishop tried to bring up more memories of his childhood excursions to Hauptmann's. "That sure sounded like a train coming through the station, but there's no place for it to go, unless . . . "

"Unless what?" Ariel and Bishop continued to make their way

through the forest of discarded trash on the basement floor, following Ez and his magic nose.

"My mom would know, but she went back to Kansas a couple of years ago. I think she told me the Hauptmann family had a private train. Fancier than the one the shoppers used. Just a couple of cars so they could get back and forth without getting stuck in traffic or having to rub shoulders with the hoi polloi. There must be another tunnel on the loop that goes off somewhere else, probably wherever they lived."

"Which was?"

"Don't know. One of those big robber baron estates built before income tax? Didn't the Vanderbilt's have their own, personal subway station in New York?"

Ariel stopped at an old display counter that was, more or less, free of junk and laid out Mouser's map of the tunnels. She traced the loop of track under Hauptmann's. Two tunnels spoked at oblique angles off each side of the oval shaped loop that brought customers to and from the store. One dead-ended. The other went straight off the end of the page.

"This one must be a utility tunnel for maintenance and extra cars. This one," she put her finger on the long tunnel. "Goes somewhere else. The question is . . ."

"Where?" Bishop finished for her.

When she looked up, Ez was waving a long hairy arm.

"He must have found something." She refolded the computer pages and stuffed them into her coat pocket. "Let's go."

"Aren't you worried about cutting your feet on something?" Bishop asked. Ariel had been barefoot since the roof, as had Ez.

"You ask too many questions," she looked down at her Raptor feet with their high arches, long toes and curved claws. "Besides, I think you're jealous."

"Trust me," Bishop told her. "If I ever want to gut a flying monkey, you'll be the first person I call."

- 2 -

Bishop gave the extra clip of demon loads in his back pocket a reassuring pat. Mouser flies, but he's still a kid. Special talents or not, they're all kids, even Ariel is barely out of her teens. Is this enough to fight people like Tesslovich and Kiriyenko, that is, if the bio-tech genius was truly involved?

The whole demon thing? Bishop was still not completely buying it. So Ez was hairy and weird. Had he ever taken a really good look at the guy before tonight? Maybe he'd always had a twelve o'clock shadow, bad teeth and a severe over-bite.

It was probably the goggles. Who doesn't look weird when they're green? And Gargoyles? A bad science experiment like Jurassic Park. Cloning run amok. Or maybe this was just a really bad dream.

Bishop liked Mouser, and the kid was missing. Other kids were missing too, there was no ignoring that. And one missing kid might lead to another---from Mouser to little Sarah Elizabeth Morgan to a growing number of others. He only hoped they were both still alive and that whoever had taken them would have the opportunity to spend some quality time with Ariel, Ez and Bishop before anyone called the cops.

Ez had found a door in the corner leading to a utility corridor. It said, "Staff Only" and had been propped open a crack with a wedge of debris from the floor. Ez opened it just enough for three of them to, pass through.

Along the corridor were doors labeled *Men, Ladies and Stock*. Further along was a door labeled *Garage*. It was locked.

Bishop tugged at his brain, getting nowhere, his mom and he always took the subway. They'd never driven to Hauptmann's, but it stood to reason some people did and would be offered the convenience of parking near, or actually inside the building. Didn't there used to be valet service at the front door?

A service stairway at the end of the corridor led downward. There were two doors at the bottom. One said *Garage, Level II*, the other *Subway*.

"This must have been the employee entrance to the platform," Bishop said. "The garage must be on more than one level." He tried the door to *Garage, Level II*. It was unlocked. He eased it open a crack, praying it wouldn't squeak and was momentarily blinded. The garage had lights. They were dim, like emergency lighting, but they were on.

He pushed the goggles up on his forehead and put his eye to the crack. Two white vans were parked by a set of open doors. The side door to one van had been left open. A jumble of what seemed to be packing blankets and utility straps were barely visible. One blanket hung out of the door like something heavy had been unloaded and dragged.

"We have company," Bishop whispered. "There are vans in the garage, but nobody in sight. There seems to be access doors to the platform. Maybe they use the train to transport goods in and out. I see rolling racks or cages by the door."

"I smell Mouser," Ez said.

Okay." Bishop closed the door softly. "See if the door to the subway is unlocked."

Ariel shook her head.

"Well there's nobody in sight. We could try for whatever's on the other side of the garage."

"I'm going," Ariel said.

"We could be stepping right into a whole gang of demons."

"Who've just abducted three terrified kids," Ariel reminded him.

"No need." Ez popped the lock to the subway door with one upward wrench on the handle.

The passageway beyond was unlighted, but the brightness that spilled through two dirty glass windows set in double doors at the end of the short corridor gave off enough light to see the way to their destination. Shoulder-high, each window was made of smoky, grey glass. Opaque enough to discourage a view back into the corridor, but with enough visibility to ensure that employees exiting onto the subway platform wouldn't open the doors into a paying customer.

Ez, Bishop and Ariel had an oblique, but almost complete view of the platform from where they stood on either side of the small windows.

Hauptmann's subway platform reflected the opulence of a bygone era. Fancy tile walls with friezes in porcelain relief celebrated both early twentieth century transportation and commerce. Steamships, trains and old-fashioned trucks brought goods to docks and freight platforms as passengers disembarked from exotic places. On another wall, well-dressed tourists shopped for rugs, jewelry and art objects in foreign market places. The blind, glass windows of empty showcases set in the walls reflected the light created by two large crystal chandeliers hung from a vaulted ceiling.

Thrumming at the edge of the platform was a four-car subway train. It was nothing like the one Bishop remembered taking to the store. This one was sleek, polished steel with the rounded lines and aerodynamic, art-deco styling of the nineteen thirties. Even standing still, the train gave the impression of elegance and speed.

The open doors of the cars showed plush, club car interiors with velvet chairs and couches, chrome side tables and lamps, except for the last car which had the stripped, spare interior of a baggage car.

A man dressed in a white lab coat, carrying a clip board was directing the activity on the platform. Boxes were being loaded into the baggage car by two over-muscled workers in coveralls who stacked them against the walls as if they weighed practically nothing. Lab-coat checked each one off against a list attached to his clip board.

Finishing the last check-off, he made a come-on gesture to someone down the platform. With a rattle, more workers appeared pushing three metal cages like the ones Bishop had seen in the garage. The cages were taller than they were wide with wheels on the bottom for easy movement. Two had huddled forms in the bottom, one curled in a fetal position. In the third a defiant boy of about fourteen stood, swaying on his feet, hands clutching and shaking the bars of the cage. It was Mouser.

"You better let me go!" Mouser was yelling. "People are gonna come looking for me. They're gonna kill you, you fuckers. You perverts are all gonna die for this. You just wait . . . "

A little man in a striped suit and bowler hat who'd been trailing the cages stuck his arm through the bars and punched Mouser in the ribs. The boy's whole body went into spasm and he collapsed to the bottom of the cage. The cage pusher laughed as Bowler Hat dropped the Taser back into his jacket pocket.

"That's him!" Bishop whispered. "That's the little freak you blew out the window in Tesslovich's office. He's still alive just like Tesslovich!"

Ariel started to surge forward, but Ez was quicker and blocked her way. "Too many," he said. "More on the train. We're outnumbered."

"They've got Mouser!"

"We can't take them all, El. We'd just be showing our hand. Right now, they don't know we know what they're doing. We still have the element of surprise. We can find out where the tunnel goes and get him and hopefully the rest of the kids back."

"I can't let them take him!"

"You have to. They don't know he's a shifter. When he comes to he can probably get out all by himself, fly right between the bars and escape before they know he's gone."

"Ez is right," Bishop agreed. "We need a plan."

Ariel was staring through the small window, watching as the cages were strapped in and the other passengers took their places in the forward cars. The little man in the striped suit was the last one aboard. He took one last look behind him, as if he sensed their eyes on his back, and stepped into the baggage car.

With a hiss, the train began to move forward. As it disappeared into the tunnel the lights on the platform dimmed, then extinguished one by one until the platform was dark.

Ariel shook Ez' restraining hand off her arm. "If anything happens to Mouser, I'll never forgive either of you."

"It's my fault." A voice behind them said. "I should have never let him go back for his shoes."

～

They all swung around. Part of Bishop's brain noticed that the ruff of hair down Ez' spine was standing up like a dog in attack mode. He heard the snick of Ariel's gravity knives falling into place and felt the weight of the Glock as he brought it up, ready to use it against whatever new threat this was.

"Don't kill me; I'm on your side." A man in a loose, brown pull-over sweater and brown pants moved toward them, arms held out from his sides, hands empty. A dark scarf covered his head, one end wrapped his neck, trailed over a shoulder and down his back. Calm, amber colored eyes in a dark face seemed to hold neither threat nor fear.

"Cassius," Ez said. "One of these days you're going to sneak up on the wrong person."

Cassius' teeth showed briefly in an unapologetic grin. "Wasn't sneaking Ezrim," He said. "I was trying to get to the boy before he got himself in trouble. Too late I see."

"They took Mouser." Ariel told him. "They caged him and put him on a train. A demon knocked him out with a Taser. There were two or three other kids. They seemed to be unconscious. We need to rescue them before they get hurt."

"Easier said than done," The brown man said. "You'd all better come with me. They'll be missing their 'goyles soon and send somebody to look around."

"We should have gotten him while we could!"

"This must be our Raptor." Cassius smiled at Ariel. He turned his attention to Bishop. "And you are?"

"Frank Bishop," Bishop said. "Professional innocent bystander."

The teeth flashed again. "A civilian." The man pushed his way through the double doors and onto the platform, pausing only once to be sure he was being followed. "There are no innocent bystanders anymore Mr. Bishop, only victims and those willing to fight back."

"I'm finding that out." Bishop stuck the Glock back into the waistband of his jeans.

Cassius pulled a metal rod with a sharply bent end out of his sleeve. "I wouldn't normally come out here, but it's the fastest way and the cameras won't pick us up if we hurry." He started for the far edge of the platform, away from the direction the train had taken. As he went down the steps to the track he explained that this tunnel was part of the loop that brought customers to the department store.

"The old train's in this utility tunnel. They just drove it in there and shut it down the day the bankruptcy court took the store. We've salvaged some parts, but mostly it's just good cover."

"Where are we going?" Bishop asked.

Cassius led them between the old train and the wall of the tunnel until they came to a rusty metal door in the wall. He stuck the end of the metal rod into a hole on one side of the door and moved it completely around in a counter-clockwise rotation, then halfway back in the other direction. The door opened silently on well-greased hinges.

"Down," Cassius said. "Into the Deeps. I think you'll find it interesting."

Even with night vision goggles Bishop soon lost track of the twists and turns of the brick and stone passages below the subway tunnels. Metal, then brick and stone stairways led down from one level to another. Small animals scurried just beyond the range of Bishop's vision, and the sound of rushing water came and went as they moved deeper.

Bishop didn't like the claustrophobic feeling of being underground and was thinking about what might be sneaking up behind them in the dark when they stopped at a rusty iron door at the end of the passage.

The door swung open. Bishop pulled his goggles down around his neck to let his eyes adjust to the light.

"Welcome to the Deeps," Cassius said. "Let's go check the security cameras."

Mouser woke to a jolting ride. The cage he was in hadn't been tightly strapped to the rings welded to the sides of the freight car. Every time the train hit a curve the cage swung forward, then slammed back against the wall. Mouser's head was already throbbing from the Taser and each contact with the wall made him feel like he was being used as a human drumstick. He was careful not to show he was awake. If he opened his eyes slightly he could see the striped legs and polished shoes of Taserman. He would bet that the ugly little demon was just waiting for an excuse to zap him again.

He had no idea how long he'd been out. He'd been stupid to go back to the surface for his shoes, but he'd traded hours of hacking to get them and next to his computer they were his most prized possession. He'd been bending over in the alley tying his shoe laces when they grabbed him. He'd had no time to shift and instinct told him that it might not be a wise move to show his hand before he knew what he was up against. If they kept him in a cage with bars like this one, he could be out of it and on his way the minute they left him alone. He was willing to wait for that chance.

Mouser had seen the other kids in their cages as he was being wheeled to the train. They looked like they were in pretty bad shape, especially the girl. Humans didn't recover from injuries as fast as shifters, that's why he was sure the demon wouldn't expect him to be awake this soon. He hoped the others were just sleeping off being stunned. Or maybe they were drugged. He didn't want to dwell too long on why they'd been kidnapped. The possibilities were too scary. What if they wanted him for . . .

- 4 -

"... Organ transplants!" Ariel was saying. "Child Porn! Sex Trafficking! Cannibalism! Human sacrifice!" She paced the large room, toenails clicking on the cement floor, black coat swirling with each turn.

"Calm down." Bishop told her. "Whatever they're doing they seem to be letting some of them go."

"One. They let one of them go and she broke someone's arm and her whole family is afraid of her."

Cassius looked up from the monitor he'd been examining over the shoulder of a young tech whose spiky orange hair glowed with strange luminosity in the light from the screen. "I don't think he's in immediate danger. Whatever Zaki wants these kids for isn't going to happen overnight. He's ruthless, but meticulous. He always plays the long game."

The room was full of salvaged computer equipment. Banks of monitors glowed from all four walls, every type from large consoles the size of old fashioned TVs to high definition flat screens. Each section was under the watchful eye of one or two people.

More computers lined the middle of the room. Some were

searching the internet, others showed street scenes, roof tops, interior rooms, offices and tunnels. Cassius motioned them over.

"This is the roof of Hauptmann's," he said pointing to the screen. "We disposed of the dead Gargoyles and bent the siding back into place. It won't hold up under close examination, but Zaki's people hardly ever go up there. Our cameras just happened to see you in the alley and we picked you up again on the roof. Nice work, by the way," he told Ariel. "And Ez, I'm glad to see you haven't lost your edge,"

Ez ignored the compliment.

"Where'd you get the demon loads?" he asked Bishop.

"I have friends. Where the hell are we?"

"The control room in the Deeps," Ariel said. "This is pretty amazing. You can see what's going on all over the city."

"Not everywhere," Cassius admitted. "But we can watch a lot of it. We're wired into the traffic cameras, building security monitors, private alarm systems. Even a tv and spy satellite. We're piggybacked onto the grid and we have ultra-fast connections. We can go anywhere that has phone, cable, TV, satellite or internet access, and it's untraceable. The only place we can't seem to get into is Zaki Industries. He has an impenetrable firewall. My guys have been trying to hack it for months with no luck. It's like a constantly moving target, almost like his system senses the threat and redesigns itself to meet it.

"Playback the platform," he told the tech.

The lights came up and the train entered the station. Several people got off after the doors slid open. Two over-muscled steroid cases who looked like they were on loan from the WWE followed the guy in the white lab coat.

Someone also disembarked from the first car. He was talking over his shoulder as he stepped out onto the platform. When his head turned Bishop could see the man was none other than

Nicolai Tesslovich, alive and dressed in one of his usual faultless four thousand-dollar suits and a two-hundred-dollar tie.

Trailing behind him was the ugly little freak in the striped suit holding an object the size of a garage door opener. A flash of current leaped across the top of the device. The little freak gave Tesslovich a nasty smile.

"Always nice to see someone who enjoys his work," Bishop muttered.

"I killed those guys less than a week ago!" Ariel told Cassius. "Two days later Tesslovich was back in court and now his ugly little enforcer is back from the dead."

Bishop pointed at the monitor. "I'll bet he's also the little shit who put a curse on me and left a goat head on my desk. He must be a gypsy demon."

"Travelers are big on curses," Cassius said, studying the image. "But they're rarely demons."

"He's still alive after going out a tenth-floor window with a demon load in his chest." Bishop said. "If that's not demonic, I don't know what is. And he works for Tesslovich. I saw the green blood when the lawyer's head went flying across the room."

"Interesting. Here are the kids."

The cages came rolling in from off-camera. Mouser's defiance and its consequence was more disturbing without sound. The steroid cases loaded each cage onto the train as everyone reentered their cars. The doors closed, and the train accelerated into the tunnel. As it disappeared, the platform lights behind it went out one by one.

"Was Mouser down here?" Ariel asked. "All these cameras and computers and stuff. This would be Mouser heaven. I can't believe he'd go back topside when he had all this to play with."

"It never occurred to me he would," Cassius said. "I would have stopped him, or at least sent someone along to make sure he made it back. I'm very, very sorry and I assure you, we'll do everything we can to help get him back. At least we know where the tunnel goes."

"Where?"

"The old Hauptmann estate. Now owned by Yamazaki Kiriyenko and home to Zaki Industries."

"Why am I not surprised?" Bishop said.

"Let's take a look at the maps," Cassius suggested. "We've salvaged, copied or rescued everything we could get our hands on. A lot of them were simply abandoned by the city and left to rot in old store-rooms. We even found a room down here full of hand drawn plans for the lowest tunnels. Once they were built, the engineers just left them behind."

They left the computer room and started down a corridor.

Bishop's jaw dropped. The Deeps was like a whole underground city with light and heat and people moving on foot and in golf carts along what appeared to be a central thoroughfare. The locals were a bit exotic in their clothing choices and their complexions tended toward pale, at least if they were light skinned, but everyone looked well fed and sane, unlike many of the homeless up above. Obviously, there were reasons why they'd chosen to live in The Deeps, but maybe they were better off in this strange place underground.

"Where do you get your food?" Ariel asked.

"A variety of places other than dumpsters," Cassius answered with a wry smile. He removed his scarf and pushed absently at the short, copper colored dreadlocks tumbling around his face.

"We have our own hydroponics garden on the level below this one. It has water, grow lights, and a small park with fruit trees. We encourage everyone down here to spend some time there to keep their vitamin A and D levels up."

He led them through a set of double doors. Inside was a huge room filled with floor to ceiling bookcases. A few kids sat at one of the many tables, surrounded by a well-used collection of books and a stack of printouts, furiously taking notes.

"This is the library." Cassius said. "I think there's a history exam coming up."

A small, wizened woman in a long, homespun lavender dress and grey, knitted shawl peered through rimless spectacles at Cassius and his visitors.

"Miranda," Cassius said by way of introduction, "is our librarian. She helps us keep our books and maps in order."

He patted an old, oak card catalogue. "We have everything in the computer, but this is Miranda's hard copy, just in case. She knows where everything is anyway. We need the map room, Miranda."

The small woman removed a large key on a chain from around her neck and silently handed it over, her bright eyes watched as the small group move through the room to a door in the back.

"She's like Cerberus guarding the gate," Cassius said as he waved them through into the map room. "Woe to anyone who hurts one of her books."

"How long has she been here?"

"Six years. One of our scouts found her sleeping on a subway grate practically frozen to death and brought her down. She hasn't said one word the whole time she's been with us, but I don't know what we would do without her."

The map room amazed Bishop even more than the library. Deep shelves divided into various sized cubicles held hundreds, maybe thousands, of paper tubes with plastic caps on the ends. Each was meticulously labeled. Tall, oak or steel document cases with shallow drawers undoubtedly held more. A huge computer screen hung on one wall, the green light on the outsized key board below it was blinking in eager anticipation.

Cassius waved a hand. "These are our maps. It's still not everything, but we have most of the underworld either in tubes or scanned into the computer." He tapped a few keys. "Let's see what we have connecting Hauptmann's to the outside world."

The monitor sprang to life. The image that came up was dense with detail; tunnel after tunnel, layer after layer, pipes, conduit, rails, switches, electrical diagrams. It was all too crowded to make sense. Cassius tapped a few more keys and multiple layers peeled away, leaving only one map behind.

Hauptmann's basement and subway platform with its entrances and exits appeared on the screen. A large loop of track circled north, intersecting another platform on the other side of the circle.

"This is where Hauptmann's customers connected with the regular subway." Cassius put his finger on the screen. "It's been sealed off, but the station on the other side is still in use. There are a couple of utility ports that give us access if we need it. Here's the utility tunnel where the old train is parked and here . . ."

His finger touched another place on the screen. ". . . is where Zaki's train veers off from the loop and heads for the estate. It's almost fifteen miles from here to there. Part of the track used to be above ground, but sometime in the last few years he dug out an underground tunnel that goes straight into the buildings on his property. He followed the old track though, so we still know where the train is going.

"Here's another interesting bit." Cassius traced his finger along the private track until he was back inside the city limits. "There's another small platform here."

He tapped the screen. "If we overlay the surface map we can see what's above it."

A transparent overlay flipped down over the subway map.

"See this foot print here? The Hauptmann family had a city residence as well as their country estate. It was built in 1912. The neighborhood started to go downhill in the late sixties, so they closed it up and moved to the country full time. It was sold when the family business started to go bad. The area gentrified in the mid-nineties and now it's the hot place to live. Guess who owns the house now?"

"Zaki Kiriyenko?" Bishop asked.

Cassius shook his head.

"Nicolai Tesslovich," Ariel said with grim certainty.

"Bingo."

"So where are they takin' the kids?" Ez asked. "The city or the country."

"I'm betting the country. There's a lot of unexplained activity out there. Plus, Zaki built several large research type buildings on the property where he can develop his 'personal projects'. No one's quite sure what those projects are."

"So, we could go in through the tunnel and get Mouser and those other kids out of there," Bishop said.

"Sorry, it's not as easy as that. Not only haven't we been able to tap into Zaki's security cameras, there are traps in the tunnel."

"What kind of traps?" Ariel asked. Bishop could sense her thinking there had to be a way to follow the track and get Mouser back.

"Besides surveillance cameras and lasers, Zaki installed steam traps. We lost two scouts before we figured it out. When the train hits a certain point in the tunnel it triggers a series of high pressure steam jets. Zaki uses the original Hauptmann train, but it's been retrofitted with watertight steel plating, thick Plexiglas windows and tight door seals. The jets are designed to hit it from all angles as it goes past. Anybody walking down the tunnel or hitchhiking on the outside of the train would be instantly parboiled."

"So, we can't get to Mouser from this direction?" Ariel said. "Can we get into the tunnel beyond the steam trap?"

"The tunnel is all underground at that point. Its concrete surrounded by solid earth, no way in from any direction."

"I can still get in from the air."

"Gargoyles, laser motion detectors, surveillance cameras, drones, wards. Very hard, possibly fatal."

"I flew over it before."

"Well, Zaki's not the president. He doesn't get a no-fly zone but believe me he has the hardware to take out anything he recognizes as a threat. If you were high enough you might not have been noticed, or maybe they thought you were just a big bird."

"So, you can get caught going in and coming out."

"Well, they've probably made some adjustment for animals and birds. Otherwise their alarm system would be going off every five minutes. Mouser might be able to fly out if he could avoid the Gargoyles."

"We should have taken them on the platform before they got the kids on the train," Ariel told Ez. She glared at Cassius. "Screw being seen!"

"I understand your feelings, Ariel, and your natural instinct as a Raptor, but there's a serious war brewing out there and hardly anyone knows about it except the enemy. Our only edge is surprise, but we need more information."

"You want to stay down here and play with your cameras and computers, fine! I can't do that. There's information about Zaki and Tesslovich on the street right now and I'm not staying down here until it filters through the grates, so you can add it to your database."

Ariel stalked out of the map room and through the library,

toenails clicking an angry staccato on the cement floor. Over her shoulder she said, "You want to know what I find out, give Ez your email. Otherwise, stay out of my way."

A few minutes later Ez and Bishop found her pacing the corridor outside the library. "Nice exit." Bishop said, tucking a short cardboard tube up one sleeve. "Too bad you had to wait for one of the native guides to lead us out of this place."

A boy of about twelve, dressed in the brownish-grey mufti that seemed so popular in The Deeps, joined them. The neutral color made him almost invisible against the stained cement walls of the underground tunnels.

"I'm here to take you out," the boy said. "I'm also 'sposed to introduce you to Old Bill topside. He doesn't move more'n four blocks in either direction. If you need to come back down he'll get you in, but he's clasterphobic so he won't come down hisself."

"Lead on, B'wana," Bishop told the kid. "Our fearless leader needs to stretch her wings."

The boy handed Ez a jacket. "We got all your stuff off the roof," he said. "That's 'goyle blood on there isn't it?" He pointed to a spatter of acid holes in the cloth. "Man, those things are meaner'n a rat on crack. You got to watch out for them when you go topside or they'll take you out."

"Not if you have a Raptor and a werewolf along," Bishop told him, and left it at that.

Old Bill turned out to be a derelict living behind a dumpster in an alley off Sixth and Franklin. He was grizzled by weather, neglect and alcohol but, if you looked beyond that Bishop thought, he wasn't all that old. His pale blue eyes went from bleary to intelligent when he realized there was a purpose to his being sought out.

"Cassius says these guys are okay," the scout told him.

"Copy that," Old Bill looked at each one of their faces for a long moment before he burrowed back into his filthy sleeping bag. "Tell them next time to bring me something to drink."

"Bill likes his Beam," the kid said and slid around the corner out of sight.

The three looked at each other.

Bishop felt like a guest who'd just found out the party was over but didn't quite know what to do about it. "Anybody need a ride?" he said.

"Never liked the tunnels." Ez raised his nose to some scent on the wind. "I'll walk."

Ariel gave Bishop an evaluative stare as if she were turning a decision over in her mind. She started to walk away. "I have a date," she said over her shoulder. "Want to come along?"

"Why?"

"You did just offer me a ride, didn't you?"

"Yeah."

"Then shut up and drive."

There was no conversation. Bishop wondered why a trip in a motor vehicle with Ariel was like waiting for a car bomb to go off--- the kind that didn't get you when you turned on the ignition but exploded just at the point in the journey when you started to relax.

Bishop glanced at Ariel's bare feet, which she'd put up against the dashboard as soon as she slumped into the passenger seat. They were filthy from the tunnels. In Bishop's imagination, he saw the claws on her toes slash deep grooves through the plastic covering into the metal itself. He'd already had to explain a couple of bullet holes in the trunk to his insurance company, replacing the dashboard because of claw marks would be a whole other problem.

"Um," he said. "Could you put those away they're making me nervous."

Ariel gave him a put-upon sigh, but retracted her nails, letting her feet return to normal.

"Look, about Mouser . . ."

"This is about Mouser, Frank, and heads up, when we go into the bar don't stare, don't order anything but beer in an unopened bottle and be the strong silent type, okay? If you go all freaky-geeky on me, we might get in a lot of trouble. Park over there," she told him, indicating the mouth of an alley. This time she waited until he turned the ignition off before getting out of the car.

"Bring the gun," she said.

- 6 -

The fog of smoke inside the bar was so thick Bishop thought he might need a lung transplant if he stayed too long. He could see a band on a small stage in one corner. The female singer had a sort of glitter-goth-metal-ska thing going with a screechy edge to it like bad wheel bearings. She was dressed in a purple prom formal with a fluffy, sparkly net overlay, black, elbow high gloves and lace up leather boots with six-inch heels. Her blonde hair was streaked with black and her eye makeup looked like she'd paid someone to punch her out and the bruises were three days old. Her back-up singers were shaped like Bowling Ball Barbies, long blond hair, long limbs and short, round bodies in pastel spandex. The lead guitar had six fingers on each hand and the drummer looked like a squid.

He decided not to look too closely at the people at the tables. It didn't take being a rocket scientist to know he wasn't in Kansas anymore.

Bishop followed Ariel to the bar. "T' Jon," Ariel said, sliding onto a stool next to a thin man in a fuchsia leisure suit, royal blue shirt and yellow silk pocket handkerchief.

The unfortunate T' Jon immediately turned a lighter shade of pale.

Bishop took the stool on the other side of the man and held up two fingers--- the universal signal for two beers.

"Polyester," Ariel said, as if appalled. "Timmy! Are you robbing trailer parks again?"

"It's retro," Timmy Jon told her, defensively. "It's all the rage in some circles."

. . . of hell, Bishop thought.

When the bartender appeared with the beer he told him, "and another of whatever our friend here is drinking."

One of the bartender's eyeballs rolled over to look in Ariel's direction.

"Go ahead," she said. "We're all friends here." Neither Timmy or the bartender looked convinced.

"Who's your butch-looking companion?" T' Jon asked, looking Bishop up and down. "Don't go for the GQ type I see. Ruff!" He gave Bishop a little bark.

"Careful, Sparky," Bishop said. "I bite."

Timmy Jon took out a short, black onyx cigarette holder, screwed an unfiltered pink cigarette into it, lit it and blew a stream of smoke at the mirror over the back bar.

"So, do I, honey. Call me anytime and we can compare the length of our incisors."

"Oh God, stop it!" Ariel said. "Get a booth" she ordered Timmy Jon. "Spot here will bring your drink."

Bishop raised one side of his upper lip in a mock snarl as Timmy Jon swished past him.

"Grow up!" Ariel hissed as she followed the psychedelic glow of the demon's petroleum-based fashion statement over to a booth along the wall.

Bishop threw a few bills on the bar, picked up his beer and scooped up the large martini glass the bartender had delivered for

Timmy Jon. Something stuck on a toothpick was bobbing in the drink's grey-green depths. Bishop peered into the glass and swore he saw something looking back.

He slid into the booth next to Ariel and pushed Timmy Jon's drink across the table. The toothpick waggled back and forth until Timmy reached out and held it against the side of the glass with one finger.

Bishop checked his beer before he took another swallow: All clear. He'd have to thank Ariel later for the warning.

Timmy Jon's eyes kept checking the room. He'd already smoked his loathsome pink cigarette down to the holder. He ground it out in the ashtray in front of him. His long thief's fingers tapped restlessly against the martini glass.

Ariel leaned forward. "I think you have some information for me," she said. "Cough it up or I'll sic the dog on you." She hoped Bishop was looking suitably threatening.

"I could get in a lot of trouble for this."

"More trouble than us taking you out in the alley and beating the crap out of you?" Bishop asked.

"Yeah," Timmy said. "A lot more trouble than that. You need to make the information worth my while. I'm used to getting beat up."

Ariel was a little surprised. Timmy Jon had always been a bit on the cringey side, but she could see the demon was genuinely scared.

"How much?" she asked.

"I need a vacation, know what I mean? Someplace warm and far away. Just for a few weeks until things blow over. I think I might have asked the wrong person, the wrong question."

"You want a plane ticket?"

"No, I want money. This information is worth a lot, but all I want is four or five thou and to keep my head."

"That's a lot of money, T' Jon. You need to tell me something that's worth that kind of cash."

Timmy looked down for a long minute, like he was considering his options and the pickings were slim. He took a big gulp of his drink and pushed it aside. Released, the toothpick started to do laps around the glass. Ariel could see Bishop out of the corner of her eye staring at it with glassy fascination.

The demon glanced around the barroom then leaned forward. "It's a resurrection bug."

"It's a bug?" Ariel repeated.

"Not a bug, bug!" Timmy Jon hissed. "It's some kind of technology that brings you back from the dead. It heals you and makes you stronger. That's what happened to Tesslovich. They sewed his head back on and voila! He's a new demon."

"And Zaki's behind this?" Bishop asked.

"He invented it. He's been testing it for three, maybe four years. Tesslovich is his front man to the demon community. It's gonna cost a lot, but demons like Tesslovich are gonna be able to buy immortality. The really ambitious ones could create an army of invincible soldiers. The guy's a maniac, he wants to rule the world."

"Lab Rats." Ariel said, her stomach twisting into a knot, heart sinking. "They're using the kids as lab rats."

She leaned closer to Timmy Jon. "We need to get onto Zaki's estate, T' Jon. Do you know how we can do that?"

The demon's eyes went wide. "Are you crazy? That place is tighter than Fort Knox's asshole. The man's a technology genius; he's got security up the wazootie, to say nothing of having attack-everything patrolling the grounds."

"He's got a friend of ours, Timmy. I need to get him back."

Timmy shook his head. "Let him go, sweetie. Even if you got him out he wouldn't be the same person you knew."

Ariel reached across the table, grabbed Timmy Jon by the lapels and pulled him toward her. "Yes, he will!" she hissed. "If he's not, I will personally kill every fucking demon in this town including you."

"People are noticing," Bishop said softly, pulling gently at Ariel's arm.

Ariel released Timmy Jon who thumped back down onto the bench. The demon quickly straightened his jacket, smoothed the lapels and adjusted his handkerchief. "This is a vintage outfit," he huffed. "You'll ruin the line!"

Ariel rolled her eyes. "Imagine how it will look on you with no head over it."

"Okay. Okay! There might be one way." He hunched forward. "Zaki's big into sports. He built himself a stadium on the property, so he can hold events; boxing, wrestling, ice hockey, soccer. Stuff like that. It's no fun if he's the only one who sees the games, so he invites important people to come watch. The stadium holds one, maybe two hundred and fifty people. Lots of security; the invitations have some kind of chip in them and you can't get in without one. Nobody's allowed to drive in, buses take people straight from the lot at the gate to the stadium. Then there's cameras, X-rays, metal detectors, bomb sniffers. It's a hard party to crash, but if you can figure out a way to get a ticket you might be able to get in."

"When's the next event?"

"Do I look like I'd be invited?"

"Timmy," Ariel warned. "You know everything that happens around here. When's the next event?"

"Saturday."

"That's three days from now. Who knows what they'll do to Mouser in three days!"

Timmy spread his hands, palm up. "I can't change the schedule, doll face. This week it's some kind of combat sport marathon. Wrestling, kick boxing, kung-fu, bare knuckles, half naked sweaty men, bruised and bloody." He fanned himself with a hand. "Zaki makes the rules, so there aren't many and there's always big betting going on. The people he invites can afford it."

"We need three tickets." Ariel told him.

"What?! I can't do that. How am I supposed to do that?"

"You're a thief, Timmy Jon," Bishop said. "Steal some."

"You get me the tickets and I'll get you your get-out-of-town money." Ariel said. "I expect them by tomorrow night." Ariel slid out of the booth and Bishop followed.

"You're going to get me killed!" Timmy hissed.

"Eye on the prize, Timmy," Ariel told him. "Picture yourself in a vintage Speedo on some tropical beach, naked kelpies bringing you Pina Coladas and roast bat on a skewer or whatever it is you eat."

"You always appeal to my baser fantasies," he sighed.

"Tomorrow night, T' Jon."

Timmy nodded, disconsolate.

As they left the bar the demon was franticly waving over a waitress to order another drink.

7

"You think he can do it?" Bishop asked as they walked back to his car.

"He's a pretty good thief."

"Do you believe Zaki's got this resurrection bug thing?"

Ariel shrugged. "I think you have other problems right now."

"Jesus! Shit!" All four tires on his car had been slashed and his windshield was spider webbed with cracks.

"Maybe this is part of the curse," Ariel said dryly.

"My car," Bishop moaned. As he turned away something flickered in the air, caught in the light from a streetlamp. Ariel's hand flew out and plucked the knife out of the air as it flew by. She whirled around and grabbed another.

"Get down, Frank!" Bishop fell to one knee and reached around his back for the Glock. Ariel swatted away another knife. They were coming from the alley.

"Step to the side!" Bishop shouted. Ariel stepped two feet to the right and Bishop fired three rounds down the alley. There was a clatter and he fired two more. Silence.

"You alright?" he asked.

"Yes. Think you got him?"

Bishop pulled out his car keys and popped the trunk where he kept his old police issue flashlight. He pointed it down the alley, holding it under the extended pistol with his left hand so he could see what he was going to shoot. The alley was empty.

Bishop lowered the gun and flashed the light around. There was blood on the cement, but no body. He squatted to take a closer look and Ariel peered over his shoulder.

"It's red," she said. "Human."

"Your blood's red."

"Okay, not demon. Look at this."

Bishop stood up. Ariel held up a fan of flat, black handled knives. "Throwing knives."

"I don't get it."

"You keep calling the guy who worked you over and probably left the curse in your office a circus freak."

"Yeah, but only because he's small, ugly, creepy looking, wears a weird suit and hit me a lot."

"He's also a gypsy. Maybe he was a knife thrower in a carnival or the circus. Maybe there's something symbolic about him trying to kill you with circus knives."

"Swell. I can't believe I only nicked the little bastard."

"We don't know how badly he's hurt, only that he managed to get away."

Bishop shook his head. "What about my car. The cops will probably be here any minute."

"Call Triple A. The cops never come to this neighborhood except on bag day. You'll be fine."

"You're leaving?"

"Things to do." She waved the hand full of knives over her head as she walked away. "I'll add these to my collection. Meet you at the Caf' just before midnight tomorrow and we'll get the tickets from Timmy Jon."

Bishop leaned against the front bumper of his car, pulled out his cell phone and hit the speed dial for Triple A.

8

When she got home, Ariel stripped off her clothes and stood in the shower until the water went cold. She dried off and wrapped herself in a ratty old terry cloth robe.

As she made tea her eyes kept going to the blue envelope on the kitchen table. She was determined not to be intimidated by it. Her worry about Mouser was bigger than her worry about herself. Maybe the envelope was just another assignment. Maybe the Guardian didn't know that Tesslovich was still alive.

And maybe pigs fly.

She picked up a throwing knife from the pile she'd dumped on the table and slit the envelope open. The message was one, hand written line: Tower, 3:00 p.m. She hoped that meant three p.m. tomorrow not today, because today was already gone.

She finished her tea, crawled into bed and thought about Mouser until she fell asleep two long hours later.

Ariel heard voices, arguing. They seemed far away at first but louder as they came closer. The voices made her feel small and afraid because it wasn't the first time she'd heard them.

Then she started to see the faces. The man was angry and the woman's face looked scared but she was yelling back. Then the man hit her, hard. Blood flew, and the woman crumpled.

Ariel knew she needed to get away. She'd been told by the woman: "Get away! Run! Hide! He'll hurt you too."

She began to tremble and sweat, fighting against hands that were holding her back: feeling caught, trapped, knowing she'd never get away in time. Then she was stumbling, falling, running. Heart pounding, knowing she'd never make it, knowing he was right behind her.

An angry male voice yelled, "I'll kill you! I'll kill you, you little bitch! Don't you run from me! Nobody leaves me. Not her. Not you. Nobody! Nobody!"

Ariel sat bolt upright in bed, gasping for air, her throat so constricted she thought she'd never get another breath. She could feel the hands, the fingers around her neck, feel the weight of him, see his eyes.

She threw the covers back and stumbled out of bed. Standing up usually helped get her breath back, stopped the dizzy darkness, quelled the fear. Sometimes, in the bathroom mirror, after she'd splashed cold water on her face, wiped the sweat away, she could swear she saw the imprint of his fingers on her throat, but in the morning the bruises were always gone.

She was always exhausted after the dream and she fervently wished she would never have to sleep again.

- 9 -

Mouser woke in a plastic box. His head was muzzy from the drug, and the lurch of nausea in his stomach made him crawl to the stainless-steel toilet in the corner of the box where he puked up what he thought of as his last pizza.

He'd faked being unconscious, but when they pulled him out of the cage he'd fought them, earning another Taser blast that made him helpless to resist the syringe full of junk they'd stuck in his neck. He had no idea how long he'd been out or where he was. There was a piece of cotton taped to the inside of his elbow. He pulled it off. They'd taken some of his blood and the bruise told him they hadn't been gentle about it.

He sat up and looked around. He was in a small cell with a Plexiglas front that had a collection of two-inch holes higher than his head and a triangle of smaller holes over an open slot further down. A narrow bunk hung on the side wall. It had been made up with sheets, a pillow and a grey blanket.

The toilet he'd just puked into was on the back wall, next to the steel sink. There were no movable parts, everything was molded into solid pieces, worked by buttons. Nothing to pull apart and use as a weapon, nothing to help get yourself out of this place.

The walls and floor of the corridor outside the cell were white tile. Everything had a glare to it. A sterility. There was no dust, no dirt or fingerprints. You could probably eat off the floor, and the drain holes implied they could hose the whole place down if they needed to and it would be like you were never there.

They'd even taken his clothes. He was dressed in a green jump suit with Velcro closures and paper slippers. There was a row of similar cages twenty feet across the tile from him. He could see a blanket covered form on one of the bunks, but it didn't move. He reached out to touch the Plexiglas wall and the contact gave him an unexpected shock. Not as strong as a Taser, but enough to throw him back a couple of feet.

He sat down on the bunk and stared at his feet. This wasn't good. This wasn't good at all.

- 10 -

Ariel's response to her dreams was either to paint them while they were still fresh or to work them off with exercise until she was physically too tired to think, let alone dream. Tonight, she couldn't bear to put her terror on canvas one more time and she was afraid that if she tried to go back to sleep Mouser would visit her next, and she was worried enough about him already without allowing her subconscious to play with her fears for him in her dreams.

She had gone to bed in draw string pants and an old t-shirt, which were now soaked with terror sweat. The large room she used for everything except eating and sleeping had a heavy punching bag hung in one corner and mats on the floor. Juke, one of the motorcycle mechanics downstairs, helped her hang it. The bikers did her small favors from time to time and never asked questions.

In return she shared with them interesting weapons and other bits of strange she picked up on assignment. Juke was into stuff like that. She'd given him a sword shaped like a scythe with two handles attached to the blade, and a couple of throwing stars. Today, she'd give him most of the knives she picked up in the alley. He was into those too. One wooden wall of his shop was scared with puncture marks made by different sized blades. She figured it was leftover biker gang stuff since Juke and Ham were older now and had obviously mellowed out. Dingo was younger, but he was still accepted as part of the pack.

They were always polite to her, even gallant at times. And since they lived behind their shop, one of them, usually Juke, was often on the front steps of the building having a smoke when she came home late at night. He'd always say he was just getting in or having a bout of insomnia and needed some fresh air. She could sympathize with that.

The Dog's colors were two snarling wolves with red eyes with the words Bad Dogs underneath. Ez would like that, and the mental picture of snarling wolves on Harleys made her smile.

Ariel taped her hands the way she had been taught by Tomas and started in on the bag with her fists. She began to alternate punches with kicks until the bag was swinging on its chain and small bits of sawdust were starting to leak out of the hole where the ring bolt was screwed into the beam.

She slowed it down, letting her muscles cool off until they were ready to accept the slower pace of a set of Tai Chi exercises, but the knots came anyway. That always meant she hadn't paid enough attention to the other part of herself, the Raptor part that wanted its release. It was in these times she craved to be out of the city and somewhere in the mountains where she could wheel and soar with the smaller, non-shifting creatures of her kind, but dawn was coming, and it was too dangerous to fly.

The other end of the room was covered, floor to ceiling, with mirrors. Maybe at one time this roof top apartment had been a ballet studio. She could almost see a line of little girls in their pink or white tutus gravely practicing the positions of the dance, but now it was her aerie and she owed it to her inner Raptor to let it out, however brief and unsatisfying that might be in the enclosed space.

Ariel knelt before the mirrors and stripped off her soaked shirt. Her tattered sweat pants hung on her hip bones, exposing the hard muscles of her flat belly. She didn't look at herself in the mirrors, it wasn't time. Instead, she slid one foot forward, curling her torso over her bent knee. Head down, she extended her other leg back as far as she could, taking the weight on her toes. She stretched her muscles, spread her shoulder blades, let the air leave her lungs until her diaphragm felt like it was touching her spine. She could feel the ripple start under both shoulder blades, following their curves as muscle and sinew parted to reattach themselves to the internal structure that supported her wings. She felt them emerge as they always did in an exquisite rush of sensation that was beyond pain or pleasure, expanding like magic, dark, lustrous, and tipped with light.

Ariel stood and spread her arms, her wings spread with them. The Raptor in the mirror looked back at her, fingers and toes claw tipped, the planes of the face sharper, cheek bones higher, hooded eyes brighter, the bridge of her nose narrower and slightly hooked over an upper lip that came to two sharp points in the middle. She smiled. This is what her enemies saw. This is what Zaki Kiriyenko would see when she came for Mouser. This was what she wished she could be in her dreams, the adult changeling she had become. Powerful and brave enough to stop the man who'd hurt the woman and tried to hurt her. Powerful enough to make the dreams stop. Powerful enough to let her sleep without fear.

Exhausted, she sank to the floor. Wrapping her wings around her like an embrace. Head on one arm, Ariel fell into a dreamless sleep.

- 11 -

Mouser suspected the slot in the Plexiglas was for receiving food and the arrival of a rolling cart filled with trays proved him right. The guy delivering the trays was dressed in white paper coveralls, a paper shower cap and latex gloves. If there was no movement inside a cell he banged on the plexi with a metal rod with a ball on one end. If that got no response he shoved the tray through a slot near the floor. If a resident, (Mouser thought 'prisoner'), made it to the wall in time, he shoved it through the upper slot. Nobody talked. When lunch-guy got to Mouser's cell, Mouser was waiting at the upper slot. "Hey," he said as the guy pulled a tray out of the cart. "Where am I? What is this place? You can't just keep me here against my will!"

The guy shoved the tray through the slot. Mouser had to grab it to keep it from falling to the floor. It was covered with a clear plastic top like they put on vegetable containers in the supermarket.

"Hey!" Mouser yelled. "I asked you a question. This is kidnapping. It's illegal."

The guy swung around and slammed the rod against the Plexiglas. Mouser jumped back even though the rod couldn't connect with him. The guy gave him a hard stare. There was something wrong with his eyes, something weird about his face and the way he moved, like all his parts didn't totally articulate.

"Back up, rodent." The guy growled. "You don't talk to me. You don't talk to nobody if you know what's good for you. Toss can hurt you bad if he wants. Toss can make you piss yourself, an' cry an' beg. Toss can even make you die!"

Toss stuck the rod through the tray slot and pushed a button in the handle. A bolt of light jumped at least two feet straight off the end of the ball. Mouser dodged sideways, barely managing to avoid it and still keep hold of the tray. He'd already thought of using as a shield if Toss took another shot at him. But the lunch demon just laughed, low and nasty, and went back to his cart to push it to the next cell.

Mouser sat down on his bunk. That had shaken him up pretty good, but he was also hungry. He pulled the plastic top off the tray. It had compartments for each different, but unidentifiable food. It all looked like slop to Mouser. A large pile of beige slop next to a smaller pile of lumpy, green slop, with some gelatinous orange slop and a piece of unbuttered bread. He'd also been given a flimsy plastic spoon and the kind of napkin you got out of dispensers in fast food restaurants. A capped plastic cup that looked like it contained juice sat in the last compartment.

He sighed. It wasn't pizza, but he had to keep his strength up if he was going to escape. He scooped up a spoonful of beige. It was virtually tasteless with a vaguely metallic edge. The orange goop was sweet, and the bread tasted like bread.

Mouser ate it all although a small voice in the back of his head told him he was probably being a fool. By the time his eyes involuntarily started to close, he was sure of it. "Crap! You stupid . . ."

The sound of the tray hitting the cement floor was the last thing he heard.

The light was so bright Mouser couldn't open his eyes. It was giving him a headache, or maybe he already had one. He tried to raise a hand to block the glare and realized he couldn't. His wrists and ankles were strapped down.

"He's awake," a voice said.

A head momentarily blocked the light, then tilted it aside so it wasn't right over Mouser's face. "I was afraid you might have gotten the wrong tray. Those dolts in the kitchen sometimes get things mixed up. That can be very unfortunate."

The speaker was wearing a white lab coat over blue scrubs and a tight-fitting cloth cap. A stethoscope was draped around the back of his neck. He looked at Mouser over half-spectacles, then referred to the clipboard in his hand.

"Interesting lab values," he said. "You seem to have a remarkable immune system even for a healthy young man. I'd wager you have interesting DNA as well. We'll need to test that before you join our little study."

"What are you going to do to me?" Mouser demanded.

"Hmmm? A few more tests. Then we'll see. You might have a remarkable future here number eighty-three, if you cooperate. But that's what you need to do—cooperate. If you make that decision there will be rewards. If you don't . . ."

"You can't make me do anything, you perv!" Mouser struggled against the restraints, then reminded himself that if he got too worked up he might shift. Instinct told him now was not the time. He needed to know more about the way out before he tried to escape.

"On the contrary," the doctor told him, looking calmly into his eyes and patting him on the arm. "We can make you do almost anything we want."

- 12 -

"I wil kil yu"

Bishop hadn't seen the message scratched into the fender on the driver's side of his car until the guy at the body shop pointed it out to him the next day. It had been dark, and he'd been too busy trying to keep from getting a knife in the chest.

"That's a paint job," the shop manager was saying. "Plus, four new tires and a windshield, comes to twenty-two fifty. Did you try to start it?"

"No."

"Good, but I think we better drain the gas tank just in case. Remember that time you were on that stakeout an' that guy snuck up an' . . ."

"Vividly." Bishop told him holding up a hand to stop the man's cough and sputter down memory lane.

"I'll give ya' a deal on draining the tank. Fifty bucks."

Sigh. "When can I have the car back?"

"Three, four days, more or less."

"I'll throw in an extra fifty if you can do it in less. I don't suppose you have a loaner I could use?"

The manager scratched his head with the business end of his

pen. "Well, I got somethin' in the back. It's not much to look at, but you bein' such a good customer, I guess I could let you have it. You know how to drive stick?"

Five minutes later Bishop was behind the wheel of an orange, '82 Ford Falcon. Except for the explosive bangs from the tail pipe when it started, the dents in the body, the moldy torn upholstery, pitted windshield and chrome skull with light-up eyes on the gearshift, it was a total piece of shit. But it was free. And he needed free because he was going to have to pay cash for the repairs to his car. His insurance agent was starting to treat him like a stalker. The last time he called him to report the latest in a series of career-related damage claims, he was sure he could hear the guy grinding his teeth through the receiver. He took that as a sign that unless the car was totaled, he'd better write a check, or he'd be cancelled.

Bishop hoped his car would be done by Saturday. Not just because the oxygen in his blood was being rapidly replaced by carbon monoxide, but because even if they got the tickets, there was no way he could drive this wreck to Zaki's estate. He was going to need a back-up plan. Bishop made a mental note to call Rain as soon as he figured out how to get the Falcon out of second gear.

The Guardian Building was a thirteen-story stone edifice on the edge of the downtown business district with a view of the lake. The bottom five stories were built in stepped layers, like a square wedding cake. A massive, heptagonal tower sat exactly in the middle of the top layer. The whole structure had been called The Braithwaite Building when it was built in the 1880s, but soon everyone was calling it The Guardian Building or The Angel Tower because of the twenty kneeling stone angels that guarded each corner of the five first floors. They were massive sculptures adorned with wings. Each one leaned slightly out over its corner, some watching the ground below, others had their heads tilted to the right or left or turned up toward the sky.

Ariel had never looked closely but she had been told that each angel had a separate, distinctive face. The fourteen angels that guarded the tower itself, stood upright, two to a side, framed by their folded wings and dressed much like Knights Templar---long, split tunics over chain mail, hands resting on the pommels of their swords, points touching the ground between their feet.

The Guardian Building was in the state registry of historic buildings and would never be torn down.

When she visited the building, Ariel always took a moment to look up at the angels. In her imagination she saw them suddenly taking flight, rising to circle the sky, swords ablaze, propelled by the graceful sweep of their massive wings to do battle with the powers of darkness.

Unfortunately, child-stealing demons weren't important enough to wake the angels, it would take a full-blown apocalypse to get them off their stony butts and into the fray. That's why there were Raptors. They took care of the little stuff so avenging angels could save their strength for the end of the world.

She pushed her way through the brass and glass revolving doors into the lobby. She had only been to see The Guardian a few times since she had been assigned to the city, and next to the angels, the doors were the best part of the visit. She was always tempted to go around more than once, but the guard at the security desk was already giving her the evil eyeball.

The ornate clock over the elevators said two fifty-five. The guard called up to the tower, then signed her in. She had timed herself, so she would reach The Guardian's office at exactly three o'clock. The Guardian considered punctuality a virtue, but he would also make her wait. His time was extremely important. Hers was not.

The Guardian's offices occupied the top five floors of a tower set on the exact center of the Guardian Building roof like a medieval keep. In actuality, offices for researchers and top officials occupied the lower tower floors. The absolute top and its roof observatory were reserved exclusively for The Guardian, a protocol that was strictly enforced. The ceilings at the top three tower levels were much higher than on other floors. It was an impressive space. The walls were lined with rows and rows of gently curving bookcases containing thousands of books and scrolls, most covered in various shades of leather. The floors were polished marble and the ceilings were painted with celestial scenes of clouds and sky and winged beings with swords or spears in their hands and grim expressions on their faces.

The effect was to make a visitor feel like he was about to have an audience with an Archangel, not a stuffy, uptight librarian with wings.

A private elevator let Ariel out on the eleventh floor. A woman sat behind a massive, antique desk directly across from the elevator. It was placed for maximum impact between broad, twin stairways that curved toward each other like an incomplete embrace.

The woman always reminded Ariel of the mother superior of some prison convent for wayward nuns. Her dark business suits were pristine and perfectly fitted, her white blouse buttoned to the neck. Pale blue eyes under dark brows carried the same warm welcome that an iceberg carries for an unwary ship heading in its direction. Her unnaturally black hair had been severely coiffed and lacquered into place. Ariel thought the style made her look like the Wolverine in the X Men comics---minus the side burns, of course.

The only acknowledgement the Wolverine made of Ariel's presence was to pick up the telephone and announce, "The Raptor has arrived."

There was no offer of a seat, a glass of water, a magazine or an estimate on how long it would be before 'The Raptor' would be graced with a few minutes of The Guardian's time. It was just another obscure lesson in humility that Ariel would allow to go right over her head. As always, she stood in front of the woman's desk, feet spread, hands clasp behind her back, and stared down at her until Brother Gregory, the Guardian's poor, overworked clerk finally came to get her.

Brother Gregory was a mouse in clerk's clothing, perhaps not literally like Mouser was a hawk, but Ariel wouldn't have been the least surprised to see him turn into something small, grey and whiskered, dashing for a hole in the baseboards.

The little man was a scuttler. Never fully erect he bobbed in place, reinforcing the lowliness of his position, then scuttled up the stairs in front of her to open a set of large brass doors at the top. On each side of the doors, the balcony was also lined, floor to ceiling, with bookcases. They gave off faint overtones of old leather, slightly moldy paper and the merest hint of incense. Ariel knew there were even more books below in a large, and very private, library guarded by the Wolverine.

The Guardian was at his desk, flanked by open balcony doors on either side of the huge room. One set faced the vast expanse of the lake that gave the city both its beauty and its commerce. The lake itself was a continuous horizon, uninterrupted by the sight of land. The other view was of the city, a forest of tall buildings behind the Guardian Building, standing as if they expected the angels to defend the perimeter against any attack while their busy inhabitants performed their own small evils in the name of business.

As she expected, he let her wait a few moments longer than necessary while he finished the page he'd been reading in the open tome that lay on his desk. Finally, he stood up and his flat, steel-colored eyes gave Ariel an evaluative look.

The Guardian was tall and lean, the way some men in their sixties tend to be after all the padding has left their frame, leaving only bones and sinew behind. The planes of his face were sharp, emphasizing his long, nose and thin, bloodless lips. Today he wore a light grey suit with a darker grey tie over a white shirt. His thick, silver hair was shot with threads of black and he wore it swept off his high forehead, barely touching his collar in the back.

"Raptor," he said. He was using his disappointed, schoolmaster voice. Ariel stood with her hands respectfully behind her back, but she refused to hang her head. She'd been ordered to kill Tesslovich, and she'd done her job. A weapon wasn't responsible for the results it caused, the one who aimed it was.

"Sir?"

"You failed your assignment. Explain this to me."

Ariel had learned through experience to never apologize to the Guardian. It only made him even more condescending than he already was.

"I beheaded Nicolai Tesslovich in his office three nights after I received the order," she told him.

"It seems from later evidence that Mr. Tesslovich failed to die."

Ariel spread her hands, "When I left, he was as dead as I could make him without burning the body."

"And now his security has tripled."

"I intend to keep trying."

"That won't be necessary," The Guardian said.

"Sir?' Ariel was startled. "But what about the children?"

"Children?" The inquiry was bland, barely interested.

"There are kids missing all over the city. Tesslovich is involved in the kidnappings. I thought that's why you wanted me to stop him!"

"Hardly. Tesslovich's minor indiscretions will be dealt with when the time is right."

Ariel was incensed at the cavalier way The Guardian was taking her information. "The time is half-past right already, sir. How can we let this go on? I think they're doing medical experiments on these kids. And now they have my messenger!"

"The hawk?" The Guardian waved a dismissive hand.

"Replace him. You have enough candidates from the riff-raff you insist on associating with at that café place."

"I don't want to replace Mouser. I want to get him back!"

"You will not question my decisions, Ariel. There is a higher plan at work here. It requires great patience and discipline—two things that you seem to lack. One misstep and all, all could be lost. If you defy me on this there will be consequences."

The Guardian looked down at his book.

"In the future," he said without looking up. "You can expect your orders to be more specific."

She was dismissed.

Ariel gave the Guardian a short bow and spun on her heel to leave. The 'consequences', as always, were undefined. As she descended the stairs, she heard the Guardian bellowing for Brother Gregory. He was the one who penned the messages and he was obviously about to hear something about his own deficiencies.

Ariel caught a small smile of satisfaction on the Wolverine's face as she passed her. Luckily the elevator was right there, waiting. She hated elevators. They were painfully slow and claustrophobic with no room for an angry Raptor to pace off her frustration.

She wished instead she could have flown away from the top of the Angel Tower, thrown herself into the air as she sometimes did, falling toward the ground like Icarus, only to catch the updraft, wings beating furiously to pull herself above the city canyons toward the open sky and the race toward home. It would have been some release from the anger she was feeling. But daylight, and the risk that she would be seen, made that impossible.

Screw the higher plan. She spun herself out through the lobby doors with a force that kept them spinning another full turn. The Guardian could take his damn instructions and . . .

well anyway, she wasn't going to just sit around while demons did whatever they wanted. She was going to get Mouser out of Zaki's clutches along with as many other kids as she could manage. Ez would help her, Timmy Jon would supply her with a way in, and Bishop, lame human that he was, was still better than no ally at all.

- 14 -

Bishop had arranged to meet Rain for a late lunch at The Forbidden City. He'd just been served his order of Mu Shu Pork with extra pancakes, General Tsu's Chicken, and spicy pot stickers with hot pepper sauce when Rain eased through the booth's curtains with a large Tsing Tao beer in one hand and a bottle of sparkling water in the other.

"Mm Mmm," he said, "all my favorites. You must want something special."

"Eat," Bishop told him, building himself a Chinese burrito stuffed with Mu Shu pork and plum sauce. "This is serious."

Rain loaded his own plate. "Tell me about it. Sister Catherine trapped the Captain in his office this morning and started taking him apart for not doing anything about her missing kids. He tried to palm her off on Missing Persons downtown, but she seems to think the kids are being sold into sex slavery to rich, foreign perverts who bring their boats across the lake to pick them up. She claims they have diplomatic immunity and that's why we're not doing anything about it. That lady is a terror once she gets rolling."

"You think there's any truth to that?" Bishop asked.

Rain shrugged. "I 'spose it's possible. Hasn't hit my radar." He grinned. "The Cap'n looked like he'd been whipped through a briar patch when the fine sister got through with him. He was sweating like a pig and his eyes were all bugged out. I thought they were going to shoot out of his face and ricochet around the room like ping pong balls. He kept yanking at his collar like she'd tried to strangle him with his own tie. The Weasel almost called 911. Cap's been locked in his office with the shades down ever since. I hope we find him in the morning with that vodka bottle he keeps in his desk clutched, empty in his cold, dead hand."

"Hope springs eternal," Bishop said. "But about that favor."

"You didn't get another goat head, did you?"

"No, and thanks for spoiling my lunch. The little mutant trashed my car. It's in the shop and they gave me a loner, but I can't drive it out to the Kiriyenko estate on Saturday. They'd laugh me out of the place."

"You got invited to the arena?" Rain asked, chopsticks half way to his mouth, awe and envy battling for supremacy in his voice. "Man! How did you manage that?"

"A friend of mine thinks she can score some tickets."

"How many?"

"Um, three."

Rain chewed thoughtfully, making Bishop wait. He took a sip of water, patted his lips dry with his napkin then used his chopsticks to pick up another bite.

"What's it going to cost me to get your car for the evening?" Bishop finally asked.

"The third ticket," Rain grinned.

"Yeah. I saw that one coming. It's a little complicated, though. First, we have to actually get the tickets, then I'll see what I can do."

"I hear some heavy betting happens at Zaki's games." Rain wasn't even listening to Bishop. "Man, I'd like to get in on that."

"It could be way out of your league," Bishop warned, thinking about the type of people Zaki might invite.

"Nothing's out of your league if you know the odds," Rain threw his napkin on the table. "Well, gotta go. Need to take the old lady to the beauty parlor. Get her ready to style."

Bishop knew he meant his prized 1962, maroon Mercedes Benz sedan. Rain treated the car like it was a dowager queen. He only drove it on weekends and special occasions.

"I'll call your cell and let you know if it's a 'go'," Bishop told him.

"Zaki's games," Rain was saying to himself as he pushed through the booth's curtains. "Mmm, mm mmm, mm, mm!"

- 15 -

The steps and curb of the runaway shelter looked like school had just let out. Kids were bunched together on the sidewalk, hanging, talking, smoking; being rowdy, cool or bored, but there was tension under the bravado and none of them were moving too far away from the building.

Bishop had to climb over a few to get up the steps and through the door. They eyed him suspiciously and somebody muttered 'cop' under his breath. Bishop thought that was better than 'perv'.

He found Sister Catherine in her office. The room looked like the same disorganized mess it had always been, but the bulletin board now held twenty photographs of missing kids and a list of names longer than that. Cate didn't look like her usual feisty self. A deep weariness had settled into her features and Bishop could smell that she'd started smoking again.

"You look like shit," Bishop told her.

"Flatterer," she said. "How many times do I have to tell you nuns don't date?"

"I'm serious, Catie." Bishop lifted a stack of files off one of the chairs in front of Sister Catherine's desk. There was no place in the office to put them, so he set them in the hall by the door. "You need to get some sleep. Have a decent meal. You can't keep going like this."

"Where are my kids, Frank? I'll rest after I find them."

"I hear you worked the Captain over pretty good today." Bishop smiled. "I wish I could have seen that. Rain said you went all Ride of the Valkyries on his ass. The squad's hoping to find him dead of a heart attack in his office tomorrow morning. Nobody's going to check on him 'til then."

"I'm going to have to confess that, you know," Sister Cate told him. "If I killed the bastard I'll be saying rosaries until I'm ninety."

"Rain says he hasn't heard anything about a child sex slave ring operating in the city."

"That doesn't mean it isn't true."

"I know, Cate. I'm not having any luck on my case either, although some possibilities have come up."

"What, Frank? If you know something, please tell me. These kids are so tough and so fragile all at the same time. They don't have anyone to look out for them. The shelter's packed. I've got them sleeping in bathtubs, in the laundry room, on every square inch of floor space. I'm letting them in whether they're using or not. I know that's going to be a problem, but I don't know what else to do. Every one of them knows somebody who's disappeared."

"Before I say anything I need to ask you a question."

Cate just looked at him over the pile of papers and abandoned Styrofoam cups of stale coffee on her desk.

"Do you believe in demons?"

"Me, personally or according to church doctrine?"

"You, personally."

"Are you serious?"

"As death, Catie. I need to know."

"Okay, but if you tell anybody about this I may be forced to commit a mortal sin on your head.

"Before I took my vows, I was a probation officer. I was assigned some pretty bad people, who'd done some really bad, unspeakable things. And a lot of them got away with it. Those unspeakable things usually weren't what they went to prison for, even though everybody knew they were guilty. They'd just sit in my office when they checked in and smirk at me, because they knew I knew and couldn't do a damn thing about it. I thought those guys must be demons, but they were only an example of how really evil humanity can become. They were the ones that made me decide to become a nun. I thought the church would help me make the world a better place.

"Compared to probation, the convent was a peaceful, spiritual place. I thought I was safe from evil until the night I saw the demon. I was praying alone in the chapel when he appeared to me. At first I thought I'd fallen asleep and was dreaming, but I wasn't."

"Did it talk to you? How do you really know it wasn't a dream?"

"He just stood there, staring at me, like he wanted to remember what I looked like. He had horns and bright red eyes. I started to pray for my soul and I think that made him smile. He reached over and touched my arm, turned around and was gone.

"Still don't believe me?" Kate rolled up one of the sleeves to her flannel shirt. Burned into her left wrist like a brand was a dark scar that looked like the pad of a finger with a small, triangular puncture about a quarter of an inch above it. "The triangle is the tip of his claw. And you know what else was weird?"

Bishop shook his head.

"He was wearing a business suit and tie. I think it might have been Armani."

Bishop shut his eyes for a moment. All of this had to be connected in some way. Kids were being kidnapped, most of them runaways. Sister Catherine was running the shelter. Tesslovich was her lawyer, Zaki a benefactor. Mouser was missing, Ariel had tried to kill Tesslovich and failed, and Bishop was the intended victim of a curse just because he was in the wrong place at the wrong time.

It still didn't make any real sense. He took a deep breath.

"I think Tesslovich is a demon," he told Cate. "I think Zaki Kirienko is also a demon, or at least he's working for them. I think he's using these kids for some kind of experiment, but I don't know any of the details. I'm going to Zaki's tomorrow night because he's holding a sports match in a private arena on his property. It will give me the chance to look around."

"Why wait?' Kate said. "Can't we call the FBI and get them to raid Zaki's estate, look for the kids?"

"We don't have any real evidence Catie. The FBI isn't going to take our word for it, they need proof. And the biggest reason is we don't know who the enemy is. There could be demons in the police department, demons in the FBI, demon lawyers, demon judges, demon senators. We don't know how widespread this is. If we show them, we know about them too soon we'll lose out advantage. I'm pretty sure the kids are still alive. I just need a couple of days to get more evidence. See how bad it really is. You need to trust me on this one."

"I'm so angry, Frank. And scared. I want to go get them right now. And God forgive me, I want to kill the people who hurt my kids."

"I just need a few days, Catie. You can break out the winged helmet and spear after that. If you're good, I'll introduce you to an avenging angel I met a few days ago. You two are a lot alike."

"Isn't there anything I can do in the meantime? It's hard to just sit here."

"You're not just sitting, Sister Catherine. You're giving shelter to a whole bunch of homeless kids who'd be disappearing off the streets every night if you weren't here for them. Keep doing that. I'll let you know what I find out."

Bishop leaned out the door, picked up the pile of charts he'd put out in the hall and plopped them back on the chair.

"Hang tight, Cate," He said.

"God bless, Frank," Sister Catherine whispered, but Bishop was already out the door.

– 16 –

It was too early to meet Ariel, but Bishop couldn't think of anywhere else he needed to go, and after seeing Sister Catherine he could use a beer. He parked down the street from the Caf'. The Falcon coughed and spasmed with asthmatic enthusiasm long after he'd taken the key out of the ignition. It was embarrassing that later that evening Ariel was going to see this pitiful piece of junk he was driving.

The energy inside the Caf' was a bit subdued. It probably had to do with Mouser. Ez was behind the bar as always and pulled a beer for Bishop as soon as he came in the door.

Bishop climbed onto a bar stool and half turned toward the room.

"I miss the kid," he said.

Ez nodded. "El's pretty upset. They told her to pick another messenger, but she refused. They told her to let Tesslovich go for now. She didn't take that very well either."

"They who?" Bishop asked, puzzled. Ariel didn't seem like someone who was very good at taking orders. He was surprised someone was trying to give them to her.

"Not my place to talk about who," Ez said.

"Right." Bishop would ask Ariel later. She was probably mad enough about Mouser to tell him.

"I stopped by the shelter. Sister Catherine has kids hanging off the walls over there. They're afraid to be out on the street at night. She needs help. You got anybody who could go over and lend a hand?"

"Speed!" Ez yelled. The bike messenger with the red Mohawk used his foot to drop a battered skate board onto its wheels and glided over to the bar.

Ez shook his head. "The next generation is going to be born with wheels instead of feet."

"Yo?" Speed said when he reached the bar. Tonight, he was wearing baggy cargo shorts that seemed to be losing their battle with gravity. An iPod in his back pocket was attached to the shorts by a long loop of chain and the headphone wire was looped around his neck.

"I need you to pick two of your best delinquents and go to the shelter. The Sister is packing them in and she needs some help keeping things from getting out of hand. Tell her Bishop sent you."

"No problemo." Speed pointed at Zoe and another boy who looked like he could take care of himself if somebody picked a fight. They grabbed their boards and followed him out.

"You think they'll be okay on the way over?" Bishop asked.

"Speed's a survivor," Ez told him. "The little one's tough as nails, and the lunk's my sister's kid. He's a wolf. They'll be fine unless lunkhead gets distracted by a shiny object and wanders off."

"Family, huh?"

Ez poured himself a beer. "Luckily they're not all as dumb as him."

"So, Cassius." Bishop finally said to break the silence. "Can you talk about him?"

Ez nodded. "The guy you met last night is Cassius Tiberius Kale. Or, at least, he used to be."

"C.T. Kale?" Bishop was surprised and impressed. "The robotics guy? I thought he disappeared under mysterious circumstances ten years ago."

"He did." Ez spoke to him as if he was slow. "He went underground."

"There was some big scandal. His company went under at the height of the dot com boom."

"Kale-Co specialized in micro-robotics, mostly for medical application."

"Nanobots," Bishop said with the relish of someone who'd grown up on junk science dished out in apocalyptic scenarios on the Sci Fi channel.

Ez nodded. "C.T. was mostly interested in micro automation. He wanted to build tools that could be programmed to locate, diagnose, and treat disease at the very earliest stages. It's about materials as well as size. His company developed a programmable, carbon-based bot the size of a molecule with a gold-plated polymer shell. It was a major breakthrough, but very expensive to produce on a large scale. He needed a partner with deep pockets."

"Zaki Kirienko?"

"The very same. Zaki already had several very successful IT start-ups. He'd studied immunology in Europe and understood bio-mechanics and the value of using nano delivery systems as a medical tool. He was rolling in money and he was very interested. But he didn't want a partner, he wanted it all for himself. Cassius made the mistake of showing him what he had and Zaki took him apart. He launched a hostile takeover, stole his patents and ruined his company."

"How do you steal somebody's patents? I thought once you registered them, they were yours?"

"Cassius didn't give up without a fight. He blocked Zaki's takeover even though it threatened to bankrupt him. Finally, Zaki kidnapped Cassius' wife and son. The price of their release was the patents."

"I never heard anything about Kale's family being kidnapped."

"Cassius never called the police, he just wanted them back. Zaki let him walk away with a couple hundred million in personal assets and some other patents he didn't care about. Cassius moved his family to France. Not too long after his wife was killed in what was ruled a one car accident, even though the police report showed that the back of her car had been hit by another vehicle. Then Kale's son disappeared. C.T. came back here where there were a few people he could trust and went underground."

"How do you know all this?"

"I used to work for him. He was one of my best friends."

"Was that before you . . ." Bishop bared his teeth and held his hands up, curled into mock claws.

"I was pack-born, you ignoramus." Ez growled. "Not bitten. You think werewolves don't need to earn a living just like everybody else? I went to college. I have a PhD in Bio-Electrical Engineering from Penn State."

"Sorry," Bishop said. "It's just . . ." He waved his hand indicating the dumpy café.

"I'm retired," Ez told him, dourly.

"I guess Zaki stole your pension fund too, huh?"

"Quit while you're ahead," Ez said.

- 17 -

Ariel came in through the Caf' kitchen. Her hair was in tangles and her cheeks flushed. She was tugging at her coat, resettling it on her shoulders, getting it to hang straight.

She looked angry but resolved. Like a woman with a plan. He suddenly saw himself from her perspective, cozied up to the bar drinking beer with Ez while some demon was doing God knows what to Mouser. He straightened up and slid off his stool. Ez rested his elbows on the bar and took another swallow of beer. He never seemed to react to Ariel's temper tantrums.

"Been flying?" Bishop asked.

"I went out over the lake," Ariel ran her fingers through her hair to take out some of the knots. "I was pretty high up, nobody saw me. I just needed it."

Ez nodded. Sometimes the beast inside everyone needed to run.

"You ready to go?" she said.

Ez pulled a fat envelope out from under the bar and placed it in her outstretched hand. She tucked it into the inside of her coat and led the way to the street.

Stopping on the sidewalk, she looked in both directions expecting to see Bishop's car.

"What the hell is that?" She asked when Bishop pulled open the passenger door to a battered orange wreck parked at the curb.

"It's a loner," he explained. "My car won't be ready until Monday."

"Oh, my God." Ariel peered inside. "It smells like feet."

The floor on the passenger side was full of soda cans, Styrofoam cups and fast food wrappers. There was a greasy wrench on the seat. Ariel grabbed it and started using it to sweep trash out into the gutter.

"Hey," Bishop said. "That's littering. It's an offense against the environment."

"This car is an offense against the environment. Ugh! Was that a dead mouse?"

"The garage guy told me it's a classic. Just needs some work."

"The Titanic just needs some work; this car needs to be put out of its misery before it gets somebody killed." Ariel threw the greasy wrench on the floor and eased herself carefully into the seat. "No seat belts," she noticed. "Nice. You can't possibly think we're going to drive this car to Zaki's tomorrow night?"

Bishop turned the key in the ignition. The Falcon bucked and banged and eventually settled down into a gasping rattle as he pulled away from the curb.

"I'm glad you asked me that. I have a backup plan."

Ariel listened as Bishop explained the bargain he'd made with Rain.

"This is your old partner, huh? Have you told him anything about what's going on?"

"He knows there are missing kids. From what he told me, I

get the idea there's a big cover up going on, directed by somebody higher up. Rain doesn't know anything about demons, or Raptors, or the rest of it. The man's a sports nut. He took me to the track where Zaki was racing one of his horses. He won a bundle. Now he can't wait to get into the action out at the arena. I figure that'll be just another part of our cover. Who'd suspect someone could bet the way Rain bets on a cop's salary."

"And how can Rain bet the way he bets on a cop's salary?" Ariel asked.

Bishop shrugged. "He has a system. He's good at it. He wins. Always has."

Bishop pulled into an empty parking space in front of the Seventh Circle. If someone wanted to vandalize the Falcon it was unlikely the damage would even be noticed.

"Don't bother to lock it," he said. "You'd have to be nuts to steal this car."

- 18 -

Timmy Jon was waiting for them in a booth along the wall. There was a different band tonight. The music had a heavy, dragging beat to it and the two couples staggering around the dance floor appeared to be in imminent danger of sliding into joint comas. The band members were all dressed in dusty black, with dyed black hair and black fingernail polish. Their greenish makeup made them look like they'd come straight out of the cemetery to their evening gig.

Bishop looked a little closer. He hoped it was makeup.

The waitress appeared at Bishop's elbow to take their order. She seemed almost normal compared to the band. Bishop ordered a bottle of beer, remembering Ariel's warning not to drink anything that didn't come in a sealed container. Timmy Jon ordered a Grasshopper rather than his usual Greyhound.

"The SPCA shut down the company that distributes canine cocktail bits," he said. "The bar's trying to line up a Canadian supplier." His neon green Grasshopper came in a large martini glass garnished with an insect stuck on the handle of a small paper umbrella.

"Did you get what we needed?" Ariel asked.

Timmy Jon hunched forward. "I took a lot of risks for this. If the individual I 'borrowed' these from finds them missing before I get out of town there'll be hell to pay. And I mean that in the most literal sense."

"How does your source happen to have a drawer full of invitations to the arena? I thought these things were next to impossible to get." Bishop asked.

"Depends on who you know. Zaki gives his closest associates a few extra invites so they can pass them out to politicians, celebrities and big bettors. I took these off the bottom of the pile. But I've got to get out of here, tonight."

"We'll keep our half of the bargain," Ariel told him. "Let's see what you've got."

Timmy Jon slid a large envelop across the table. "There's three invitations in there. Special paper, special watermarks and each one has a magnetic strip imbedded in it, so it can be scanned on your way in. You'll also be given a plastic bracelet to wear during the games that can't be removed until you're on your way out.

"If you take it off a signal will be sent to security. Zaki wants to be sure everybody who comes in leaves. He doesn't want anybody wandering around, getting into places they shouldn't."

Ariel pulled out one of the invitations and checked to be sure the other two were identical to the first. She looked at Bishop.

"The bracelet's going to be a bit of a problem."

"Stop waving those around," Timmy Jon hissed. "Gimme a break here, I kept my part of the bargain."

"You did, T' Jon. Fair's fair." Ariel took the thick envelope out of her coat and slid it across the table to the demon.

"What's in here?" Timmy Jon asked. "It's what I asked for, right?"

"It's a round trip ticket to Tahiti and thirty-five hundred dollars in cash."

Timmy Jon covered the envelope with his hand and shut his eyes for a moment.

"Praise be," he said and shoved it into the inside pocket of his jacket. "You leave first, I'll slip out a few minutes later. Can't be too careful these days." He downed the rest of his drink.

Ariel and Bishop made their way to the door. As they went out they failed to see the waitress arrive at Timmy Jon's table and set a drink in front of him. Timmy Jon frowned. "I didn't order this."

The waitress gave him a bright, waitress smile. "Oh, this is from that gentleman over there," She pointed to a little man in a striped suit sitting at a table in a shadowy corner of the bar. "He told me to tell you, you were going to need it."

- 19 -

"Do you trust Timmy Jon?" Bishop asked Ariel after they'd gotten into the car.

"He's a demon," Ariel said. "Demons only tell the truth when it causes more trouble than lying. But I think Timmy Jon really wants to leave town and the invitations are his way out. I picked the destination because I wanted to know where he was going. That way he knows I'll be right on his tail if he gave me counterfeit invitations. Still, I don't know how we're going to get around the bracelets."

Bishop pulled the car over to the curb in front of an all-night convenience store.

"What are you doing?" Ariel asked.

"Ez told me Cassius is some kind of computer genius. We're going to go see him, but I have to pick something up first."

Bishop got back in the car with a paper bag in his hand.

"What's in there?"

"A pint of Jim Beam."

"You need a drink that bad?" Ariel asked.

"Not me," Bishop said. "But I was told to bring a bone for the watch dog, so he'll take us to Cassius."

"We're going back into the Deeps?"

"I don't see any other choice if we want to get into Zaki's and find Mouser."

"I guess it's better than being stuck in an elevator," Ariel said.

Old Bill was happy with the pint if not the hour. He crawled out of his sleeping bag and led them into the cellar of an abandoned building. Its ancient cistern hid the entrance to a tunnel guarded by a young runner who could take them to Cassius.

"I won't be where you found me when you come out," Bill warned them. "Gotta keep moving, confuse the enemy. 'preciate the drink."

"We move around a lot," The runner told them, handing Bishop a second set of night vision goggles. "Different gates on different days. Random pattern. Don't ever try to come in on your own. If the booby traps don't get you, one wrong turn and you can be lost forever down here."

As they moved, the runner swept the laser light on his rifle back and forth across their path.

"Are you expecting trouble?" Ariel asked.

"Rats," the kid said. "They get really big in the Deeps. Keep an ear out behind you."

He turned around and swept the corridor they'd just traveled.

"Did that one time over by the main sewer line and there must a' been fifty of the ugly bastards sneaking up on us. We had to open up on 'em. Still gives me nightmares."

"Booby traps, hopelessly lost, giant rats. Check." Bishop said. "Old Bill it is."

Cassius met them in the computer room. He looked a little rumpled, as if he'd been roused from sleep. But he didn't seem surprised to see them again.

Bishop apologized for coming back so soon after being introduced, but Cassius waved the apology away.

"I was just catching up on my reading," he said. "Living underground is a little disorienting. We keep military time, so we know whether it's day or night topside, but in truth, eventually you make your own time. Sleep when you're tired, eat when you're hungry, work or play in between."

He listened to the problem of the invitations with the same calm attention he seemed to give everything.

"Let's see them," he said.

Ariel handed over the envelope.

Cassius laid all three out on a light table and started by running a black light over them. They fluoresced with a bright purple-white glow.

"This isn't paper," he told them, "It's rag bond." He turned a light on under the glass. "Practically the same stuff they use for currency. There are even flecks of color in it and look at the watermark. It's Zaki's logo with a magnetic strip running through it. Let's see what it has on it." He ran a hand-held scanner over the invitation then hit a few keys on the computer next to it.

"It's just like that strip on the back of a credit card. It carries a small amount of data, easily retrievable by a standard reader. The programming seems pretty standard. It has two code words on it. One probably identifies the person who gave out the invitation, the other is anybody's guess. Do you know where these came from?"

"We only know it was a close associate of Zaki's. He doesn't know we have them."

"Well, I hope that guy isn't attending the same games you are and gets alerted that his 'guests' have arrived."

"So, they're the real thing?" Bishop asked.

"The paper would be pretty hard to fake, so all three invitations seem to be genuine. But, here's another risk. If I were

Zaki, invitation or not, I'd take a finger print or ask you to show a driver's license before I let you in. That way you could be run through a database to make sure you weren't any threat to him and he'd also end up with a list of who's been to the arena and when."

"Another fly in the ointment," Bishop said. "Is there anything you can do about that?"

"Funny you should ask." Cassius waved a young tech over. "Olivia here will snap a couple pictures for the driver's licenses, we'll order up the necessary thumbprints and you'll be good to go in twenty minutes."

"Apparently, we also get a bracelet that goes off if we wander away from the arena." Ariel added. "I was hoping to take a look around while everyone's distracted by the competition."

Cassius nodded. "I would guess the bracelet will be made of flexible plastic with a wire running through it that completes a circuit when it's locked on. If the circuit is broken it sends out a signal. The trick will be getting the bracelet off, while keeping the integrity of the connection."

Cassius pressed a button on a small intercom next to the computer. "Gary, bring me some of that filament tape from electronics. Make it the five-eighths. Minutes later a young man appeared with an envelope and a pair of scissors.

"Two inches should do nicely, thanks." Cassius held up the cut tape. "This is a conductive foil tape with paper backing. Peel each end back and stick them to the bracelet. Leave a big loop so once you cut the bracelet you'll have plenty of slack. The tape maintains the circuit and voila, you're free. When you come back, join the ends of the bracelet as tight as you can, and press the tape down over it. Hopefully they won't inspect them too closely on the way out. I hope you're not planning to try and break your friend out tomorrow night. It would be suicide."

"We just want to get familiar with the layout," Bishop said.

He could see that Ariel was hoping to take it farther than that, but she didn't contradict him.

"You know," Cassius said. "Yamazaki Kiriyenko is kind of a hobby of mine." He spun in his chair and tapped into another keyboard. An aerial view appeared on his flat screen monitor.

"This is a satellite view of Zaki's compound. These buildings between the house and the arena are research labs and offices. As far as I can tell, the train comes in under this building here." He pointed to the top of a large building that backed into the woods and shared the far end of the parking lot with the arena. Pipes, conduit and vents covered the roof. "But it could go as far as the arena."

"Considering all the stuff on the roof, I'm thinking that's the main lab. You can see the earth rises up to cover the first floor on three sides. The train used to stop at a little platform by the house but Zaki changed the route, so it can enter the property without being visible. If he's still experimenting with nano-biotics I imagine the clean rooms are also underground." He hit another key.

"That was a stored image. This is real time." The second view was darker and suffused by the greenish haze that the use of infra-red, night vision filters produced. Bright globes of light spotted the perimeter of the buildings and parking lots.

"This is from a spy satellite. It can get close enough to see people moving around on the ground. The property is patrolled by armed guards with dogs. And occasionally at night, we see something the size of a small chimpanzee with wings flying around. They seem to feed on the deer Zaki keeps on the property."

"Gargoyles," Ariel said. "Like the ones on the roof of the Hauptmann store."

"I'd really like to know what Zaki is up to, since he 'retired'"

Cassius said. "I hope you'll come back and let me know what you find out."

"Will you help us stop it?" Ariel asked.

"I've watched demons and their collaborators insinuate themselves into the power structure of this city for the last ten years. Demons and technology have all the makings of a holocaust for the human race. If you can convince me we can stop it, you have my total support."

"Cool." Ariel said. She was admiring her new thumb print. The polymer resin clung to her finger like a second skin. "This should do the trick. What about your friend, Rain?"

"I think he'll be fine as himself. They'll just think he's a corrupt cop with a gambling addiction. Especially when they see he's with us, a guy who's mobbed up and his bimbo girlfriend. You do have other clothes, don't you?"

"Please," Ariel said. She read off the fake license Cassius had given her. "Candi Banderoni. You can tell what she'd wear just from the name."

"I'm thinking Spandex." Bishop started to round the corner onto the street where he'd parked the orange Falcon.

"Holy shit!" he said, backing up. "There are cops everywhere."

"What?" Ariel tried to get around him to take a look, but he pushed her back. "There are cops all over my car. The trunk's open."

Ariel took a cautious look around the edge of the building. "They're loading a body onto a gurney," she reported. "Looks like somebody small wearing a striped suit. Whoops, they just zipped him up." She thumped Bishop on the arm. "You drove us around with a body in the trunk? What were you thinking!"

"I didn't put a body in the trunk. I never opened the trunk. It was hard enough opening the doors. Why would I put a body in the trunk of my car?"

"To get rid of it? It did look familiar."

"I didn't kill anybody and put them in the trunk of my car!"

"Shh! The police are right there. Let's put some distance between them and us."

When they were several blocks away Ariel said, "You know, you might have killed that knife thrower in the alley last night. I know we couldn't find him, but there was blood and he might have died later. Maybe it's him."

"If he died how did he get into the trunk of a car he didn't even know I was going to be driving?"

"Maybe the car repair guy put the body in the trunk. Or maybe it's part of the curse. Dead midgets in striped suits do seem to be following you around."

"He's not a midget, he's a short gypsy. And how do we know he's going to stay dead? He hasn't before." Bishop winced. "That car has my fingerprints all over it. I need to get back to my apartment and report it stolen---or maybe not. If I was already home how would I know it was stolen? Maybe I should wait until morning? Damn! I was a cop. They'll identify me from my prints in an hour. Then they'll come to my apartment to ask about the car. I really need to get home. And you need to take this."

He handed Ariel the Glock. "If he died from a bullet wound I want this gun as far away from me as possible.

He started to jog toward the subway entrance. "Pick you up at the café at six thirty," he called over his shoulder. "Remember, wear something sexy."

Ariel was left on the street, shaking her head.

- 21 -

Bishop entered his apartment without turning on the lights. It was two o'clock in the morning and he was supposed to be asleep in his bed, oblivious to the fact that his loaner had been used to transport a dead, homicidally inclined, knife throwing, circus freak.

He tore his clothes off, threw on his sweat pants and a t-shirt and rolled around under the covers of his bed, trying to make it look thoroughly slept in. Eventually he drifted off into a fitful sleep.

The doorbell rang at five thirty a.m. Whoever was down at the front door was leaning on the bell. Bishop staggered over to the intercom. "What?" he said.

"Frank Bishop?"

"My name is right next to the bell, pal. Are you drunk or something?"

"Mr. Bishop, this is Detective Suskin from homicide. I'd like to ask you a few questions."

"Who's dead?" Bishop asked, hoping he was sound sufficiently puzzled.

"Sir, if you'd please let us in we can discuss that in person."

"Come up," Bishop said, pushing the buzzer. "But I'm warning you I'll need coffee first."

Detective Suskin and Detective Carter took seats at Bishop's small kitchen table and accepted cups of coffee. Their eyes probed the parts of the apartment they could see.

Bishop poured himself a big cup. He didn't need to fake being tired, all the missed sleep had been adding up, he needed caffeine.

"What's this about?" he asked Suskin. "Who's dead?"

"What kind of car do you own, Mr. Bishop?"

"A Honda Accord. But it's in the shop."

"So, what have you been driving?'

"My mechanic gave me a loaner. It's an orange, '82 Falcon. It's parked at the curb. I can't wait to get rid of it, it's a death trap."

"What time did you get home last night?"

"Eleven, eleven thirty. Why are you asking me this?"

"At twelve twenty-seven 911 got a call from an individual who claimed he saw a man putting a body into the trunk of an orange Falcon. He gave the dispatcher the license number."

"What? You're welcome to take a look at the car. I've only had it for twenty-four hours. I've never even opened the trunk."

"We've already looked at the car, Mr. Bishop. A deceased male was found in the trunk."

"There's a dead body in the trunk of my loaner, parked at the curb in front of my apartment?" Bishop got up and looked out the window. "Oh," he said. "Where's the car?"

"Patrol found it parked on Third Street. The trunk was unlocked. The car is registered to one Tony Torchetti. He owns a car repair shop. We found your fingerprints on the car. They were in our database. You used to be vice."

"Right, the good old days. Now I'm private. The last I saw

the car it was parked in front of this building. Can I ask you again, who's dead?"

"We haven't identified the body yet." Carter pulled out a photograph. It was the knife thrower in the striped suit. He was definitely dead.

"Never seen him before," Bishop said, wishing it was true.

"M.E. says he's been dead about 24 hours."

"Well somebody must have stolen the car to dispose of the body. I didn't kill him, and I don't know who he is. A '82 Falcon must be pretty easy to hotwire."

"That's the strange part, Frank. Can I call you Frank?" Carter asked. Bishop gave him a weary nod, hoping the good cop would hurry up and turn the questions over to the bad cop so they would finish up and leave. "The wires were intact. Whoever drove it must have had a key. Do you still have the keys to the car, Frank?"

Bishop went into the bedroom and fished them out of his trouser pocket, Carter was right on his heels. "Take them," he said. "The car is a hazard. I'll get a rental."

"Do you have a gun?" Carter's eyes took in Bishop's clothes on the chair, the condition of the bed.

"Yes, and a license to carry it."

"Were you carrying it last night?"

"No, it's locked in a box in my closet. Would you like to see it?"

"Wasn't fired or cleaned recently," Suskin said after thoroughly trashing Bishop's closet.

"Unloaded." Carter added.

Bishop yawned. He wasn't faking it.

"Anyone see you last night, Frank?"

"I'm investigating the disappearance of some kids. I went by the runaway shelter and talked to Sister Catherine. Stopped in a couple of other places, asked some questions. Routine stuff. Did you find any of my finger prints on the trunk or anywhere inside it?"

"No." Carter said.

"Well, there you go."

Suskin handed Bishop back his gun. "Don't---"

"Leave town," Bishop finished. "I'm going back to bed, detective. Make sure the street door locks behind you when you leave. It needs to be adjusted or something."

Once the two cops were out the door, Bishop lay down on the bed, but he didn't sleep.

22

Rain pulled the Dowager Queen into the loading zone in front of the Caf'. Bishop could see Rain had some serious doubts

"What is this place?" he asked.

"Kind of a neighborhood hangout. You know, computers, coffee, bad food. Ariel works with some of the kids that come in here. I'll go get her."

Ariel saved him the trouble by appearing at the top of the stairs at almost the exact moment Rain turned off the ignition. She had taken Bishop seriously about dressing up.

The Raptor's black skirt was tight across her hips but the rest of it, what little there was, was cut in such a way that it flirted across her thighs as she walked, exposing long legs that ended in red, four-inch heels. Her low cut, red blouse had the same effect, clingy but draped so it swayed back and forth with the motion of her breasts. A single gold chain adorned her throat and her earrings sparkled against the sleek darkness of her hair.

Rain gave a low whistle as Bishop stumbled from the car to hold the door open for her.

"Gentlemen," she said, sliding into the passenger seat of the old Mercedes.

Bishop noticed he had suddenly come into possession of a small evening purse, three invitations and a red silk shawl, all in an instant of total distraction. He got into the back, making awkward introductions over the leather seats.

"How did you two meet?" Rain asked, pulling away from the curb.

"We got involved in the same case," Ariel told him, cutting off any explanation Bishop might have come up with.

"You're a P.I. too?"

"In a manner of speaking."

"Ariel's a fan of the martial arts," Bishop added. "She, uh, teaches kids self-defense."

"I have a black belt," Ariel said, smiling sweetly over her shoulder at Bishop who changed the subject.

"So," he asked Rain. "Did the Captain survive the night?"

"You didn't hear?" Rain said.

"What? You mean he didn't survive? Sister Catherine will be very upset. She hates having to perform acts of contrition."

Rain grinned. "You wish. He got a visit from the boys downtown. I have the feeling he's not holding up his end of something, at least not to their satisfaction. The weasel's been scurrying around whimpering and wringing his hands ever since. He doesn't know whether he should jump ship and start sucking up to someone else or hang in and hope everything blows over. It's hard being a career rodent, nobody cares if you get your tail caught in a trap."

"Any word on the kids? Sister Cate is swamped with runaways who don't want to be out on the street at night."

"I don't think they can stonewall this much longer. I smell Task Force, made up of the usual spin doctors, toadies, boot lickers and other expendable incompetents. That'll give them time to figure out who to blame and come up with something to explain it all away."

"Who's going to be in charge?"

"My money's on Ted Bourman. He's the Chief's spinmeister. Remember the way he handled that underage hooker thing for the mayor? He'll probably announce that all the missing kids joined the Foreign Legion and are alive and well living in the Moroccan desert."

Bishop shrugged. He'd had contact with Ted Bourman when he was working Vice. The man had lizard eyes and the ability to make almost any lie seem like a plausible explanation.

"Speaking of putting money on something," Ariel said to Rain. "Frank says you have a fool-proof system."

Rain loved being recognized as a player. Bishop watched as he preened a bit at Ariel's compliment. Then he sighed. The next fifteen minutes were going to be a recap of Ray Mann's greatest bets. Thankfully, that would probably take the rest of the trip.

The entrance to Zaki's estate was a hive of activity. A red jacketed valet relieved Rain of the Dowager Queen and a five-dollar bill with the aplomb and prestidigitation of someone whose living is built on tips. Another red coat scanned their invitations with a hand-held device and passed them though the gate.

Bishop took a covert look at the large, grey Gargoyles sitting on the top of the pillars flanking the entrance. They gave no indication of being anything other than stone statues, but he noticed Ariel kept her head down as she went through the gate.

Inside, a crowd barrier had been set up with a single point of entry. A guard fed the invitations into a machine as each guest pressed his thumb to a glass plate. A blue light swept quickly underneath the plate and ten seconds later a translucent plastic strip inched out through a slot and dropped into the guard's waiting hand.

The strip was reminiscent of the self-locking ties that were sometimes used in place of handcuffs. Once on, it would have to be cut off. The guard made sure each bracelet was securely fastened and pointed the trio toward a waiting bus for the five-minute ride to the arena.

On the bus, Ariel examined her bracelet. Several thin strips of wire ran through it. Cassius' intuition had been correct. She hoped she would have the opportunity to slip out of it and take a look around.

Not much was visible from the driveway except trees. Eventually, the road split and the driver took the left fork. It ended at a large parking lot shared by the building Cassius had pointed out in the satellite photos and one other, set further back into the woods by the lakeshore. The Arena.

The arena had been constructed as a wide, stone oval with a glass dome for a roof. The whole effect made Bishop think of a Roman coliseum on steroids, complete with an arched colonnade, topped by super-size niches holding statues of anatomically correct gods and goddesses with a few Gargoyles thrown in for good measure.

Although it wasn't dark, yet everything was brightly lit, including a set of Kliegs that crisscrossed the sky with blue-white beams of light. Buses were disgorging passengers at the entrance.

Everyone seemed to be in a party mood. It was hard to distinguish those who had money and had come just to enjoy themselves, from those who had come to place serious bets.

Bishop thought he recognized a few famous, and even infamous faces, including some politicians, a lobbyist whose name was usually attached to companies with large government contracts, and a couple of movie stars well known for their bad-boy ways. The women were mostly decoration, although Bishop spied a few who had a hard, business-like set to their faces. No one looked incapable of placing a substantial bet.

Inside, the building was even larger than it appeared from the outside. The lobby ringed the top of the game floor with sheer walls of glass; alcoves framed by faux Roman pillars allowed observers to stand or sit and watch the action without entering the stadium. Beyond the glass, tiers of plush theater seats descended at least two stories below ground level. High on the walls, glass-fronted celebrity Skyboxes seemed to hang in space, affording their occupants a bird's eye view of whatever was happening below.

Bishop estimated the arena would probably hold three hundred people, but only about half the seats were filling up.

Tables of food and drink had been set up around the lobby circumference, everything with the compliments of the host. Bishop, Rain and Ariel loaded their plates with exotic goodies, collected drinks and went to find three seats with a good view of the floor. An usher handed them programs and assured Rain that because the combat ring was an oval there were no bad seats.

"Most of this building must be underground," Rain said as they took three seats in a middle tier.

Ariel insisted on the aisle seat, explaining that she had a touch of claustrophobia in crowds.

Bishop set his beer in the convenient cup holder in the arm of his chair and flipped up a small, laminated table top for his plate. Cocktail waitresses were walking the aisles taking drink orders from seated guests. "I could get used to this," he said.

Rain opened his program. "It starts with three kick boxing matches, followed by a Sumo wrestling competition, then something called Kuk Sool Won. And finally, Ultimate Fighting. Not for the faint hearted, it says. All fighters have signed a release of liability for serious injury or death."

"Is that legal?" Ariel asked.

Rain shrugged. "Combat sports are rough. Sometimes players are crippled or even killed. It depends on the circumstances whether it qualifies as a crime or not."

A moment later the lights dimmed, making the ring a bright circle of light in the middle of the arena. A man in a black suit with an embroidered gold vest slid between the ropes to grab a microphone descending on a cable from the ceiling.

"Ladies and gentlemen," He announced, pacing a circle so that he would only have his back to any of Zaki's guests for a few moments at a time. "Welcome to the Yamazaki Kiriyenko Sporting Arena. This is a private facility and you are our honored guests. Please feel free to feast at our banquet tables and drink freely of the beverages we provide. Our hosts and hostesses will be circulating throughout the arena all evening and will be happy to replenish your beverages and comestibles.

"As Ringmaster, it is my duty to warn you that what you see tonight may shock you. What we present here at the Sporting Arena are the ultimate in ultimate sports matches. There are few rules. We do not use a point system or stop our contests because of injury or concession. You need not worry about the opinion of judges; the winners will be obvious to all.

"What I can absolutely promise you is that there will be blood, and there will be pain or worse. If this becomes too much for anyone, please notify one of our ushers and we will gladly provide you with assistance or transportation home.

"The rules for our audience are: One: Although you may become caught up in a moment of enthusiasm, please do not approach the ring for any reason. Two: You may, of course, bet among yourselves but we also provide you with the opportunity to bet against the house. Please place or increase your bets at any time before or during the match. For your convenience, our bookers will pass among you. Simply wave anyone in a red and silver vest down and place your bet. The odds will be on the big screens at each end of the arena. Three: Finally, do not, at any time, attempt to leave the building. Armed security staff accompanied by trained canines patrol this property and we would hate to see anyone injured in a misunderstanding. Smoking is allowed in the lobby, and oxygen will be provided if you feel the need for a breath of fresh air."

There was general laughter at this remark.

"We will start the program with some of our youngest contenders. These youngsters are still in training, but I think you will enjoy their enthusiasm."

Tipping back his head, the ring master let out a final, booming pronouncement.

"Let the games begin!"

A blast of sound and huge screens set at intervals along the walls of the arena sprang to life, showing a panorama of the arena followed by close-ups of the ring. Betting odds scrolled across the top of the screens, designating the contestants as red or blue. Even the youngster's matches could be bet on.

Two adolescent boys appeared from the tunnels at opposite ends of the arena. They were dressed in black pants, a red or blue t-shirt and sported lightly padded boxing gloves that allowed more hand movement than traditional gloves. They stepped into the ring and joined the announcer in the middle. He said a few, inaudible words to them and slipped between the ropes onto the arena floor.

The boys tapped gloves, the bell rang, and the fight began.

It was a kick boxing style Bishop didn't recognize, not that he gave kick boxing much attention. When he and Rain were partners they'd hung out with people who frequented illegal matches where there was always betting and drugs. Initially, the fights had some style to them. The participants were often Asian fighters, trained in a certain style, with a certain set of rules, but this type of fighting quickly deteriorated into free-for-all matches where anyone who thought they could kick and punch were allowed to compete until someone was knocked unconscious.

The first two kids were evenly matched. They'd obviously had training, but not a lot of time in the ring. What they lacked in skill they made up for with enthusiasm, punching and kicking until one caught the other with a roundhouse kick to the jaw, knocking him out. The crowd clapped politely while the downed fighter was carried from the ring.

In the next match, the boys were older, and one was larger than the other by twenty or thirty pounds and three inches in height. Surprisingly, the smaller of the two won. He worked at his opponent like an attack terrier until he managed to get behind him and put him down by springing into the air and delivering a solid punch to the back of his head and a kick to the lower spine as he was pitching forward onto his face.

The crowd cheered as the winner raised his gloved hands in the air in a victory gesture. Even the announcer gave him a quick pat on the shoulder as he left the ring.

Rain hadn't placed a bet yet and neither had most of the spectators. They knew this was just the warm-up. They'd probably never seen the combatants before and didn't want to waste their money on them. The few bills that did change hands were mostly friendly bets between guests.

The third match sparked a lot of enthusiasm. The fighters were female, still in late adolescence and dressed like the boys, although instead of t-shirts they each wore a red or blue colored sports bra with a wide X-strap which allowed for free range of motion in the shoulders. The bras also showed off their lean muscles and the outline of their young breasts to the crowd.

If anything, the girls were more ruthless than the boys, going for the face, knees and kidneys with brutal efficiency. It almost seemed like a grudge match and the more they savaged each other the better the crowd liked it. Soon they were both bleeding and beginning to stagger under repeated blows.

Finally, the blue fighter caught her opponent with a vicious upper cut to the jaw. The red girl's head snapped back and to the side and a spray of blood arched into the air from her open mouth. As she started to crumble to the mat, the blue girl kicked her legs out from under her, then kicked her unconscious body twice in the back, causing her to roll over onto her face.

The crowd went wild, but the blue fighter didn't raise her fists in triumph. Instead, she walked a single, contemptuous circle around the fallen girl, as if she was savoring the beating she had delivered more than the spectator's applause. She quickly slipped between the ropes and was gone.

"Whoa," Rain said. "Wish I'd put my money on her."

Ariel leaned forward, a slight frown on her face. "That wasn't an exhibition match, and what they're being taught isn't a sport."

In the ring the loser was handed through the ropes to what appeared to be paramedics in white scrubs. Her body had an unsettling, boneless quality to it and her head lolled as if it had been loosened from the rest of her spine. But she was quickly taken away and the men in white scrubs seemed unconcerned as they loaded her onto a rolling stretcher.

The announcer climbed back into the ring, grabbing the microphone as it dropped from the ceiling. "That was Lena, winner and one of our five furies. L-E-N-A. I suggest you write it down. This girl will be back!"

The ropes began to sink into the floor. The announcer moved to the edge of the platform. The middle of the circle shifted down and sideways. A tray of white sand surrounded by low bales of straw emerged and stopped three feet above the surface of the ring.

"And now," the announcer intoned, circling the tray, "for the heavy weight part of our program."

The large screens were suddenly filled with the image of two huge Sumo wrestlers in their traditional mawashi, or loin cloth. Each man weighed well over four hundred pounds, all of it on display in overlapping mounds of naked flesh except for the minimal amount covered by the mawashi. One of the wrestlers had the rich, dusky skin of someone of African descent.

"Oh, sweet Jesus!" Rain muttered. "I haven't seen that much wrinkled booty since my Auntie Violet tripped going down the church steps and rolled to the curb with her skirt over her head."

"On the east screen," the announcer continued in a louder voice. "Weighing in at five hundred and twenty-two pounds, is Nioarashi Nozumu of Japan. In his country, Nozumu-san holds the Sumo title of Sanyaku, or champion.

On the west screen, at four hundred and eighty-six pounds, the formidable Akuma Isogoro, a champion in his own right, trained and sponsored by our host, Yamazaki Kiriyenko.

The sport of Sumo wrestling may be unfamiliar to many of you. As you can see by the size of the rikishi, or wrestlers, Sumo is a contest of strength that has been practiced in Japan for over a thousand years. The combat ring or dohyo is made of clay and sand. Matches are won by one rikishi forcing the other out of the ring or causing him to touch the sand by any part of his body except his feet.

"Tonight's series of five bouts will be overseen by a traditional referee or gyogi."

Bishop noticed some excitement in the stands. There seemed to be a contingent of Japanese businessmen who were already enthusiastically motioning for a bookman to come take their bets.

"Something for everyone, I guess," he told Ariel.

"I think this is my cue to go find the ladies room."

"Are you . . ."

"I might walk around a bit. Can I bring you anything back from the bar?"

Bishop frowned. He didn't want Ariel going off on her own without a better feel for what the possibilities might be. "But you'll miss all the excitement."

Ariel looked up at the screens and shuddered. "Don't worry, I won't be gone long. There seem to be other guests who aren't Sumo enthusiasts taking the opportunity to stretch their legs."

"Well, that would include me," Bishop said. "Feel like some company? Rain?"

"You two go on. I have to see what a brother that size can do."

Ariel was right, quite a few of the guests had decided the Sumo contest was the perfect time to take a break, freshen their drinks and graze the splendid array of offerings on the buffet tables.

The Raptor threaded her arm through Bishop's and the two of them started to make a circuit around the lobby, just one more couple enjoying an evening watching human beings beat each other up.

"This place is locked down pretty tight," Bishop murmured, letting his eyes roam over the locked doors, glass walls and high ceilings.

"Mmmm," Ariel leaned her head against his shoulder. "We need to look for a back way out, or at least a way into the lower level where the fighters hang out before bouts. I'm sure there's a connection between the two buildings."

"But even if we got over there and actually found him, how would we get him out?"

Ariel started to say something about air ducts but then, to Bishop's great surprise, she suddenly pivoted into his arms, spun him into an alcove so his back was to the lobby and firmly planted her lips against his. It was entirely unexpected but not at all unpleasant.

He let his arms go around her back. Her lips were firm and warm and seemed to fit naturally against his. She smelled like ginger, sandalwood and lime, something he'd never noticed before – maybe it was a scent she'd put on because she was dressing up, but he liked it. In fact, he liked the whole experience, but he could tell from the slight tension in her body that she had embraced him for a reason that had nothing to do with wanting to kiss him.

"What?" he murmured against her lips, reluctant to break contact, his exhalation mingling softly with hers.

"Look over my shoulder into the window."

Bishop shifted his head slightly to the side. It took his brain a second or two to pull back from looking through the window to looking at what was reflected in the window. Behind him, a small man in a yellow and black stripped suit and bowler hat was coming down the stairs from the celebrity box level. He had a thick, eight and a half by eleven size envelope under his arm. He wasn't exactly rushing, but there was a brisk, determined purpose to his movement. He flashed a card at one of the security guards at the door and the man opened it just enough for him to slip through.

"Ow," Ariel said, slightly breathless, and Bishop realized he'd gone from enjoying an unexpected kiss to gripping his partner against him in some sort of death lock.

"Sorry," he let her go and turned to watch the little man hurry out of sight into the parking lot.

"Him again!" Bishop said. "What is he, some kind of cat with nine lives? You blew him out a ten-story window, the police found his body locked in the trunk of my loaner car, and now he shows up at Zaki's arena like nothing ever happened."

Ariel straightened her blouse which had become somewhat disarranged by Bishop's vigorous clinch. "Maybe there's more than one of them."

"Like clones? Kill one and another pops up to stalk me and leave death threats on my car? There has to be a way to make it stop."

"That's what we're here to figure out," Ariel said in a low voice. "Zaki's either a demon himself or he's helping them develop some kind of regeneration technology. They're testing it on kids and probably some demon volunteers. The only way we can figure out how to stop it is to get into that big building where the train stops. But right now, Mouser is my priority. If I can figure out how to get to him tonight I'm going to do it."

"What if breaking Mouser out blows the whole thing? What if we can never get to Zaki again? They could move the entire operation beyond our reach. We'd lose the element of surprise just like Cassius said."

"Mouser is family!"

"The other kids have families too, Ariel. People who care about them. We don't know enough yet. Think about it!"

"I did not!" Ariel said loudly.

Bishop looked up. The security guard was paying them more than passing attention.

"I was only being friendly. It didn't mean anything, baby, you know that."

Something in Bishop's brain ticked over. He raised his own voice

"I saw the way you were looking at him, and I don't like it!"

"I'm going to the ladies room." Ariel announced. "Get yourself a drink with ice in it--you need to cool off!"

She flounced away from Bishop, down the hall, butt swaying, her skirt doing a furious fandango around her thighs. After a mutual moment of appreciation, Bishop made eye contact with the security guard. He shrugged.

"Women!" The guard said, one guy to another.

"Yeah," Bishop agreed. "They sure are sexy when they're angry."

He strolled off toward one of the bars and ordered a large scotch on the rocks. The security guard seemed satisfied that all he'd seen was a couple having a jealous tiff.

But that wasn't the reason Bishop was asking for extra ice in his drink.

Ariel ducked into a nearby ladies room just in case anyone was still watching. She had started to tell Bishop about her plan to explore the heat ducts in the building when the little man showed up and distracted her. As much time actors on television seemed to spend crawling around in heating ducts, she was surprised how often real-life security firms ignored these systems.

The grill over the duct in the ladies room was high on the wall and looked like it would be a tight fit. Ariel could imagine herself right in the middle of trying to wiggle into the opening only to have a gaggle of women open the door to be greeted by the sight of her butt and legs dangling from the wall. She needed a more private place, and she needed to leave her bracelet with Bishop, so no one would be able to track where she was going.

Locking herself in a stall, Ariel removed a thin blade from the spine of her small purse and started to work on taping and cutting the bracelet. She hoped it didn't have a heat signature as well as a contact alarm.

She applied Cassius' strip of copper tape with just enough slack in the middle, so she could cut the bracelet, slip her wrist out, but not break the contact. She dropped it into her purse, flushed the toilet for effect then fluffed her hair and applied fresh lipstick at the mirror over the sink. It wouldn't do to ignore the appearance of her fake personality even though she had something much less glamorous in mind.

Ariel made one full circuit of the lobby before she joined Bishop and Rain back in the arena. She intended to leave her purse and bracelet with Bishop while she crawled around in the heating system. She'd worn a lot of bright, clunky bracelets on that wrist to disguise what was now missing from her arm. They, like the clothes she wore tonight, had been bought in thrift stores and garage sales where she almost stopped thinking about being a Raptor and let herself pretend she was a real live girl.

When Ariel settled back into her seat the Sumo wrestlers were still at it. Bishop's look of pained bemusement told her he couldn't wait until this part of the entertainment was over. Rain was counting a small sheaf of bills. He stuck them in an inside pocket and leaned over Bishop to tell her what she'd missed.

"It's like watching two elephants run into each other," he said. "I don't know anything about this Sumo stuff, but I bet on the brother, and the brother was good to Rain."

"This is the last match," Bishop said. "Akuma's already the winner on points. You missed all the slapping and grunting that happened in the last round. Nioarashi is pissed and he has nothing to lose, so this bout is pure grudge."

Ariel could see a lot of agitation in the Japanese seats. A few countrymen seemed to be getting a lot of flak from their fellow gamblers. She guessed it wasn't considered okay to bet against a Japanese wrestler, especially if you won.

Each wrestler performed the usual ritual, throwing salt into the ring, spitting water insultingly close to each other's feet. They squatted simultaneously, lifting one massive knee after the other to pound a foot down onto the sand.

All at once, both wrestlers lunged forward. The sound of their naked flesh coming together was like a giant, reverberating slap accompanied by an explosion of sweat in all directions. Spectators in the front rows actually threw up their arms or ducked to avoid the splatter.

"Holy shit!" Bishop said.

"Now it's just brute strength," Rain explained. "One of them has to push the other out of the ring or make him touch some other part of his body to the sand."

The struggle went on. Mountainous flesh quivered with effort, naked buttocks clenched, toes gripped at the sand for purchase, sweat rolled, threatening each man's grip on the other.

Suddenly, Akuma's grip shifted. With lightning speed for such a large man, his hands plunged to Nioarashi's hips to grip his mawashi. In an amazing feat of strength, he used the wrestler's own momentum to spin him off his feet and toss him out of the ring, over the bales of hay and onto the floor three feet below the platform.

In the moment of stunned silence that followed, the sound of Nioarashi's body hitting the ground was almost indescribable. Ariel imagined she felt the ground under her feet heave with the impact. Nioarashi lay completely still. Akuma, the winner, stood alone on the sand inside the ring, accepting the whistles and cheers from the audience with a small, quickly suppressed smile of triumph on his lips.

Bishop's jaw dropped, Rain was trying for sang froid, but only managed to look dazed, until he realized he'd won his bet.

"That's what I call game!" he yelled to no one in particular.

"That's impossible!" Ariel said.

"What? Is that some kind of foul?" Rain asked. "You mean the brother didn't win?"

"No, he won. It's just impossible that someone, even someone equally matched, could toss that kind of weight fifteen feet."

Paramedics were swarming over Nioarashi. It was like watching pygmies trying to resuscitate a giant. The announcer climbed into the ring with Akuma. He was speaking into the microphone, but his words were lost in the general swell of noise caused by the audience. A screech of feedback shut everyone up long enough for the announcer to call a ten-minute break while they set up for the next competition.

Ariel glanced over her shoulder as she, Rain and Bishop headed up the steps toward the lobby. The paramedics had called for a fork lift to help them move the unconscious wrestler.

If that doesn't work, she thought. You're going to have to use a chain and a tractor.

She'd seen that once on the Discovery Channel when a Circus vet had to pull an unconscious elephant out of his stall, so he could be examined and treated. It was a disturbing picture and a further humiliation for the champion of an ancient martial art who had come to compete in America with no idea of what he was up against.

Even Rain seemed more subdued in the lobby. "Man," he said. "I've never seen anything like that. If you'd told me about it, I'd say you were lying. Those dudes were as big as my mother's entire side of the family. What do you think they get paid for that?"

"Probably not as much as those fake wrestlers on American TV get paid for acting like idiots," Ariel said. "Sumos are well respected in Japan because what they do is real not faked. Except for tonight."

"You think that was faked? I heard somebody say that guy must have been attached to wires to be thrown like that."

"It wasn't wires." Ariel said. "They're taking him out of the arena on a fork lift. Aren't you glad you bet on the right guy?"

"I guess I should go cash in," Rain said. "Tell you the truth, this win doesn't taste quite as sweet as I expected."

Bishop and Ariel watched him go. Ariel handed Bishop her purse. "Take this. It has the bracelet in it." She rattled her bangles. "No one will notice I'm missing."

"Where are you going?" Bishop asked.

"I want to see if I can find a way over to the other building. I'm sure the fighters come from that direction. There's probably a tunnel, but I'm going to see how far I can get through the ventilation system. If I'm not back by the time this is over leave without me. We'll hook up later."

Bishop took her arm. "I don't want you to do this alone. These people are seriously dangerous. If they get their hands on you, who's going to get you out?"

"Tell Ez to get Tomas. Tomas will know what to do." She shook Bishop's hand off and started to walk away.

"Who's Tomas?" Bishop said, mostly to himself.

He looked down at the red purse in his hand. As usual, a woman had left him holding the bag.

Ariel made her way through the crowd in the lobby. She milled around with the rest of the guests for a bit, then a bell sounded signaling the next match, and people began to move back into the arena.

On her previous circuit of the lobby Ariel had identified a restroom located out of the traffic pattern. It wasn't near one of the more popular entrances to the seats. It had no food table or bar nearby. It was even down a small hallway, next to a janitor's closet.

As soon as she was alone she slipped inside and locked the door. It was clear why this one-room, facility existed. It had been built to satisfy disability requirements and offer access to those confined to a wheel chair. Since the only disabled individuals Ariel had seen since she arrived were beaten and unconscious contestants, she assumed she would be undisturbed.

The air vent over the sink was set in a drop ceiling made of large acoustic tiles suspended on a metal frame. Ariel balanced herself with one foot on a safety bar, the other on the edge of the sink and pulled at the screen over the duct. It swung down, revealing a space much too small to crawl through.

She managed to slide the tiles next to the duct aside and pull herself up into the crawl space above. There was plenty of room up there, but it was precarious. Dividing walls poked their tops above a vast sea of fragile tiles, metal ducts ran in every direction only to end at the support wall for the giant dome. If she wanted to get to the other building she'd have to find a way around the dome.

Ariel nudged the tiles back into place, took off her high heels, and set them on the nearest duct so she could find her way back. Barefoot was better. Her Raptor toes were meant to grip, something human feet couldn't do.

She moved from wall to wall, aiming for a place at the far end of the dome where the ducts, pipes and cables all came together to disappear downward to somewhere below.

The shaft of the duct was bigger here and it had a maintenance grill. She hooked her fingers into the metal squares and pulled until it popped loose. She could make out a bit of light below, but it was coming from a long way down -- two or three stories at least. If she was careful she might be able to fit into the space next to the pipes and use the strength in her hands and feet to lower herself down the shaft.

Ariel rolled the waistband of her short skirt over several times so that it wouldn't catch on things as she went down. Maybe a lacey red thong hadn't been the best choice for crawling through heating ducts.

After a couple of tight squeezes, the shaft widened, and the bottom became visible. The light came from a grill. It was high on the wall of a wide corridor. Under it, the duct turned again, becoming an empty, horizontal tunnel. As Ariel lowered herself to the metal floor to peer through the grill, she heard the sound of footsteps, then voices, coming along the corridor.

"Remember," a voice was saying. "He likes to use the chuks, but he also likes to show off his flashy moves to the crowd. Go for his knees and ribs. Joints and bones are more fragile and take longer to heal than cuts and bruises. He got clipped a good one in the eye today, it may not be back to 100%. It was the left. Yeah, left is good 'cuz you're right handed. See if you can hit him on that side of the head. Stay away from his feet unless you're sure you have a good opening."

"Shut up." Another voice said. "I know what I'm doing. If you were any good in the ring you'd be out there yourself, not carrying my towel and yapping at me like one of those little rat dogs."

The two speakers drew parallel to the grill. One was a boy of eighteen or nineteen. Naked from the waist up, he was lean and muscular with a hard face currently set in a scowl. His companion was younger, smaller, trying to keep up with the older boy's longer stride. His movements were jerky, and one side of his face had a nervous tic that pulled his cheek toward one eye in a series of rapid spasms.

Ariel wondered if he'd been hit in the head one too many times. And if they'd done that to this kid, what were they doing to Mouser? She dropped to her knees and started to crawl along the horizontal duct.

A nearby grill offered her a view into what looked like a small dressing or treatment room. A glass-fronted cabinet held bottles of alcohol, liniment, packets of gauze, splints, liquid medicines in clear vials and individually wrapped syringes. A rolling stand held the debris of someone's recent injuries, bloody gauze, scissors, a suture kit.

A teenage boy lay much too still on the treatment table, half covered by a sheet, his face was swollen and distorted. He seemed to be unconscious, maybe dead although no one had bothered to pull the cover over his face.

Ariel's hands explored the grill. It was fastened from her side with wing-nuts tightened down on the ends of heavy screws. Ariel loosened them, swinging the grill up on its hinges, easing herself into the room without a sound.

She knew she was taking a big chance, but she needed more information. If the boy was dead at least she would know what happened to homeless kids Zaki kidnapped off the streets.

The boy's head moved. His eyes were swollen shut from the pounding he'd taken. Blood trickled from his broken nose. His lips were mangled and split, but he managed to open his mouth.

"Who's there?" The words came out as a croak.

Ariel quickly pulled her skirt down to a more modest length and moved over to the side of the table. She grabbed a water bottle from the stand and held the bent straw carefully to the boy's lips. "I came to check on you," she said. "Try some water."

The boy's lips couldn't manage the straw, so she squeezed the bottle letting a small amount of water slide into his mouth. He swallowed and coughed, then groaned and moved one hand to his ribcage. "Go away," he said.

"Can I do anything for you?"

The boy let out a strangled laugh, then clutched his side again. His eyes were bloody slits. Ariel knew he couldn't see her.

"Yeah, Nurse Nancy," the boy said. "You can get my pink and fuzzy tail the fuck out of here. I'm tired of getting beat to shit, healed up, and beat to shit again. If you can't let me go, just put me down, okay? A common lab rat gets better treatment than this."

"Believe me, I'd like to get you out," Ariel told him. "Maybe if you gave me more information. I'm looking for somebody."

"In here? You're crazy, babe. This place is the Hotel California. They check you in, but you can never leave. That means you, too."

"His name is Mouser. About fifteen, brown hair. Do you know him?"

The boy started to shake his head, but quickly though better of it. "How long?" he asked.

"A few days."

"He's probably still up in the cages." The boy's sudden cough turned into a groan

Ariel tried to give him more water, but he waved her away. "I'll be fine in a few hours. Maybe a day the way my ribs feel. You better get out of here, they like to check in and see how fast we heal. It's got something to do with the shit they shoot us up with."

"Where are the cages?" Ariel asked.

"Y'all can't get there from here, it's like super security. Glass walls, lights always on. Cameras. It's better when the training starts, but you still can't get out."

"What about the heating ducts? They seem to run--"

The boy's hand shot out and grabbed blindly, connecting with Ariel's arm. She pulled away from his grip.

"Don't use the ducts!" The boy said. "A few of us tried. They got some kind of death ray set up in 'em. It really fucks up your shit! They showed us the bodies."

"It's been okay so far," Ariel told him.

"The farther you go, the riskier it gets. You're lucky you got this far. It's probably cuz you're still in the arena."

A door shut somewhere along the corridor outside.

"Go!" The boy said. "They're checking on us."

Ariel's eyes went to the rolling stand. She grabbed a latex exam glove, stuffed a handful of the boy's bloody gauze into it and tucked it into the waistband of her skirt to free up her hands. Kicking a chair under the grate she pulled herself up into it.

"Watch for the dead rats," the boy called after her.

She closed the grate behind her and spun a couple of nuts onto the bolts to hold it in place in case anyone tried it.

"I'll come back for you," she told the boy, but she thought she might have said it too softly for him to hear.

Dead rats? live rats, Gargoyles, things that slither and bite maybe. But what's the problem with a dead rat?

Around the next turn she found out. Three dead rats lay in the entrance to a connecting duct, twisted forever into a rictus of rodent agony. Their bodies appeared to have exploded outward, scattering their organs and entrails onto the walls of the duct.

The floor around each one was stained with the dried fluid that had exited their bellies and orifices in a boiling torrent. The traps the boy had warned her about started here, and since she couldn't see what triggered them, there was nothing she could do to safely get past them.

Ariel cursed silently. She'd have to find another way to get to Mouser. In the meantime, she had to get back to the arena and Bishop.

Getting back up the duct proved to be a lot harder than going down.

23

Ariel took the drink she'd been offered.

She'd come back in through the ladies' room ceiling, washed the dirt off her hands and knees, splashed some water on her face, stepped back into her sexy red heels and tried her best not to look as upset as she was feeling as she made her way through a mostly deserted lobby to the entrance to her seat.

She must not have been entirely successful. As she passed one of the waitresses who ferried drinks back and forth to patrons watching the matches, the woman asked,

"You okay Hon?"

Ariel nodded, hoping to just keep going, but the woman balanced her tray on one hand and patted her on the arm.

"You're not the only one finds that stuff in there hard to watch. I've seen people come tearing up that ramp and barely make it to the rest room in time."

She rotated her tray a half turn. "I got a double Jack on the rocks here. I was about to take it inside, but you look like you need it more than the guy who ordered it. I'll get him another."

"Thank you."

"No problem. You take care now, Miss." The woman bustled off.

Ariel downed the drink in one gulp and started down the steps into the arena.

"You all right?" Bishop whispered as she took her seat. Rain's chair was empty.

"I wish people would stop asking me that!" Ariel snapped, taking her frustration out on Bishop.

Bishop held his hands up in a gesture of surrender. "Sorry. You were just gone for a while. I wondered."

"I can take care of myself, you know."

"No argument there." Bishop gave her back her purse.

Ariel stuck the rolled-up glove into it and slid the bracelet back onto her wrist.

"When does this end?" She asked, eyeing the giant metal cage that now occupied the center of the arena. Two men in overalls were inside raking the sand so there would be a smooth surface for the next match.

"Just as soon as the first three Thunderdome winners finish beating each other senseless in a final, free-for-all grudge match. That apparently determines who gets the title of meanest, most ruthless mutant on earth. I hope you brought your barf bag."

"A waitress in the lobby made me drink a double Jack Daniels before she'd let me come back to my seat."

"Good choice." Bishop said. "What do you think they do with all the dead bodies?"

"Apparently they just let them lie around until they heal."

"Not possible." Bishop told her. "There weren't any decapitations, but I was in the Army, and I was a cop. I know dead when I see it."

Ariel shook her head. She kept her voice low, so no one would overhear what she had to say.

"I got as far as the place they keep the fighters before matches."

Bishop's eyebrows went up.

"I talked to a kid from one of the early fights. He looked pretty bad, but he said he'd heal because they gave him something that makes that happen."

Ariel rubbed her forehead. The frustration was giving her a headache. "He didn't know Mouser, but he thought he knew where they were keeping him. I tried, but I couldn't get any further because there are traps in the duct system set to fry anything with a pulse."

"Jesus. What can do that?"

"Lasers, microwaves, a death ray from outer space. I don't know. The point is that Zaki does have some drug that causes rapid healing. He kidnaps street kids and teaches them to fight each other, lets them get the shit beat out of them, then sees how fast they recover. It must work on near fatal injuries as well, at least for demons. It also makes people a whole lot stronger than normal. The question is why?" Ariel shrugged. "The kid didn't know so I grabbed a sample of . . ."

Rain slid into his seat. He was humming.

Ariel gave him a look.

"What?" He said.

"People are getting beaten into an ugly stain," Ariel said to him. "And all you care about is winning money." She crossed her arms under her breasts and slunk down in her seat, disgusted.

Rain looked over her head at Bishop as if to say: This is what happens when you bring women to watch combat sports.

Bishop shrugged. When Ariel got mad, it was better to keep your thoughts to yourself.

- 24 -

Mouser sat with his back to the wall of his cell. He'd been totally stupid going out alone, hoping to impress El by showing her he could handle himself. That's what had landed him here in this stupid cell.

Fighting back had also gotten him nowhere. They just drugged him up, which meant he woke with a headache and tape on his arm with needle sticks underneath. He didn't know if that meant they were taking something out or putting something in. He only knew when he woke up his skin itched---on the inside.

The kid in the cell across from him had been here longer than he had. When nobody was in the corridor, they talked through the holes in the glass walls, compared notes, told each other which one of their tormentors was highest on their list for revenge. Mouser said he knew people were going to come after him, get him out.

"Give it up, Man," the kid said. He was a little older and had been on the street longer, past the age where somebody was going to stand up for him like El had with Mouser. "The more you fight 'em, the worse you end up."

"So, you're telling me to cave? Do what they want?"

"No man, I'm tellin' you to do whatever you need to do to survive. Let 'em think they got you. Wait for your moment, then run like hell."

The next time Mouser woke up, the kid across the hall was gone and nobody had replaced him. He missed him. His jailers refused to talk to him. Except for shoving meals through the slot in the wall, they left him totally alone.

He tried to eat less because he was afraid of drugs in the food, but then he stopped caring. He found himself waking up, still tired, with no idea how long he'd slept. He began to wish for an end to the unrelenting presence of light.

When he wasn't sleeping Mouser found himself pacing the small steel and plexiglass rectangle that defined the parameters of his world. He wondered if El was looking for him. But why should she? She was a demon killer and he was just a stupid kid. Even Ez barely gave him the time of day.

Maybe both sides had abandoned him. Not worth the trouble. He pressed his forehead against the thick Plexiglas. He missed the kid across the corridor. He missed having someone to talk to. He missed coffee, he missed pizza, he missed his computer.

His mind desperately needed something to do. He found himself surfing the net in his head as he paced, fingers twitching, racing through the rhythm of the keyboard on the seams of his pants. He revisited all the conspiracy theories he believed in. What was the key to all manipulation? It was that the bad guys always messed with your head. And these bad guys were currently messing with his.

His missing cell mate had been right: Survival was everything. You have to grab on to that. Give yourself a goal.

Mouser resolved to mess with them back. When he got tired of pacing, he lay on his bunk and dreamed of flying.

When they came for him again, he went willingly. He could tell they assumed he eventually would.

- 25 -

The final match of the day had been designed for maximum intensity. Instead of fighting in pairs, all three combatants were going to fight at the same time. Two of the three were in their late teens and seasoned fighters, matched in skills, strength and ruthlessness. They carried the scars of their battles like badges. The third, a woman, was younger and less scarred but proved to be very, very good in her previous matches that evening.

The fighters circled each other. Kicks and punches were thrown. Each one tried not to leave their back exposed to the second opponent while they were fighting with the first.

Weapons were thrown through the bars at random intervals, poles, chains, brass knuckles—nothing sharp and pointy seemed to be allowed. The attackers switched off by some sort of silent assent: two against one, then that one partners against the rotating third person. As soon as someone's energy flagged he was turned on no matter what the previous alliance had been. Finally, only two were left standing.

A halt was called while the third fighter's unconscious, or

possibly dead, body was dragged from the ring. This pause started another furious round of betting.

Ariel had been watching everything very closely. This was no carefully crafted act, no smoke and mirrors. It was savagery and pain. Like the fighters, she was glad for a few moments to catch her breath. She looked sideways at Rain.

"Not betting?"

He shook his head.

"Why not?"

"Bad odds," he said.

"Now that they're down to two, the odds look pretty good."

"I mean my odds," Rain said. He motioned to a passing waitress for another sparkling water. "The trouble with being on a winning streak is you start to feel invincible. Like no matter what you do the gods are with you. You know your luck won't turn and that's just not true. The odds always turn. Nobody beats that sacred rule of mathematics forever. I've won enough tonight. I can just relax now and enjoy the fight because I know I'll be leaving with all my winnings in my pocket. Others won't."

"So, you don't think you know who'll win this match?"

"Sure I do. I'm just not going to bet on her."

A bell rang, and the match started up again.

The male fighter chose a long pole from the weapons lying on the sand. He'd used it in the previous match but this time, with only one opponent, he obviously thought he had time to give the crowd a thrill. He began to twirl the pole around his body, circling his waist, flipping it over one shoulder and under the opposite arm, letting it spin like a pin wheel through his fingers; letting everyone in the audience admire his skill.

The second fighter watched him, head tilted, face filled with boredom and contempt, a chain hung from one hand. Suddenly it whipped out, and the pole fighter found his wrists tightly wrapped in steel links. One tug and the two were face to face, the pole angled between them.

Before the man could react, the woman grabbed one end of the pole in both hands. Her foot came down and broke it in half leaving a ragged point at one end. She twisted the point around and thrust it deep into her opponent's belly. His legs went out from under him as she drove him onto his back, her weight pushing the sharp stick through his flesh until his body was pinned to the sand like a dead bug.

Medics ran for the cage. The woman pushed her way through them and out the cage door.

The ring master grabbed her hand and held it over her head. "No worries, ladies and gentlemen," he announced. "He'll be fine. But here's our winner, the fabulous Lena, Mistress of the Cage!"

The crowd went wild.

"Thought so," Rain said as they filed up the steps to leave.

"You thought she'd win and you didn't bet on her?" Ariel said, looking confused.

"You ever see a kid pull the wings off flies?"

"No."

Rain went on as if she hadn't answered. "Nobody likes the fly, but it's such a cruel thing to do, it just doesn't seem fair."

Rain offered to drop Ariel off at her apartment, where ever that might be, but she insisted on going back to The Caf'. When they stopped in front, Bishop told Rain he'd be right back knowing, hoping anyway, that Rain wouldn't want to leave the Queen all alone on the street in a neighborhood like this.

"Two minutes," he said.

When they got inside he asked Ariel, "How are you planning on getting home?"

"What are you, my mother? I can. . ."

". . . take care of myself. I know. Just don't tell me you're planning on flying home in that outfit. I don't think my imagination could take it. And you're not taking the subway dressed like that either."

Bishop shoved a twenty-dollar bill into her hand. "Take a cab," he said gruffly.

"Make sure she does." He pointed at Ez. "I'm making that your responsibility." He left before El could give him an argument.

"Nice girl," Rain said as Bishop got back into the Dowager.

"Thanks, Dad. Does that mean I can borrow the car next Saturday night?"

Rain snorted. "Fat chance. "My Queen don't drive for nobody but me."

- 26 -

The cab dropped Ariel at her apartment building. She was greeted with a low whistle as she sashayed up the walk. It wasn't her fault she thought, embarrassed, it was the way her fancy shoes made her hips swing.

Juke was sitting on the top step of the porch having a smoke. His tattered denim jacket hung open and his elbows rested on his knees. He took one last drag and flicked the cigarette toward the curb.

"Hot date?"

"Just work," Ariel said, sitting down on a lower step. She pulled her shawl closer around her. The nights were getting cooler. The moon was starting to fill the sky with harvest light. Autumn was almost here.

"You seem to spend a lot of time out here after dark."

Juke shrugged. "I'm in the shop all day. Lots of engine noise, customers wanting to shoot the shit about their bikes. I like having some quiet time."

"Night's the best part of the day," Ariel said.

A sudden alteration to the way the light was hitting the walk made them both look up. Three winged shadows crossed the moon and dove straight out of the sky toward the building.

Juke and Ariel jumped to their feet. The biker pulled an old, wide bore revolver out from under his jacket and pointed it at the lead shadow. He pulled the trigger unleashing a series of huge bangs and two Gargoyle bodies exploded less than ten feet from the ground. The third one lost a piece of wing but kept coming. Its injury forced a crash landing but didn't slow the beast down. It scrabbled forward, straight for Ariel.

Ariel threw off her shawl. She had no weapon, except . . . She snatched the shoe off her left foot and smashed the four-inch spike heel straight down into the top of the Gargoyle's head.

The animal's eyes rolled up in their sockets. It let out a soft, Eeeping whistle like the sound of air escaping from a punctured tire, fell over onto its side, twitched once, and died.

"Nice work," Juke told her. "I'd love to see what you could do with an actual weapon." He looked around to make sure nothing else was coming at them before inserting his gun between the waistband of his jeans and the small of his back.

Ariel reached over and pulled her shoe out of the Gargoyle's head. All the red leather surrounding the spike heel had been eaten away by the creature's acid brain matter and the back of the shoe was starting to blister.

"Damn it!" she said. "I really liked these shoes."

"We better get these little mothers off the lawn before somebody calls the cops." Juke said.

He went into repair shop and came back with a pair of heavy leather gloves and a shovel. Inside Ham was rolling an empty oil drum up to the open garage door.

"Any idea how these guys knew where to find you?" Juke asked, grabbing one of the Gargoyles by the wing and dragging it over to the drum.

Ariel limped over to the porch steps on one shoe and dug

around in her purse. She pulled out the two halves of the tracking bracelet. "I thought this had stopped working when I cut the connection. I was going to show it to a friend of mine."

"Ham?"

Ham took the bracelet and motioned Ariel inside the garage. He switched on a bright tensor on one of the workbenches and held the bracelet up to the light. In addition to wires there was a small chip embedded in the plastic tongue where the bracelet locked on.

Ham lifted a small sledge off its hook on the wall and smashed it down on the chip. He threw the rest of the bracelet into the drum with the three dead Gargoyles.

"Their acid'll take care of the rest." He looked at her one bare foot and motioned her to sit on an old wooden stool by the bench.

"Thanks," Ariel said, a little dazed by the matter-of-fact way Juke and Ham were dealing with the Gargoyle attack.

She heard the sound of a truck starting up.

"Dingo's bringing the pick-up around," Ham announced. "Better move these guys as far away as possible."

"Can he drop me off downtown?" Ariel asked. "I've got to get something to a friend before it goes bad."

"I don't think it's a good idea for you to go out again tonight." Juke told her. "Somebody sent those 'goyles after you. Maybe something else is still out there."

"I have to go. It's complicated. I have to find a guy, who can take me to a guy who can get what I have to somebody else. And I have to buy a pint of Beam on the way."

"You lookin' for Old Bill?" Juke asked.

Ariel frowned.

"It's okay," Juke told her. "Bill and I go way back. I'll take him the things."

Ariel gave the idea some thought. She knew these guys looked out for her. She'd thought it was just because she was young and living alone in a bad neighborhood. But Juke had taken out two Gargoyles without batting an eye and he and his guys were prepared to dispose of them as if they did something like it every day. Maybe that thought shouldn't bear too much scrutiny.

She pulled the glove she'd stuffed with bloody bandages out of her purse. "I should probably put this in another bag."

Juke took the glove without comment, dropped it into a zip lock bag from a roll he had on the work bench and stuck it in the pocket of his jacket.

"It needs to get to the third guy," Ariel said.

"No problem."

Ham and Dingo, the third and youngest Dog, picked up the drum to heave it into the back of the pickup. Juke moved Dingo aside and took his end

"See she gets upstairs okay," he told Dingo. "Lock up first." He jumped into the cab with Ham.

"I don't . . . "Ariel started.

Dingo swung the garage door shut and threw the bolt. "You want to get me in trouble?" He asked.

"Nope."

Ariel pulled off her remaining shoe and looked at it. It was red, it was sexy-hot, and its mate had given its life to save hers. It was time to say good bye. She threw both shoes into the trash barrel and followed Dingo up the steps to her apartment.

Pounding.

At first Bishop thought the noise was in his head. Then someone started ringing the doorbell. He opened one eye and looked at the clock. Six-thirty in the morning. Visitors. Ah, joy!

He rolled out of bed and dragged an old sweatshirt that was lying on the floor over his t-shirt and pajama bottoms. He wasn't psychic, but people pounding on his door at the crack of dawn were always a bad thing. Last time it had been homicide about the body in the trunk of his loaner. Maybe he was about to be under arrest.

As he passed through the kitchen he pushed the start button on his coffee maker. He'd set it up, ready to go the night before. Must have been a premonition. Maybe he was psychic after all.

Bishop pushed the intercom button. "What?" He said.

"Frank Bishop?" A male voice asked.

"If I said no would you go away?"

"Police, sir, we need you to open the door."

Bishop pushed the door button. "I hope you brought donuts."

Official looking men in suits followed by uniforms swarmed into the apartment.

"Missing Minors Task Force," one of the suits said, flashing paper. "We have a warrant to search the premises"

Bishop poured himself a cup of coffee, opened the frig and added milk. "Now what?"

"We understand that you have been illegally investigating alleged abductions of minors that have not been reported to the police. This warrant allows us to search your premises and seize your files and computer records."

Bishop threw out his free hand and yawned. "Seize away," he said. "But you're a little late. Most of my files were at my office and that's already been hit by thief or thieves unknown. They also took my computer. I filed a police report."

"Why do you think they did that, sir?" The suit asked, opening note book.

"Coffee?" Bishop asked.

"No sir, I'm on duty."

"Jesus," Bishop muttered. "Do you belong to one of those religions that think caffeine gives you a boner?"

"Sir?"

"Never mind." Bishop topped off his cup. "I'm going to be right over here sitting in my comfy chair, drinking coffee until I achieve consciousness. Feel free to search your decaffeinated butts off. Just remember, I have a lawyer from hell. You break it you've bought it."

That was a total lie of course, but maybe he could hire Nicolai Tesslovich to sue the city for harassment and violation of his civil rights.

An hour and a half later most of Bishop's possessions were on the floor.

One of the suits came back to his chair. "We'd like the keys to your office. Mr. Bishop."

Bishop yawned and slapped himself on both cheeks trying to wake up from his doze.

"It's open"

"You leave your office unlocked?"

"Nothing left worth taking, although I am rather fond of the desk."

"You seem to have a rather casual attitude toward this warrant Mr. Bishop."

"Harassment only works if you can actually do something to me, dude. The fact that you had to form a task force means the Chief is clueless about these kidnappings. You guys are two minutes from the FBI taking it all away from you. Then heads are gonna roll. Good luck with that."

"Do you know a family by the name of Corbin, Mr. Bishop? Their eleven-year-old daughter Jennifer was missing for a while."

"I was never hired by the Corbins," Bishop said. "But I know their daughter came back, seemingly unharmed. They decided to home school her, she seemed to be having some problems adjusting back to her old life."

"Sometime last night, Mr. Bishop, neighbors heard screams coming from the Corbin house and called the police. What they found wasn't a murder. It was a massacre. Jennifer Corbin was the only one still alive when they arrived. They had to chase her down and put her in restraints. She put one of the officers in the hospital with a broken jaw.

"So, I wonder, can you tell me Mr. Bishop, why an eleven-year-old girl would murder her entire family? How someone that age could have physically accomplished that?"

"Oh, my God," Bishop said, remembering Jennifer's five-year-old sister and her flip flops. "Millie. She killed her sister Millie too?"

"She doesn't deny it. In fact, it's hard to get a word out of her longer than four letters. If I were you Mr. Bishop, I'd strongly consider whether you might have information that could be helpful to us in solving this crime."

The suit handed Bishop a card. Lt. Ronald Martin, it said, Missing Minors Task Force. Bishop had never heard of him.

Bishop put his head back and closed his eyes until the door of his apartment shut with the predictable more force than necessary. He should be used to this stuff by now. But this was way too close to home.

He thought about poor little Millie and the still-missing Susan Elizabeth Morgan, he thought about the kids in the photographs, he thought about Sister Catherine and how the police had totally ignored her when she'd tried to get something done about it. But most of all, he thought about Mouser.

He'd seen kids last night, only slightly older than the young hacker, beating each other's brains out for other people's entertainment. And Lena, 'Queen of the Cage', ramming that broken stick into her opponent's gut with almost no emotion whatsoever, unconcerned whether he lived or died. Bored by the win.

What would make kids do something like that? What would make Jennifer, damaged as she might have been by her kidnapping, suddenly kill her parents and her younger sister?

He pried himself out of the chair. His house was trashed, drawers hanging open, clothes and paperwork everywhere. Chairs over turned, the mattress half off the bed.

He kicked his way through the mess and started to pick up the things he usually kept on top of his dresser; keys, wallet, cell phone, the junk from his pockets. The dresser had been swept almost bare by the searchers whose goal was not just to find something, but to intimidate and annoy the person whose home was being searched by creating a maximum mess.

The only object they'd left on his dresser top was that stupid charm on a string Madame Zebella had given him. She said it got warm when there was a demon nearby. He'd dumped it on the dresser that night along with the loose change in his pocket and never picked it up again.

He tried to move it aside, but it seemed to be stuck to the wood. He used the side of one of his keys to pry it loose. As it popped up and turned over, a whiff of charred wood came with it.

Bishop stared at the dresser. The coin had burned a perfect twin image of itself into the oak like a brand. It was a head sprouting two curling horns.

Bishop touched it. It was still warm.

He grabbed his cell phone and called El.

"Mmpfh?"

"This is Frank. Meet me at The Caf' in twenty minutes. This is serious."

Bishop hung up and threw on his clothes. Just before he left the apartment he reached under the seat cushion of the comfy chair and pulled out the two files he'd been sitting on all through the search.

That's what happened when cops didn't drink coffee, he thought smugly. It made them miss the important details.

Forty minutes later Ariel opened the door to The Caf'. She looked annoyed.

Bishop pushed a latte he'd ordered across the table toward her. It was probably cold by now. Served her right.

"I have things to do today you know."

"Remember Jennifer Corbin?"

"Of course," Ariel said. "The creepy child."

"Well, she apparently slaughtered her whole family last night in a blind rage. I made a couple of calls. Sedation isn't really improving her mood. They have her in a straitjacket and a padded cell. Just like some old fifties horror movie."

Ariel sank into a chair. "Mouser."

"Yeah. We have to get him out of there, but I can't think of how. Zaki has too much clout to call a raid. Even if we convinced the task force he was selling minors to the kiddie porn industry, the Mayor and the Chief would never go for it. There's also the possibility he's ruthless enough to kill any kidnapees who haven't been turned into total psycho-bots, then pretend he's just running a school for disadvantaged youth or something."

"I didn't get a chance to tell you last night," Ariel said. "I took some bloody bandages from the room that kid was in and sent them to Cassius. I thought he could analyze the blood and find out what's in it that makes people able to take that much punishment and recover like nothing happened."

"Good thinking."

"Also, I'm afraid I was followed home last night. I didn't dump my bracelet like you and Rain did. I thought Cassius might be able to replicate it or something. I took the tape off, but I guess the tracking chip was still working. They sent Gargoyles."

"But you're okay?" Bishop asked.

"I wouldn't have been, but my neighbors helped me out."

"Is that a good thing? I mean except for the you-not-getting-hurt part. Didn't they freak about the Gargoyles?"

"Luckily, not so much. They're bikers. I don't mean like Hells Angels or anything. They have a motorcycle repair shop next to my apartment building."

"Oh. Well, I guess if you're a biker you tend to be more flexible about the occasional attack by strange looking creatures."

"You seem to have adjusted."

"Actually, I'm convinced this is all just a bad dream. I'll wake up soon and my mom will be there ready to feed me chocolate ice cream and Fig Newtons and tell me happy stories about Christmas and puppies."

Ariel made a face.

"My dream, my food, my holiday choice," Bishop told her. "Now what?"

"I think we should go see Cassius. Do you have your car?"

"I have two. One in the shop and one in the police impound lot. We'll have to take the subway. I think there's a liquor store on the way."

- 28 -

The Bad Dogs had been a little more generous with Old Bill than his usual customers. He was snoring like a buzz saw under his tarp. Bishop couldn't get any more out of him than "Wazzat?" and, "Go'way."

"Jesus," Bishop said. "I hope nobody throws a match into this alley."

"Excuse me,"

The voice made Bishop jump. He heard the snick of a blade falling into place at the end of Ariel's coat sleeve.

A kid of about thirteen, with dirt on his face, wearing a ratty sweater and a long scarf wrapped a couple of times around his neck slid out from behind a nearby dumpster. "You the ones with the Beam?"

Ariel fumbled in her coat pocket and showed him the pint they'd bought Old Bill.

"Don't have the liver he used to," the boy said, lifting the tarp and tucking the pint of Beam into the sleeping bag next to Old Bill. "He'll wake up and think the Tooth Fairy left him a present."

"I heard that, boy," a voice said from deep inside the bag.

"Get yourself outta here and let an old man sleep!"

"Grouchy too." The kid made sure the tarp covered Old Bill's nest. "Follow me please. Mr. Kale is expecting you."

Cassius Kale looked the same as Bishop remembered. Maybe a little more tired, his shirt a little more rumpled. His face was definitely grimmer, and his lab was hopping.

Bishop hadn't the first idea what all the equipment did, but serious, scientist-looking people and younger Deepers, whose enthusiasm just screamed 'tech support, seemed to be intently involved in several projects at once.

"Juke said this blood came from one of Zaki's Foo Fighters." Cassius said.

"Fresh from being badly beaten up, unfortunately." Ariel said

Cassius turned on a wall screen. It showed a crowd of moving circles of various sizes interspersed with the occasional unidentifiable squiggle.

"What's that?" Bishop asked.

"Your fighter's blood cells on a microscope slide," Cassius told him. "Cells, which I might add, should be inert by now."

"You mean dead?'

"Exactly. As soon as blood leaves the body it loses oxygen and starts to degenerate. Normal blood carries a large amount of red blood cells," Cassius moved to point to the bigger circles on the screen. "White blood cells, platelets and a few other stray cells like monocytes and eosinophils can be found in any blood sample. The healthier an individual is, the slower his blood degenerates outside the body. However, no matter how healthy this kid is, by now the cells in his blood should be totally dead."

"But they're still moving," Ariel said. "The boy told me that as badly as he was hurt, he'd heal within a few hours and be capable of fighting again another day. How can that be possible? Is this because of some drug they gave him? Or some kind of virus?"

"Nope." Cassius tapped the key board. Another huge flat screen on the wall lit up. "Something a whole lot scarier than that, I'm afraid."

Bishop and Ariel looked at the screen and then at each other. The picture Cassius put up looked like a huge alien landscape, or possibly a giant assortment of hard candy. Raft size, spongy red disks with dimpled centers bumped up against spiky white puff balls. Smaller, colored disks and lozenges were scattered in among the larger pieces. Over, around and in between them were tiny, luminescent creatures that seemed to have tiny propellers or fins and sometimes even tentacles attached to their miniscule bodies.

"What are we looking at?" Bishop asked.

"Nanites" Cassius said. His tone grim. "Better known as nanobots. Miniscule, man-made machines inside this boy's body that are obviously capable of producing enough oxygen to keep a small drop of blood alive even though it's been separated from its host for almost . . ." he turned to Ariel.

"Fourteen hours," she said. "Oh, my God."

"The cells are dying," Cassius pointed to the first screen. "They've begun to slow down, and some have already stopped moving."

"What about the bugs, I mean bots?" Bishop asked. "Can they get out and infect other people?"

"I don't think so. It's a symbiotic relationship. When their ability to manufacture oxygen stops, they should also die. Or at least become inert. I have to run more tests."

"And there's something else that's interesting here." Cassius picked a couple of pages out of a printer.

"I can hardly wait," Bishop said.

"When I tested it, the pH of this blood was 8.2, well over the average of 7.3, which means it's abnormally high in alkaline. That indicates lowered carbon dioxide and elevated oxygen production, oxygen being the factor that causes hemoglobin to turn red. Demons . . ."

". . . have acid blood," Ariel finished. "If you could make their blood more alkaline it would not only raise their pH but make their blood red instead of blue or green. If they were injured they could still pass for human."

"As long as no one ran a blood analysis or took a closer look at it under an electron microscope. In addition to alkalosis, the bots in the boy's blood seem to be of mixed type. Each type may have been built to perform a different task inside the body."

"So," Ariel asked. "If a demon were to have his head cut off, both parts of the body could live long enough to be put back together. Would that demon heal up, good as new?"

"Theoretically it is possible. One set of bots might keep his brain going, and another set his body alive long enough to allow some kind of surgical repair. Other bots might be tasked with reattaching nerves, muscles and ligaments, restoring vessels, reattaching bones and skin, then support rapid healing until the body could function on its own. Demon physiology is different from ours to begin with. They live much longer than we do, heal faster and their limbs, even heads have been known to stay alive for an hour or more after being separated from their bodies. That and healing bots might be the perfect combination."

"I'll try to remember that the next time one attacks me," Bishop said, thinking about the constant reappearance of the ugly little man.

"Total spontaneous regeneration is very rare."

"Not anymore," Ariel said.

"So why experiment on homeless kids?"

Cassius shrugged. "Zaki Industries has a lot of defense contracts. Maybe it's not all about demons. Maybe this is about building the perfect human soldier and selling him to the highest bidder. Or maybe he's already sold this technology to the highest bidder. Maybe he's sold it to the demons, so they'll be able to pass for human or regenerate if attacked."

"If it is about building the perfect demon," Ariel said, "holding them back will be harder than ever. They've already infiltrated governments, businesses and professions all over the world. Look at Tesslovich, he's a lawyer, although I guess that's a more understandable match. A war against some sort of super demon army would be catastrophic. The human race would die by the millions."

"My technical forensic team is taking the bots we salvaged apart." Cassius told them. "If we find out how they're built and what they're supposed to do, we might be able to postulate what Zaki is really trying to accomplish."

Cassius pushed a key and both screens went dark.

"I'd say Zaki has been in the development stage for a while, but now he's flaunting the results of his experiments without actually revealing what he's done or why. He must be close to making a big move, something that will take the entire world by surprise. Whatever it is he needs to be stopped before he goes global."

29

Mouser twisted around in the metal chair, so he could see what the room looked like. There wasn't much to see. The chair was white, the walls of the room were white, the desk in front of him was white and devoid of any objects on its surface except a folder that looked like medical chart. The number 83 had been written on the tab in heavy black marker.

Mouser was also aware of the man who stood behind him. He was dressed in white coveralls and held a plastic stick that Mouser recognized as a Taser. He guessed that was in case he tried to escape.

But Mouser was more interested in the man behind the desk. That man was tall and thin with perfect grey hair combed severely back from his high forehead. He was wearing a white lab coat over an expensive looking grey suit. It was unmarred by stains, a name badge or pens in the breast pocket. The man's long-fingered hands were clasped loosely together on the desk top. Beautifully manicured fingernails gleamed in the too bright overhead lights.

Mouser reminded himself that he had to work this just right. He only had to give them what they wanted until he found a way to escape. That didn't mean he wasn't going to lie his butt off if he had to.

The man unclasped his hands and dragged the chart in front of him with one finger. "I don't think it's necessary to continue to refer to you as number 83," he said. "I'd like you to tell me your name?"

"Mouser."

"That's what they call a street name isn't it? Don't you have another, more adult name that would suit this conversation a little better?"

Mouser thought a moment. Way in the back of his memory another name surfaced. He had no idea where it came from, but it felt right.

"Theodore." He said.

"Just Theodore?"

"It's all I remember," Mouser told the man, and that was the truth.

"Then it will have to do, won't it?" The man smiled slightly. It looked as if he had practiced the expression in the mirror.

"Would you like something to drink?" The man asked.

Mouser shook his head.

"It's perfectly safe, I assure you."

"No thank you."

"Manners." The man said. "How nice. Then let's get down to business, shall we? I have a few questions." The man opened the file and pulled out a pen from the inside pocket of his suit coat. It was gold.

"Do you have parents?"

Mouser shook his head.

"Siblings? Grandparents? Any other close relations?"

"No"

"Where do you live?"

"Around," Mouser told him.

"You have no single place that you sleep?"

Mouser scratched the back of his neck. "There's squats," he said. "I move around. Stay in one place for a while, then maybe try another. Sometimes the cops roust us out, take our stuff and throw it away. Then I have to start over."

"How old are you?"

"Fourteen." Give or take Mouser thought.

"How do you support yourself?" The man asked.

"You mean get money?'

Nod.

"Different ways. But mostly I hack."

"Really?"

"What? You don't think I'm smart enough to do that? 'Cuz I'm good at it. I look for information, you know. Credit card numbers, names, addresses. Stuff like that. Sell it to people for good money. I don't have to beg or do stuff I don't want to do."

"Where's your computer?"

"Gone now, I'll bet. I left it back at the squat with my stuff when I went out. I don't know how long I bin in this place but it's a no brainer that my stuff is somebody else's now."

The man flipped over a page in the chart. "I'm going to ask you some other questions that might seem a bit---unusual. I need you to answer them with absolute honestly. If you lie, there could be serious physical consequences for you in the near future."

"You mean old sparky back there?" Mouser asked, jerking his head in the direction of the man with the Taser. "I think I'm getting used to it. I might even be starting to like it. Breaks up the monotony."

"It will have nothing to do with Nile's little toy, Theodore. I can assure you the consequences will be worse, much, much worse."

30

Before they left Cassius said he had something he wanted to show Ariel and Bishop.

"Not the solution," he said. "But a step in the right direction. I've been hiding down here too long. Look at what I've almost let my old partner get away with, a war against the human race."

"Isn't that a little apocalyptic?" Bishop asked. "Maybe they're just tired of Raptors cutting their heads off."

"It's not like we're out there randomly hacking away," Ariel snapped. "It's a matter of maintaining the balance. I just follow orders."

Bishop and Cassius both gave her a look, which was dangerous since the three of them were zooming along at high speed in a day-glow purple electric golf cart through tunnels and corridors lit by curly fluorescent tubes wired into cables strung along the ceiling.

"Okay, even I know that sounded totally Third Reich," Ariel said. "Besides, I'm already going against everything I was ordered to do, which unfortunately consisted mostly of nothing."

As they sped on, sensors turned sections of the light tubes on, then off again as they passed through. Cassius had explained that the less energy the lighting took, the less chance the Deeps energy use would be detected.

Bishop found the effect creepy. It was as if the dark was chasing them, always just one step away from catching up.

"What about the rats?" Bishop asked as they'd made the transition between Cassius' labs and living space to the nearly deserted tubular highways of his underground city. As they went further, the frequency of distant banks of light sensors going on and off, indicating someone else was using the 'road', stopped.

"Intermittent, high frequency sound waves keep them out of these tunnels." Cassius said. "Higher up they're still a problem. But then somebody would notice if the rats completely disappeared. Most people have a primal fear of rats. In a way they help keep us safe."

"Orders?" Bishop asked Ariel. "Is that why you went after Tesslovich?"

"You know the principle 'an eye for an eye'?" Ariel said. "Well, it's like that between us and demons. They take one of ours, we take one of theirs. They cross the line, we push back. There's at least one Raptor in every major city or region throughout the world. Raptors are the instrument that maintains the balance. Most of the time I don't even know what the demon did to make us hit back. I have nothing to do with the 'why'. I get my orders, I do my job. Until now."

"But you didn't get Tesslovich?"

"The bastard resurrected. How am I responsible for that? The Guardian called me on the carpet about it, then he tells me to back off. He didn't care about all the kids who have disappeared. It's 'none of my business'. Do what I'm told. Higher purpose, blah, blah, blah, fullness of time, yata, yata, millennial agenda and all that crap. He also told me to forget about Mouser. I'm not going to do that."

"So, what's he going to do when we declare war on Yamazaki Kiriyenko?"

"I don't know. Arrest me. Kill me. Send me back where I came from?"

"Where's that?" Bishop asked.

"I have absolutely no idea."

31

"You have some very interesting blood test results, Theodore. Do you consider yourself a healthy person?"

"Yeah. Sure. I don't get sick much." Or ever, Mouser thought.

"Have you ever had any childhood illnesses? Measles, chicken pox, frequent colds or flu?"

"No."

"Ever been hospitalized? Any operations? Tonsils, appendix?""

"No."

"What's your best childhood memory?"

"Getting my laptop," Mouser told him.

"I mean before that Theodore. Any memories of family events? Christmas? Toys, gifts? Going to church, living in a house with adults? Pets?"

"I had a rat once that seemed to like me. He came out at night in the squat. I fed him scraps from the dumpsters that were too rank for humans to eat. He didn't seem to mind."

"That's it?"

"Yeah."

"What about dreams?"

Mouser sighed. He had no idea where this was going. Everybody dreamed. Sometimes his were bad. Living on the street was hard and scary. There was never enough to eat, and people tried to hurt you, or mess with you on an almost daily basis. You never knew where you were going to sleep that night or if it would be safe to close your eyes. Sometimes the dreams were good, especially since Ariel, Ez and the Caf'. And of course, his computer.

"Do you ever dream of being an animal, Theodore?"

Oops. "What? No." This was going in a bad direction.

"How about flying? Have you ever dreamt you could fly?"

Careful here. Mouser had often dreamed of flying before the first change happened. Then, after suddenly finding himself a small brown bird, he'd felt totally terrified, even of pigeons, until he'd fallen asleep and awakened, naked in an alley, changed back into a kid. Luckily his clothes weren't that far away.

Ariel had told him even regular people sometimes dreamed of flying, but she and Mouser were the lucky ones. They actually could fly.

"Sure, he said. "But I know I can't. It's just a dream."

The man wrote another note in the chart.

"I don't want to fight." Mouser told the man.

"What?" The man looked up at him, amused.

"I don't want to fight," Mouser repeated. "I'm too small and I wouldn't be good at it."

"Is that what you think we have in store for you, Theodore?"

"Yes," Mouser said. "That's what you make everybody do, right?"

"Not everyone, Theodore. You're right, you're too small to be a fighter. And it would be a pitiful waste of your true potential. We have something much better in mind for you, my boy. Something special."

32

Cassius stopped the cart at a large steel door. Several other brightly painted carts were parked nearby. Each made an artistic statement, except for one. That one had once been white but what was left of the paint had turned a grubby ivory. What also made it unique was the number and severity of the dents and patches it sported. It was also missing both fenders.

"That belongs to the engineer," Cassius said. "He's not much on style. As long as it runs, he's happy. He pushed the steel door open. On the other side was a tile platform above a subway track.

"Come on," Cassius said. "Before the train leaves the station."

Within a hundred feet the platform broadened into a station. It was an old station by the look of it. Unused for decades, possibly an entire century.

"Wow," Ariel said.

"Holy cow," Bishop said. "Where is this place?"

"Under a really bad neighborhood," Cassius told them. "It used to be a posh address about a hundred and thirty years ago. Its residents wanted to use the new underground transportation system, but only in their own fancy train from their own fancy neighborhood station. This place has long disappeared off all the existing maps. They built it deep and no other trains ever came through here except their three-car luxury express."

"Crystal chandeliers," Ariel said. "Marble walls, mosaic floors, mirrors."

"The fixtures are gold plated," Cassius told her. "There's a bar that still has bottles of liquor and champagne, crystal glasses and amazingly, running water. The elevators no longer go up to the houses. Too dangerous in this day and age so the shafts have been filled with rubble. I'm afraid most of the furniture has lost its upholstery to time and rodents but there are still some sturdy benches made of exotic wood inlaid with ivory and brass. There was no income tax back then, you know. The rich could spend their money as they liked on fancy toys and fashion."

"What's that?" Bishop asked. What he was looking at sat on tracks next to the platform, each car was rounded on top and painted an azure blue with curly, brass accents and gold striping. The cars had elegant interiors, couches instead of seats, wood paneling and murals on the walls. Dusty but elegant Persian rugs still covered the floors.

"Amazing, isn't it? Magnificent actually. Runs on either electricity or steam generated by burning coal oil. We're modifying that to a modern hybrid system so that the train can function on newer electric tracks or switch to bio-diesel, but that's another project."

Beyond the blue train at least twenty workers were crawling over another, more modern, set of subway cars armed with a variety of tools. Bright sparks were flying from the steel plates being fitted over the windows.

An elderly man in overalls and a striped cap came up to Cassius. His grease streaked hands held a clipboard filled with papers. "Movin' along Sir," he said as Cassius stepped nearer.

"Engineer Jeorge McCullen," Cassius said in way of introduction.

"It's another train" Ariel said, as if no one had noticed.

"Oh, aye lass," Jeorge said. "She's a beaut too. Plenty of power and a heart of iron. Used to take passengers from the main line to Hauptman's store. We brought her down here to work on her. Once we get the plates on we'll be able to make it through Zaki's steam trap, no problem. The lads have been going at it twenty-four seven. The gun mounts are nearly done."

"You're going to run the tunnel into Zaki's compound," Bishop asked.

"Hopefully," Cassius answered. "The steel plates and gaskets will protect us from being boiled alive by the steam. We've mounted heavy artillery on the engine and roof of the cars."

"Zaki put something that makes rats and people explode in the heating ducts of his stadium," Ariel told Cassius.

"Most likely microwaves," Cassius said. "Thank you, Ariel, for that information. We'll incorporate it into our defenses. And thank you for those sketches of the compound,"

Bishop had missed that slight-of-hand. Sneaky Raptor.

"What's your timeline here?" Bishop asked.

Cassius looked at his engineer.

"Forty-eight hours, Sir." The engineer said.

"Two days, then?"

"Tops."

"You're not going without us!" Ariel said.

Us?

"Of course not," Cassius told her. "The fate of the world and Mouser are at stake. Come on, I'll show you the quick way out."

As they started back down the tunnel Cassius handed both Bishop and Ariel flat, steel cell phones. They looked banged up, as if they'd been well used.

"I already have a cell phone," Bishop told him, surprised at the number of bright green bars showing in the corner of the small screen.

"Not one like this. This one has thumb print activation, just slide your thumb across that little window there, push nine and it will remember it. Scan your thumb every time you want to make a call. It also has a scrambler, a GPS, and it works underground. Kale.net has its own towers and satellite relays, kindly hosted by the Pentagon although it doesn't know it. Since things are heating up I thought you might need to get in touch faster than using Old Bill. They're fully programmed. I'm number three on the speed dial. One is Hot 'n Fast Pizza. Two is Discount Liquor & Smokes. They know Old Bill. We like to make sure he eats as well as drinks."

Once out of the Deeps, Bishop's own cell phone started to make the ring tone that signaled he had messages.

The first one was from Rain. "She's dead, man," he said. "Jennifer Corbin died a couple of hours ago in Memorial's security nut ward. There'll be an autopsy, but they think it was some kind of drug reaction. Or a brain aneurism. Anyway, they're still waiting for the tox screen. Hopefully the autopsy will tell us why she went all Freddy Kruger on her family. I'll let you know when I find out more. Watch your back, bro."

The second call was from Sister Cate. One of her missing kids had just stumbled into the shelter, wild eyed, shaking and disoriented. He'd been missing about three months. She'd taken him to Mid-City Memorial. He was in the ER.

"I've got to go," Bishop told Ariel. "Jennifer Corbin just died and one of the missing shelter kids turned up at the shelter acting weird, so Sister Cate took him to the hospital. I think I'd better check it out."

"You want me to come?"

"No point. I'll stop by the hospital, then I need to make a

few calls. So far, two formerly missing kids have shown back up with serious medical problems. And your fighter's blood was over oxygenated and full of bugs. Things are taking a bad turn. I need to check on Susan Elizabeth's family. Who knows, maybe she'll show up next."

Bishop punched up the directory on the Kale.net cell phone. "Hey," he said over his shoulder. "You're number four on my new speed dial. We'll stay in touch."

- 33 -

The hospital was a quick cab ride. Bishop found Sister Mary Catherine in the ER waiting room. She began to fill Bishop in before he'd had a chance to say hello.

The kid's name was Jip Gustov. He was fifteen and he'd put on twenty pounds of muscle since Sister Cate had seen him last. He'd been incoherent when he showed up; sweating, shaking, yelling at anybody who came too close.

Sister Catherine had gotten him into her car by reciting the rosary with him over and over until he calmed down. The ER doctor had sedated him. He was going to be admitted. Cate had no idea what was wrong with him. They were running some tests at the moment and then she'd be allowed back in the cubicle to sit with him. She wasn't family, but she was a nun with attitude and her determination had been so fierce the docs had given in.

"He just showed up on my doorstep," she said. "He couldn't tell me how he got there. It's like somebody dropped him off. He was really fucked up. Scared, then angry, then scared again. Wouldn't let anyone touch him. I'm worried that while I'm here more of my kids will show up at the shelter. Maybe they're letting them all go. What if they show up and I'm not there?"

"You can call in and check, Cate. Let's worry about this kid right now."

"They don't allow cell phones in the ER, Frank. I need you to go by the shelter and make sure everything's all right. I left Tony in charge. He has my list. He'll let them in if they show up after hours."

"How about I step outside and call Tony? Then I can stay with you and you won't have to worry."

"I'd really appreciate that."

The entrance to the ER was lit up like a used car lot. Ambulances were coming and going, distraught looking people were rushing in, or limping out. Bishop used his own phone to call the shelter. Tony told him nobody else had shown up and everything was under control from his point of view. Bishop gave him his cell number. He'd leave his phone on and if it went off they could throw him out while he answered it. Doctors got pages all the time in hospitals. He sincerely doubted his cell phone conversation would crash some patient's pacemaker.

Then he thought about what Cassius had said about alkalosis being really dangerous. He'd been out of the Deeps twenty minutes and already he was pushing number three on his secret spy phone's speed dial.

Cassius answered on the second ring.

"I think we have a couple more problems, C.T." Bishop said.

Cassius listened to what Bishop had just learned about Jennifer Corbin and Jip Gustov's sudden appearance at the shelter and what Bishop knew of his symptoms.

"I have a couple of contacts at Memorial," Cassius told him briskly. "When a doctor named Jason Bender shows up to take over the case, follow his lead. And get back in there and make sure that kid isn't taking oxygen."

The line went dead.

Bishop trotted back through the automatic doors and into

the waiting room. Sister Catherine was no longer sitting where he'd left her. In fact, she was no longer in the waiting room.

Bishop walked up to the triage desk and flashed his PI identification open and closed under the nose of a harried looking aid.

"Detective Bishop," he said. I understand a Jipper Gustov, fifteen, was brought in here within the last hour. The kid's been missing and feared kidnapped for the last three months. The Shelter Director who brought him in called us. What's his room number?"

The Aid looked at Bishop. Her lips parted, and Bishop just knew she was going to refuse to tell him or ask to see his ID again. But she was too busy, and too tired to care. "Room eight," she said, consulting a list and motioning to a set of double doors with her clip board. "Bed three. The lady he was with just went back there."

Bishop hustled down the hall.

Sister Cate was sitting in the visitor chair at the side of the bed. There was barely room for Bishop to crowd in between the curtain separating Jip's bed from the one next to him. The kid had wild black hair and an unhealthy pallor. His entire body was in the throes of a continuous series of jerks, tics and tremors, and underneath closed lids, the kid's eyes were rolling in their sockets as if he was terrified by a bad dream. His mouth and nose were covered by an oxygen mask.

"They let me back here," Sister Cate said. "They don't know what's wrong with him. They gave him an anti-seizure drug, but it doesn't seem to be helping so they tied his hands and feet to the bed. I don't know what to do, Frank except pray for him."

"I called a friend. He's sending over a specialist. We need to take off the oxygen."

"They said he needs it."

"It's the first thing they give everybody who comes in here

whether they need it or not. It's standard CYA. My friend says his problem might be too much oxygen in his system. More could be really dangerous for him."

"What if he's wrong?"

Bishop knew that if they turned off the oxygen on C.T. Kale's say so, he was trusting the word of an eccentric genius he hardly knew over the entire medical establishment. In turn, Sister Catherine would be trusting him, someone who had no medical training whatsoever.

"What if he's right?" He said.

Sister Catherine looked at the boy for a moment. He was obviously suffering and so far, no one had helped him stop. Without a glance back at Bishop she stood up, leaned over the bed and turned the oxygen valve on the wall to off.

The boy's muscles started to relax, if only slightly and his eye movements slowed to a less frantic pace.

"We'll leave the mask on," she said. "That way these idiots won't notice we've turned it off."

Not more than ten minutes later there was a commotion at the door. A man wearing a white coat over a three-piece suit gave the curtain a vigorous push so that it rattled in its track as it slid back almost to the wall. He was followed by two orderlies pushing a gurney.

"Dr. Bender," he announced. "I'm taking over this young man's case. We need to move him to another floor." The boy was untied and transferred onto the rolling cart.

Sister Cate stood up. "What . . .?"

"It's okay," Bishop said. "This is the specialist."

The orderlies rolled the cart out of the room and down the hall in the opposite direction from the ER waiting room so fast Bishop and Sister Cate had to jog to keep up. They passed through two double doors and out an emergency exit into the parking lot where an ambulance waited with its engine going and its back door open.

Sister Cate jumped into the back of the ambulance with Jip and the doctor before they could stop her. She tossed her car keys to Bishop as the doors closed.

"Blue Toyota in the front lot. Follow us!"

The ambulance pulled out, lights and siren blazing. Bishop ran for the front of the building and into the rows of parked cars. He pushed the auto unlock button until a car blinked its lights at him, then jumped in and started the engine. As he burned rubber out of the lot he realized he had no idea which way the ambulance had gone.

Then a terrible thought hit him. What if he'd just given a sick, unconscious kid and Sister Mary Catherine to the wrong guys?

After being underground, Ariel desperately wanted to fly; let her wings out; feel the air in her face as she climbed and rolled and dove into its currents high above the lake. But it was still light out, so she'd have to settle for a run. Maybe after dark she'd be able to get her flight.

She changed into sweats, making sure her jacket had a hood. She hoped to prevent being identified from the air if there were any Gargoyles hanging around the neighborhood.

Still, she made sure she had something up her sleeves in case they did come after her. All she wanted to do was 5K, just enough to take the edge off, let her think.

The fact that she hadn't gotten any orders lately disturbed her. Was the Guardian holding back, embroiled in his own devious strategy? Or was he waiting for exactly the right moment to strike? Maybe he'd just lost confidence in her.

There was nothing wrong with her skills, but despite following her instructions to the letter Tesslovich had survived. She wondered if the Guardian had any idea what was about to happen. She was tempted to go tell him, but that hadn't worked out so well the last time.

When it became obvious she'd struck out on her own, there'd be hell to pay. Being 'fired' as Raptor of the City was going to be the least of it. She told herself she was past caring, but only just.

The run took longer than she expected. When Ariel rounded the corner toward her building, long shadows had already begun to form on the sidewalk. Shortly, it would be dark.

Dingo was waiting for her on the porch. He was in his early-twenties and still had some adolescent shyness about him. It didn't matter. She felt baby sat and her prissiness was starting to rise. It was going to be all she could do not to tell him off.

"Just wanted to let you know," Dingo said as she climbed the steps. "We did a few things to your apartment."

She stopped.

Dingo could feel the vibe coming off her. "Not much," he said, backing up. "Just a bar for the doors and, um, a panic button in case of another 'goyle attack. If you think you need backup that is."

Ariel took a deep breath. The Dogs had helped her out the other night when she needed it. They were just trying to help now. Don't alienate your friends, she thought, especially when they're a lot like you.

"Thank you. I probably won't need it but thanks."

When she opened her door, she decided maybe she'd said 'thank you' too soon. The wooden door into the apartment now had a steel bar on the inside that dropped down into two brackets. That only helped if she was home. The door onto the roof top had the same arrangement, a less impressive security feature considering the door, in fact practically the whole wall, was glass.

There were two unattractive red panic buttons. One just inside the glass door, and one by her bed. The Dogs had also loaded two of her crossbows, added a supply of quarrels and left them by the roof door 'just in case'.

"Great!" Ariel said out loud. "I'm all set to go to the mattresses."

It was almost full dark now and she was hungry, but first she wanted a shower. She ran water into her biggest sauce pan, threw in a handful of spaghetti and lit the flame underneath. By the time she got out of the bathroom the noodles would be done.

She had just started to pull her sweatshirt over her head when there was a huge thump out on the roof and the sound of breaking glass.

"Shit!" She tugged the shirt down and ran for the roof door, hitting the outside light switch as she passed it.

Something large with wings had hit the glass wall and rebounded onto the roof. The creature was still rolling with the impact.

Through the broken panes Ariel could hear the shrill cries of hunting Gargoyles. Without stopping she scooped one of the crossbows up in one hand and swung the iron bar out of its braces with the other.

The thing on the roof tried to get to its feet.

Ariel could see it better now. Although it was at the periphery of the circle of light from the outside lamps her enhanced vision made it out clearly. The man was a study in black on black with one damaged ebony wing that was getting in the way of it trying to rise.

He was somehow familiar. Tomas!

Ariel hit the panic button, grabbed the other cross bow and kicked open the door. She didn't know what she'd expected, a siren, bells—nothing happened. She ran to Tomas' crumpled figure. The Gargoyles were big ones and they were coming in fast.

"Tomas! Get inside!"

"Can't," the Raptor gasped. "Give me a bow." He had one hand clutched to his side and his face was covered in blood.

Ariel handed him the second bow, her eyes never leaving the 'goyles in the sky.

"What happened?" She yelled over the noisy cries of Gargoyles and the leathery flapping sound of their wings.

"Trap," Tomas said. "Hurt."

She gave him one, quick glance. There was a cross bow quarrel in his leg and one in his arm. A dark stain was spreading across his stomach although it was hard to see on the black t-shirt.

"I've got the leader," Tomas told her. "You take the next one."

Tomas lay almost flat on his back, wings and legs askew. He was holding the cross bow with one hand, its butt propped against the flat surface of the roof. He'd clamped it between his upper arm and ribcage, so he could move it in an arc.

He raised his head, waiting until the lead Gargoyle was almost right over him and pulled the trigger. The bolt hit the 'goyle dead center.

The beast screamed and clawed at the shaft, trying to rise away from Tomas' line of fire, but collapsed onto the wounded Raptor instead. Still alive it clawed at Tomas' body and spit acid at his face. Raising a clawed hand, it was about to rip into the downed Raptor's throat when it was hit by the body of a large dog and dragged squealing across the roof.

Ariel fired at the second 'goyle, hitting him with two quarrels in quick succession. Behind her, a large caliber pistol fired and another 'goyle went down.

Ham jumped in front of her holding a four-foot metal pipe in his hands. He swung at one of the 'goyles like Babe Ruth aiming for the fence. The 'goyle made a wet, burst melon kind of sound and disappeared over the edge of the roof.

Ariel ripped off her hoodie, leaving only her sports bra and the gravity knives strapped to the inside of her wrists in place.

Wings unfurled from the dark shadows along the inside of her shoulder blades. With one beat she was in the air.

The combat was too close for comfort. She didn't want to block someone else's shot or get herself nailed in the confusion. Instead of trying to get close enough to use her knives or claws she barreled straight into one of the bigger 'goyles.

The surprise of it and their combined body weight took the goyle off to the side. Before it could use its claws, she buried a knife in its stomach and ripped upward, spilling ropes of acid coated 'goyle guts onto the tar paper.

Spinning quickly, she grabbed a double fistful of 'goyle wings and smashed the creature two or three times against the brick chimney of the building's heating system. Its green blood left a large, gooey starburst on the brick.

As she turned back toward Tomas, another Gargoyle went down. She saw Juke standing, pistol extended like Doc Holiday at the OK Corral picking off the last of the Clantons.

The dog, which at second glance turned out to be a wolf, tossed a dead goyle over its shoulder. The 'goyle's disjointed appearance implied it had several broken bones, including its neck.

Ham was checking out an unconscious Tomas. He motioned the wolf over.

A few seconds later a naked and blushing Dingo was grabbing Tomas' feet, helping Juke and Ham maneuver him through the doorway back into the apartment. The Raptor's unfurled wings proved to be a bit of a problem.

Ariel surveyed the roof. Five, no six Gargoyles lay in various positions of death. A seventh was still twitching. It hissed at Ariel when she leaned in to finish it off.

That was a large hunting party for one Raptor, she thought. And what was Tomas doing on her turf? She already knew the answer, but she was going to make him tell her anyway.

A quavery voice called up from a window below. "What's going on up there? Should I call the police?"

Ariel pulled in her wings and leaned over the roof wall. Mrs. Avery's untidy grey head stuck out of her third-floor window.

"Raccoons on the roof, Mrs. Avery," she said. "Big ones. We had to chase them off, but everything's okay now. We're going back inside. You can go back to your programs."

Mrs. Avery was practically deaf and had her television on at full volume most of the time. If she'd heard the noise, Ariel couldn't imagine what the rest of the tenants in the building thought was going on.

When she went back inside Juke had already gone down to the lower floors to spin whatever story he'd come up with to anybody who wanted to hear it. The building housed a pretty weird collection of renters. Things happened here all the time, like Ralph-the-Inventor's exploding soap incident, the buttered popcorn in the dryer experiment, and the Pockart's famously creative weekly fight-nights in 2B. People usually blew noisy events like that off and went on with whatever they were doing, unless there were sirens and flames.

Tomas was lying on one of Ariel's mats. Ham had straightened his wings, so he could lay him flat and get to the hole in his side. Tomas moaned when Ham pulled the Raptor's hand away from the wound. He was only half conscious.

"Nice one, boy," Ham told him. "Deep and nasty. That and these two bolts sticking out of you make you a regular portrait of sainthood. Nice acid burn on your face too."

"Is he going to be okay?"

"Don't know yet. Dingo run downstairs for a pair of pants and my medical kit. When I get my stuff we'll see, you Raptors don't die easy."

"You're a doctor?"

"Naw, Army medic. Saw a lot of combat. I'm real good with wounds."

"What about his wing?' Tomas had a hole in one wing and the spines of the nearby feathers were bent and broken at odd angles.

"Don't know squat about feathers. Wish he could pack those things up so I could work on him better."

"He can't pull in a broken wing. It will just do more damage. It's better to let it heal outside the body."

"You know this guy?"

"He was my combat instructor when I was in training. He lives in a different city. I don't know why he's here."

"Well he landed on your roof with one bad wing and multiple bogies on his tail. I'd say he was looking for help."

An instant later a shrill siren broke the relative silence of the apartment.

"Is that the panic button again?" Ariel glanced around, looking for a missed Gargoyle.

"More like your smoke alarm, missy."

"Damn it!" Ariel yelled, as she ran for the kitchen and the column of smoke coming off the stove. "That was my dinner!"

35

Cages!

Mouser hated cages. Every time he saw some poor bird behind bars he wanted to let it out, so it could fly away. Now he was the canary in the cage.

"Good afternoon, Theodore," the grey man said.

"I'm not some dumb kid," Mouser told him defiantly. "Let me out of this stupid cage." He remembered the pet shop owner telling him the birds really didn't mind being caged when he'd objected to the way all the birds in his shop were locked up. He didn't believe that for a second.

"Not until we do a little experiment, Theodore. It shouldn't take too long although some have told me it feels like an eternity."

"What are you going to do to me you perv?"

"Just provide you with a little incentive, my boy."

"Incentive to do what? Just ask me, I'll do whatever you want except, you know, the bitch stuff. You're not giving me a chance to cooperate."

"Oh, but I am. Change for us, Theodore."

"Change what?"

Precisely. Change into what you really are. Show us your true self."

"This *is* my true self," Mouser yelled. "I'm me! This is what I am."

The grey man sighed. "You're making this much harder on yourself than you need to. But we shall see what we shall see."

"I don't know what you're talking about," Mouser yelled. He wasn't going to change for them. His ability was his ace in the hole; it was his only chance to get away.

Mouser looked down. The cage swung from an overhead chain. It had bars on all sides. They'd taken his shoes and his feet felt greasy, like he'd stepped in slime.

He grabbed the bars. There was nothing to hang onto that wasn't steel. His feet started to tingle. The sensation increased. Small shocks began to run up his fingers. He snatched his hands away. Soon he was shifting from foot to foot. The current was going higher.

"No!" he yelled.

The grey man picked up a heavy wooden rod and gave the cage a push. It turned on its chain and swung back and forth throwing Mouser into the side bars.

The first shock to his arm threw him in the opposite direction, slamming him into the other side of the cage for a second jolt. He screamed and sank to his knees trying to get cloth between his skin and the electrified floor. The shock of that brought him back to his feet.

He danced with the pain and the motion made the cage swing even more, knocking him from wall of bars to wall of bars, where current pulsed in alternating intensities. The shocks increased his momentum as he rebounded from one side of the cage to the other. Tears were streaming down his face and the shrill noise in his ears was coming from his own throat, from his gut, from the very depths of his soul.

Somewhere inside the pain Mouser could feel it coming. No! He thought. Then, Yes! Yes please, just stop this! Please.

Suddenly, he was in the air, wings beating frantically as he tried to stay in the middle of the cage where no part of him would touch metal. His avian vocal cords let out an angry, scream of rage. He wanted to go for the grey man's eyes, rip his throat out, open his belly and devour his entrails until he'd eaten his way into his heart.

A wooden dowel attached to two pieces of rope fell through the bars from the top of the cage.

Mouser saw it and realized his captors knew he couldn't maintain flying in place like this for long. He landed on the perch, hating himself for this humiliating act of defeat. His feathers were sticking out in all directions. He began to smooth them with his beak, ignoring his tormentor.

"See how much misery you could have saved yourself," the grey man said, "if you'd just been honest with us in the first place." He reached out a hand to steady the cage. It brought him close to the bars.

Mouser threw himself at his tormentor with a screech, his head darted through the gap trying to get to the grey man's face, take out an eye, bite a piece out of his smug, self-satisfied flesh.

The grey man stepped out of reach, chuckling softly. "I like your spirit, Theodore. A mere human would be groveling on his knees after all that. Really, I'm not your enemy. In fact, as we spend more time together I think you'll find we have a lot more in common than you ever thought possible.

"Well. You must be hungry. I'll order you a couple of nice live rodents for your dinner. Food tastes so much better when you kill it yourself."

36

Tony and Bishop had plenty of time to perfect their routine. The two of them alternated pacing the front hall of the shelter waiting for the reappearance of Sister Catherine. Bishop had tried her cell phone, but she must have turned it off at the hospital and forgotten to turn it on again. He'd left messages--- four so far and was tempted to try again. It was three a.m. and he was trying hard to stay focused, but he couldn't ingest one more cup of Shelter coffee without doing himself serious damage.

At the moment, Tony had the chair and Bishop was walking in a circle on the foyer's well used rug. He'd decided to try leaning against the wall for a while when he heard the sound of a key in the lock.

An exhausted Sister Mary Catherine pushed open the door, only to jump about a foot when Tony leaped to his feet and Bishop appeared from nowhere to grab her in a tight hug that made her drop both her keys and shoulder bag on the floor.

"Thank God!" Bishop said.

Tony shifted from foot to foot behind them, not sure what to do. He and Sister Catherine weren't on hugging terms. In fact, Sister Catherine wasn't the sort of person you grabbed up in your arms no matter how happy you were. She struggled out of Bishop's grip.

"What's wrong?" She asked. "Did something happen? Have more kids arrived?"

"We're just glad you're okay," Bishop explained. "You've been gone for hours. We were really worried."

"I thought you were going to follow me."

"By the time I found your car the ambulance was out of sight. I thought maybe you'd been kidnapped too."

Sister Catherine dropped into Tony's chair. "Not exactly," she said, "although it's been an interesting night. Tony, you look really tired. It's okay if you go to bed now. I really appreciate you waiting up for me, but Frank and I have to talk."

"Coffee?" Bishop asked as soon as Tony had gone off to his room.

"Thanks, but I'd like to be able to get to sleep sometime in the next two weeks. Tony's coffee is the gateway drug to methamphetamine use. I usually dilute it by half even in the morning. Come into my office."

Once they'd settled in chairs Sister Catherine said, "I don't know where I went tonight, Frank. The ambulance windows were tinted so dark I couldn't see out. By the time we stopped it was parked inside the engine bay of some old fire station. After that I just followed the gurney. There was an elevator and corridors and another elevator and suddenly we were in some kind of infirmary with bright lights and beds, machines and medical people who'd obviously been waiting for us."

"So, how's he doing?"

"They took a bunch of blood, hooked him up to all kinds of monitors, gave him an IV with something in it I don't remember the name of and then we waited. When I left the twitching had almost stopped and he was sleeping. They made me ride in the back of the ambulance on the way back, so I couldn't see where

I'd been. Who the hell are these people, Frank? Why isn't Jip in a regular hospital where they can find out what's wrong with him?"

"They work for C.T. Kale, and a regular hospital can't fix his problem."

"And a dot com guy can? Anyway, I thought C.T. Kale was dead."

"C.T.'s a biotech guy. He owned a large research lab in partnership with Yamazaki Kiriyenko. Apparently, a few years ago Zaki stole Kale's patents for nanotechnology and got the board, which he'd probably stacked with demons, to take the company away from him. C.T.'s wife died in a suspicious accident and his son disappeared. C.T. had to go underground, literally, to stay alive. He thinks these kids are full of experimental nanobots and Kiriyenko plans on using the bots to make demons into a super race. Problem is, the bots aren't compatible with human physiology. They enhance these kids into serious fighting machines, but eventually the changes make them really crazy, or really sick.

"Kiriyenko holds matches on his property where he fights his lab rats for sport, or maybe he just wants to see if they can take the punishment and recover. I don't know why he's letting some of them go. Maybe to confuse the mayor's task force about whether they were really kidnapped, or maybe it's because he's so close to some major play that he doesn't care."

"Demons. You really think this is about demons? Even the church has moved away from believing in that kind of stuff." Sister Catherine said.

"You told me you saw a demon once. He marked you."

"Maybe I was delusional. Religious hallucinations aren't uncommon when you're in an isolated, intensely faith-based environment."

"Catie, you are the sanest person I know. And I'm telling you that in the last two weeks I have seen things that I never thought existed except in an Ozzy Osbourne acid flashback. Some of the people I've met are on our side, and some are hoping to make people like you and me their permanent bitch. All I know is that when it comes down to it, the good guys have got to win."

"What do I do if more sick kids show up?"

"Call me. I'll get them picked up. C.T. Kale and his guys are working 24/7 to come up with a solution."

"This is all really crazy, but I trust you and I know you're working in the best interest of my kids."

Sister Mary Catherine walked Bishop to the door. He'd already stepped out on the porch when she said, "Frank, that girl who killed her family, do you think the demons took her soul?"

"I don't think there's any lab test for that, Sister. I sincerely hope not."

"Be safe, Frank. I'll pray for you."

37

"If you're going to breath down my neck while I'm working, at least make yourself useful. Hold this retractor so I can get this piece of metal out of him. Dingo keep that light aimed where I'm working or I'm going to take you back to the pound."

Tomas had been stripped of clothing and weapons and laid out on Ariel's kitchen table. Because of his height, his legs dangled over one end and his arms hung over the sides. His wings had gotten in the way until Ariel smoothed and straightened the feathers allowing them to fold properly without more damage. Then she'd persuaded a minimally conscious Tomas to let go of his defenses, so he would change. Ariel had thrown a towel over him for modesty sake.

"You found Dingo in the pound?" Ariel grabbed the handle of the instrument holding Tomas' torn flesh open so that Ham could get to whatever was still in the wound.

"Yeah. He was just a pup. Some hunter had killed his family but missed him because he was out running around like young pups do. Juke and I followed his trail. Animal control had taken him in as a stray. We claimed him, and he's been a pain in the ass ever since. Aim it to the right, boy! There it is."

Ham pulled the forceps out of Tomas' side. The serrated tips held a large shard of broken metal covered in a layer of flaky green scale. The shard glowed with a sickly blue green fluorescence.

"Verdigris. It's a poison that oxidizes bronze. This is the tip of a demon-forged blade. They're deliberately coated with an enhanced form of the poison. Even a small wound can cause debilitation and death. I'm amazed he was able to get here with this in him."

"He has a really strong will. Does removing the piece reverse the effects?"

Ham held the fragment up to the light. "I can't tell you the exact kind of weapon this came from, but it's probably something called an Angel Slayer."

"Angel Slayer? But we're not angels, we're Raptors. Shape shifters just like you guys."

"Whatever. It's an old weapon from an old war that neither side has ever won. It obviously works on Raptors just like it did on angels. Do you have some baking soda?"

"In the back of my refrigerator," Ariel said. "I think it's been there since I moved in. I'm not much for baking."

"Dingo? I'll need some more water too."

Ham carefully poured the contents of the crumpled yellow box into the wound. "Baking soda will neutralize the acid in the poison. Pour the water in slowly, boy. Somebody better hold him down."

As soon as the water hit the wound the white powder turned into pink foam that frothed and bubbled out of the hole in Tomas' side onto the old linoleum floor, causing its brittle surface to dissolve where it touched. Tomas gave a convulsive twitch. Ham caught his wrists just before the Raptor's hands could reach the wound. "It's okay, son. It'll be over in a second, then I'll stitch you up. We're going to pull those arrows out of you too."

Ham had clipped off the pointed end of the shaft protruding out of Tomas' arm with wire cutters before he'd started on the bigger wound. The feathered piece was still stuck in his bicep. Ham reached over and yanked it out. Simultaneously, Juke clipped and pulled the quarrel out of Tomas' leg.

"Ow!" Tomas' yelled. The pain had brought him back to consciousness.

"Quick is better," Ham said as he filled a syringe with local anesthesia to prepare for stitching. "Turn the radio on would you, missy? This is the tedious part."

38

"E l?"

"What?" Ariel sat up. She cursed herself for having dozed off. Tomas had begun to spike a fever shortly after his injuries were stitched and bandaged. He was soon unconscious, his skin blazing with heat. The Dogs had put him in Ariel's old-fashioned claw foot tub and sent Dingo out for bags of ice.

"It's the poison," Ham said. He clipped open a couple of stitches and inserted a piece of rubber tubing into the wound causing it to drain a greenish-black fluid into the melting ice water. "As soon as it starts running clear he'll be over the hump."

"Ariel?" Tomas asked. Ariel had rolled a sleeping bag out on the tile, so she could sit on the floor next to the tub and hold Tomas' hand. Ham checked the drain every ten minutes. At the sound of her name, Ariel rolled to her knees.

"Can I get out of this tub?" Tomas asked in a weak voice. "I'm freezing."

"You're awake. Ham!"

Ham came into the bathroom and leaned over the tub. "It's running clear," he said. "Fever's gone. Let's get him up, dry him off and put him under some blankets."

In a few minutes Tomas was asleep in Ariel's bed. While she'd been in the bathroom with Tomas, the Dogs had disappeared the dead Gargoyles and put plywood over the broken windows.

"Ez set me up, right?" Ariel asked Juke. "He arranged for you guys to keep an eye on me."

"We're guard dogs, not spies." Juke told her. "We kept an eye on you, but we had no intention of getting in your way unless you needed us."

"I guess this qualifies. Thank you."

"If your friend takes another bad turn, push the button. It's almost dawn, I don't think there'll be another attack this morning."

Ariel dragged her sleeping bag into the bedroom. When Tomas woke up for real they were going to have a talk.

39

Bishop slept late, drank a pot of coffee and went to pick up his car from the mechanic. It was ready, and amazingly enough the orange Falcon was back in the garage.

"Sorry about the dead body and the police confiscation," Bishop said.

The mechanic shrugged." You have no idea what people leave in their cars. The wife and I ended up with a kid for two weeks because his parents forgot he was in the back seat and not at grandma's while they went off on a cruise. It's insured. With your track record I was hoping you'd total it."

While Bishop was writing a check, his steel cell phone rang. It was C.T. Kale. "Any chance you could get me a demon blood sample?" he asked.

"Well there might be some dried stuff in the back of a car I have access to."

"A fresh tube of it would be better, but I'll take what you can get."

Bishop had a flash of the demon bar Ariel had taken him to. "I might be able to get you both. No promises."

"Sooner is better." C.T. hung up.

"Can I check the trunk of the Falcon?" Bishop asked. "I might have left something inside."

40

Ariel's living room was completely trashed: glass everywhere, blood on the mats. She couldn't face cleaning up. Her kitchen smelled like scorched noodles and melted linoleum. Somebody had cleaned up the blood and foam, scrubbed the blood off her table and put the noodle pot to soak in the sink. Probably Dingo.

She had just poured her first cup of coffee when Tomas' limped into the kitchen, her comforter wrapped around him, toga style.

"I smelled the coffee," he said.

"How are you feeling?"

"I think I have frost bite in unmentionable places, but other than that I'm good." He pulled the blanket aside and showed her his ribcage. He'd removed the bandages. The wound was still red and angry looking, but the skin had healed shut and the scar had the shiny look of a two-week-old incision. Acid burns and claw marks on his face, torso and arms showed bright pink against his dark skin.

Ariel pulled a chair up to the table, so he could sit down, and poured him a cup of black coffee. She topped up her own. "What are you doing here Tomas?"

"The Guardian sent me orders. He wanted me to take out Tesslovich.

"Really? And you didn't call me to ask why he asked you to do something like that in my territory?"

"I got the impression it was urgent, and you weren't available to handle it."

"And how'd that work out for you?"

Tomas winced, pulling the comforter closer around his body. "I scoped out his house. It looked pretty quiet. Two guys in the courtyard, couple of 'goyles on the gate pillars and some on the wall in the back. I thought it would be him and me and maybe a bodyguard or two. I got in through a balcony window. Place was lousy with demons. They were everywhere. It was like a demon convention and I walked right into the middle of it. And Tesslovich has a weapons collection you wouldn't believe. There was something on every wall. I had to fight my way out."

"And you brought their little monsters straight to me. Thanks so much."

"I'm sorry. I was trying to warn you."

"I came to you for help and you sent me packing."

"I didn't . . ."

Ariel's cell phone rang. "Sorry. I have to take this. I'm expecting an important update about the end of the world. Where are you, Bishop?"

"My office." Bishop sighed as he looked around.

The task force had tried to make a mess, but they were amateurs compared to whoever had left him the goat head. He'd put his remaining files in a storage cage in the basement after the first break-in. The cabinets in the office were empty, the computer was already gone, but the rusty blood stains were still very visible on the wood of the desk top. He was going to have to have that refinished. Or maybe he'd leave them. Let clients speculate on who had bled all over his desk and why.

"I called Susan Elizabeth's mother and she hasn't reappeared. I warned her to call me the minute she shows up. That there might be complications." Barbara Morgan's hope was heart wrenching. He wondered if calling her had been a good idea, but he didn't want a repeat of the Jennifer Corbin debacle.

"I'm a little busy here, Frank. Is there something else?"

"C.T. called wondering if we could bring him a fresh blood sample from a demon. Since you seem to have connections . . ."

"Demon blood? Are you serious?"

"What about Timmy John?"

"We relocated him to Tahiti, remember? For stealing the fight-night tickets."

"There must be somebody else at the Garden who'd be willing to give it up for cash."

"I think we have bigger problems right now."

"You know, I really hate that phrase."

"All right." Sigh. "Do you have your car? I'm going to break rule number three in the Raptor Rule Book and give you my address. If you meet some bikers on the way in, just tell them you know Ez."

"What's rule number one?" Bishop asked when Ariel opened her door.

"Never let a civilian know what you are."

"Too late for that, how about rule number two . . ."

Bishop caught sight of Tomas. He sat at the table wrapped in the quilt, one bicep circled by gauze. He was eating peanut butter toast with jam.

"Am I interrupting something?"

"Tomas is part of our new Guest Raptor program." Ariel said. "He tried to take Tesslovich out last night and got his ass kicked all the way to my backdoor."

Bishop raised his eyebrows. "Didn't El tell you what happened when she tried to kill him?"

Tomas gave El a narrow eyed 'who-the-hell-is-this?' stare. "There was some concern she might not have been as thorough as she could have been," he said.

"Thorough?" Bishop said. "She took his head straight off his shoulders. It bounced across the room. I was there, I saw it happen. Three days later he's back in court with a stiff neck."

"I guess I was misinformed." Tomas said through clenched teeth. "Why are we talking about this in front of a civilian?"

Ariel slammed down into her chair and leaned across the table. Bishop decided he was safer leaning against the sink. He'd said what he saw, and he was sticking to it.

"Do you have any idea what's really going on here, Tomas?"

"There seems to be a heavy infestation of demon activity in the area. They seem very organized." Tomas said.

"Organized? They're here to plan a takedown of the human race, you idiot! That's why all the kids are missing. Zaki Kiriyenko has been using them to test ways of engineering a demon super race."

"How do you know that?"

"I know people who know things like that, okay?"

"Him?"

"No, not him. Don't be silly."

"Standing right here," Bishop said, miffed.

"A scientist. Zaki's ex-partner. He's a biotech genius."

"Have you told the Guardian this?"

"The Guardian made it very clear that he's not interested in my opinion."

"So, a Raptor, a few wolves and a 'biotech genius' have decided to take on a bunch of super-demons by themselves?"

"I was hoping you'd help now that you're here."

"I'm helping." Bishop said, but no one was paying attention to him.

"Ariel, the Guardian called me in because he didn't think you could be trusted to follow orders. You can't bring other Raptors in on this without his permission."

"Well, I guess the old fart was right. I'm through waiting for him to get a clue. You haven't been here Tomas. You haven't seen Zaki's arena, or how he brutalizes these kids. You haven't seen that he's created a way for demons to achieve a world-wide domination of human beings. Maybe even an annihilation. The Guardian is used to having his Raptors take out a demon or two at a time, maybe a whole nest if they're threatening enough. They tip things in the wrong direction, we tip it back. Good balances out evil. Well, good and evil don't weigh the same anymore, Tomas. Evil is about to move all the weight to their end of the teeter-totter and we have a miniscule window of opportunity to stop that from happening."

"I need more proof than a bunch of well-dressed demons swilling champagne and trading stories about the good old days." Tomas countered.

"We'll take you to see our guy. He can show you proof. I need your help on this Tomas."

Tomas scrubbed at the unburned side of his face, His short copper dreads looked frayed. He was healing fast, but he had a way to go.

"Clothes?" he asked. "Weapons?"

"Dingo left jeans and a sweat shirt for you in the bathroom. There's soap and towels. If you need some help, let me know."

Bishop raised one eyebrow. It was a talent.

"Shut up." Ariel told him. "We'll be ready in a minute."

"And the plan is?"

She struck it off on her fingers as she headed for the bedroom. "Demon blood, C.T. Kale, rescue kids, kick some demon ass."

41

"That was quick." Bishop stopped his car across the street from the Seventh Circle to let Ariel out. It was late morning, but Ariel assured him that Hell never closed. When he was a kid, the parish priest had told him the same thing.

Ham had given Ariel a syringe and a special test tube that had preservative in it for the blood. He'd given her a general description of how to use it.

Bishop made a mental note to never let her try to stick a needle in him.

In five minutes Ariel was back in the front seat. "For twenty bucks, the guy drew it for me himself. Thought it was kinky. I hope the fact that the blood's fifty percent alcohol won't ruin the sample."

She held up the tube. It was the color of one of Timmy John's Grasshoppers without the bug garnish. "Guy was blasted. Hopefully he'll forget anyone asked him for this."

"Where are we going?" Tomas asked without enthusiasm.

"Underground. We have to be a lot more careful now. C.T. said we should take the eastbound train from Jefferson Station until someone tells us to get off."

After changing subway trains twice, the Deep's guide, who looked like a college student on her way to classes at the local university, eased them toward the end of the station platform and through an almost invisible opening in the wall. Once off the platform and into the tunnels she stopped and quickly assembled one of the Deep's automatic weapons, complete with infra-red scope, from pieces stored in her book bag. Then she gave Bishop a pair of night goggles that matched her own.

Bishop eyed the rifle. "We're going through the rat tunnels, aren't we?"

"Sorry." The guide swung the bag back over her shoulder. "We've stepped up security and the rats tend to discourage being followed. Last in line watches everybody's back."

"If they attack," Bishop promised. "I'll try not to scream like a girl. Although if one of us does scream, that will be me."

The girl gave him a grin and pushed the safety to full automatic.

"You guys armed?" Bishop asked Ariel and Tomas.

"Never leave home without something sharp and pointy," Tomas answered. "Are we expecting something larger than rats in these tunnels?"

"Demon activity has picked up in the last couple of days," the guide said. "They've got guards on the subway platform at Hauptmann's and Tesslovich has some kind of ogre guarding his stop on the line since last night. You never know how far demons may have penetrated the perimeter."

"Ogre?"

The Raptor waved a dismissive hand. "All muscle and no brains," she said. "They're used as guards and most of them moonlight as bouncers in the demon bars."

"Is that what that guy was?" Bishop was thinking about his

first trip to The Seventh Circle with Ariel. "I thought he was just big and really, really ugly."

"They have the brains and vocabulary of a house pet. If one of them attacks you, just throw something shiny and yell 'fetch!'"

"I'm only a private detective you know," Bishop said, glancing sideways at Tomas. "Maybe I should write that down."

42

Cassius received their little group in his study. The walls were paneled in dark wood and lined with bookshelves. It was as if the entire room had been transported from some old mansion or exclusive gentleman's club to the Deeps. Some books looked really old, others seemed to be about history, or technology, but a whole shelf was full of popular novels. A few reference books and unrolled maps were open on the large table in the middle of the room. The floor was covered in old, but impressive looking oriental rugs, and the chairs were deep and inviting. There was even a fireplace, though it burned gas instead of wood.

"Wow." Ariel said.

"Our scavengers got the room from an old house that was being torn down," the guide explained. "Seemed a shame to let it go to waste. Here's your guests, C.T. I'll see ya' later in the 'sitch room."

Cassius was at his desk with his head down, typing something into his laptop. "Sorry, I'll be done in a second." Then he looked up. Several expressions moved across his face in rapid succession. He stopped typing and stood up with an unexpected suddenness.

Ariel put her hands out. "It's okay, Tomas is a Raptor. He has important information that we thought you should hear."

"Tomas?" Cassius came around the desk and held out his hand, his eyes never left the Raptor's face. "Your---addition to the guest list startled me that's all. Welcome to the Deeps."

"Nice to meet you," Tomas said. "This is some place you have here."

"It wouldn't have been my first choice, but I've gotten used to it. Being down here gives me more quiet time to do my research. What happened to your face?"

"Goyle blood. I tried to get Tesslovich last night. Never came close. I was stabbed and shot up pretty good. Ariel and her friends saved my life. But I may have stirred up a hornet's nest by accident."

"Tesslovich's house was full of demons," Ariel said.

"What does 'full' mean?"

"A lot," Tomas said. "Thirty, forty, it was hard to tell. Everyone was dressed up as if it was a special occasion."

"Then it's begun" Cassius waved everyone to a seat and leaned against the front edge of his desk. "We've noticed more cars parked in the Hauptman garage, more activity on the subway platforms, guards patrolling the tunnels nearby. Zaki is about to unveil his master work."

"Ariel told me if I came along I'd find out what's about to happen and what you plan on doing about it."

"First the bad news." Cassius went back behind his desk and tapped a key. A section of bookcase pivoted around revealing a flat screen.

"What are we looking at?" Bishop asked.

"Blood chemistry. The numbers on the left are the boy you and the Sister rescued. The next column is Jennifer Corbin's blood sample. And the third is the blood from the adolescent Ariel found badly beaten after his bout in the arena. Luckily, we have connections in the coroner's office. All samples are off the charts for steroids. Cortisol levels, which show the body's reaction to extreme stress, run from two hundred to over four hundred. The blood also contains a variety of toxic byproducts including a mutant form of e-coli. According to her sample, I would postulate that Jennifer Corbin was in a state of toxic steroid rage when she went after her family. She may not have even known who she was killing.

"The boy in the hospital was headed in the same direction. Plus, he was in a dangerous state of alkalosis that would have short circuited his nervous system within a few hours. I can't imagine the demons thought he would be found alive. They probably hoped finding his body would distract and confuse the task force.

"We also isolated some of the nanites in their blood. My techs were able to disassemble them. There are at least two distinct types."

A new picture appeared. Nanites the size of Tonka toys prowled the screen. Some had a golden carapace with a flagellum for a tail. Others were transparent, lit up like small, blue neon insects allowing the observer to see tiny circuit boards inside their shells.

"Of course, they're magnified thousands of times on the screen. Each one is smaller than the size of a molecule which allows them to travel freely around the body through the circulatory system. An appropriately programmed nanite has the ability to manipulate and rearrange the body's mechanisms so it can go everywhere it wants and do whatever it needs to do; repair cell damage, stop the aging process, prevent death by natural causes or severe physical trauma. Run by ultramicroscopic computers they can operate independently or be networked into a master server that tells them what to do. Considering how little energy they consume, scientists think that nanites might be programmed to last for hundreds, even thousands of years."

"That's a scary thought," Tomas said. "Especially under the circumstances."

"Well, to be truly successful any nanite has to be non-toxic to the host. Zaki used my model of carbon atoms bonded into tiny spheres and coated with 24 carat gold to avoid toxicity. Unfortunately, he's expanded that concept to engineer compatibility with demon physiology by creating a molecular vehicle made out of a previously unknown acid resistant material with an unidentified bacterial propulsion system. This material seems to attract, or even manufacture proteins that eventually become toxic to the humans who carry it.

"Those blue nanites make the body stronger, faster, more aggressive, the gold nanites repair the cell damage caused by toxicity and trauma. But eventually the healer nanites can't keep up with the constant rearrangement of molecules necessary to keep a human body alive. Serious injury doesn't get repaired, mutations occur, toxicity increases, internal organ systems start to fail causing physical as well as mental symptoms. This may not happen in demons. The proteins the demon nanites produce might have beneficial effects for them, and their nanites have been built for survival in a highly acid environment that already contains poisons toxic to humans like arsenic, strychnine and chlorine. Gold is also impervious to acid so the healer nanites are compatible for use in demons."

"So, this is going to make them much harder to kill?" Tomas asked.

"Consider the fact that Tesslovich himself not only survived a nanite infusion, they saved his life when Ariel beheaded him. The only permanent solution may be to dismember the carriers and burn the bodies at high temperature until there's nothing left."

"You said you wanted a sample of demon blood to see how the nanites react to it." Ariel said.

Bishop pulled a crumpled paper bag out of his pocket. "This is a piece of carpet that has blood on it from a dead demon. I'm afraid it's a few days old."

"I got a fresh tube." Ariel held it out. "My guy was pretty drunk, but it's the standard green stuff, nothing exotic. I think he was a lesser Strixian, they're easily addicted to all kinds of drugs and they'll do anything for a few bucks."

"If you don't mind I'd also like a sample of Raptor blood."

Cassius pushed a button on his desk. A young man opened the door holding a plastic carrier filled with tubes, packages of syringes,

"No problem," Ariel said, starting to roll up her sleeve.

"Actually, I'd prefer blood from Tomas. He's been injured recently and that means his immune system is highly activated. That would give me a chance to analyze Raptor blood and its physiological response to injury."

Tomas shrugged and rolled up his sleeve.

- 43 -

Mouser woke up back in a plastic cell. It wasn't in the same place he'd been put when first abducted, it was in the grey man's lab. The clear Plexiglas wall of the cell was flush with the other walls of the room but had been hidden by a sliding panel.

Mouser didn't remember anyone bringing him mice for dinner, but he did remember being hit with a dart and falling off his perch in the cage. He'd lost consciousness before hitting the floor.

Now he was back in human form, naked and very thirsty. A fresh set of clothing had been left on his bunk. They resembled the scrubs that doctors wore. His were orange, the same color prisoners wore in county jail. The waist of the trousers had a draw string and he had to tie it tight then roll the excess cloth over several times to keep from tripping on the cuffs. A sandwich wrapped in plastic and a bottle of water had been left on the floor just inside the cell. He tore into them, chugging the water followed by a ravenous attack on the sandwich.

When he finished eating, he threw himself on the bunk. He'd blown it! He'd revealed his secret, his ace in the hole. They'd never give him the opportunity to escape now. He'd just become another lab rat.

He looked at the crease in his left arm. There it was, a fresh needle hole. Had they put something in, or taken blood out?

Ariel had promised him she'd always watch his back. Where was she now? He'd thought of her as a super hero, like in one of the comics he shoplifted from the local bookstore. Someone who came to the aid of people at the mercy of diabolical villains.

What was more diabolical than this? If she didn't hurry, when she finally found him he'd be dead.

There was another knock on the door of Cassius' office. A young man poked his head into the room and announced, "Captain Greggs has his group assembled in the situation room."

"Thank you, Neal. Tell them we'll be there in a minute." Cassius looked at Bishop and the two Raptors. "I've been planning for something like this to happen for a couple of years now. I didn't know exactly what the event would be, but I thought someday the Deeps would need to defend itself. It doesn't surprise me that Zaki is involved, I just didn't expect he'd have demons as allies."

"Is it possible Zaki is a demon himself?" Ariel asked.

"He certainly acts like one. I never suspected it if it's true. I thought he was just a sociopathic thief and murderer. He killed my wife, you know."

"We know," Ariel told him. "Your wife and your son. I'm sorry."

"Not my son. They found his blood but no body. I have faith he's still alive, but I've never been able to find him." He looked at Tomas. "He'd be about your age now, but that's a problem, for another day. Let's see what we can do to ruin Zaki's plans."

The situation room had more space, larger screens than the study and a shallow platform at one end. About forty men and women of various ages were sitting on an eclectic collection of chairs, stools and benches, or standing in groups waiting to be briefed. An undercurrent of anticipation moved through the gathering when Cassius appeared.

Cassius introduced his security chief Mallory Greggs to Bishop, Ariel and Tomas as an Iraq war veteran and former Army Ranger. Greggs introduced his sector chiefs, scouts, and soldiers, then turned the process back to Cassius for the various scientists, techies and engineers. It was news to nobody that demons were the enemy and they'd finally crossed the line.

Someone had erected a war board. Maps of the Deeps were pinned up as sequentially as possible. Some were just sketches of unmapped territory that had been enlarged and taped together to give a larger picture.

Jorge McCullen, the engineer, raised a hand. "Bringin' in the train tonight, sir. Close as I can get it to a place where we can load up without the demons noticin'."

"Guns are mounted," Greggs said. "We have small arms and automatic weapons for about forty of us. The rest have cross bows, swords and a few sling shots. My explosives expert is cooking up some surprises, plus we have enough C4 to blow the buildings if we put it in the right places."

"Our people will ride the train," Cassius said, pointing out the route. "Through the Hauptmann station, down the tunnel past Tesslovich's platform and past the steam trap to the underground entrance to the arena and the labs. We don't know what we'll encounter here," he tapped the map where the track ended. "But we'll probably have to stop behind Zaki's train. That will block their escape route back down the tracks, but it means we'll have further to go until we're in the building. We've tapped into their cameras in the tunnel. We'll run a loop, so they don't see us coming. Sometimes large animals or the occasional homeless person sets off the steam trap. We have some footage of that happening that we've cut into the loop so when the trap goes off they won't suspect they're about to be under attack."

"Large animals?" Bishop asked.

"Coyote, deer, raccoons, other---things."

"I expect we'll encounter security force resistance," Greggs added. "Some human, some not. We can't worry about the distinction. We're hoping to keep the fighting confined to the arena, but there will be staff and guards at the front gate and in other buildings. A special team will escort the tech crew into the labs."

"What about the prisoners?"

"Extraction teams will find them and get them to the train. We won't know who's human and who's a ringer until we have more time to sort them out, so we're not bringing them back here. We'll take them to a holding area and infirmary we set up below the old fire station on the south side.

"Tomas and I will round up as much air support as we can," Ariel added. "We have some other resources as well although they'll be on the ground. As soon as we clear the front gate we'll let them in and re-block that exit. Nobody shoots a wolf, okay?" She made sure she held Gregg's gaze for a few seconds.

"Some of Tesslovich's visitors have already been taken to the estate by train using his entrance to the tracks." Cassius said. "More will go in the same way tomorrow. Others will come by car, maybe even by boat or helicopter. We think Zaki's going to be using the big screens in the arena to show off the bots and make his pitch. His customers will want proof before they buy so I anticipate he'll have an exhibition match or two.

"He has a satellite hook-up, which means if he's broadcasting to demons in other parts of the globe we can intercept the signal and see and hear what he's saying."

Greggs took over. "I imagine he's wining and dining his investors tonight. Sort of pre-sale congrats fest. He had about a semi-truck's worth of wine and liquor delivered day before yesterday and plenty of demon delicacies that tend toward the raw and disgusting. After the ruckus last night Tesslovich tripled his guard for himself and those who are still at his place. I guess they're the ones who are here to buy, not sell.

A special squad will break off and go for the prisoners. Science and tech will go for his servers, the object being to copy what we can, then corrupt and destroy his data. It's a closed system and this is the only way we can get to it. Tech has rounded up and checked out most of the coms we've been using in the Deeps. They'll be handed out to squad leaders and various other key combatants, so we'll be able to communicate with each other. As soon as we've gotten the prisoners out we'll start blowing the buildings. You'll have floor plans and pictures of some of the missing kids but be careful. As I said, there may be ringers in the bunch."

"Particularly one called Lena," Ariel said. "She's tough, she's vicious and I'd bet anything she's a demon."

"We're going to get Zaki and Tesslovich on this one, people. Study their pictures, we can't let them escape. Once this starts they may try to make it to the lake. Zaki has a couple of fast boats docked there and a helicopter pad on site."

"How much other support can we expect?" A woman in the crowd asked.

"So far, two Raptors four werewolves and a civilian," Ariel told her. "We're hoping for more and we'll bring what arms we have. Warning: Tesslovich has a collection of ancient demon blades. His guests may or may not be allowed to bring them onto the estate. If they do, be careful. They may look old and no match for modern arms, but they can poison anyone they cut."

"After we leave here," Tomas said. "Ariel and I will be going to see the Guardian. We don't know what his priorities are at this point but we're going to try to convince him to help."

"Is this your whole army?" Bishop asked Cassius as he looked around.

"There are at least twenty or thirty more who aren't in this room," Greggs said. "We've sent the word out and may get a few outliers signing on. We also have quite a few pissed off kids who want to go fight, but we're not taking anybody under sixteen on this mission. Plus, a few of our soldiers need to stay here to guard the Deeps, just in case."

"I'd like permission to have Sister Mary Catherine from the runaway shelter taken to the infirmary," Bishop said. "She knows a lot of the missing and can help identify them. Plus, she'll have me excommunicated if I don't get her in on the rescue."

"We'll send a car for her."

"We all have things to do before tomorrow," Ariel said. "The three of us need to get topside. We'll stay in touch through Kale.net. If the Guardian won't back us up you still have Tomas, me and the wolves."

"And me," Bishop said. "Standing right here." It was beginning to feel like his mantra.

One of the runners made his way through the crowd and handed a piece of paper to Cassius, who motioned Bishop over.

"Mr. Bishop, I think you should know that the blood on the carpet you gave me was human."

"Nanites?"

"No."

Bishop shook his head. "Any insight on why a human being who's been shot dead twice won't stay down?"

Cassius shrugged. "Maybe you're dealing with more than one guy."

PART III

"Hello?"

Mouser raised his head. The voice was young, light, female.

"Hello?" he said.

"Where am I?" the voice asked. "I think they moved me while I was asleep. I don't know this place."

Mouser put his mouth up to the holes in the Plexiglas. "Where were you before?"

"In the Angel Dorm," the voice told him. "With the other younger kids. I was trying really hard to get it right, so I could go home."

"What were they asking you to do?" Mouser asked.

"Take the medicine to make me strong. I tried to be strong, but other kids got chosen over me."

"Chosen for what?"

"To learn to be angels. To help save the world and then go home. I want to go home, why didn't they pick me?"

"They did choose you." Mouser said. "They've chosen me too. But they aren't angels."

"What are they?" the little voice asked

"Bad people," Mouser told her. "People you shouldn't trust. People who are definitely not angels." He paused, he didn't want to scare her. "What's your name?"

"Susan Elisabeth Morgan," the voice came back. "My mom calls me Suzee with two e's. I'm almost six, and I'm really, really scared."

- 2 -

"If you want we can meet later tonight at my place, Frank. Tomas and I just have this errand to do before we come back."

"I have an errand of my own," Bishop said as Ariel and Tomas piled out of his car in front of the Guardian Building. "We need everyone we can get, right?"

"Four o'clock tomorrow. We'll leave from my apartment, unless you want to go in on the train."

"I'd rather stick with people I know. I'll go in with you and the Dogs."

"Frank," Ariel said. "You don't have to do this. Tomas and I, it's what we're meant to do, but you . . ."

"It's my world too, El. You think now I know what's going on I can just pull the covers over my head and ignore it?"

"It would be the smart thing to do."

"There you go," Bishop said. "Of all the people who know me, the only one expecting me to make an intelligent choice is you."

"See you tomorrow, Frank."

Bishop watched her follow Tomas through the revolving doors of the Guardian Building as the sun slid down its facade like a receding tide, leaving shadows in its wake.

- 3 -

Bishop's cell phone rang. He looked at the number. It was Rain, just the person he was thinking of calling.

"Rainman," Bishop said.

"Bro," Rain said, his voice low and guarded. "Just listen. The taskforce issued a warrant for your arrest."

"For what?"

"Four counts of Murder One. They found your finger prints at the Corbin house. The coroner says a girl Jennifer's size couldn't possibly have done the amount of damage they found on the bodies, let alone on the house. They think she had help."

"Are they crazy? Sure, I was at the Corbin house, I was interviewing the family because I'm working a similar case. What possible reason would I have to kill the Corbin family let alone leave Jennifer behind as a witness?"

"Jennifer's brain was totally blown, Frank. They'll say, why not leave her there? She was hysterical, covered in blood and not tellin' anybody anything except how she was going to rip out their entrails and piss in their eyes an' other crazy stuff. Then there's that body they found in the trunk of your car."

"It was a loaner. I didn't put a body in the trunk. I can't

believe you think I'm running around out here killing people, Rain."

"I don't, but Lieutenant Martin does and he's the one with the warrant. It'd be better if you turn yourself in man, get a lawyer, work this through."

"I can't do that right now. Not for a day or so. People are depending on me. If it all works out," or not, "the warrant won't be an issue anymore. You have to trust me on this."

"Really, Frank…"

"One last favor for old time's sake. Did you ever get a fingerprint match on the knife in the goat head?"

"That's the other thing, man. The prints match the missing dead guy in the Falcon's trunk. He was apparently part of a knife throwing act in a visiting Romanian circus. He jumped his visa three years ago along with his two brothers. But here's the kicker . . ."

"Yeah?"

"The brothers—they're triplets."

Bishop hung up. If the warrant had just been issued he still had maybe an hour to get off the street. Going home wasn't an option. He could probably make it to Ariel's, but they'd have his license plate and a description of his car. Unless he could hide the car fairly quickly it could lead them right to Ariel and the Dogs.

He was closest to the Caf'. He'd park the car a few blocks away, check in with Ez and let him know what was happening, then catch an Uber to Ariel's neighborhood. There wouldn't be an APB until the cops had spent a few hours looking for him with no success.

He pulled over to the curb. It was a four-block walk. He was dressed in jeans, a t-shirt and his old leather jacket. He always carried a couple of hats in his trunk and two or three different colored t-shirts in case he had to follow someone.

Bishop rummaged through the archaeological layers of stuff in his car trunk. He threw a bag of half-eaten, totally forgotten and petrified fast food over his shoulder, then felt guilty about it. He decided to retrieve it and throw it into the first trash can he came to.

First he chose a red ball cap then stuffed a clean navy-blue t-shirt into his jacket pocket to change into at the Caf'. He was about to reach up and shut the trunk lid when a stabbing pain hit him in the back of the neck. A quick shove from an unseen assailant and he tumbled forward, halfway into the trunk, tongue numb, limbs useless, body spasming uncontrollably.

Someone leaned over him and fumbled under his jacket, checking to see if he had a gun. Bishop managed to control the fluttering in his eyelids long enough to see Lieutenant Martin straighten up and pocket his Glock.

"Give him the shot," Martin said. "The Taser's starting to wear off."

Another figure took Martin's place. He was shorter with black hair. He smelled faintly of garlic and grease and some other spice Bishop couldn't identify. Worst of all he was wearing a badly-made yellow and black stripped suit and holding a syringe. He smiled an ugly little, brown toothed smile and jammed the syringe into Bishop's leg. The last thing Bishop heard before everything went black was a low, evil chuckle.

- 4 -

Ariel and Tomas straight armed the revolving door and blew by the guard station in the lobby, headed for the elevators.

"Hey!" the guard yelled. "You can't do that! I'm calling upstairs."

"Emergency," Ariel called over her shoulder. Tomas held the elevator door open for her and followed her in before the guard could lift the phone.

"There's a camera in here," Tomas remarked. "They'll see us coming."

"Good," was all Ariel had to say. She pulled her boots off and shoved them into the pockets of her coat. Her toes flexed, claws scratching on the marble of the elevator floor.

Tomas glanced at her feet then up at her face, a slightly puzzled expression on his face.

"We're having this conversation as Raptors," she said. "Maybe he'll listen to what we stand for, even if he won't listen to us."

The doors opened. The Wolverine was standing behind her desk, outrage radiating from every pore. "This is totally unacceptable!" She snapped. "The Guardian is very busy and cannot be disturbed."

"Really?" Ariel leaned over the desk and pushed the intercom button. "Two Raptors to see you, Sir. It's about the end of the world. They thought you might want details."

There was a pause, followed by a testy voice. "As long as you're here, Ariel, you might as well come up."

Ariel gave the Wolverine a tight smile and got a glare in return.

Brother Gregory was scuttling down the stairs from the Guardian's Tower, robe flapping, hem swishing as it slid from one step to the next.

"This is most irregular," he was saying over and over, ringing his hands. "The Guardian is extremely displeased with this intrusion."

"Then maybe you'd better stay down here where it's safe, Greg. We wouldn't want you caught in the middle, would we?"

Ariel tilted her head back and forth like she was working out a kink. Her wings blossomed from the vents in the back of her coat but stayed furled against her sides, their tops rose above her shoulders like a collar of sable colored feathers.

Tomas sighed. In for a penny. His wings tore through the back of his sweat shirt. He spread the right one slightly, examining the place where the feathers had been broken. They were as smooth and black as the rest of his wing.

Brother Gregory pressed his body against the banister, letting them pass. "Oh, dear," he said, mostly to himself. "This is entirely against protocol. Entirely against it!"

∼

The Guardian stood behind his desk with his back to the door staring out the tall windows at the city below. His suit was a muted brown. His hands were clasped behind his back, his arms mimicking Raptor wings.

Mine are bigger than yours.

This sort of pose used to make Ariel feel small and inadaquate, now she was just pissed.

By unspoken agreement she and Tomas stood quietly, waiting him out. She knew when he finally turned he would act mildly surprised to see they were already in the room.

But this time there was no surprise, merely annoyance.

"Both of you?" He said, as if disobedience was contagious like the flu. "Tomas, I'm extremely disappointed."

"I'm afraid Ariel is right, Sir. There's much more going on than meets the eye."

The Guardian shook his head. "One simple kill---"

"Not a simple kill," Ariel told him. "Tesslovich can't be killed by usual means. He's been treated with a new technology that allows him to regenerate, even after decapitation. He did it after I killed him. He can do it again."

The Guardian frowned. "You're telling me that a demon has discovered a way to sustain his life even when mortally wounded."

"Not necessarily a demon," Tomas said. "He's a biotechnologist named Zaki Kiriyenko. He invented the process and is more than willing to sell it to demons on a large scale. Scions from many of the first families are already gathering to bid on it. Tesslovich is in the thick or it. He's either Zaki's partner or his connection to the demon Familia. At any rate, he'll have a lot to gain from both sides. He's heavily guarded and surrounded by powerful demons waiting to see Zaki's product."

"Tesslovich has been very careful about this," Ariel added. "The demons slipped into town a few at a time. Some are already staying with Tesslovich or on the Zaki estate. The big unveiling is tomorrow night in Zaki's arena, complete with satellite link and surround sound."

"And if this so-called technology spreads into the demon population . . .?" The Guardian asked.

"We won't be able to kill them," Tomas said. "They can use this invention to regenerate, overwhelm opposition and enslave every human on earth. It's their dream come true."

"Coincidently," Ariel said. "Zaki has also been experimenting on humans. Kidnapping runaways and injecting them with nanobots to see what happens. Eventually the demon bots kill their human host, but not before the host goes insane. I don't think that was his original intention. I think Tesslovich encouraged him to infect and program children to go back to their families and wait for some signal to do something to help the demons."

"Reports are coming in about missing children being returned unharmed with some story about angels." The Guardian said.

Ariel nodded. "One has already killed her whole family. I think she knew she wasn't an angel. I think she was so damaged she didn't care."

The Guardian had been pacing for the last several minutes. He stopped. "When is this auction happening?"

"Tomorrow evening."

"That's very little time."

"Tomas and I have joined forces with the Deeps. Their people are going into Zaki's estate through an old subway tunnel built by old man Hauptmann back in the twenties. Tomas and I will attack from the air."

"Just the two of you?" The Guardian asked dryly.

Ariel shrugged. "It's better than none of us. We have a few wolves signed on, but there will be lots of demons. I have no idea if there are other Raptors close enough to get there before this goes down. That would certainly change the odds. The important thing is to try and stop them before it's too late. That's what we're here for right?"

"Why didn't you tell me about this before now?" The Guardian demanded."

Ariel turned and started for the stairs, Tomas close behind. "I tried," she said. "You wouldn't listen."

"That went well," Tomas said, his voice brimming with sarcasm. "I thought we were going to ask for help?"

"You don't ask The Guardian for help. It has to be his idea. If demons win this one, it's going to be his fault. That doesn't change anything for us, we're going to try and stop them anyway. Right?"

"Ours is not to reason why, ours is but to do or die," Tomas quoted.

"What?"

"Alfred Lord Tennyson. Charge of the Light Brigade. Classic Movie Channel."

"You mean you think we're gonna die without The Guardian's help, but you're still with me on this?"

"Right."

Bishop came back to consciousness with a bad taste in his mouth and the mother of all headaches. It didn't help that he was, once again, duct taped to a chair. He promised himself if he ever met the guy who invented duct tape, he was going to punch his lights out.

When he finally managed to raise his head, he discovered he was in some sort of home office. The walls were paneled with wood and lined with shelves of law books, and there was an incredibly tasteless, but very expensive wooden desk whose top seemed to be supported by naked maenads with clawed animal feet.

Unfortunately, there was also a medical examination table with a restraining strap hanging from each corner. The ugly little man in the striped suit was standing in front of the table poking through the former contents of Bishop's pockets and examining his cell phones. Bishop's gun, still in its shoulder rig, was tantalizingly close but out of reach for a man whose wrists, torso and legs had been thoroughly taped to a chair.

"What's this?" The little man asked, holding up the Kale.net cell phone.

"I'm on call for the circus freak eradication program. It's part of the new effort to Make America Great Again."

The little man took a step forward and casually backhanded Bishop across the face with the hand that wasn't holding the phone. He didn't bother to look away from the open phone.

Déjà vu all over again, Bishop thought, spitting a little saliva mixed with blood at the little man's feet. He missed.

The little man was pushing buttons on the key pad with his thumb. "Why doesn't it work?" He asked.

Bishop shrugged. "Sunspots?" He wasn't going to tell him that it took his finger print to activate a call. Everyone on his call list was safe, at least for now.

"This one works." The little man held up Bishop's personal cell phone.

"Yeah," Bishop said. "Push three. The person on the other end is just dying to meet you."

"Who's El?" Bishop had put Ariel's name and cell number in both phones, just in case.

"Tesslovich introduced her to one of your brothers. She tried to teach him to fly but he wasn't a quick learner."

"The Raptorrrrr." Bishop was surprised that even a person with a thick Romanian accent could roll an R out quite that long and with such venom.

"I push three, she answers me, yes?"

"Probably, unless she's having her nails sharpened or something. You know how women are about their claws."

"She answers, maybe I put on speaker phone and she listen to me make you scream and beg Connie for mercy."

"Your name is 'Connie?'" Bishop asked, feigning disbelief.

The little man drew himself up to his complete height, which was about the same height as Bishop sitting in the chair.

"Is Constantine, very old, very famous Romany name."

"Connie," Bishop snorted. "In this country that's a girl's name."

Connie hit Bishop again. Bishop wanted to tell him he hit like a girl, but he was too busy counting his teeth with his tongue.

- 6 -

When Ariel and Tomas arrived at Ariel's apartment building it was full dark. Light was showing through the cracks around the Dog's Garage door and the sound of muted activity invited Ariel to knock on the smaller side door so that she and Tomas could bring the Dogs up to speed. An eye appeared briefly at the peep hole, then Ez opened the door.

"Ez. This is Tomas."

"Heard of you," Ez said, shaking Tomas' hand. "You're the combat trainer, right?"

"And visiting Raptor," Tomas said with a smile. "I've heard of you too."

"Come on in. I guess you've already met the rest of the pack."

Tomas looked around. The wall on one side of the garage had been rolled open. Inside a shallow alcove, weapons of various sizes and shapes were hanging on wall to wall black peg boards. The arsenal was impressive in both its quantity and variety.

Dingo stood in a chest-deep hole in the floor handing Ham and Juke automatic rifles, hand guns and artillery that looked very much like Mk32 MGL grenade launchers and possibly a bazooka or two.

Hey, guys," Tomas said. "I never got a chance to thank you for saving my ass last night."

The Dogs each raised a hand in acknowledgement but kept at their task.

"Holy crap," Ariel stared at the stash. "I'm glad you guys are on our side."

"Tooth and claw is all very well," Ez told her. "But werewolves have to move with the times."

"That's it," Dingo said, huffing a box of grenades over the edge of the pit onto the floor.

Juke reached down and gave him a hand out of the hole. "Is it bite, then shoot, Ez? Or shoot then bite?" He said. "I keep forgetting."

Ham tossed a combination automatic weapon and grenade launcher to Tomas. Tomas grabbed it out of the air and began checking it over. "Sweet!" he said. "What's its range?"

"Fifteen hundred yards," Ham told him. "More if you're aiming down."

Juke walked over to Ariel holding a double holster shoulder rig and two handguns. "I modified the rig to accommodate your wings. These have an eleven-shot clip filled with demon loads. The loops in the front hold extra clips." He turned toward Tomas. "I have one for you too." Ariel tried hers on.

"Also, Kevlar vests," Juke said.

Dingo rooted around in a trunk and pulled out various sizes of black Kevlar.

"If we jerk the straps tight," he said. "This one should fit you." He tossed a vest toward Ariel.

He looked at Tomas. "You're more standard issue, so no problem. The back of the vest leaves your shoulder blades free in case you need to get a wing on."

Ariel fussed with her rig. "I don't want to wear a vest."

Tomas examined his vest. "Will this stop a knife or a sword?" he asked.

"It has a layer of titanium mesh between the layers of Kevlar. That should do it."

"But . . ." Ariel started.

"Angel Slayers?" Tomas reminded her, "Plus, Zaki's security force will probably be shooting at us from the ground. Wear the vest."

Ariel bristled at being ordered around, but a look from Ez made her turn her reaction into a shrug. "Fine." She said. "I'll wear mine if everybody else wears one."

Tomas looked at Ham." Um," he said. "Wolves in vests?"

"Only 'til the shooting stops." Dingo dumped an armful of black vests that looked like something a doting pet owner would put on his poodle for a walk in the rain if the poodle happened to be working for Blackwater in Iraq.

"The demons would have to have silver bullets anyway," Ez said. "Getting shot with regular bullets would slow us down, maybe take us out of the action, but not kill us."

"I don't think Zaki is expecting wolves," Ham said. "But you never know. He might have munitions for all contingencies."

"That's more than four vests," Ariel said.

"Yeah, that's the next thing. We have two more packs coming in tonight. The Rabid Road Dogs and a bunch that just call themselves 'The Pack'. That will bring our number up to about twenty-five wolves."

"Aren't the Rabid Road Dogs all lawyers and CPAs?" Ez asked.

"And you're an engineer, so what's your point?" Juke asked.

"An engineer can take a CPA any day!"

"Chill." Ham said. "We're all wolves and we need all the fur we can get. Besides, I saw the Road Dogs do some pretty severe damage to a bunch of investment bankers at an office picnic one time. Remember, most of them are vets since that kind of service runs in the wolf line."

"Dingo raised a hand. "I solemnly swear not to growl, bite or pee on another wolf's bike until we win. Then the pee will be mostly beer."

Ariel's cell phone rang. She fished it out of her pocket. "Bishop?"

"Not Bishop," the voice on the other end said. "Although Mr. Bishop is right here and would love to say some few words to you. This phone is using speaker. Please to do that with yours so we can, as you Americans say, fully communicate."

"Ariel switched her phone to speaker. "Who the hell is this?"

"Patience, Raptorrr," the voice said. There was a sound like a sharp slap, a grunt, then Bishop's slightly slurred voice yelling, "Fuck you, you little mutant! I'm going to sue your dwarf ass off when I get out of here. Don't try to find me, El! There's more imp . . ."

There was the sound of a chair crashing over and nothing more from Bishop.

"I think Mr. Bishop has become temporarily unconscious," the voice said. "And I am not dwarf."

"Who are you? What do you want?" Ariel yelled.

"Revenge," the voice said. "Long, very painful revenge. First Mr. Bishop, then you Raptorrr. I am professional with knifes, you know. And fists. A man can die, slowly, slowly from many cuts and bruises. It can take days. Sleep well Raptorrrr. We stay in touch."

～

Ariel looked at her phone. "First Mouser, now Bishop. I am profoundly pissed."

"Zaki has him?" Ez asked.

"Not Zaki. If it was Zaki Bishop would have said something about kids. I think he's at Casa Tesslovich."

"Who was that on the phone?"

"A knife throwing, mutant Romanian Gypsy who works for Tesslovich. Bishop and I have tried to kill him twice, but he keeps bouncing back. He put a gypsy death curse on Bishop that seemed to have something to do with furniture and a goat head. But mostly he's mad because I blew his ass out a nine-story window after I tried to kill his boss."

"Sounds complicated, and a little kinky." Juke said.

"Are we going after Bishop?" Dingo asked.

"You bet your furry butts we are, but timing is important. We have to wait until the demon express leaves Tesslovich Station. Too soon and we walk in on a bunch of well-armed demons. Too late and we miss the party at Zaki's estate."

"Can Bishop last until tomorrow afternoon?" Tomas asked.

"Revenge is either really fast or slow and deliberate." Ez said. "I think we have a methodical revenge practitioner here. He'll draw it out, make it last. Bishop was a soldier and a cop. He's tougher than he looks. He can make it, but it won't be pleasant."

"And the mutant?"

"First I'm going to kill him." Ariel said. "Then I'm going to kill him again. Then I'm going to set fire to his remains. Then I'm going to scatter his ashes over running water until every molecule of his being sinks to the bottom of the lake to be eaten by snails and fishes."

Tomas looked at his sister Raptor. Ariel's face was all sharp planes, set mouth, jutting chin and cheek bones. It was pale with fatigue, but limned on the edges with an angry scarlet flush

"Jeeze," he said. "If we live through this, remind me to stop pissing you off."

- 7 -

"Suzee?" Mouser was sitting wedged in the front corner of his cell where his cage met Susan Elizabeth Morgan's. His mouth was pressed against a hole in the Plexiglas. "Are you awake?"

"I can't sleep," the small voice said. "I'm too afraid."

"Are you warm enough?"

"I have my blanket and they gave me a pillow. I'd rather be in this corner where I can hear you than in my bed."

"Me too," Mouser said, trying to convince himself that he was on the floor wrapped in a blanket rather than trying to sleep on the narrow shelf-like bed in his cell because Suzee was five, and he was fourteen and he had a responsibility to comfort her. In truth, he valued her small voice in the darkness as much as she valued his fake bravado and reassurances.

"Do you think your parents miss you?" Suzee asked.

"I don't know who my parents are," Mouser said. "But I'm sure your parents are doing everything they can to find you. I know for a fact they hired a private detective to help them. I met him. He's really good at finding people. Also, a friend of mine, she's like a superhero with wings. She defends kids like us against bad angels and evil scientists. I know she won't stop until she finds us and gets us out of here."

"She has wings?"

"Yes. Beautiful wings. I've seen her fly. She's very fierce and she cares about all the kids who've disappeared."

"So, she's a real, true angel?"

"Absolutely," Mouser said. "The real thing, with a fiery sword and everything."

"I hope she hurries," Susan Elizabeth said with a quaver in her voice. "I don't know how long I can stay brave. Sometimes I cry."

An unwelcome, embarrassing tear rolled down Mouser's cheek. "Don't cry," he said. "We can help each other stay brave. If you can't sleep, I'll tell you a story. I know a lot of them."

"Okay."

"Once upon a time in a land far, far away there was a brave princess named Suzee . . ."

Consciousness came slowly. The pain came right along with it, reminding Bishop why he'd passed out in the first place. He was hoping to do that again very soon, and with minimum preamble. Although his head was still fuzzy and lolling on his chest, he could hear Connie moving around.

The room door opened and shut. Then two sets of footsteps crossed the carpet. A hand grabbed his face by the chin and lifted up his head.

Bishop blinked. His eyelids seemed to be working in slow motion, one of them wasn't cooperating with the other. That probably had to do with the last punch he'd taken.

Lieutenant Martin turned Bishop's face from side to side, examining its condition. He seemed pleased with Connie's workmanship.

Nicolai Tesslovich was standing a few steps away, probably to avoid getting blood on his suit. "Has he told you how to find the Raptor yet?"

"He's harder to convince than Connie thought," the little man said.

Bishop hated people who talked about themselves in the third person. Since he really, really hated Connie, it wasn't much of a stretch to add that little quirk to the shit list he was building against him. When he finally killed the little mutant, he wouldn't feel a shred of guilt. It would be a public service.

"He's bleeding on my rug. This carpet was six hundred dollars a yard."

"Is red," Connie said. "Nobody notice.

Bishop heard a slap. "Okay, okay. Sorry. I put down newspaper before I start again."

"Plastic! Put down plastic you idiot, newspaper will just soak through. Why are you doing this in my office anyway?"

"People everywhere," Connie complained. "Come. Go. Get me this. Get me that. I am professional artiste, not servant. I need quiet place to do my work. This room soundproof. Nobody bother me here."

"We need to get going, sir, Lt. Martin said.

Tesslovich sighed. "Unfortunately, Connie, I need to take you away from your playmate for a few hours. I need you to do some errands for me before tomorrow. It's going to be a big day, and everything needs to go perfectly." Tesslovich kicked Bishop in the ankle trying to see how far gone he was. "Are you almost finished with this?" he asked the little man.

"No. No. No truth yet, only bad words and disrespect. More pain is needed. More pain is deserved by this one before he dies."

"Well," Tesslovich said, "I imagine he'll keep. Give him a shot before you go out. Wouldn't want him getting ideas."

Connie gave a snort of laughter at the very idea that Bishop might get away from him. "Is good," he said, "for this man to have plenty of time to think about what I do to him when I get back."

After Tesslovich left, Connie opened one of the wall panels behind the desk. The shelves were full of pill bottles, small vials of liquid medication, bandages, bright steel instruments and a few large jars of various body parts swimming in preservative.

"Connie know you awake," he said.

Bishop watched through swollen eye lids while the little man filled a syringe from one of the small vials.

With total disregard for technique, he stuck the needle into Bishop's leg, right through his jeans, and emptied the contents. It hurt. A lot. But not as much as some other things Connie had done to him.

"It must be nice," Bishop mumbled, as he started to drift off into unconsciousness, "to have a job you really enjoy. . ."

- 9 -

Ariel held the phone in her hand all the way up the stairs to her apartment, so she wouldn't miss it if Bishop's kidnapper called back. Tomas dumped the vests and the grenade launcher on the kitchen table, filled the kettle and put it on for tea.

He poked around in the refrigerator and cupboards looking for food. "Looks like pasta with," he looked closer at the jar he was holding. "---tequila garlic tomato sauce. Do you have any parmesan?"

Ariel pointed to a cupboard.

"Are you all right?"

"No. I hate sitting around when demons are holding my friends captive. I know we can't do anything until tomorrow or we might warn them we're coming. But I feel like I should be doing something. I don't even know if Mouser is still alive."

"Well, you know Bishop is alive because the guy who has him said he'd call you back and let you listen in."

Ariel dropped into a chair and set her cell phone on the table top where she could reach it."

Tomas turned the gas on under a large pot of water, threw in a fist full of pasta and a dollop of olive oil. "You might as well eat something," he said. "I had breakfast, but I haven't seen you take a bite all day. You don't want to faint from hunger in the middle of slaying demons, do you?"

The kettle started to whistle. He snatched it off the burner before it hit that excruciating high note than only dogs and Raptors could hear.

"Tea?"

Ariel picked at the plate of pasta. Tomas was a good cook. She remembered that from combat training, although he tended to err on the side of quantity because he was usually feeding a whole class.

"So, how long have you known this Bishop?" Tomas asked.

"Since the night I tried to kill Tesslovich. He was already there getting slapped around by the lawyer's gypsy minion. In fact, it was the same guy who's got him now. Cassius says he's human, but we've killed him twice and he just keeps coming back."

"Carries a grudge, huh?"

"Bishop does tend to piss people off."

"No wonder you two get along so well."

Ariel laughed. "Is this jealousy?"

"Of course not."

"Bishop told me about the missing kids. He pulled the whole thing together, so it made sense. He bought Mouser espresso and pizza and listened to all his conspiracy theories. I owe him."

"They're collateral damage, El. We have other priorities."

"Collateral damage? That's shit, and you know it!"

"Our responsibility is to stay on mission."

"I get that, but if we start writing humans off as collateral damage who are we protecting? Or has this always been a war between angels and demons with humanity just a bunch of cattle caught in the crossfire?"

"That's stupid."

"Really? Think about it for a minute. A demon is kidnapping homeless kids for medical experiments. The Guardian refuses to do anything about it. Yeah, he put a hit out on Tesslovich but that could have been because he'd become too high profile The Guardian needed to make an example of him, let demon-kind know they were trying to climb farther up the ladder than they deserved to go. Then suddenly there's a real threat: Booga! Booga! Super demons! Demons who could pose a real threat to the order of things. Now the guy upstairs is listening, and he's decided to throw a little cannon fodder at the problem, see what shakes loose before he gets involved."

"You're saying we're expendable."

"Dude!" Ariel channeled Mouser. "Have you been paying attention? How long have Raptors been around?"

Tomas shrugged.

"Centuries? Millennia? Eons of uncounted time? How big are your combat classes?"

"Eight or ten fledges every three to six months."

"And are you the only combat trainer?"

"No."

"So why are so many newbies being trained all the time? There's only one Raptor to a territory. It has to do with the balance, Tomas. The demons overstep, we retaliate. Sometimes they die, sometimes we do. Can't you see Raptors are only a tool? Tools are expendable, one breaks you get another. For the Guardians it's as simple as that."

"We're not human, Ariel. We exist for only one purpose."

"We're not human now, but what if we used to be?"

Tomas got up and cleared the table, setting the dishes

carefully in the sink. "It's the dreams, right?" he said. "I told you before, you can't believe dreams have anything to do with reality."

"Do you remember your childhood?"

"We don't have childhoods."

"Okay. Do you remember anything past four or five years ago?"

"No."

"Well, I do. It's the same memory, over and over again. There's a man, a woman and a child. I think the child is me, only much younger. I think. . . I think the woman is my mother. The man hits the woman, hard. Maybe even kills her . . . then he tries to hurt me. At the end of the dream I'm always running away. Running for my life."

Tomas frowned. "I never dream. I meditate. I teach. I kill demons. I sleep. I never dream."

"You're lucky."

Tomas found a towel and dried his hands. "You still mad at me?"

"No."

"Yeah you are. Not about our relationship, but because I wouldn't listen to you when you came to me for help."

Ariel shrugged. "If you're apologizing Tomas, I accept. But it's not necessary. What we had was nice, but we both moved on. I'm not trying to bring that back. As far as help goes, you're here now. That's what counts."

Ariel looked at the cell phone. It just sat there on the table, pregnant with silence. "I guess we should get some sleep."

"The tub is a little short for me. If you have some extra blankets, I'll sleep on one of the mats."

"Sleep in the bed," Ariel said. "There's plenty of room and your virtue is safe with me."

Tomas smiled. "Thanks, I could use a good night's sleep."

"Me too."

"Really," Tomas said, following Ariel into the bedroom. "I never dream."

～

Ariel lay on her back staring at the ceiling. Tomas lay next to her, on his side, snoring gently. She envied him his serenity and the simplicity of his commitment to being a Raptor. He'd tried to teach her meditation as a way to calm her volatile nature, but Ariel cherished her anger like a small votive flame, fearing that if she let it burn out she would lose her purpose in the world.

Tomas twitched in his sleep. No, it was more than a twitch.

Ariel sat up, alarmed.

Tomas trembled and thrashed at the covers, his face was covered in sweat.

Ariel dodged an out-flung arm and put her hand on his shoulder, hoping the touch would settle him. The touch electrified Tomas. He flung himself to the side, falling out of the bed, scrabbling toward the wall, taking the covers and pillow with him like a shield.

She lunged for the bedside lamp, knocking the cell phone to the floor in her haste.

Tomas blinked owlishly against the light. His bare feet pushed against the floor in an attempt to get further from the bed. He looked down at the blankets and pillow as if he didn't know why he was holding them so tightly, then closed his eyes and let his arms drop. His head thunked back against the wall. He sat perfectly still until his breathing slowed to a normal rate.

Ariel could almost see him mentally picking up the scattered pieces of himself and putting them back where they belonged.

"What happened?" He asked at last.

"You had a nightmare," Ariel said.

"No."

"Believe me, I know a nightmare when I see one. It's something you have no control over. It just comes no matter what you try to do."

Tomas scrubbed at his face. "I can't . . ."

Ariel got up and came around the end of the bed. Gently she pried the covers away, threw the pillow back against the headboard. "Get back in bed," she said. "It's cold in here and you have all the blankets."

Tomas let her extricate him, getting to his knees to let her pull the sheet out from under him. "I don't think I want to go back to sleep right now."

"Not a problem We can talk."

Ariel pushed the pillows up against the headboard and pulled the covers over both of them. Tomas sat against his pillow, but she crossed her legs and sat facing him Indian fashion, curious and concerned.

"What was it you saw?" She asked.

"There was a crash and then a man." Tomas shut his eyes, trying to hold the threads of the dream together long enough to remember them. "He was trying to tell me something, but there was no sound coming out of his mouth. He was holding a woman in his arms. She was covered in blood, not moving, but I couldn't see her face. Then I was in an alley. Someone hit me and kept on hitting me. I could hear yelling, then I couldn't hear anything at all, just like I couldn't hear what my dad was saying . . ."

"Fuck!" Tomas' fist thumped the mattress. "That couldn't be right." He was quiet a minute, thinking, letting the idea that he'd had a dream settle in. "Is this what it's like for you?"

"Pretty much, slightly different scenario. Something triggers it. My dreams started after I saw this guy backhand a woman on the street in front of a bar. I knocked him down, but she wouldn't leave him. Just kept screaming at me to go away."

"I don't know what my dream means," Tomas said, "but I don't like it. The man and woman were black like me. Maybe that's what you do in dreams, make people look more like yourself. I never saw the ones who were hitting me in the alley, although I felt like I'd really stirred up a nest of trouble and they were getting me back for it."

"You'll probably be fine for the rest of the night," Ariel told him.

"I don't know. If this keeps happening I may never want to sleep again."

Tomas stared straight ahead. He wasn't looking at her, but she was looking at him, a line of concern between her eyes. She leaned over and kissed him on the cheek.

It startled him, but he turned his face toward her and she moved her mouth to his lips, probing gently at first, then as he responded, urging her tongue deeper. She rose to her knees, straddled his legs, and put her hands on his shoulders, trying gently to massage out the knots his nightmare had put into his muscles. He slid his hands under her t-shirt, moved them up the smooth skin of her back until he reached the faint scars that followed the inside curve of her shoulder blades. All Raptors knew this was the center of their power, the opening to their wings. The scars were exquisitely sensitive. Opening them triggered a burst of adrenalin that heightened their senses and doubled their strength.

Ariel arched her back as Tomas touched her. Something between a growl and a moan rumbled softly in her throat. Tomas pulled the t-shirt off over her head and leaned forward to nip gently down the naked line of her throat to her shoulder. Her fingers dug into his biceps urging him on. In seconds they were tearing at each other's clothes, working it off over arms, legs and heads while barely breaking contact. Tomas rolled Ariel onto her back. Their hands and mouths roamed each other's body, touching, licking, biting all the sensitive places, old and familiar spots, but somehow new again. The bed covers slid unnoticed onto the floor.

Tomas' muscles were hard and defined, honed by years of martial arts. Ariel's body was lean and taut from daily practice. Her long legs tangled with his, her small breasts filled his hands, their nipples erect. The taste of them was sweet on his tongue. Ariel touched Tomas in return. The skin on his sex was tight and silky under her fingers. His breath moaned against her mouth. He grabbed her wrist, pulling her hand away, not trusting himself to be able to wait.

Tomas kneeled between her legs. His tongue trailed hot and wet down her body, searching gently for other places, other tastes. Ariel reached behind him, stroked his shoulder blades, ran her fingers back and forth along his scars. A cry burst from his lips as his scars parted. Wings unfurled from open flesh, feathers spread dark and wide over the two of them like an exotic tent of blue-black silk.

"Now," Ariel whispered.

Tomas slid both hands under her thighs. He lifted her and watched their bodies join as he entered her. She was moist and hot and tight. Her legs circled Tomas, heels pressing insistently against the back of his thighs. She rose to meet him, pulling him deeper with each stroke until they were moving to a rhythm that became so exquisitely unbearable they had to let go.

For a long moment there was no here or there, no time or space, no fear or regret, only blind sensation that made no judgment and asked for nothing in return. They collapsed into an exhausted tangle of limbs and wings. Each knew that what had just happened hadn't been for love or lust, but for comfort, for sensation without thought, for an exhausted mutual peace and a few hours of dreamless sleep.

- 10 -

"Bill?" The man who stood on the corner of Fourth and Lincoln was clean shaven, hair cut to a stubble and wearing a wrinkled but clean and patched set of fatigues.

"Surprise, huh?" he said in a familiar voice. "Mr. Kale said I could get on the train as long as I was sober enough to hold a gun and know who to point it at." He pulled a half pint of vodka out of his shirt pocket and took a small sip before putting it back. "That's just to keep off the shakes and hallucinations. Don't want to mistake a 'goyle for one of my flying monkeys. I've kinda gotten used to the little buggers and I don't want to shoot one by mistake."

Dingo flashed a good grief kind of look at Ariel behind Bill's back. "We need to get below," he told Bill. "We got a tight schedule."

Bill gave the roof tops and doorways a good going over as he backed into the alley. Ariel and Dingo followed his lead. In a moment they were behind a dumpster and through a hole in the wall that Bill quickly closed up with a piece of plywood. After that it was just the usual confusing twists and turns, dark tunnels and ladders leading down, level after level.

"You think Bill is a good idea?" Ariel asked Cassius.

"He really wants in on this. He's an experienced combat vet and he's been semi sober for three days. He's done his best to adjust his blood alcohol level from blotto to functional. Except for one bad bout with pink bats, he's been doing fine."

"Monkeys," Ariel said. "Pink monkeys."

"Whatever. Where's your friend?"

"Tomas? He's with the Dogs. I'll meet up with him after I get Bishop."

Cassius flipped on a wall mounted screen. "Zaki's train is loading up now. There hasn't been a new car entering the Hauptman garage or Tesslovich property for at least an hour. They're picking up passengers from both platforms." The screen split. "There's Tesslovich playing All Aboard."

"And there's his gypsy knife thrower," Ariel said. "That's good news. I want to be sure both of them get on the train. As soon as everybody gets off at Zaki's end I'm going into the house."

"That's a pretty big troll," Cassius said.

Ariel pulled a dart gun out of her coat pocket. "You know what they say: The bigger they are . . ."

It was at least half a mile from the Hauptmann platform to the smaller one that accessed the mansion. It was nothing more than a large rectangle covered in early twentieth century tile backed by flaking mirrors mounted over carved stone benches. The Hauptmann's probably spent very little time on the platform waiting for their private train to pick them up and take them to the store or their country house. Ornate gates closed off the stairway to the first floor of the house, but they were open now because the troll was still on guard and the only place that would support his gigantic butt was the three bottom stairs.

Dingo and Ariel stayed close to the wall, walking single file on a narrow, cement utility ledge that ran along the side of the tunnel from one platform to the other. Ariel had cautioned Dingo to not make a sound. Trolls might be dumb, but they weren't deaf.

When they got to the bottom of the Tesslovich platform several rusty rungs provided access to its surface five feet above the tunnel floor. Ariel could hear the troll shifting his vast bulk as he whistled tunelessly through his teeth.

Dingo's foot landed on a stray track cinder making a sound like a twig being snapped. Both he and Ariel froze, which meant they could hear with perfect clarity the sound of the troll getting to his feet. It wasn't a quick process. And if the swearing and farting that accompanied the move meant anything, the troll wasn't happy about it. But he was still going to take a look.

Ariel motioned Dingo to flatten himself against the platform wall where he wouldn't be seen. She pulled herself quickly up the rungs, and stood on the tile, holding the dart gun behind her back in one hand.

The troll came out from between the gates and stopped when he saw her. A lone woman wasn't what he expected, and he paused, his small brain confused by this anomaly. The troll was a good seven feet tall and at least four feet wide. His bullet head was a lumpy, hairless cylinder that seemed to sit directly on his shoulders without the benefit of a neck. His eyes were dark and beady. Small, ruffled ears were stuck to the sides of his head like some strange fungus that grew on logs that had spent too much time on the forest floor.

"Hi." Ariel said. "I guess I missed the train." She pulled the gun around and shot him with a dart in the general vicinity of his invisible neck. The troll frowned.

"Shit! Shoot him in the leg Dingo."

Dingo had his elbows on the edge of the platform holding Ariel's crossbow. He pulled the trigger and the quarrel hit the troll just above one knee. The troll gave no indication it hurt, but it did get his attention. He bent over to pull it out and Ariel shot another dart into the side of his head and a third into the inside of a tree-like thigh, thinking there had to be an artery in there somewhere.

The troll stood up holding the quarrel. He batted vaguely at the dart sticking out of his meaty temple, rolled his eyes toward heaven and promptly fell over on his face. A huge puff of subway dirt rose up at the impact and settled back down onto the tiles in a rain of dust and crushed cinders. Ariel put a hand over her nose and mouth while Dingo sneezed.

"Shss!" Ariel hissed.

"Are you kidding? Seismographs just went off all over North America and you're worried about a sneeze?"

"Upstairs! Now!"

The door into the house was as open as the gates. After all, who was going to be able to sneak past a troll? The top of the subway stairs had its own little green tiled foyer where family and guests could leave their coats or take a last look at themselves in the ornate mirror over an antique Bombay chest. There was a porcelain umbrella stand that seemed to contain a riding crop, a number of canes and two Samurai swords. Ariel tossed one to Dingo who mouthed the word 'Cool' as he admired the first six inches of its shiny blade. She pointed a finger to herself, then upward toward the second floor, meaning she would look for Bishop up there.

Dingo nodded and made a circle with a raised index finger, meaning he would scope out the first floor and take out any possible baddies. Ariel traded him the tranc gun for the crossbow and put a finger to her lips. They were going to do this as quietly as possible.

The main entry hall was also tile but the stairway to the upper floor was carpeted in thick, red pile. Not a color choice Ariel would have chosen for the beautiful old Beaux Arts mansion, but she wasn't a demon. Tesslovich also seemed to favor weapons over art. A fan of medieval pikes adorned one entry wall and a collection of ethnic weaponry hung from the wall next to the stairs. Ariel heard the distant pfhuut of the tranc pistol followed by a thud, but she kept going. Dingo could take care of himself.

The upstairs hall was clear as far as she could see, but it made a sharp right turn about halfway down the width of the house and she had no idea where that led. She stepped to the corner and took a quick glance down the adjoining hall. A bored looking demon with blue skull ridges and spiky ears, wearing a badly fitted tweed sports jacket and grey slacks was sitting in an uncomfortable wooden chair outside a closed door.

Bingo, she thought. Bishop was still alive. This was going to be a piece of cake, but stealth was still important. No way to tell if there was anyone behind other closed doors. She considered her weapons while she took another quick peek. Definitely the crossbow.

Ariel swung around the corner and pulled both triggers, one after the other. One quarrel hit the demon in the ribs, the other in the side of the head.

"What the fuck?!" the demon said, jumping to his feet. The feathers of the quarrel were right up against his blue skull, the metal point stuck out of his opposite ear.

Ariel looked from the demon to the crossbow as if it had somehow malfunctioned. Downstairs, a gun went off. Then it went off again.

"Ariel!"

"Up here!" Ariel yelled. She dropped the bow and pulled both of her pistols. Stealth was out, artillery was in. She stepped into the junction of the two hallways. She could see in both directions, so she pointed a pistol each way, one at the demon, one at the top of the stairs. There was a thump and the demon started to stagger down the hall in her direction. She shot him in the chest. He lurched back, looked down at the spreading green stain, looked at her, and fell over on his back.

Feet thundered up the staircase. Ariel swung both guns in that direction. Dingo's face appeared above the top step.

"Sorry," he said. "The housekeeper turned out to be a Wizek and I ran out of darts. Bottom floor's clear. Did you find Bishop?"

"I think he's down the hall." Ariel stepped over the blue demon. His sports coat had fallen open. On his belt was a gold police badge in a leather clip. Ariel reached over and grabbed it, holding it up for Dingo. "This can't be good."

"Is he dead?"

Ariel shot the demon in the head just to make sure. "I think Bishop's in here."

She opened the door the demon had been guarding.

The man in the chair looked up at the sound. The flesh around one eye was dark purple and the eye was swollen nearly shut. His lower lip was split down the middle and a stream of blood from one nostril had dried on his upper lip and chin.

"Shit."

"Lo El," Bishop said. "We've got to stop meeting like this."

Ariel's feet made crackling sounds as she walked across the square of plastic under the chair. She slid out a gravity knife and slit open the tape holding Bishop's arms, legs and torso. He tried to raise his arms but settled for shaking his hands to get the blood flowing to his fingers again.

"Can you walk?" She let the knife drop back into her sleeve. "We haven't got much time."

"Ribs hurt, and I think my legs are asleep. If you can get me upright I can probably get them going again."

Dingo grabbed Bishop under one arm, Ariel the other, and they both lifted him out of the chair.

"Ow," he said, tottering a little. He tried stamping his feet to get the circulation going. "Ow! Ow! Ow! Pins and needles!" Bishop hobbled over to the small lavatory, moving like a very old man, turned on the faucet and threw water into his face, rinsed out his mouth, and drank several swallows out of his cupped hands. When he came out Ariel helped him into his shoulder holster and jacket. He picked up his wallet and swept the change off the desk into his pockets.

"One more thing." He went over to the panel where Connie had gotten the knock-out drug and syringe. There were plenty of other pharmaceuticals to choose from. He began pulling them off the shelves onto the floor until he found what he was looking for.

"What are you doing?" Ariel asked. "We have a train to catch."

"Vicodin." Bishop said pouring three white tablets out of a brown plastic bottle into one hand. He stuck that bottle in the pocket of his coat. "Amphetamines." He dumped out two more pills from a second bottle, popped the pills into his mouth and dry swallowed.

"When I was in Vice we used to call this a Suburban Speed Ball. Give me five minutes and I'll be fine."

Dingo was out in the hall pouring something white and granular into the demon's chest wound.

"What's that?" Bishop asked.

"Kosher salt. It's been blessed by a rabbi and demons are

allergic to salt. If this cop has nanites, we're hoping it will help keep him dead."

"He's a cop?"

Ariel held up the shield she'd taken off his belt.

Bishop looked closer at the body. "Hard to tell who he is, him being all blue and shot up, with an arrow through his head. Nice work, by the way."

Dingo felt around in the demon's jacket for a wallet. "Says his name's Sergeant Ralph Danziger, Missing Childrens Task Force."

"Yeah. I met his boss, Lt. Martin, a couple hours ago. He's also a demon. The good news is he interrupted the mutant from poking me with small, sharp objects including his fists. The bad news is, he's planning on framing me for kidnap and murder, then kill me as I try to escape. He was going to plant a couple of dead kids in the trunk of my car. I hope nothing's happened to them yet. One was going to be the kid I was trying to find, Suzee Morgan."

"We need to get down to the tunnel." Ariel hustled Dingo and Bishop down the stairs. "I was going to put you on the train to the compound, Frank, but you look pretty bad. You sure you can handle it?"

Bishop squared his shoulders and twisted his neck to work out a kink. "I'm fine," he said. "The drugs are kicking in and I wouldn't miss this party for the world." He looked at Ariel. "Those are the stakes, right? The World."

The three of them crossed the front hall into the small foyer that led to the platform. Bishop made a face as he caught his reflection in the mirror. Ariel pulled the other daiko out of the umbrella stand and handed it to Bishop. Just like Dingo, Bishop pulled the blade out a few inches to admire its edge.

"That's really sharp," Ariel warned him. "You could lose a few fingers if you aren't careful."

"Hey. I saw the Seven Samurai at least ten times when I was a kid. Used to practice sword fighting in front of the mirror with an old broom handle..." Bishop dropped the silk rope attached to the sword's scabbard over his head, so the sword would hang at his back. "I had some moves, and I'm sure they'll all come back to me just before some demon with flames coming out of his ass bites off my head."

Mouser knew something was up. People had been hurrying up and down the halls for several hours. Doors opened and closed. He could hear people talking in stressed voices. Orders being given. One time there was a serious scolding in a language he didn't recognize, and the sound of a vicious slap. For an hour or more now there had been silence. Then he heard voices again. These were unhurried. Feet moved at a leisurely pace. Someone was explaining something. Murmurs followed.

The door to the lab opened. The grey man held it wide, letting a group of six males and three females precede him into the room. They were all expensively dressed. The women's ears, necks and wrists glittered with beautiful stones that brought out the color of their eyes and skin. Mouser could see they weren't human. Although two women and three of the men maintained their glamour, the other four had dropped all pretense as to what they were. Two of them seemed to be bodyguards; one of the other three was obviously a very important person. Instead of Armani, he was wearing a long robe of elegantly embroidered silk with a high rolled collar. His dusky violet skin was stretched tight across abnormally sharp cheek bones. Yellow eyes topped a hooked nose and a jeweled circle pierced one nostril. The stones on the circle matched those in his ears. He seemed to acknowledge nothing that was going on around him but was seeing everything.

"So, these are your failures?" He asked, walking up to the Plexiglas wall of Mouser's cell. For once, Mouser was glad the wall existed. He'd never felt so close to being devoured alive just by the power of someone's eyes.

The grey man immediately stopped talking to another demon and moved quickly to his side.

"Failures, yes," he said. "But we have learned important lessons from these two. Ironically, this one is a shape shifter. We had no idea when we picked him up off the street that he contained that little surprise. His animal form is nothing much: a common hawk, brown, boring. But when he shifts from human to hawk the mechanisms we implanted to control him completely disappear. It's as if even this minor power of his is strong enough to cleanse his blood."

"And this one here?" The demon glided over to Susan Elizabeth's cage. "Does this one change form as well?"

"This one, My Lord, is even more of a puzzle. It's usually so easy to take control of the small ones. Virtually like stealing candy from a baby." The grey man gave a nasty little laugh which stopped abruptly when he noticed a twitch of annoyance from the demon. "This child's soul will not come loose no matter what we do. Our best collectors have tried. And the nanites, they simply vanish from her blood. We do not know what this child is, but she could be very dangerous. After the celebration, they both will be destroyed."

"Leave us alone!" Mouser heard Suzee tell the demon. "You're a bad, bad, evil man."

The demon leaned over to peer down at the defiant child.

"My dear," he said, mildly. "Your little brain cannot possibly conceive how astonishingly bad, bad, evil I can actually be."

- 11 -

Yamazaki Kirienko looked down the long, Zebra Wood table that ran the length of Zaki Industry's board room. He counted off the eight demons in his head, so he would remember the names of each one. The exotic wood of the table had been waxed to a deep luminous shine that made its black stripes appear to float hypnotically over a core of deep purple heartwood. It had been outrageously expensive, but the cost was insignificant compared to the deal he would strike today.

If the table was a deliberate distraction, the Brioni suit Zaki wore was a calculated understatement. Compared to the demons sitting in the chairs on either side of him, he would be considered downright drab.

The Lords of the House of Eight were resplendent in exotic gowns, silk robes and flashy designer suits. Each represented one of the eight most important demon families in the Northern Hemisphere. Between them, they controlled a hidden empire of vast power and influence. Their supernatural roots had not prevented them from moving with the times. Each had assets beyond measure. Together, they controlled corporations, commodities, heads of state. They were advisors to kings, queens, dictators, and presidents, but they were still vulnerable to their own internal politics. The Eight had managed to maintain an uneasy peace within their Familia while continuing to deal ruthlessly with outsiders, usurpers and traitors within.

Nicolai Tesslovich sat to Zaki's left. The demon lawyer was the architect of many of Zaki's corporate plans and ambitions, but by no means his friend. Zaki had no friends. He survived by his own twisted genius and ruthless ambition. Today, he was here to negotiate the deal of the millennium and he intended to walk away with much, much more than he intended to give. He knew The House of Eight thought they would get the best of him but, as always, he had created a scenario that would assure he won while appearing to not have thought through the implications of what he was placing into their hands.

Greed, he thought. Demon's believed they were much cleverer than men, but they were only more vengeful, sly and greedy. What they wanted was totally predictable: more money, more trinkets, more sex, more death, more souls, more slaves, more power. Zaki had seen this from both sides of the fence.

"Your father," Bezla, the violet demon asked. "Is he well?"

Zaki's father had been one of Stalin's nuclear scientists. He'd been purged as an enemy of the state after a particularly self-indulgent bit of destructive exuberance. Luckily Zaki and his mother were already in Japan. He had dismissed any attachment to his father a long time ago.

"He's dead." Zaki said mildly as if seventy years in the past was yesterday.

"And your mother?"

"An amazing woman, but only human, Lord Bezla. When her famous beauty faded away, so did she. Had she survived a few decades longer, I could have kept her alive and beautiful forever."

"Is that what you're offering us?" Zovan asked. "Forever? We pure bloods are already immortal."

"But still vulnerable to a knife in the heart, a sword across your throat, or an exotic poison."

With this last comment, Zaki inclined his head in Alameil's direction; she was renowned throughout the demon empire for both her beauty and her skill with poisons. Her only flaw in Zaki's eyes was she favored Versace, a designer whose couture reminded him of Fredrick's of Hollywood.

"My product can heal even the worst injury. Nicolai, please show our guests."

Tesslovich loosened his collar, revealing the wide scar that circled his neck.

"Nicolai was beheaded by a Raptor. Emergency medical intervention was obviously needed, but both his body and head were kept alive by my little machines until they could be reunited."

Zoven and Nob, got up to look at the back of Tesslovich's neck. Zoven, in strapless, midnight blue Valentino, traced the scar with one long, red fingernail causing Tesslovich to leer at her over his shoulder.

"And your fighters?"

"A prototype for an army of slaves and soldiers---human and demon. A renewable asset that can take great punishment yet heal to work or fight another day. Their will and actions can be controlled by wireless signals from a central, or even portable, source. With this technology, the Eight can control the human race or annihilate it as you will."

Nob smiled. "If we destroy them, what will we play with when we're bored?"

"Besides," Yellow horned Zoven added, "Destruction of the human race has been tried before. Several times. Humans are like cockroaches; they suffer, they die, but they always find some way to survive."

"What I offer is not magic." Zaki told them. "It's science. Hard, cold, technological virtuosity."

"And the secret to making this science?" Bezla asked.

"Remains mine, and mine alone."

"And in return for your---virtuosity?"

"I want my own house within the Families and the wealth to run it. I will keep the technology and continue to improve it until it is everything you wish it to be."

"What about your own scientists? The ones who produced the machines. They must know how these things are made. Why don't we just buy one or two of them? After all, we are obscenely rich, we could easily provide them with all the equipment they need to duplicate your technology for ourselves."

Zaki had perched his elbows on the arms of his chair and entwined his long fingers during this discussion. He threw his hands apart.

"Too late." He said.

"Sorry?"

"It's too late to do that. I'm not a fool. All my scientists are dead, or soon will be. The celebratory lunch I just gave them was poisoned. Death is so much cheaper and more reliable than a pension plan or non-competition agreement. And I really don't have a use for them anymore. All I need now are a few assistants who don't have the whole picture to help me move my equipment and set up somewhere else."

Alameil gave him a predatory smile. It was too bad he couldn't trust getting closer to her. She liked her little hobby far too much.

"Besides, you wouldn't want to do my work. It would be tedious and boring for Lords of your station. Just pay me for the results and provide me your protection from my enemies."

"You have enemies?" Bezla asked, amused by his own question.

"My Lord," Zaki answered him. "Don't we all? I'm offering you the ultimate in protection against them: the antidote to death itself."

"And families outside of The Eight?"

"Have also been invited to bid. The house that wins controls my product, and perhaps, in time, the entire world." Zaki smiled. "Who can say where this will go, the possibilities are endless."

"We could kill you right now and take your data." Nob told him.

Zaki shrugged. "It's encrypted. It will self-destruct if tampered with." He waved a hand as if dismissing the idea as absurd. "The Lords of Eight are many things, but none of you are fools."

He stood up. "Nicolai will escort you to the arena. Your private Skybox is well supplied with food, drink and other potential amusements. There will be entertainment and a fascinating presentation. Your bids, if you wish, can be confidential."

"Have you met with the other families the same way you've met with us?" Nob's voice was harsh.

"Of course," Zaki said. "But few others have the vision and resources of The Eight."

As the demons filed out of the board room Bezla turned back to Zaki. "I'm afraid I cannot stay," he said. "I am old enough to have wearied of bread and circuses, and I have other business that needs my attention."

"You aren't concerned about what the other lords will do in your absence?"

"The family has my vote. Each one of us is as ruthless as the next but we recognize when something is of mutual advantage." Bezla gave Zaki a small smile. "I have no worries about who will ultimately win."

A few moments later, from the window of the board room, Zaki watched as The Eight's helicopter took off over the lake.

Well done, Zaki thought. Bezla was Patriarch of The Lords of Eight. His departure was just a ploy to make The Eight appear less interested in the nanotechnology than they actually were. Zaki shrugged. He'd watched their eyes as he explained what his little beasts could do. There was no price they wouldn't pay to have control of his invention. And, devious as they might be, not one of them had any idea that Zaki would always retain ultimate control over what they did with it.

- 12 -

"The helicopter is taking off," one of the techs informed Cassius. He turned to another screen. "Zaki has entered the arena."

Cassius looked at the second screen, one of three mounted in the front of the first car of the train. The ultimate showman, Zaki was rising out of the arena floor on a round platform which stopped when he was six feet above the lowest row of seats. He had a microphone in his hand. Huge screens covering all four walls of the arena magnified him until he was a giant, god-like replicant of the puny humanoid on the platform below.

"Turn up the sound," Cassius said. He knew this image would be on the screens in all cars of the train.

". . . ladies and gentlemen." Zaki was saying. "I hope you have enjoyed the bouts of combat, feats of strength, victory and defeat you have seen here today. But what you have seen is merely the beginning. . ."

"How big is his audience, would you say?" Cassius asked the tech.

"Two hundred or so in seats," the tech said. "Most of the ones on foot are security or catering staff. But there's also the Skyboxes. We can't tell how many have demons in them."

"The ones on the floor are probably small fry. Minor families, retainers and pilot fish. The power families are in the Skyboxes with their body guards. That adds maybe thirty or forty more. And we don't know who's in the other buildings. They could be another source of resistance." Cassius frowned. "Who got on the copter?"

"Some violet colored dude in a fancy robe. He was by himself."

"Odd. But we can worry about that later. With the copter gone it gives them one less means of escape.

". . . ground breaking technology," Zaki continued. Giant nanobots started to crawl across the screens. ". . . powered by self-replicating bacteria, their life span can be calculated in hundreds of years, possibly millennia."

"Poisonous bacteria, you bastard!" Cassius said. He looked behind him. The train car was full of rag tag, but well-armed Deepers. He adjusted his wireless head set. "Everybody on board?" he asked. Captain Greggs gave him a thumbs up.

Mr. McCullen?" The engineer was in a closed compartment at the head of the train. "Let's roll this train. If Mr. Bishop and the Raptor are on the secondary platform we will stop and board them."

". . . what I have to offer goes beyond immortality. It promises enhanced strength, faster reflexes, and most important of all, regeneration at the brink of death, and beyond."

The train slowed to a stop. The doors of the first car slid open. A shaky, but determined looking Bishop, flanked by Ariel and Dingo, was waiting on the platform. Behind them, a giant mound of flesh was giving off a sound like an asthmatic water buffalo with a head cold.

"You found him!" Cassius said, meaning Bishop.

"Piece of cake." Ariel stayed on the platform while Bishop and Dingo stepped on board. "I'm going to hook up with the Dogs." Ariel said. "We'll come in through the front gate or over the wall. Try to keep your fight inside the buildings. From the amount of 'goyle activity we've seen lately, Zaki must have a roost on the property. If somebody lets them loose, that will be just one more thing to contend with."

"Let us know when you hit the gate."

Ariel tapped her headset. "Good luck," she said. The train doors slid shut.

"You need a medic, Mr. Bishop?" Cassius asked.

Bishop knew he looked like someone who been thoroughly worked over, twice. "Not yet." He thumbed the cap off one of the bottles in his pocket and threw down another pill. "I'd take an ice pack if you have one handy."

Over Cassius' shoulder Bishop could see the video feed from the arena. Two brightly painted slant boards were being set up, facing each other on the arena floor. They had straps attached to them in a configuration that implied something with four limbs would soon be restrained at ankles, wrists and waist. It reminded Bishop of the set up for a knife throwing act in the circus, and that thought led to one that was even worse.

Zaki's voice continued. "In a short while, my associate and I will show you irrefutable proof that what I'm offering you actually works."

A little man in a striped suit stepped onto the arena floor and began to check over the boards and straps.

"See that guy in the ugly suit?" Bishop asked no one in particular. "I want him really, really bad."

- 13 -

As the train pulled away from the Tesslovich platform, heavy steel shutters slid down over windows and doors, hopefully sealing the cars off from the lethal consequences of the steam trap and any microwaves aimed at the train. Ariel knew that Cassius had already activated a continuous loop for the security cameras showing an empty track. The train would take about twenty minutes to reach Zaki's estate. She had to hurry.

The fastest way was back up the stairs, through the first floor of the mansion and out the back door. If she went airborne from the alley there was less chance of being seen leaving the ground. Ariel's feet pounded up the stairs and across the hall tiles. She skidded around a corner into the dining room, where a display of old weapons covered the walls. Several were missing, leaving faint outlines behind.

Damn! she thought. Some of the demons were armed, and by the look of lesser weapons left behind, they had taken all the Angel Slayers. Were they expecting trouble? And why would they expect it to be the kind of trouble that called for Angel Slayers? She couldn't worry about that now. There were two particularly nice spears mounted on either side of the door to the kitchen.

She pulled them off the wall and shouldered her way through the swinging door into a room full of bright white tile and shiny stainless steel. A walk-in refrigerator with glass doors took up almost one whole wall of the industrial size kitchen. Ariel didn't want to speculate on what kind of animals the sides of meat hanging inside might be from. Because she was looking at the refrigerator, she narrowly avoided stepping on a body surrounded by crushed condiment containers, lying on the floor near the sink. It was dressed in checked pants and a starched white chef's tunic, but the limbs and accessories protruding from the openings in the uniform weren't attached to anything a gourmet was likely to see preparing the sauce at his favorite bistro. The demon looked totally dead with a dash of sea salt, just the way Ariel liked them.

The kitchen door opened into a small backyard surrounded by a stone wall. Two small Gargoyles faced outward, perched on posts on either side of the alley gate. They were obviously leftovers from the pack that had pursued Tomas. Ariel leaped into the air, unfurling her wings with a loud snap. The Gargoyles hadn't expected a threat from inside the wall and their reaction time was slow. As they began to pivot on their posts, Ariel flipped the spears, so they were parallel to the ground and rammed them straight through the 'goyles leathery torsos. The spear points exited their bellies with a crunchy sounding splot.

"The shish-kebob is particularly good tonight," she told the dead 'goyles, as she shook their bodies off the spears into the yard where they wouldn't be seen by a passing neighbor. If the Deeper and werewolf attacks were going to happen simultaneously, she had to get to the Dog's campground as quickly as possible.

She launched herself into the sky, hoping that multiple sightings of a giant bird wouldn't make the seven o'clock news. Her experience told her that if someone saw her they were likely to dismiss it as some kind of urban hallucination.

~

When she reached the campground on the lake, Ariel had no trouble identifying which section of sand and beach grass had been claimed by the Dogs. The parking lot was lined with Harleys. Riders in leathers and sleeveless jean jackets with pack colors were perched on wooden tables and benches in the group picnic area. A few barbeques were still smoldering, the remains of hot dog lunches and dead six packs were stuffed into overflowing garbage drums near the small pavilion and rest rooms. The Dogs were a mixed group: both men and women riders, some with passengers. Once changed into wolves, sex wouldn't matter; they'd all be equally scary. Ariel could see weapons tucked here and there in waist bands and shoulder rigs, but the bulk of firepower was under the tarp of Juke's old pickup truck. Tomas was talking to a couple of long haired accountants but stopped when Ariel dropped down onto the sand. She tossed him one of the spears.

"Saddle up," she said. "We have a gate to crash."

"Steam trap fifteen seconds. Best move to the center of the car."

It took Bishop longer than anyone else to get up off the bench and grab one of the poles provided for standing passengers. Although he could feel the painkillers and the speed working out the terms of their agreement inside his body, sudden moves and deep breathing still made him grit his teeth. I can do this, he thought, wrapping his fingers around the cool metal pole. Then he heard the steam come on. It sounded like multiple explosions of air under extreme pressure. They hit the old train car with enough force that it began to rock from side to side. Wisps of wet heat forced their way through cracks between the retro-fitted steel plates and the old metal sides of the cars, causing boiling condensation to flow in streams down the inside of the doors and windows to form puddles on the floor. His fellow passengers squeezed closer together trying to keep their feet from contact with the steaming puddles.

"Everybody okay?" Cassius listened to his headphone for a few seconds. "Minor burns," he announced. "We're through."

The secondary screen switched to an aerial view, then went thermal. Bishop could see bright red, yellow and orange bodies moving around the buildings, their appendages were visible as long as they didn't stand too close together. Bodies in the arena gave off a huge thermal signature that coalesced into a giant, pulsating red blob surrounding four smaller blobs in the middle. Zaki's house had only a few blobs inside. The bodies moving about the grounds could only be random security on patrol, and there were Two bodies on the subway platform at the end of the tunnel. There were three blobs at the front gate.

Greggs stood at Cassius' shoulder, his eyes moving from building to building. "A Team will move down the tunnel on foot and take the station," he began. Then, "What's this?"

A large room in the lab building showed multiple immobile green blobs in rag doll poses. Some were lying flat out, probably on the floor.

"Maybe unconscious, probably dead," Cassius told him. "Green means their body temperature is lower than normal. We'll have to check it out."

On the first screen, two young, shirtless men had been strapped to the slant boards. One had pale blue skin and two small horns right above his hairline, the other looked human. The little man in the ugly suit had removed his jacket, displaying deep sweat stains under his arms and a set of gaudy green sleeve garters. The boards started to spin in an anti-clockwise direction. He took a stance about fifteen feet from the board holding the blue demon and started to throw knives at him. His objective wasn't to miss his target.

A knife sunk into the young demon's body just below his collarbone, another hit his abdomen dead center. The demon writhed with each impact, then suddenly went slack, head lolling to the side. Streams of yellow blood ran down his chest and belly. The Great Constantini strutted over and wrenched each knife out, displaying the wounds to the crowd. The big screens made them look cavernous in size. Within a moment the blood flow stopped, and the lips of the wounds quivered and started to seal themselves. The right side of the huge screens began to display eight, then nine, then ten-digit numbers.

The car went silent. "Jesus!" Somebody said. "They're bidding on what's keeping that guy alive!"

"Twenty seconds to drop point," Engineer McCullen's voice echoed through the car. "Prepare to hit the tracks and deal with the security Mr. Greggs. I'll give you four minutes lead time then I'm parking this train on Zaki's bumper."

- 14 -

Ariel and Tomas led the phalanx of biker Dogs from the air. Directly under them was Juke's pick-up truck, loaded with artillery and the jeans, boots and helmets of semi-naked werewolves on Harleys. Some Dogs had kept their colors, others wore Kevlar vests. Because riding a bike took a mostly human shape, the Dogs hadn't totally transformed. Most were hanging somewhere in the zone between not quite human and mostly wolf. The partial transformation had elongated their bodies, causing arms and torsos to hunch over the handlebars. Their faces were all snout and fangs, their hands and feet like weapons, tipped with claws.

Ariel signaled that she and Tomas were going on ahead. She knew from the drive-by with Bishop that the gate was flanked by pillars with one large Gargoyle on each post. A security booth just inside contained at least one uniformed guard. If she and Tomas couldn't take out the 'goyles and open the gate before an alarm could be raised, Juke would have to blow it open with a grenade and that would not only alert Zaki that an invasion was on the way but create one more easy escape route for the demons inside.

Tomas signaled Ariel to break left. They had already decided they would loop around and attack the 'goyles from the back, then Tomas would take out the guard and open the gate. The Dogs were to hold back until that was done.

Ariel was swooping down on her 'goyle when she heard a shout from inside the gate. The guard was halfway out of his booth, pointing at the Raptors and yelling at the 'goyles. Ariel flew over the booth.

"Take the guard!!" she yelled into her headset. Tomas abandoned his 'goyle and dove for the booth. The guard tried to pull the door shut before Tomas could reach him, but he was seconds too late. Tomas did an air somersault a few feet off the ground and landed a sweeping side kick to the door, slamming it back open and propelling the startled guard back into the booth. The guard hit the control panel and scrabbled for the alarm button just as Tomas landed full force on his back. As the guard was going down, Tomas grabbed his head and gave it a hard twist. He shoved the crumpled guard out of sight under the console and hit the "Open" button with the heel of his hand.

Ariel rammed her spear into the nearest 'goyle's back. The 'goyle turned toward her with an expression of mild surprise that quickly became annoyance. Twisting his torso, he ripped the length of wood out of her hands and reached around with one scaly claw to break off the shaft. The splintered nub sticking out of his back began to smoke and blacken as the acid in the creature's blood dissolved it. He flew at Ariel, his small red eyes glowing with fury. Ariel reached over her shoulder and grabbed the handle of her sword, pulling it free of the sheath strapped between her shoulder blades. Her wings beat faster to hold her in one place, she swung the sword with both hands. Its razor edge split open the 'goyle's belly causing ropes of steaming viscera to pour out of the wound toward the ground below. The wounded 'goyle shrieked, more in rage than pain. One clawed hand grabbed at the escaping intestines while its head darted back and forth on its skinny neck, trying to get beyond the Raptor's guard to deliver a poisonous bite. The second Gargoyle left its pillar and darted at Ariel, causing her to spin sideways to avoid an attack from both sides. But the second 'goyle wasn't as brave as his companion, so it hovered, growling and spitting, its eyes following the tip of her sword as it tried to figure out how to reach her without losing its guts.

Tomas ran from the booth and jumped into the air. He dove toward the second 'goyle. Seeing him, the creature bolted toward the estate, flying as fast as his leathery wings would take him, Tomas on his tail. Ariel finished off the first 'goyle and landed on the grass just as Juke's pick up squealed through the now open gate and pulled to the side to let the Harleys, two and three abreast, enter the estate. The sound of the bikes heavy engines was accompanied by a rumbling chorus of growls and excited howls from the riders. A furry, but upright Ez stood in the back of the pickup tossing swords, semi-automatic rifles and grenade launchers at the passing bikers who snatched them out of the air with long, clawed fingers.

"There's five guards still loose on the property." Ez was yelling as the bikers passed him. "Take their heads. Gut them! Do as much damage as you can so they can't heal! Check the house, the lab and any other buildings you see. Keep the occupants from getting outside into open space. Keep runners away from the lake and the gate. I need two volunteers on the gate and four at the lake."

Two female Dogs slipped off their rides, guns raised over their heads. Four other hands went up, volunteering for the lake.

Juke backed the truck around until it was sideways to the gate and got out of it while Ham leaned into the booth, to press the large button that closed and locked it. He was carrying a tank with a metal hose attached. Ariel heard a clicking sound and fire exploded out of the bell-shaped nozzle. Juke let it wash over the control panel, melting buttons and switches into flaming piles of goo, buckling the panel until it sagged like an old hammock. One of the women who'd volunteered for gate duty glanced from the flaming booth to the dead 'goyle lying on the ground next to it. Alive, the body had been three feet tall with a six-foot wing spread. Now it was just a pile of ugly skin and bones, its deflated belly spilling yards of stinking, bluish-green intestine. The wrinkly face still held an expression of outrage and surprise at being killed so quickly and with such little effort. The woman smiled wolfishly at Ariel, revealing a very impressive set of teeth. Ariel grinned back. It was a moment of silent acknowledgement; one scary bitch to another.

"Platform's clear," McCullen's slightly tinny voice echoed through the car. He felt the tap as the old train was hit by the bumper spring of the cars behind it. Steel panels retracted, and the doors of each car slid open. Deepers poured onto the silent platform, forming teams that Greggs quickly dispatched with a series of complicated hand signals. Cassius brought up multiple views of the arena up on the monitors inside the car. Silent videos of adolescents beating each other to the ground in the day's earlier combat matches played on the big screens on the arena walls. Side bars with time clocks in the corners showed fast forwards of fighters regaining consciousness, their injuries healing with cartoon swiftness so that they could be thrown back into the ring to do it all over again. Some fighters who were obviously demons, died over and over; stabbed, shot, decapitated only to come back as hollow eyed and hopeless as their human counterparts. Looking over Cassius' shoulder, Bishop wondered what multiple resurrections did to a person. Did a bigger and bigger piece of you get left behind each time you died, until you were just a hollow creature of meat and bone held together by a scurrying army of invisible healers? And what would happen to this violated flesh after it was rescued? If the person it used to be was only an insane shadow of its former self wouldn't it be better to let it die along with the soulless creatures that made it live?

"If they're human we have to save them," Cassius said to him. It was almost as if he'd read Bishop's mind.

"You're staying here to watch the screens?" Cassius nodded. He popped up a floor plan in the corner of his monitor and printed it out. "Mouser is probably in one of the lab buildings. It's not secure yet so you might have to take one of the utility stairs under the arena, then follow the passageway south."

Bishop stepped onto the platform where there was more room to pull his daiko out of its scabbard. He felt slightly silly with a sword in his hand, like some miscast hero in a bad kung fu movie with lame choreography and an out-of-sync sound track.

"Don't forget to lock the doors behind me," he told Cassius. "You never know which way a trapped demon will run."

As Bishop made his way down the platform, he was glad to see that a few armed Deepers had been posted to guard the train. Several had climbed onto the top of the first car to man the mounted artillery in case they were attacked. McCullen was sitting on the steps to the engine compartment having a smoke. "Find our kids," the engineer said as Bishop passed him. So far, only Mouser and Susan Elizabeth Morgan had names, but all the kids waiting for rescue had already been adopted into the Deeper's underground family.

Ariel followed the driveway, past the main house to the large piece of open ground that led down to the lake. A pack of Dogs had managed to flush a small group of security guards and were chasing them back and forth across the lawn for sport, their long bodies thrust forward, heads jutting between furry shoulders, snouts snuffling up the heady scent of fear. She was about to leave them to it when Tomas suddenly burst into the sky from a break deep in the trees, trailing an explosion of leaves and twigs in his wake. Behind him poured a swirling cloud of shrieking, growling creatures with leathery wings and eyes like burning coals. Someone had opened the 'goyle cages. Below her, Dogs and guards stopped to watch the leathery tornado spin out across the sky.

The Gargoyles seemed intent on getting as much distance as they possibly could from the confines of their roost. The smaller ones immediately sought cover in the leafy canopy of nearby trees. It was the behavior of animals being chased by something larger and scarier than themselves. Ariel climbed higher in the air. She could see what was scaring them now. Behind the 'goyles came creatures of more distinct threat. They were large and brightly colored in red, blue, yellow and green, with spiked, snake-like tails, lizard bodies and scaly wings that seemed much too small to support their weight. Large heads darted left and right, as saucer-sized eyes looked for their escaping prey. One lizard grabbed a small 'goyle in its lipless mouth, tossed it into the air like a piece of popcorn and swallowed it whole. Another swiped one out of the air with a clawed foot, casually biting off body parts as it flew along. Its forked tongue darted in and out searching its snout for any morsels it might have missed as the 'goyle went down. Behind these two flying monsters was another and another, and another, all searching for something to eat.

Ariel could feel the wash of Tomas' wings behind her. "Jesus," he said through her headset. "It's like Dr. Doolittle's Zoo from Hell. The big gate 'goyle managed to open the cages before I took him down and these lizard things came out of somewhere in the back. Uh oh, I think they've spotted the wolves."

The lizards began plowing relentlessly through the cloud of fleeing Gargoyles toward the larger, more meaty sources of food on the ground.

"How many lizards are there?" Ariel asked.

"Six, eight?"

"Well, I think two of them just put us on the menu."

The wolves scattered. Several of them had semi-automatic rifles. They started firing at the lizards, but the bullets bounced harmlessly off their boney chest plates. One bullet penetrated the wattle of skin under one lizard's jaw and exited through the flesh of its cheek. The lizard barely flinched. Its only reaction was a darting purple tongue that came out to lick away the small clumps of gelatinous fluid spattering its muzzle and jaw. The lizard flying closest to it gave it a speculative glance but was warned away by a throaty bellow. The wolves melted into the woods, leaving the security guards to their fate.

Three of the lizards swooped down on the guards, knocking them to the ground, biting off their heads and ripping at their bellies with great clawed feet. Once the guards were dead, a squabble broke out between the scaly predators over possession of the meal. Clawing, biting and bellowing at each other, they started bumping chests, hip blocking and smacking each other with their tails.

"What ever happened to good manners?" Ariel switched her attention to the lizards bearing down on her and Tomas.

"Get above them," Tomas yelled. "Try to land on its back, behind the head."

Ariel swerved to the right. She intended to go higher but didn't want to telegraph the move too soon.

Tomas broke left, luring the lizard closest to him farther away from its buddy.

Ariel was getting a much more detailed look at the monster bearing down on her than she wanted. The creature was acting as if nothing else existed in its world except the tempting piece of flying meat that happened to be her. Its large, yellow eyes were almost hypnotic. Their iris seemed to be spinning slowly around a bottomless vortex of darkness where moments ago there had been a pupil. Ariel's wings began to feel incredibly heavy. It was hard to keep them moving. She was tired of trying to stay in the air. She could feel herself start to drop toward the ground.

"EL! EL! SNAP OUT OF IT!" Tomas voice yelled. "Look away! Get behind it. NOW!"

Ariel's head snapped to the side. She blinked to clear away the fog and dove upward just as powerful jaws snapped shut on the empty air where her foot had been only half a second ago. Ariel spun around and landed on the creature's back, the claws on her fingers and toes extended to get a better grip. A quiver ran through the lizard's skin as it tried to shake her off. She threw herself forward, claws grabbing the folds of flesh around the creature's neck. She held on as tight as she could while the lizard went into a series of twists and barrel rolls trying to dislodge her. She let it tire itself a bit, then realized if it landed it could easily roll over on its back and crush her. Reaching back, she drew her sword with one hand, and slowly straightened until she was standing almost upright, toes firmly hooked into the creatures hide. Holding the sword in both hands, she drove it to the hilt into the soft spot behind the creature's head. The monster screamed, twisting its head, trying to bite the thing causing it pain. Ariel hung onto the sword, working it back and forth in the wound. The creature rolled upside down, still trying to shake her off. Yellow ichor ran from the wound and from the corners of its mouth, spattering Ariel with burning fluid. The lizard began to plunge toward the ground, beating its wings, trying desperately to right itself before impact. Ariel tried to dislodge her sword, but the ground was coming up too fast. The creature made one last effort to flip over and Ariel let go, using the lizard's momentum to throw her clear. A second later the creature hit the ground.

Tomas' lizard was no more than thirty feet away and obviously dead.

"My sword," she called to Tomas. "Help me pull it out"

Luckily the lizard had fallen more on its side than its back. Tomas planted a foot in its neck and gave the sword a good yank. It took two tries, but it finally came free.

"Look at that." Ariel held up the sword, so Tomas could see what she was talking about. The bright shine on its blade had turned to a dull, tarnished silver.

"Metal's still okay," he flicked it with a finger. "It did the same to mine. I hope there aren't too many more of these things. They're a bitch to kill."

"Where are the rest of them?"

"Still having lunch."

There was a sound like escaping swamp gas and Tomas' lizard carcass rolled over on its back.

"I thought yours was dead." Ariel hissed.

Tomas hefted his sword. "It was. Maybe it's just a post mortem cadaver spasm."

"You've been watching way too much CSI." Ariel held her sword with both hands and began stepping sideways toward the dead lizard.

"I don't watch television."

"Liar."

"Okay. The History Channel and an occasional CSI re-run

marathon when I'm not training. There's this blond super-hottie on the team in Miami."

Tomas paced her, moving around the lizard's head until he and Ariel were standing on either side of it. Ripples were moving up and down the animal's abdomen as if there was a small, angry pond inside trying to get out. The ripples turned into a heaving motion. The lizard's stomach started to bulge, straining the flesh until it was totally taut like a massive balloon made of skin.

Tomas poked the body with his sword. "It's still dead," he pronounced.

"Then what's happening?"

"I don't know, but I think it's about to blow. Run!"

The lizard exploded with a resounding Woomph! Ariel felt herself carried aloft by a shock wave of hot, fetid air only to be deposited on her face several yards away. She quickly pulled into a ball, covering herself with her wings until the rain of mud, grass and lizard innards stopped. After the last plop, she crawled to her feet and began shaking goo and other chunky bits of lizard out of her feathers.

"Tomas?"

"Here." Tomas was eyeing the second lizard. "I think we should put more space between us and your lizard. If the back flip it just did is any indication, we're in for another blessed event."

"Blessed Event? I must have missed the first one because It was raining lizard parts and I was face down in a pile of goo."

"My dead lizard just had a baby by involuntary Cesarean detonation. It's the size of a Mini Cooper and the more of mom it eats, the bigger it gets." Despite the explosion, Tomas looked remarkably un-gooed.

"Great." Ariel pushed a few strands of sticky hair out of her face. Her wings hadn't protected her from everything. She was tempted to throw a nice big chunk of raw lizard at Tomas and see how he liked it. "They replace themselves. I thought I spotted two other dead lizards on the edge of the woods, thanks to the Dogs. I wonder if they've exploded yet."

Tomas was hovering impatiently. "We're going to need much bigger weapons and more air support to take these guys out completely."

Ariel looked up. The sky was clear but, in an hour or so it would be dark. If they stayed outside they'd soon be fighting things they could barely see.

The throaty roar of motorcycle engines echoed across the grass, followed by a large explosion. She smiled. You couldn't mistake the sound of a Harley or the sound of a grenade going off for anything else. She rose into the air and turned around for one last look at the rapidly bloating lizard. Its stomach was quivering like it was in the throes of a grand mal seizure. Tomas was already flying toward the sound of breaking glass.

"I'll get back to you," Ariel told it. "Or whatever you leave behind. Right now, I have to go kick some demon ass."

- 15 -

Bishop soon found the stairway that led to the arena. According to the map, there was a second exit from the platform to the labs, but Cassius told him it was blocked at the top by steel security doors. The arena stairway had wide steps and a tall, slanted ceiling, all of it was covered in white subway tile. Strips of fluorescent lights ran along each side of the ceiling creating such a glare it was hard to see much detail, except for the blood. It started with a few bright red drops that got bigger as Bishop's eyes followed them up the stairs. Something was huddled against the wall a few steps up, it looked like a bundle of old rags wearing a ratty hoodie and a pair of black high-top sneakers.

Bishop put the daiko back in its scabbard and felt around the top of the oversized jacket for a neck and a pulse. The pile of rags groaned at the touch and raised its head to show the pale, pinched face of an adolescent boy. Bishop unzipped the hoodie and moved his fingers over the kid's chest, looking for a wound. It was there under his ribs, a bullet had gone straight through the flesh, from one side to the other.

"What happened?" Bishop asked. The boy didn't look any

older than Mouser, although it was hard to tell from a face that was bunched with pain.

"Wanted to fight demons," the boy said, weakly. "A security guard shot me. Tried to make it back to the train, fell down the steps. Nobody noticed." The boy's eyes fluttered, and his head started to drop. "Am I going to die?" he asked weakly.

"No, you're not." Bishop knelt next to the boy and heaved his limp body over one shoulder. The kid was heavier than he looked but Bishop managed to get back on his feet by grabbing the railing along the wall for leverage. He could tell by the boneless sprawl that the boy was unconscious, which was probably a blessing. The armed Deepers guarding the train saw him the minute he came around the corner. One pounded on the door of the third subway car and two heads poked out of the opening to see what was going on.

"Bring him in," one of the heads said. The guards helped Bishop lift the boy into the car. Most of the seats had been removed to make room for pallets lined up side by side and covered in clean sheets and blankets.

A familiar voice said, "Put him here, Frank." The speaker was dressed in a faded Loyola sweatshirt and jeans.

"Catie!"

"Mr. Kale called me," Sister Mary Catherine told him. "He thought I should know the Deepers were going to get my kids back and I insisted he let me come along. I wanted him to give me a gun and let me fight the monsters, but he said I'd be more helpful taking care of the wounded. I'm still not above doing some serious damage if I have to. I'll worry about penance later."

Bishop smiled. "Sister Catherine, you are the scariest nun I have ever met, and that includes Sister Mary Teresa who taught Geometry at St. D's School-For-Boys-Destined-To-Be-Damned-To-Hell-For-All-Eternity. And may say, as far as guts go: Boo Yah!"

An older man in green scrubs looked up from examining the boy's side. "Through and through," he said. "Losing more blood than I'd like, but we can stop that. I'll stitch him up and give him some antibiotics. As long as he doesn't go into shock, he'll be fine in a couple of weeks."

"It's Taylor Brown," an older woman in patched scrubs said. "He's just fifteen and too headstrong for his own good. His mother's going to ground him until he's twenty-five after this little stunt."

"Let him be, Gwen," the doctor told her. "He was trying to help, and he's only the first of the wounded we're going to see tonight. We should thank God it wasn't worse."

On the wall of the car, one of the monitors suddenly switched from Zaki standing below a video of swarming nanobots to a wide-angle view of the arena floor. Zaki's face took on a look of alarm. A demon in the back row stood up, his suit coat splitting at the seams as his chest swelled and his arms lengthened to inhuman proportions. Before he could make a move, something spinning too fast to be seen took his head off at the shoulders. Other demons began to leap from their seats. A cocktail waitress dropped a full tray of drinks and started to run for one of the exits, only to be trampled by a group of screaming caterers. The big screens in the arena switched to a bird's eye view of Greggs' troops pouring into the stadium from the tunnel, firing their weapons as they split into smaller groups. More demons shed their human glamours, ripping off most of their party clothes to free wings, horns, claws, second sets of arms. The fact that no sound was coming through the speakers made it more shocking and surreal. Even the doctor couldn't look away.

On the stage, Zaki dropped his portable microphone and reached into his suit jacket, bringing out a small metal tube. He compressed a button at the top and the stage around him started to sink into the floor. The little knife thrower was quick.

Grabbing his jacket, he leaped onto the descending platform just as Zaki completely disappeared from view.

"Gotta go," Bishop said. "Take this." He pressed the coin the fortune teller had given him into Sister Cate's hand. "Put it in your pocket. It heats up when it gets close to a demon." Bishop stepped out the door and almost collided with Cassius who was standing right outside the train, cloth satchel over his shoulder, a cross bow in his hands.

"I'm coming with you," Cassius said.

"What? Who's going to watch the screens?"

"I've got people. And the live feed is coming through my phone. I can't let Zaki get away."

"What if Zaki sees you, but still gets away? He'll know you're alive."

"I'll deal with that if it happens. Right now, I'm joining my crew on the surface. End of discussion."

"I'm going after Mouser," Bishop warned.

"Fine with me," Cassius told him. "I hear the kid's quite a hacker. I might need some extra help getting into Zaki's files."

Zaki and the Great Constantini stepped off the descending platform as soon as it came to a halt. They were in the staging area under the stadium where performers and the heavy equipment could be sent topside without going through the tunnels. Zaki pressed the button at the top of the metal tube one more time. The platform started back up, sealing off and locking access to the floor below. There was a control room under the stage. It housed his security monitors and special effects team who managed the technical parts of his events both on the grounds and inside the arena. A bank of computers controlled the sound boards, the lights, the big screens, staging effects and even access to the building when necessary. The techs appeared frozen with shock at what they were seeing on their monitors. They swung around when Zaki slammed open the door to their glass paneled cubicle. Constantini hung back, almost unnoticed. Zaki pushed two of the techs aside to make room for himself at the control panel.

"Show me the grounds," he ordered. A tech roused himself and pressed a few keys. "And shut that fucking klaxon down right now or somebody's going to lose their head!"

Several views of the grounds came up the monitors. Wolves carrying automatic weapons were running across the parking lot toward the arena, some were firing into the air at a cloud of Gargoyles who were being chased by adolescent flying lizards. One wolf stopped to aim a small rocket launcher, blowing a descending lizard to pieces in the air. Lizard parts bounced off the asphalt and a few small 'goyles were knocked to the ground by the concussion.

"What are the lizards doing out of their cages?!" Zaki demanded. "And where did all those God-dammed werewolves come from?"

"An alert went off at the Zoo, Sir." One of the techs said. "Somebody threw the switch that opens all the cages. There's about thirty or forty Gargoyles out there and maybe twenty exploding lizards. There seems to be something else in the trees, but we haven't gotten a good look at it yet. If the wolves find a camera, they take it out."

"Seven Hells! The lizards are exploding. They must be binge feeding. Too much food stimulates them to reproduce. At this rate they'll be having twins any minute. Do you have any idea how much their DNA modifications cost me? Where's security?"

"I think they split, Sir. When they saw those things on the monitors they hit the siren and ran down that tunnel. We're the only ones down here now."

"You." He pointed at one of the techs. "Turn the perimeter lights on and open the stadium roof."

"But, Sir . . ."

Zaki back handed the tech, knocking him to the floor. "Do. It. Now!" he yelled.

"We need to get out of here," another tech said nervously, typing in the commands. "We're geeks not soldiers, we won't last five minutes if those guys get down here."

"Which guys?" the tech on the floor muttered. "It's a free-for-all up there and I don't think it's a costume party."

"Then get out!" Zaki had taken the chair vacated by the tech on the floor and was typing rapidly on his keyboard. "Before I kill you myself."

"But, where . . .?"

Taking one hand off the keyboard Zaki reached into his jacket, pulled out a small automatic and shot the man on the floor in the head. Eyes back on the screen, he fired a second shot into the ceiling. His left hand had never stopped typing. The remaining techs fell over each other trying to get out the door of the control room.

"I'm surrounded by fools and idiots," Zaki muttered.

"I sincerely hope that won't interfere with our business arrangement," said a voice behind him.

Zaki spun in his chair. A tall, orange demon in a spotless blue silk robe stood in the control room doorway, several other demons were clustered behind him. He seemed unruffled by what was going on upstairs.

"Of course not. I have everything I need to deliver the product. I'm just making sure no one interferes with that." Zaki extended a finger to push the final key that would execute the commands he'd just typed. He touched it and the screen went blank. He frowned. He'd just entered the sequence that would delete all his research data and crash the system, but what just happened seemed improbably fast. He attempted to reboot. Nothing. The entire system had gone down, but it seemed to have done it a millisecond second too soon. Impossible. He'd planned too carefully for this day. The bidding was just for show. He had already negotiated the terms and his price. He didn't want to appear too greedy A trillion dollars was a very good price. For now. In any case, he was done here. His eyes landed on the knife thrower. Zaki had always found the Gypsy brothers repulsive, but useful. He had no idea which one of them this was, but it didn't matter. Tesslovich had told him they were interchangeable.

"You," he said, "my guests need transportation. I still have a few more details to take care of. Escort them to the boats. I'll meet you at the heliport on the north shore."

Connie gave a brief nod. Once again, he would survive his stupid brothers. Fate had allowed him all the luck in their family. It was a sign of the greatness that would come.

The glass roof of the arena was blazing with light. A loud emergency siren was making an unbearable racket. On the ground, two dozen werewolves had begun to howl along. As Ariel watched, something hit the roof from the inside. It was beating at the glass like a trapped moth. It was soon joined by other 'moths' carrying what looked like clubs, metal poles, and in one case, a stadium seat. They were pounding uselessly against the panels when suddenly the roof began to roll back, opening the building to the sky. The moths pulled themselves toward the gap, huddling together impatiently until it had spread wide enough for them to breach the space.

Ariel watched the demons escape. Someone inside had thrown the switch to let them out. Below, the outside doors to the arena crashed open and more demons poured out into the night followed by a rag tag group of humans armed with automatic weapons, rifles, swords, cross bows and clubs.

"Oh, crap," she said, mostly to herself.

Once up the stairs to the arena lobby, Cassius and Bishop followed the noise. The piercing wail of the klaxon was echoed by the howling of werewolves and angry demons. Bishop led the way to one of the lobby alcoves where the two of them could look through a glass wall to the floor below. The stadium was total pandemonium. Small groups of Deepers were fighting their way across the floor toward the tunnel to the training rooms and lab buildings using swords, crossbows, and axes. Others were doing their best to block demons from getting up the stairs to the lobby and out onto the grounds.

The demons were ripping up seats and pulling apart railings for weapons. Small arms fire and the sound of an occasional automatic weapon added to the din. Blue emergency lights were blinking in sequence with the klaxon, giving the chaos a surreal, silent movie jerkiness.

Bishop watched as several hunched, ape-like demons leaped onto the backs of the top row of seats and began to run back and forth, taking swipes at invading Deepers with pieces of furniture, drink trays, claws. Two of them heaved a dead colleague into the middle of a group of Gregg's soldiers on the tier below them. A bullet pinged off the pipe one demon was carrying and ricocheted into the demon next to him, causing him to fly backward on a trajectory that that took out a walk-up bar and three cases of champagne. In the middle of the floor, Zaki's demonstration subjects were struggling to escape the restraints used to strap them to their boards. Ignoring the young men's pleas to be cut free, demons were pulling out the knives Connie had stuck into their bodies to use as weapons.

Cassius pulled out his GPS. "There's a utility stair further down the lobby to the right. It should take us to the space under the arena. Maybe we can get to the other side that way."

When they got there the metal door was bolted shut. "Move back," Bishop pulled a Glock, curtsey of Dingo, out from under his coat and fired at the lock. A hole appeared in the door the size of his fist. Lock parts could be heard bouncing down the metal stairs. "Demon load," he explained, deadpan. It was a great line. He'd been waiting to use it.

Behind them the klaxon finally went quiet. The last thing Bishop saw before pulling the utility door shut behind them was a crowd of demons crashing through the lobby doors with several of Greggs' men behind them.

They met no one on the stairs. The passageway at the bottom led straight to a large space under the middle of the arena. The door to a glassed-in control room hung open. Chairs had been tipped over and there was a body on the floor. The bank of computer monitors inside was completely dark.

"Zaki came down here and now he's gone."

Cassius felt one of the monitors. It was still warm. He tapped a few keys. "Looks like he took down part of the system before he left."

"He's not leaving by air. A car would be stopped before it made the gate. The train is being guarded. What else can he do?"

"Take a boat," a voice said. "I heard him order somebody to get it ready." A young man in jeans and a wrinkled t-shirt crawled out from behind the console. His glasses were smudged, and his hair and clothing were covered in dust balls and fragments of stale corn chips.

"What were you doing behind the console?"

"Mr. Kirienko was really angry. He knocked me off my chair. I crawled under the console. Stuff falls behind the board all the time and people pull out the wires trying to get it back. If you don't know what you're doing you can plug something into the wrong outlet."

"You the only one down here?"

"Yeah. Right after that Zaki fucker shot Jeff the rest of the guys split. Is Jeff dead?"

Bishop glanced at the body. "Yeah, I'm afraid so. What did he do to piss Zaki off?"

"He kept talking. Jeff always talked too much at the wrong time, in the wrong place. Man, he's dead? He got me this job."

"Did you know you guys were working for demons?'

"Not 'til tonight. Everybody on the crew assumed the effects were CGI. I know CGI and I thought there might be something extra weird going on, but weird is what FX techs do. We come in, set up, do the job, and get out. Booze and food is one of the perks. Dave tried to get upstairs earlier and score some brew, but the door was locked. We couldn't get out."

Did Mr. Kiriyenko crash the servers?"

"That seemed to be where he was going. He was crazy tweaked, muttering to himself like it was a mantra or something."

"So, he deleted the database?"

"Naw," the kid was looking at his friend's body. "We brought in a backup server and linked it into the main system, so we would have a double control of the mechanics. I waited until he was almost done, then I shorted out the monitors. He thought his server was purged. The data's still there if you can figure out how to get to it."

"You said boat?" Bishop interrupted.

"Yeah. This little stripey guy and a bunch of freaks went down that passage. Mr. Kiriyenko said there was a heliport on the other side of the lake."

Bishop touched his ear piece. "Ariel? Ariel!"

"Little busy right now, Bishop."

"This is important. Zaki's got boats. Demons are headed to the lake through a tunnel that connects with the arena. We've got to stop them before they get to the heliport on the other side."

"Any suggestions? . . .Oh, no you don't! Yeah, that hurts, doesn't it. . .? Bishop, you still there?"

"Ez, Ham, or Shep the Wonder Dog have rocket launchers. Do you know how to work one?"

"I'm a quick study. And it's Juke not Shep. Stop that!"

"Can you stop playing with the demon and find him! We don't have much time."

"Just a sec. There! Now who's sorry?"

Ariel scanned the ground for Juke. It was hard to tell one Dog from another from the air. She tapped her headset. "Juke?"

"Here," a growly voice answered.

"Zaki and some demons are headed to the lake. I need a rocket launcher."

"Got one. Meet you on the dock. We've been using 'em on these damn lizards. You gotta blow their shit totally up or you just get more. And there's demons and 'goyles all over the place. Any chance of reinforcements?"

"I wish. But I think we're on our own."

"We surprised 'em, El. But there's too much coming at us at once."

Juke was waiting on the dock with a long tube in his paws. He was upright but very much a wolf. The silver fur on his chest and muzzle was matted with blood. The grey-pink skin on his belly had four, long diagonal scratches that had already begun to heal. Under the scratches, an elaborate blue tattoo traced a pyramid of swirling lines and angular symbols upward from his groin to end in one final tendril just below his breast bone. Except for two heavy revolvers in a double shoulder rig, he wasn't wearing another thing.

"No boats?" Ariel frowned. Her insides had made the tiniest little humming sound for a fraction of a second before her concentration returned. Tattooed naked werewolves. Distracting.

"I don't think they'd leave 'em out in the open. There must be a boat house or another dock somewhere. Once out on the lake they'll be hard to miss.

Juke set the rocket launcher on Ariel's shoulder. Standing behind her he reached around, flipped open the laser sight and showed her how to aim and fire.

"You've got four small rockets in there." His muzzle fur tickled her ear. "The next one will load as soon as you fire. Lead the front edge of your target, point and shoot. Keep the back end of the tube away from your wings when you fire or you'll . . ."

"I got the picture."

The sound of boat motors echoed from the far end of the beach. Juke tilted his head, listening.

"Two," he said. "Lots of power. They'll be fast. I'll wait here as long as I can."

Two boats came flying out of the reeds at the far end of the beach, one after the other. They were long and low to the water with powerful engines and a wide, flat wake. One was moving faster and quickly overtook the other. The second driver seemed less skilled at driving a boat, or at least one that moved that fast. Ariel left the ground, repeating what Juke had told her about aiming and wind speed and letting the rocket lead the target just slightly. Someone in the back of one of the boats saw her tracking them. She could hear a shout and the first boat broke to the right, leaving its slower companion behind.

Ariel made a choice. She was going after the fastest boat, reasoning it was more likely to get away if she didn't take action immediately. The boat was cutting back and forth across the surface of the lake, trying to become a more evasive target but only succeeding in causing huge rooster tails of spray that glowed in the setting sun like plumes of blood.

Muscles screaming, Ariel closed the distance. Although the boat remained yards ahead of her it was time to take the shot.

Gripping the rocket launcher, she hovered, took aim, folded her right wing out of the way, breathed out, and fired. The recoil knocked her back a few feet and she almost dropped the tube. She watched the rocket overshoot the boat and explode harmlessly twenty feet off its bow. The small boat rocked violently in the wake created by the explosion and the driver spun it away from the turbulence. Ariel counted four or five passengers, not including the driver. It was impossible to tell if one of them was Zaki. She hovered and aimed a second time. Not rushing it, conscious of the beat of her wings, making sure she led the boat in the sight, but not by too much. She fired again. Everything seemed to stop for one long immeasurable moment and then the boat exploded in a massive fireball. She clutched the hot tube and spun in a circle looking for the other boat.

The second boat had taken off diagonally, trying to hug the shoreline until it was safe to make a break into open water. Right now, everyone in that boat would have their eyes riveted on the explosion. Ariel moved higher in the air, circling back to land, intending to come up behind the second boat. She could see wolves running along the shore, howling and barking at the boat, trying to keep it from landing where its passengers might escape into the woods. Ariel swerved around until she was directly above its bow and leveled the rocket launcher. The driver raised his hands. Other passengers quickly followed suit.

Now what? Ariel thought. We never thought about taking prisoners.

"Bring the boat in," a growly voice instructed from the shore. Three wolves waded into the lake to grab the gunnel as the boat floated into reach. "Let's see what they have to say first. We can eat them later." The driver made a small, whimpering sound and one of the older demons gave him a hard smack across the head.

"You heard him," Ariel said. "You're going to show us how

you got this boat onto the lake. Any funny stuff and I'll blow you into bite size pieces."

As soon as the boat was tied up at the mouth of the tunnel, Ariel gave the rocket launcher back to Juke. "Find out where this tunnel ends up, maybe we can get around behind them."

"What do you want me to do with the prisoners?" Juke asked. "Most of them look like they'd be more dangerous attacking a pizza than our guys."

"There must be someplace you can lock them up. I need to find Tomas and Bishop."

"You can't stay here," Bishop told Cassius. "There's no lock on the stairway, anybody could get down here. You want to play with the computers, you'll have to do it in the lab building. Find us a way to get there."

Cassius pulled out his PDA. "The fastest way is across the arena floor and through a tunnel that connects both buildings. Or, there seems to be another tunnel that goes from down here to series of rooms bisected by corridors. The floor plan indicates stairs and elevators to what looks like an administration complex."

The tech peered over Cassius shoulder. "When my crew split they went the other way. Nobody's come back yet."

"That could be good or bad."

"I vote we invite . . ." Cassius looked at the young man.

"Michael," he said.

"Michael along with us. No telling what happened to his friends if the demons took off in the same direction."

"Your choice, kid."

"Nice," Michael muttered. "This gig paid really well, too. Cash."

"The lesson is," Bishop said, prodding the young man ahead of him, "if something seems too good to be true, it usually is."

The arena basement was a labyrinth, but Cassius kept them on a path that took them under the arena and up a staircase that exited into a connecting tunnel to the administration wing of the lab building. Gregg's soldiers had built a barricade across the corridor.

"Cassius," someone called. "Jesus, Sir, get over here before they come back." Hidden hands started to remove several pieces of furniture so the three could slip through.

Bishop hung back.

"Frank?"

"You go on ahead," Bishop said. "There's something I have to do first."

- 17 -

Zaki stood, arms folded, looking through the glass of the Skybox window. Below, on the arena floor, was a scene of pure chaos. Demons from the cheap seats, as Zaki liked to think of the minor demon families and their tag-alongs, had reverted to their primordial forms. The fight with the invading humans wasn't a match between equals, but desperation often drove weaker opponents to amazing acts of bravery and sacrifice. Besides, the demons in the arena hadn't been enhanced with nanobots and were soft from centuries of easy living and rich food.

Zaki had used his private elevator to get to this special box that could only be accessed by a unique key. That key also triggered the decent of the Skybox to the arena floor.

The House of Eight demons who awaited him had expected the possibility of a Raptor or two attempting an assassination during the presentation, but not an all-out assault by armed humans and rampaging werewolves. Still, they seemed unruffled by the scene below. When Zaki arrived, several were standing at the windows making small wagers on the fighters, or on how many bodies a lizard could eat before it exploded. The monitors in the box were tuned to the security cameras outside. Zaki had seen the first boat explode. It had been a happy coincidence that the Raptor's rocket had preceded the remote detonation of a bomb the boat already carried. The second boat carried no one of any consequence. Zaki thought some of the passengers might even have been the techs from the control room under the arena. As informants they were useless. They had little or no information to give away.

The yellow skinned demon next to Zaki began to remove the formal robe she'd worn to the meeting in the board room. Underneath the expensive silk was a hardened leather vest and leggings covered in plackets of blue steel patterned like the scales of a dragon.

"I sincerely hope this minor distraction won't interfere with our business arrangement," Zoven said, adjusting the buckle on her sword belt. The scabbard was empty as requested.

Déjà vu, Zaki smiled. Demons were so focused on their own assumed superiority that they rarely saw the forest for the trees.

Zaki directed a token bow in the demon's direction, the gesture was a legacy of his mother's culture. *Arrogant bitch, you have no idea what arrangements I've made. When this is over, all annoying distractions to my plans will have been removed, including you and your pretentious progeny.*

"Of course not, My Lady." Zaki said out loud. *This chaos is just what we hoped for. The Raptors and the rest of this rabble will be blamed for your rival's deaths, you and your people will have avenged them, and your family will be hailed as heroes. Then we---and by that of course I mean you---will get on with a more important task.* Nicolai!"

Nicolai Tesslovich motioned his men forward. The bundles they carried clinked dully as they placed them on the box's long banquet table. The lawyer had been waiting hours to finish this one small task. He hated being treated like an errand boy, but the rewards he'd been promised would more than make up for the humiliation and the inconvenience of being treated like a servant, not to mention a brief but painful decapitation and the loss of two of his most loyal minions. As he twittered over the parcels, he could barely stand the thought that there might be damage to his beloved antiques. He'd only half-heartedly volunteered them, before the walls of his house were stripped of the most prized pieces in his collection. At least he'd managed to lay them out as tradition demanded before battle, on the unfurled skins of long dead demon warriors and their more delicate, but still colorful consorts. He straightened a scaly pelt. Everything was ready for the final confrontation.

"Angel Slayers." The female demon's voice was low and husky as she reached out to caress the elaborately twisted hilt attached to a scabrous green blade. Tesslovich cringed, thinking about the acid in the oil on the tips of her fingers. "No Raptor can stand against a weapon such as this. Our truce with the Guardians is finally at an end. We will kill the two young Raptors that have been causing us so much annoyance tonight, and then we will drive the rest of their kind from the face of the Earth. Your science will make us unstoppable. Earth, sky, water, every stone and flame in this world will soon be ours for the taking."

"As is your family's right, My Lady." Tesslovich sounded like the villain in a bad horror movie.

Zaki was barely able to conceal his contempt. "My only wish is to continue to improve my inventions under your protection."

As Zaki backed away from the table, he spread his hands, inviting all the demons in the slowly descending Skybox to take their choice of blades. The female demon hefted her choice of sword. It was obvious she had become impatient with irrelevant detail. This was her opportunity to finally kill an angel, something she hadn't attempted in millennia. She could hardly wait.

- 18 -

Bishop jogged back toward the arena. Most of the fight had moved outside. The dead and wounded littered the floor and two large, ugly lizards seemed to be eating their way through the remains. Bishop ran down an aisle toward the stage and jumped onto the platform. No one seemed to pay him much attention, especially now the lizards had started to fight over possession of the choicest bits. Most of the fight had moved outside. He used his sword to cut the straps that held the human boy upright on his board. The boy still had one throwing knife buried in his naked shoulder although the bleeding had stopped. Bishop pulled it out and lowered the boy to the ground. Then he started on the young demon's straps.

"Are you going to kill me?" the demon asked. There was more weariness in his voice than fear. His bare torso was covered in scars some new, some old.

"Not unless you make me."

The demon slid to his knees when the last strap split and started to crawl toward the wounded boy.

"Will," he said. "Will, you okay?" The other boy moaned softly.

"Help me with him, mister," the demon pleaded. "We got to get out of here. This place is hell on earth."

Bishop grabbed the half-conscious Will under the arms and tried to pull him to his feet.

"Why do you care?" he asked. "He's human."

The demon got his shoulder under one of the boy's arms and lifted. "He's my friend. I may be a demon, but I never wanted to hurt anybody. I just want my life back."

Bishop shouldered the other arm. "C'mon, we'll drag him out of here. I have a few friends I'm worried about myself."

"Look out!" The shout came from above their heads.

Bishop spun around. A huge demon had exploded out of a big pile of wreckage just off the stage. One arm still around the semi-conscious boy, Bishop fumbled under his coat with his other hand, reaching for the Glock. The demon was at least eight feet tall, with abnormally long arms that could probably reach them without him moving a step. His bloodshot, yellow eyes promised an immediate, painful death.

Bishop's gun hand seemed to be moving in slow motion. He wasn't going to be able to make the shot before the demon's huge hands closed the distance. Too fast, the demon swung his arms wide in what was going to be a crushing bear hug. Instead, he arched his back and crashed down flat on his face inches away. Half the length of a sword quivered deep in the demon's back.

"Had to throw it," Ariel announced, her clawed feet landing square on the demon's vast posterior. Bishop pulled the trigger. The Raptor's hands flew to her chest feeling for the wound. Behind her, something heavy hit the ground.

"There were two of them." Bishop re-holstered the gun.

Ariel gave the second demon a cursory, over-the-shoulder glance, Bishop had blown away most of its head. "I saw you through the roof. Are you crazy? You need to get out of here." She dragged the barely conscious boy to the edge of the stage by his belt and pointed. "Take the tunnel straight ahead of you. It leads to the training rooms. I think there's access to the lab building from there. Then get yourself off this property."

"I'm not leaving without you and Mouser." Bishop told her.

Ariel gave him a grim smile. "I thought you said your mantra was 'Don't be a hero.'"

"Oh, yeah. I forgot. But, since I'm already hip deep in demon goo and lizard snot, I thought I'd stay and see how this all turns out."

"Trust me. If I'm telling you to run, Run! We didn't know Zaki had this much wildlife on board. We're fighting 'goyles, lizards and demons, who, as you can see, are now uncontained and really pissed off. Tomas, the Dogs and I may be able to hold them until the prisoners are rescued and the Deepers get clear, but after that I think we're fucked."

Over Ariel's shoulder Bishop saw the tinted windows of the largest, cantilevered Skybox light up like a stage set. The box had to be twelve or fifteen feet across, supported by a metal track attacked to the wall.

"Uh oh." Bishop reached down and dragged a now somewhat conscious Will to his feet, so he and the young demon could get him moving.

The lights in the box became brighter the closer it moved toward the floor. Like deer in the headlights Ariel and Bishop stood and watched the box slowly descend until it hit the floor with a thump. Its glass doors began to retract to either side, revealing the interior one foot at a time.

As soon as the opening was wide enough, a demon in body armor stepped out of the box onto the arena floor. She was holding a sword; its blade was covered in the cancerous green mold Ham had called verdigris. As the windows moved farther apart, another demon joined her, then another and another, each armed with a weapon covered in deadly poison. It seemed impossible there were that many of them in the glass space, but like a clown car act, they just kept coming.

One by one, the smaller Skyboxes also began to move, beginning their own slow ride toward the arena floor.

"Angel Slayers." Ariel whispered. "Bad has just gotten a whole lot worse."

"Go!" Ariel yelled at Bishop. "They want me, not you." She sprang for the opening in the stadium roof.

Bishop threw Will across his shoulder and ran for the tunnel, the young demon jogged at his side.

"Down this way!" The young demon said. "We can barricade ourselves in one of the training rooms. There'll be medical supplies and stuff."

The light in the tunnel was dim. Emergency back-up lights had taken over the illumination giving the tunnel a cave-like effect. Ahead of him Bishop could hear pounding and yelling. The tunnel opened into a wide hallway with closed doors on either side. Behind them he could hear voices yelling "Hey! Let us out!" Open up!" "Help!"

The young demon tried a door. "Locked," he said. "It's electronic. They all lock-down at the same time for security."

Bishop laid Will down on the floor. "Wood or steel?" he asked.

"Steel."

"Okay, watch this. You inside! Get away from the door!" he yelled. "Move to the side and cover your ears." He held the Glock in both hands and pulled the trigger. The door exploded inward, leaving a large, smoking hole where the handle used to be.

The room was full of adolescents in their early to late teens, some older ones in their early twenties. Some were demons, the rest human. "Garl!" somebody said. Both Will, and his demon friend were hugged and patted on the back which made Bishop feel a whole lot better about rescuing him. Will was soon scooped up and placed on a padded table so someone could attend to his wounds.

"We heard noise and fighting. Explosions. We yelled but nobody would let us out."

"What's happening mister? Are you a cop? FBI?"

"Can you get us out of here?"

"We were kidnapped. They used us for experiments. Some of us are sick or hurt bad."

"They killed my best mate."

"We want out!"

"Slow down," Bishop said. He had to say it five or six times.

"This is a rescue but I'm not a cop. There's a big fight going on between the demons and the rescue team. I don't know who's winning, but it's really dangerous out there. We can either try and find a way out through another building or barricade ourselves in here and wait."

"Out!" "Out!" "Out!"

"We can fight."

"They trained us to fight."

"We want to kick some ass!"

"We'll take those fuckers apart. They can't fight all of us"

"Fight!" "Fight!" "Fight!"

"Okay," Bishop said. "Show of hands. Kicking some ass, it is. However, there's a few things you need to know. First, the werewolves are on our side."

"Werewolves?"

"Cool," somebody else said.

"Second. Avoid the giant lizards at all cost. And I mean that. They'll eat anything that moves and then they explode."

"Exploding lizards," A girl with pierced eyebrows and stars tattooed on the shaved skin above her ears repeated. "Check."

"Third. There's a new group of demons with really dangerous swords covered in green poison. They're after two friends of mine called Raptors. The Raptors look human, but they have wings like angels. Don't hurt them, okay?"

"And fourth, I'm looking for a friend of mine named Mouser. He's about this tall, fourteen, smart mouth and a wizard with computers. He can turn into a hawk, but probably hasn't in here because that would give him away."

Bishop could see lots of shaking heads except one kid.

"I think he was in the lower cells when I was there. The guards kept Taseing him because he gave them so much shit. One day they moved him. I don't know where. Sometimes they take certain kids to the labs. Then you never see 'em again. Sorry."

"So, there's more of you somewhere?"

"Yeah. Below here."

"Can we get there from here?"

"There's locked doors, an' guards an' stuff."

Bishop tapped his ear. "C.T.? C.T.? Can you hear me? Are you still receiving?"

"Bishop?"

"Yeah. I'm down in the training rooms. Just let a whole bunch of kids out of a locked practice room, but there's more locked doors."

"Okay. I can see your heat signatures. And now you're up on the monitors."

"These kids say there's cells below this level, but we can't get into them either. Everything from here on is electrically locked down."

"I'm in Zaki's office. Michael was right, the system didn't crash. There's a full bank of monitors for the security system up here. I can unlock the training rooms and the cells. Access to the lab building is going to be a little trickier, but not to worry. I see heat sigs in a few of the rooms and I'm almost live on the internal camera system. It's not part of the regular security system and I'm going to have to override the iris scan."

A series of clicks sounded along the corridor. "Hey," a new set of voices called. "Where's everybody been? Why are we out? Are they letting us go?"

"Thanks, Cassius. Tell me the best way to get them to the train."

"No way man," a voice said. "First we're going to liberate the cells. Then we're going to kick some demon ass."

"You're not the boss of us, you know."

"We have scores to settle, dude."

"Okay, fine. Fine!" Bishop had to yell to be heard above the din of voices. "How do I get to the lab building?"

Fingers pointed.

"Be careful."

"They got traps, man."

"Yeah. They got lasers and microwaves and stuff that'll fry your skull and toast your . . . things."

"Don't trust nobody, dude, 'specially if they're wearin' a white coat."

"Kill them scientist bastards for us, huh?"

"Hey!" somebody yelled. "The weapon locker's open!"

The announcement was followed by multiple shouts and cat calls.

"Be careful," Bishop yelled as everyone stampeded down the hall.

"Form a line," an older boy yelled. "We're splitting into two groups. Group one, you guys under sixteen to the cells. Group two, grab a weapon and follow me to the stadium."

"Hey," a voice said behind Bishop. It was the young demon from the arena. He had his friend Will by the arm. Will was looking better, although still a little shaky. "We wanted to say thanks. Nobody does what you did for us kids. Nobody straight ever risked their life for us. We, um, 'preciate it." Will nodded.

"Are you guys going to be okay?"

"Better all the time," Will managed.

"Watch your backs, huh?" Garl said.

"Watch yours, dude. We'd like the chance to return the favor sometime."

"Uh, gotta go. Find Mouser."

"Luck," Garl said. Bishop tapped the kid's extended fist with his own.

Both kids jogged backward for a few steps, then turned to join their friends at the weapon locker.

Luck, Bishop thought to himself. We're going to need it.

Ariel burst through the opening in the stadium roof looking for Tomas. She wanted to warn him. The fact was, they stood a better chance together against the Angel Slayers than alone. Tomas was on the ground, fighting three demons armed with swords: regular everyday swords, long, sharp, pointy and unpoisoned. Three on one was starting to look like a piece of cake. The demons were good, but Tomas was better. He lured them closer by concentrating on the one in front of him, letting the other slip behind and to the side. Suddenly, he dropped into a crouch, spinning on the ball of one foot, using the other leg to sweep the feet out from under the first demon while simultaneously extending his sword arm to drive its length through the one behind him. Ariel dove grabbed the third demon by his knobby spinal ridge and slammed him to the ground.

"Thanks," Tomas said, casually eviscerating the first demon while Ariel finished off the third.

"Bad news," she said. "We have a new set of warriors armed with Angel Slayers.

"How many?"

"Fifteen, twenty? House soldiers and their masters. From the livery I would say they're House of Eight. They obviously waited until we spent most of our energy on this lot, then joined the party. Where are the wolves?"

Tomas shrugged. Heard some whistles and most of them just faded into the woods by the lake."

"They ran?"

Another shrug. "Some of the demons have started to pull back toward the stadium. Bastards have iPhones. They're texting each other."

"That's because the demon dream team just arrived. Bishop and Cassius are inside somewhere. The Deepers are regrouping. The wolves are missing. I think we're on our own."

"So, in about five seconds, twenty demons are going to come through those doors looking for blood?"

"Yup. It's the fate of Raptors Tomas. No past, no future and dammit, not much of a sex life. Every time one of us gets a city it's because the last Raptor just bought the farm. If this is going to be our death, we might as well make it count. . .." Ariel paused. "How was that?" she asked.

"Inspiring. Really. I feel so much better, except about the sex part."

"Call it."

"Air."

"I'll take ground," Ariel said. "They already know I'm out here."

"Check."

"I really thought we could do this."

Tomas started to rise. His wings lifted the breeze they created lifted the hair around her face. "Doesn't matter."

"Tomas . . ."

"El, this isn't your fault. Somebody had to stand up for those kids. Besides you and me. Twenty demons?! Piece a' cake. Home by dinner." He smiled at her. Tomas rarely smiled. And when he did it stopped her heart.

Ariel turned away, dug an elastic band out of a pocket and tied back her hair. She could feel her sword, strapped and ready against her back. She bent slightly. The knife she'd attached to her calf was still there. She had the gravity knives. The guns were her last resort. She turned to face the arena doors, waiting. When the first demon in armor appeared, she let the gravity knives fall into place. Now there were demons on the roof as well. They stepped off, floating to the ground on small leathery wings. The swords they carried glowed a sickly green in the darkness, the color of infection and death.

- 19 -

Cassius ran a hand over his face. Bishop was liberating Zaki's kidnapped street kids. C.T. had seen their heat signatures in the training rooms, but he'd chosen to leave them there, thinking they were safer locked up than running loose. Now it was anybody's guess.

Zaki's office had been a find. His personal computers were hooked into everything and Cassius had been furiously inputting code, trying to unlock their secrets without erasing the contents or setting off a trip wire put there for just that purpose. The computer system had been compartmentalized with separate servers and firewalls. Zaki's server had a triple lock system which he was working on breaking now. He was more and more convinced that the locks were decoys, especially when one blew up, fried his key board, melted the insides of equipment that was connected to that server and, took down half the indoor lights. There had to be to be a back door to Zaki's server, its most valuable documents, schematic's and equipment lists. There also had to be recipes and samples of the mother cultures for the bacteria he had used in the bot's propulsion system. Zaki probably had that on his person. It was easier than creating the cultures all over again. Things sometimes go wrong.

Greggs had assigned Cassius three bodyguards who were taking their duties very seriously. He'd kept Michael with him to monitor the security cameras while he was breaking into the rest of the system. The guards had barricaded the doors with furniture and were keeping up a constant rotation of two guards patrolling the perimeter while one stayed with him in the inner office. It wasn't bad duty. The offices were plush. Zaki had spared no expense with the furnishings, works of art or stocking the refrigerator and bar full of treats. The collection of ancient Samurai swords alone must have cost a fortune. Blank outlines on the wall showed that he had taken the best with him.

It was almost full dark outside now. The view at dusk had been magnificent. One whole wall was floor to ceiling glass so Zaki could look out over the manicured, rolling lawn down to the lake. Now the glass was a growing black void that occasionally sparkled with brief bursts of light caused by muzzle flashes and explosions. Its thickness implied it was bullet, and probably rocket-proof.

After talking to Bishop, Cassius turned his attention to the security screens. Since the outside flood lights had come back on, he had been tracking Tomas with the mounted cameras outside and watched him as he fought the three demons. The Raptor was all grace and fluidity, no motion wasted even when fighting multiple opponents. Tomas' style was a good balance to the female Raptor's bursts of controlled fury. They made a good team. He was the disciplined martial artist. She was the rogue Samurai warrior.

He saw the two of them finish off the three demons, but almost immediately both Raptors glanced up at the arena's open roof. Cassius zoomed a camera out for a wider view and keyed up the inside of the arena so both views appeared simultaneously in the upper left and right corners of both his computer screen and the Sixty-five-inch TV on the wall across the room. A group of armed demons could be seen moving up the aisles toward the lobby level, and the front gate. Others were emerging from the open roof, their small leathery wings beating rapidly to keep them aloft. When he zoomed back, Tomas had disappeared, but Ariel was holding her ground. Cassius felt a small surge of relief at Tomas' absence, but he knew Tomas wouldn't abandon a fellow Raptor when she was outnumbered twenty to one.

"Greggs," Cassius yelled into his com. "Where are you? We've got a surge building. Zaki just dropped a bunch of new, well-armed demons into the arena. They're being joined by other demons and stragglers. Several with wings are on the roof and on the lawn, their target seems to be the Raptors."

"Acknowledge," Greggs voice said. "We've experienced significant casualties, Sir. The medics have been using the wounded who can still walk to get the worst cases back to the train. I'll pull everyone who can still fight back to the arena area and send more outside. The demons seem to be headed in that direction anyway."

"Another heads up, Greggs. Bishop just freed most of the kidnapped kids. Some are demons, but young and subjected to the same abuse. They're not what you're fighting. He tried to send them to the train, but they want a piece of the fight. If you can, see if your men can get them moving out of the line of fire or at least give them some backup."

"Are you okay up there, Sir?"

"My babysitters won't let me out of this room, thanks to you."

"Yes, sir. You can kick my ass for that later."

"And the odds I'll get the chance?"

"Slim. We're outnumbered, we've lost contact with most of

our patrols and we seem to have lost the wolves completely. I never thought they'd cut and run."

"I'm watching the monitors. A circle is starting to form on the lawn." Cassius zoomed in.

Ariel stood in the middle space. Her coat was long gone. She had rips in the legs of her black jeans and shirt, cuts and scratches on both arms and a smear of blood across her face. Her hair was gathered into an unruly knot at the back of her head. One of her two gravity knives was strapped to her left arm and fully extended. Her right hand held her sword. She still wore the Dog's Kevlar vest, and had her guns strapped in cross-draw holsters at her sides.

The appearance of the new demons seemed to be attracting a crowd. Some had human captives. Cassius recognized Deepers among them. Others looked like catering staff, office help, hired parking valets, even a security guard, all of them experiencing their worst night at work ever. The crowd parted as three of the new demons made their way down the arena steps toward the waiting Raptor. A round of betting started, some demons were using their human prisoners as collateral for their wagers.

When the three demons reached Ariel, they began to circle her in opposite direction. Two were men who looked drab in contrast to the female demon. She had small horns and pointed ears pierced with gold rings and jewels. Her skin was the yellow of hotdog mustard and she wore burgundy colored hardened leather armor. Her sword was definitely an Angel Killer.

A noble. Cassius thought. Probably House of Eight. She looks like she can't wait to kill a Raptor and take her head home to put on her trophy wall. In contrast, Ariel calmly began to turn herself, keeping the three in sight, but moving slowly enough to avoid becoming dizzy. It almost looked like she was smiling. The crowd started to close in.

- 20 -

Great! I've been adopted by the road company of 'Lord of the Flies'. Bishop had made it to the double steel doors at the end of the tunnel leading to the lab building. He was trailed by seven armed adolescents who were watching his every move. Three were girls; no sexism in the land of nanobot-enhanced lab rats. The group had told him that 'Lab Rats' was their chosen tag. After a few weeks in captivity on Zaki's estate you had to declare your affiliation, or you ended up somebody's lunch. A few of Bishop's posse even had homemade tattoos of a rat standing on its back feet striking a variety of martial arts poses. They were actually pretty good, considering.

"Blow the doors, man!"

Bishop was taking a good look at the doors, all the way from their shiny silver bottoms to their tightly sealed top. They were eight feet tall and solid steel. Too thick to even think about using a demon load. There was an optical scan machine mounted to the wall on the left side. He touched his com.

"Cassius?"

"Here, Bishop."

"I'm at the doors to the lab building. They look pretty solid, probably pneumatic. . ."

Behind him one of the boys launched himself into a running leap at the doors. He hit one of them with both feet, causing an electric blue outline to zip around his body, illuminating it like a cheap neon sign. He was instantly propelled backward, landing on his back and sliding across the floor until he crashed into the opposite wall. His mates pulled him to his feet, dazed but alive.

"Whoa!" the kid said. "What a rush!"

". . . and definitely electrified. There's a retinal scan thingy on the wall."

"No problem. I can authorize your scan from here. Put your right eye up to the lens."

"Are you sure I'm not going to get a laser beam through my unauthorized skull?"

Cassius paused. "Doubtful. Just follow my instructions. Put your eye up to the reader. A light will flash. That's the camera taking a picture. Step back. Give me a minute to store and authorize, then let it read your eye again and the system should let you through."

Bishop took a deep breath. "Okay, go."

The large doors made a whoosh sound and separated soundlessly into the wall on either side of the entrance.

"C'mon," Bishop said. "We've only got a few seconds." The rats crowded through with him in the middle. There was pushing and bitching, and someone felt Bishop's back pocket for a wallet.

"Chill!" He hissed once the door had closed behind them. "You keep making that much noise we might as well just run up and down the halls yelling: 'Lucy, I'm home!' until some mutant scientist comes out with a big stick and beats our brains in."

Shuffling ensued. "We could take 'im," somebody muttered.

Bishop tried the closest door in the long hallway. Locked.

"Look." he said. "Most of the rooms have a glass panel in the door. Pair up. Spread out, see what you can find. Do it quietly. If you spot kids in a room pass the word back and I'll have my wizard open the door. If you spot anybody else, hide."

"We want to kick some ass, man."

"Fine . . . Don't say I didn't . . ."

"Mr. Bishop?" One of the girls was looking through the window into one of the rooms. "I think these guys are dead."

Bishop pushed his way through the kids suddenly crowding the door's window. The room was obviously some sort of large banquet/meeting room. There were several round, banquet tables covered in white linen, topped with half eaten plates of food, silverware and half drunk or tipped over glasses of wine. Bodies were sprawled every which way. Most were dressed in white lab coats. One man had fallen by the desert table, a big slice of pink mousse cake shoved half way into his open mouth. A woman had toppled face first into her food. Several bodies had simply fallen to the floor or had slid from their chairs under the table. Each face had a livid blue tinge and protruding black tongue. Bishop could see it must have been a killer meal.

"Cassius? Can you unlock the interior doors in the lab building? We have a bunch of bodies down here. No blood. No visible wounds." Locks clicked up and down the corridor including the lock on the banquet room.

"Wait!" Bishop said, opening the door to the room. It was like telling a herd of buffalo to hold on just a minute before starting their stampede.

"Don't touch anything!"

"Wow. What happened?"

"I think they were poisoned." A plate shattered.

"When I say don't touch anything . . ."

"I was just smelling it. We never get fancy stuff like this to eat."

"I'm sure these guys wish they hadn't gotten fancy stuff like this either."

"These guys were major dicks, but this is wack."

"I think their boss was ready to make his big move and he didn't want any copyright infringement," Bishop said, mostly to himself.

"Hey," another voice put in. "We can't do nothin' here, right? So, we need to find the cages."

"Level Two," the girl with the stars said. "The guards were always talking about Level Two when they disappeared somebody."

"I'm going upstairs," Bishop said. "You guys go back into the hall and check for prisoners down here. And don't leave this building, it isn't safe."

Somebody made a rude sound with his lips.

"And by the way, a psychotic circus mutant took all my cash last night when he was torturing me for information, so whoever has my wallet can give it back." Bishop pulled the door of the room firmly shut.

In the back of the banquet room a body rose slowly to its feet. He was tall and thin, and once he discarded the lab coat, it was apparent he was an extremely fastidious dresser. His expensive suit was most notable for its restraint. All accessories had been carefully coordinated by hue. It was an elegant fashion statement if you were overly fond of the color grey.

- 21 -

The yellow demon made a feint in Ariel's direction. The Raptor didn't rise to the bait. Instead, she used her peripheral vision to watch the demon on her right. Yellow wasn't going to jump in right away and risk breaking a nail. She'd let the Raptor be worn down by her soldiers, then she'd take over, finish her off and claim the glory.

The demon to Ariel's right made his move with a flat sweep of his sword just as Ariel expected. She blocked it easily with her knife. He backed off, sliding his sword along her blade, making sparks. Ariel heard a sound behind her. She swept her knife in that direction, spinning, countering the second demon's blade by blocking it to her left, leaving her over-confident opponent open to a fatal right thrust to the throat. The skewered demon rose on his toes as she pushed the blade home. She planted a taloned foot in his stomach and gave him a push to loosen the blade. He fell over on his back, dead, green blood spilling onto the grass. The freed gravity knife snicked back into its sheath letting her scoop up the demon's angel killer.

"The poison has no effect on us, Raptor," the yellow demon said. "The blade is useless to you."

Ariel hefted the sword, testing its weight and balance. She smiled. "Rumor disagrees. Besides, I've always believed it's fairer to fight my enemies with their own weapons. It levels the field. Otherwise we're merely talking about a messy execution."

Another demon with a green blade stepped into the ring

"I see this isn't combat by elimination, it's musical chairs. Where's the sport in that, yellow face?"

"You object to me because of my color? In my world yellow is the color of kings."

"In my world it's the color of cowardice and liver failure."

The yellow demon spat at her. Ariel bared her teeth and thrust the green sword backward under her arm into the gut of demon number two. The verdigris bubbled and spit, sloughing off the blade where it touched the demon. Ariel held the blade up for everyone to see. "Sweet," she said. "And I thought I was lying my ass off."

Two new demons stepped in to the ring. The yellow demon ignored them. Ariel threw the poisoned sword at one of them. He took it in the gut and fell backward into the crowd. The yellow demon swung her sword and Ariel countered with her gravity knife. Two more demons stepped into the ring.

Ariel glanced at them. "Reinforcements. Scared, huh? I know I'm quaking in my boots." She looked down at her feet. "Oops, no boots."

"I don't know why I should lower myself to fight you," the yellow demon said. "The House of Eight deserves combat with its ancient enemies, not their disposable lackeys."

Ariel gave up on the knives and concentrated on her sword work. Six against one was pushing her skill.

"C'mon," she taunted. "Fight me, just the two of us. One-on-one. Winner takes all."

"We already have it <u>all</u>," the demon hissed. "Killing you is just taking out the trash."

- 22 -

"Don't you want to hunt demons with your friends?" Bishop asked the girl with the star tattoos.

The girl continued to trudge the stairs behind him. She'd chosen a wooden staff from the weapons room and currently held it with both hands, draped over her shoulders like a yoke. She shook her head.

"There doesn't seem to be much action in this building," Bishop said.

"You need someone to help you."

"It's probably more exciting downstairs."

"Don't care."

"I don't want to be responsible for you getting hurt."

"Been hurt. I'm probably a better fighter than you are. You need me."

Bishop sighed. "Do you have a name?"

"Starr."

Bishop glanced back at the star tattoos on the left side of her temple and cheek and nodded.

"Is Mouser your kid?"

"No. He's just . . . this kid. He's really important to a friend of mine."

Starr kept silent.

"Okay, I'm lying. I got kind of attached to him over this kidnap business. Him and Susan Elizabeth Morgan, this little girl I was hired to find. I think Zaki took her both of them. Have you seen any younger kids here?"

"How young?"

"Five. Six?"

Starr shook her head. "They'd be too young to fight. Maybe they took them to Level Three right away."

"What about you? Do you have a family? Somebody who's worried about you?"

"I got the Rats."

"It must be hard to live on the street. I have this friend . . ."

Starr held up a hand. "Been there, dude. Foster care, group homes, juvie. Been there, around the block and back again. The street is better. I just need to get out of this place and I'm cool."

"The train . . ."

"Not until we find Mouser. The Rats owe you that."

Level Three was a wide hallway with more doors. Bishop and Starr each took a side, looking through window panels into rooms filled with strange machines: microscopes, computers, white boards covered in mathematical symbols, surrounded by colored markers and wadded up pieces of paper thrown carelessly on the floor. One room had a warren of empty Plexiglas cages. Some cages had blankets on the floor, plastic bottles of water, a doll.

"Sssst." Starr had moved further down the hall. She pointed to a window and motioned Bishop over. Bishop could see the room was smaller than the other labs. One side was taken up with two floor-to-ceiling Plexiglas cages. Bishop saw movement inside one of them, but the angle of the window prevented him from seeing through the Plexiglas with any clarity. A desk sat across the room from the cages and narrow table occupied the space in between. The table had padded restraints attached to all four corners. A tall, almost human looking demon in a grey suit was standing at the table drawing a milky fluid from a glass vial into two small syringes which he placed in a small tray next to a dart gun. As Bishop watched, a figure in the first cage threw its body against the glass yelling words Bishop and Starr couldn't hear.

"It's the Grey Man." Starr said.

"Who's the Grey Man?" Bishop whispered.

"He picks the ones that go to Level Three. Some kids call him the Reaper, 'cuz nobody ever comes back after he takes 'em away."

"Stay here, I'm going in."

"No way! I got the bugs inside me. I'm younger, faster and stronger than you. I can take him. I wanna take him."

Bishop slid the daiko slowly out of its sheath. The Glock would have been easier, but Bishop dismissed it. Somehow, in this instance, a sword seemed more appropriate.

The Grey Man was making a toneless humming sound as he prepared the injections. It was an unconscious habit that surfaced when he was particularly pleased about something. When he caught himself doing it he usually felt annoyed, but not tonight. He had gone to the banquet along with the other scientists and lab assistants. The invitation had indicated that Mr. Kiriyenko was celebrating the debut of his invention and wanted to show his appreciation to everyone who had worked on it. All the scientists knew their famous boss employed a Parisian chef and had an impressive wine cellar. That alone was enough to ensure that everyone would attend. The Grey Man, however, had always worked exclusively on his own special projects so although he had things in common with the primate zoologists and bio-technicians, he rarely mingled with those who spent their time peering at computer screens and into microscopes.

The fact was, the Grey Man disliked being around other people, human or demon, and he especially disliked the combination of crowds and food. At the banquet he was careful to drink only bottled water that came with the seal still intact and to eat only from his own container which held, as usual, organic black rice topped with a handful of tiny pseudopodius crustaceans which the Grey Man favored not just because they were a rare and expensive treat, but because they were animals that reproduced asexually through the release of spores, thus eliminating any need for physical contact with each other. The Grey Man ate them alive, shell and all. He liked to hear them scream.

Sitting in a far corner, out of the way, the Grey Man watched with great interest as the poison, provided by the ever inventive Alameil, took effect. After a brief latency period to allow for mass ingestion, the substance hit its victims like a freight train, dropping greedy science staff like poleaxed cattle. The stricken frothed, shuddered, blushed an unpleasant shade of blue, stuck out their tongues and died. For the Grey Man it was an enthralling event. Unfortunately, when he tried to leave the room after the final death throes, the door was locked. He had to wait locked in the room feigning death until a group of repulsive juveniles managed to bypass the security system and open the door. After that it was merely a matter of staying where he was until they left, then slipping out and taking the back stairs to Level Three and his private lab.

The Grey Man was pleased to see his prisoners were still there, oblivious to the chaos around them, awaiting his pleasure. His only problem now was who to kill first? The hawk boy was very annoying; loud, rude, abusive; unbowed and unrepentant. The boy's physiology had rejected the nanobots with ease. The Grey man was still curious as to how he could overcome that, but the time for further experiments had obviously run out.

The girl was the same, more malleable because of her age, but still impervious to control. But, who to kill first? Did he kill the girl and let the boy watch? Or did he kill the boy and watch the girl's grief and fear as she realized she would be the next to die? The grey man paused. What would give him the most satisfaction? He shook his head. So very hard to choose.

Preparation put off the choice a little longer. He fondled the vial he'd just removed from a locked cabinet. He liked this poison, it varied slightly from the first in that it could be injected which made it act much faster, but it was also immeasurably more painful. He'd perfected the dose over time by experimenting on monkeys. He knew exactly how much to give, relative to both children's body weight. He'd kill the girl first, he decided. The boy had become attached to her. His grief would make it all the sweeter when it was his turn. He picked up the dart gun. It was loaded with tranquilizer. He could open the cage, knock the girl out if necessary, strap her to the table and be ready to administer the poison as soon as she woke up. There would be no funny business of course; he wasn't that kind of demon.

- 23 -

"Open Level Three." Bishop whispered into his com. The doors all along the hall made a soft click.

The Grey Man had already opened the far cell and was dragging a small, blond girl into the room. The child was struggling frantically to break the man's grip on her arm. Starr pushed past Bishop and flung open the door to the room.

"Susan Elizabeth!" Bishop shouted. The girl looked exactly like her picture except her hair hadn't been combed in days and she was wearing pink flannel pajamas and only one slipper. Bishop moved quickly to Starr's right, intending to take Susan Elizabeth away from the demon. The demon calmly pointed the dart gun in his direction and pulled the trigger. Bishop saw Starr's staff blur across his sight line. A small, blue feathered needle was quivering in the wood. Starr twirled her staff rapidly in a circle, picking up two more darts. Then she flipped it forward, aiming to bring one end down on the Grey Man's head. The demon tilted his body out of reach and pulled Susan Elizabeth in front of him, using her as a shield.

There was a large red button on the wall just inside the door. What the hell, Bishop thought, and hit it hard with a thrust of his elbow. The door to the other cell slid open. A brown hawk burst into the room screaming with fury. It went straight for the Grey Man's face, slashing with its beak, ripping and tearing at the demon's throat with its talons. Its wings beat at the demon's head obscuring his vision and knocking him against the table. Susan Elizabeth pulled free, scooting backwards until she was up against the far wall.

The Grey Man's hand scrabbled blindly across the table top. Too late, Bishop saw the hand land on one of the syringes. The demon thumbed off the needle guard and plunged it blindly into the body of the attacking hawk. The bird faltered. It managed one last beat of its wings then fell away. By the time it hit the floor it was a naked, fourteen-year-old boy, writhing in pain, his frothing lips and pale flesh slowly turning an unhealthy shade of blue.

"Mouser!" Susan Elizabeth screamed. The child threw herself across the room, landing on her knees at Mouser's side. Tears were streaming down her face as she frantically tried to stop the boy's convulsions.

Freed of the hawk, the demon was trying to clear the blood from his eyes, so he could see. Without another thought, Bishop took one long stride and plunged the daiko two-handed into the Grey Man's murderous heart. Bishop abandoned the blade to the falling body and spun toward Mouser, a terrible grief rising in his chest. Susan Elizabeth was still frantically trying to help him. As he watched, helpless, the child seemed to gather herself. She closed her eyes, took a deep, deliberate breath and put her small hands on either side of Mouser's face. Her own face screwed itself into a tight expression of extreme concentration. Within moments the blue in Mouser's skin began to recede, fading downward, away from the place she was touching with her hands until it was gone.

Starr took a step forward, but Bishop's arm went out, willing her to stop so there would be no risk of breaking Susan Elizabeth's concentration. They could hear her singing what sounded like a rhyme very faintly under her breath.

Suddenly, Mouser gave a wrenching cough, pulling gulp after gulp of air into his lungs. Susan Elizabeth threw her arms around his neck in a tight hug and dissolved into tears. One of Mouser's hands floated upward and began to pat her gently on the back.

"Suzee," he managed. "You're strangling me." The little girl let go, grabbing Mouser's hand, holding it as if he might suddenly try to leave her grip.

"What happened?" Starr asked.

"He tried to hurt Mouser," Suzee told her. "I made the bad medicine go away."

Bishop leaned over both of them. "Are you okay?"

Mouser frowned. "Bishop? Where's El? What took you guys so long?"

"The freeway was jammed with demons and exploding lizards. You need a hand getting up?"

"Suzee," Mouser said. "You need to shut your eyes."

"Why?"

"I need to get up and I'm, um, naked. You shouldn't be looking."

Suzee dutifully put both hands over her eyes, but she was smiling. "Already did," she whispered. Then she giggled.

Mouser staggered a bit when he finally managed to stand, then ran for his cell. Seconds later there was the sound of violent retching followed by a massive explosion of vomit. Bishop was about to go in to see if he was all right, when Mouser called out; "I'm okay. Don't come in. At least I think I'm okay, I never puked blue before."

"How'd you do that?" Starr asked the young girl.

Suzee shrugged. "I don't know. I did it before, when my dog was hit by a car. My mom freaked. Please, please don't tell her, she'll get mad. She says I get all my bad stuff from my daddy's side of the family."

"We need to go," Bishop announced once Mouser was stable and dressed. "We'll find a safe place to hole up until we know what's happening out there. Where's your other shoe?" He asked Suzee. She shrugged. "You ride then." He picked her up in one arm.

"Which way?" Mouser asked.

"That way," Starr said.

All the rooms looked like labs except one on the end, which looked more like some kind of dorm. It was lined with two rows of small, single beds, recently used but now empty and unmade. A lone teddy bear sat against a metal leg, abandoned and forlorn. Starr opened the door.

"Anybody here?" Bishop said. No answer.

Starr walked down the middle space between the two rows of beds. Two or three beds had blankets that spilled over the side touching the floor. She used the end of her staff to lift one up. A small, bare foot was instantly drawn out of sight.

"Hey," Starr said softly, dropping down on her haunches. "It's okay. We're the good guys. We're here to rescue you." She leaned over sideways to get a better look. Two sets of frightened eyes looked back. "It's okay, really. C'mon out."

The boy was the first. He was about three, dressed in grubby pajamas with no shoes or socks. His eyes were scared but he was trying to be brave.

"Down," Suzee ordered Bishop. He let her slide down his arm until her feet touched the floor. She ran over to stand by Starr. "They're telling the truth," she said to the boy. "They just rescued me. He killed a demon." She pointed back at Bishop. And

Mouser, he's a really fierce bird. And Starr hits bad guys with her stick."

The boy reached out one finger and touched Starr's staff. "It's okay, Neelie," he said to someone behind him. "It's safe." A little girl about the same age crawled out from under the same bed.

"Are you the only ones here?" Starr asked.

The little boy shook his head, "You can all come out now," he called as if it were the end of a game of hide and seek. Three more children crawled out from under other beds.

"I'm hungry," one announced. The first little girl motioned Starr to lean closer, so she could whisper. "I have to pee."

Bishop sat down on one of the beds. I have five children under six," he thought, plus a shape shifter; a child with magic powers and a scientifically enhanced Kung Fu Lab Rat barely into her teens. How did he suddenly get elected Kindergarten Cop?

"Okay," he announced. "We're all going to move to a safer place. So, everybody needs to pee before we leave this room because we can't stop on the way. Do you all have slippers?" There were shrugs. "Then try to find them, okay?" To Starr he said, "This would go faster if we knew where the rest of the Rats are."

"I'm on it," Starr told him.

Mouser looked at Bishop. "Go," Bishop said. "Be back here in five minutes, Rats or no Rats. It's not safe out there."

"Why do we need Rats?" he heard Mouser ask as he followed Starr out of the room.

Amazingly, everyone found their slippers, including an extra one for Suzee.

∾

"Bishop?" It was Cassius on the com. "Where are you?"

"Still in the lab building. I found Mouser, Susan Elizabeth and a bunch of three and four-year olds locked in some sort of dormitory. I'm trying to corral the older ones who came in with me. What's happening out there?"

"The Raptors are in big trouble. Zaki had some super demons in reserve and there's a big showdown forming on the lawn."

Cassius checked his monitor.

It showed a lone Deeper suddenly bursting into the ring from inside the crowd of raucous spectators: he had a table leg in one upraised hand, his eyes were wide, mouth open in a soundless howl. One of the circling demons almost casually cut him down with a mortal blow to the neck, then motioned impatiently to have his still twitching body dragged out of the away. The death caused the circle to widen, demons pressing back from the fighters, giving them room.

Tomas was nowhere in sight.

"I see where you are," Cassius said. "I'm sending one of my men to bring you to us. We can decide what to do with your charges once you get here."

"Thanks. Tell him we'll be the ones with the teddy bears."

- 24 -

Where were all the demons coming from? Ariel asked herself. The ones in black leather armor pushing their way to the front of the crowd hadn't taken part in the initial fighting. Zaki must have been holding them in reserve. Each group had a different colored stripe running diagonally across their jacket that seemed to designate which demon Familia they belonged to. The stripes also seemed to designate the wearer's rank and status in the hierarchy of hell.

The other demons visibly deferred to the House's authority, but no coercion was necessary here. A sense of excitement was building, a sense that the next few minutes would bring a decisive demon victory, a symbolic win of massive proportions against the army of light. Much more was at stake here than kidnapped children. Something was about to change forever, the death of two Raptors was merely a showy detail.

The yellow demon swung her sword in a circle over her head. The crowd of demons moved back even further, jostling for position, larger demons shoving and elbowing their way to the front to get the best view. Once through the crowd, the armored demons spread themselves around the inside of the grassy ring, shoulder to shoulder with the members of their own house.

Ariel took a deep breath. She expected to feel alone and scared, but the truth was she felt acutely alive. Her senses seemed to have sharpened even beyond a Raptor's natural enhancements. The darkness didn't matter; her eyes saw everything in acute clarity. She could actually feel the blood rushing through her veins, the oxygen pumping in and out of her lungs. The bones in her face were shifting, cheeks becoming higher and sharper creating dark hollows beneath. Her forehead pushed forward forming a broad V, exaggerating the deepness of her brow and the predatory set of her eyes. Long fingers with pointed, curved nails wrapped the hilt of her sword. She let her wings unfurl. She was tired of the ground, she would take this fight into the air, see how high a demon could rise on those ugly flaps of skin they called wings. Raptors didn't run. They fought to the death, making room for the next one of their kind to do the same. And the next, and the next, until the end of time.

The gust of wind pulsed behind her, chasing a few fallen leaves across the grass. Tomas had come back to fight with her. She felt his heat as his wings touch hers, a brief brush of greeting. They stood back to back.

"You should have kept going," she told him.

"There's a plan in the works. We only need to hold them for five minutes, El. All their attention has to be on us. Every demon, every blood shot eyeball. You think we can do that?"

"Sure. No problem. And Tomas? The yellow bitch is mine."

"Do you have any food? These guys are hungry." Bishop set the child he was holding down on the carpet; out of the way of the adolescent Rats and the strays they had picked up from the cells that were piling in behind him. The child tilted his whole body backwards to look up at the tall man who'd opened the door. Cassius leaned over and picked the boy up. The child reached out a tentative hand to touch Cassius' rusty colored dreadlocks, his brown eyes looked shyly into the adult's gold ones.

"You hungry?" Cassius asked. The child nodded solemnly. "Then let's see what we can do."

Several of the Rats were also holding children. They'd cheerfully volunteered to carry the smaller abductees, comforting and joking with them, quickly turning their fear into an enthusiasm for adventure. One fifteen-year-old Rat with wildly spiked hair and a scar under one eye had two teddy bears strapped to his back and a little girl asleep in his arms with her head on his shoulder. He laid her carefully in an overstuffed chair and joined the rest of the gang milling about Zaki's office.

The Rats were full of shameless curiosity. They began opening drawers and cabinets, claiming space on the two couches, wandering through the suite into the conference room and back again. The built-in bar and refrigerator were quickly raided. Cassius' guards did their best to relieve the Rats of anything alcoholic or unsuitable for human consumption, but it was like taking booty away from marauding Huns.

As soon as he knew Suzee was safely inside the room, Mouser had eyes only for the computer. He took over Cassius' empty chair behind the big desk, his eyes fixed on the flat screen in its recessed storage compartment in the wooden top, his fingers were already tapping the keys.

"Access problem?" Mouser asked as soon as Cassius extracted himself from the Rats and their endless stream of questions. Starr had already promised Mouser that Suzee would get her share of the available food.

Cassius seemed unperturbed by the boy's boldness. "I can't crack the final access to the server," he told him. "I've gotten through the initial encryptions but I'm not having any luck with the last password. I think it opens the back door."

"You knew this guy?"

"Pretty well, I thought. Except for how ruthless he actually was and the lengths he was willing to go to get what he wanted."

"You know his birthday? His sign? Did he have a pet? Kids? A hobby? A hero? Someone or something he really connected to?"

"I don't know. I think he was close to his mother."

"Did you try her name?"

"No luck. Birthday either. He's a Scorpio."

"What else?"

Cassius leaned over Mouser's shoulder, watching the code the boy was entering with great interest. The kid was good.

"We were partners, but we didn't have a personal relationship. I know he liked old monster movies. Had a whole collection of original films from the twenties and thirties. Things like Dracula,

The Wolfman, Black Cat, but his favorite was Frankenstein. He sometimes ran the sound track in the background while he worked. He once told me it inspired him. That he'd always admired the doctor's obsession with overcoming death. That's what Frankenstein was trying to do. It was a prime example of how the success of scientific experimentation justifies the means: that society's concept of morality, religion, personal property, even acts of murder pale in comparison to the positive impact of a scientific breakthrough.

"I should have known what I was dealing with then, but I thought he was just talking. We both wanted to engineer a giant leap in medical technology. I never understood what he actually had in mind for our little bots until it was too late."

"Frankenstein. I saw that movie a few times." Mouser began typing again. "They always play it during a Nightmare Theater Classic Horror Marathon. It was cool, but everybody always thinks Frankenstein was the name of the monster." Mouser typed *frankenstein, drfrankenstein, and madscientist* including instructions to convert certain letters to caps and common number substitutes. Nothing. He stopped for a moment, deep in thought, then typed *itsalive!* in the password prompt.

"Numbers are easy to break, numbers, letters and symbol combinations are much harder, but he probably didn't want to make a backdoor password too hard to remember . . . and, voila! You're in."

Cassius nudged Mouser out of the chair. He inserted a thumb drive into the USB port and initiated a high-speed download. The data flew across the screen in a blur.

Mouser looked up. Everyone except the exhausted three and four-year olds were at the window. He pushed his way through the bodies until he stood next to Bishop and Starr.

"Shit! Are those guys all demons? Why is El just standing there? Who's the other Raptor? Why don't they just fly for it?"

"They'd never make it," Bishop said.

"Demons fly too," Starr told him.

"Look at those dudes in the leathers. They seem to be telling everybody else what to do."

"It's Custer's Last Stand," Bishop said. "Too many Indians, not enough Cavalry."

"What's going to happen?"

Bishop shook his head. He didn't want to say what he thought was going to happen. It was the classic tragedy scenario. First there would be the hero's death in battle, followed by the traditional massacre of all prisoners, and then the beginning of the end of the world as they knew it.

Probably won't live long enough to see that part, he thought.

Something made him look over his shoulder. He saw Cassius' hand fly to his head set. Bishop tapped quickly through the channels on his own com. ". . . coordinated attack. . ." was what he heard. ". . . wolves . . . woods. The sky . . ." He spun back around. Lights had suddenly appeared in the sky over the lake; small, blue-white flames moving in loose formation, getting brighter and brighter as they closed the distance. Not helicopters; definitely not a plane. More demons coming in for the kill? Aliens landing? Nothing would surprise him at this point.

Below, on the lawn, a roar went up loud enough to be heard through the soundproof glass. It had nothing to do with the lights over the lake, not one creature down there was looking anywhere but at the two Raptors and the six demons in black, suddenly rushing toward them. The last stand had begun

$\sim$

Ariel and Tomas launched themselves into the air, ancient Angel Slayers swished uselessly under their feet. Their attacker's momentum carried them to the opposite side of the circle where they slid to awkward stops. Ariel snickered. If she was lucky, maybe she'd die laughing. The few seconds advantage gave the Raptors the opportunity to attack from above. Between them they slashed the heads off three demons and mortally wounded another before the rest could regroup, but the advantage was fleeting. Demons were also capable of flight; leathery wings quickly expanded from a dozen shoulder blades and the battle was rejoined.

Luckily, the air wasn't a demon's best element. Their wings were made of a thin, skin-like membrane on a boney frame. They unfolded like half of a badly constructed umbrella, a design that lent itself more to flapping in menacing circles than dogfights.

Demons seemed to prefer flying straight toward their target, heads in the upright position, feet trailing along behind. They were counting more on mass in an attack than dexterity. In contrast, Raptors fought like agile birds of prey. They dove and turned, twisted and spun upside down and sideways, tumbled head over heels, extending and retracting their wings as necessary, using their talons to slash and tear at every opportunity. Tomas and Ariel attacked the flying demons from all angles, trying to disarm, disable, and kill.

They went for the demon's wings. The bat-like membrane tore easily if ripped by a sword or claw. Ariel saw Tomas land on one demon's back, hack off a wing and ride the spiraling creature to the ground. But as soon as one demon plummeted to earth, there was another to take its place.

Blood was soon running into Ariel's eyes from a cut on her forehead. She wiped it away with the back of one hand and countered the sweep of a blade with the other. Tomas was still fighting below her; he had one demon by the tail and was using it to swing him around into two armed demons, knocking all three out of the fight. The action caused a momentary halt while the demons took a moment to re-strategize their attack. The betting on the ground increased.

Ariel dropped down a level where she and Tomas hung, panting, a few feet apart. Tomas' face had shifted into a battle mask just like hers.

"How many?" She asked.

"Lost count, but there's plenty more where they came from."

"Should we try to run for it?"

"No chance, especially for both of us. You go. I'll hold them off as long as I can."

"Yeah, right. That'll look good on my resume. You go. I still have a few moves I haven't shown these guys and I'd hate to miss the chance now that I'm all warmed up."

"I liked the punch to the jaw you gave that spotted blue Fnorath. He never saw that coming."

Ariel grinned. It was a scary sight. "He called me chicken face. I don't take that kind of crap from someone with a snout and tusks."

"Uh oh. Here they come again. Stay close."

The next few minutes were a blur. Blood flew in all directions. Ariel barely noticed she was bleeding freely from a wound in her side. She'd lost a clump of feathers from one wing and a long cut on one leg that burned like a trail of fire; the flesh around it was rapidly turning numb. She assumed the wound had been poisoned by an angel killer. There was nothing she could do about it right then, so she ignored it. After all, she didn't need to stand up to fight. She'd stay in the air until she could no longer lift a wing.

She swung around, looking for the next demon. The movement hurt, and her vision swam for just a moment. When it cleared she could swear she still saw trails of light, streaking through the night sky toward her side of the lake. Below her, the party atmosphere paused as the sound of revving engines began to echo off the outside wall of the arena. A ragged half-circle of Harleys suddenly tore out of the woods heading straight for the demons on the lawn. Their furry riders were whooping and howling while equally furry passengers on the back brandished a wide assortment of weapons. The missing wolves were definitely back. On the other side of the lawn, armed screaming humans were running down the arena steps knocking any demon within reach to the ground. Some of them were too young to be Deepers and those showed a reckless enthusiasm for the fight that made them stand out in the crowd.

The House warriors waded through the confusion, cuffing and threatening any demon who tried to run. They'd taken their losses from the Raptors but they still had the numbers to crush this attempt to disrupt their plans, but they couldn't do it alone. They needed foot soldiers to take the brunt of the attack. Many of those foot soldiers were drunk, having gotten into the caterer's alcohol to celebrate the Raptor's certain defeat by the Houses. None of them had been betting on "if" the Raptors would lose, they'd been betting on 'who first?' and 'when?'.

A hand grabbed Ariel's wrist. She startled out of her daze, back into the moment and began to twist around, determined to free herself from whoever had hold of her.

"Don't! It's me. You were starting to drop." Tomas pulled her higher and she let him, hoping the fog would clear. He shifted his grip to her sword harness, using his wings to keep both of them aloft.

"The lights . . ." Ariel said. "The noise . . ."

"Reinforcements." Tomas told her. "The Guardian must have decided to help us. Look at them! Their swords are brighter than glory. And the wolves and Deepers were just waiting for a better opportunity to launch a surprise attack."

The sky overhead was suddenly crowded with Raptors, the sound of their wings was like the beating of a hundred temple drums. Each held a sword limned in blue flame and their faces were grim with purpose.

Among the Raptors were a few larger figures dressed in white tunics and chain mail covered by a belted red tunic with a white cross on it. Their massive wings were the color of snow. One passed close to Ariel and Tomas. He seemed oblivious to them until the massive head turned slightly to reveal eyes like blazing sapphires in a face of stone. The angel reached out to touch the Raptor's swords with his own, igniting the same blue flame they could see on the other Raptor's blades. A burst of energy traveled up Ariel's arm, her head cleared, and the pain in her leg became a minor annoyance that she quickly disregarded.

"Let me go," she said to Tomas. "I'm okay now."

A cloud of winged demons was rising into the air to meet the invading Raptors, among them the yellow demon from the House of Eight. She was splattered with blood of various hues, some of it red. Her carefully arranged hair had come unbound and was swirling around her head like a nest of furious snakes.

Not so high and mighty now, Ariel thought. You asked for angels to kill, and here they are. But you, my lady, are mine, all mine.

Tomas rose to join the other Raptors. He'd trained some of them and they quickly made room. One of the wing leaders dropped back to give Tomas his place, but Tomas waved him back, slipping himself easily into one arm of the V formation with a tilt of his wings.

Ariel hung back. She had only one target in mind and trusted Tomas to pass the word.

26

"I have what I came for," Cassius announced. I think we should try to get to the train while everyone has their eyes on the sky."

"Sir . . ."

"You need to understand something. I have everything Zaki knows, or thinks he knows, right here in my pocket. I can use this information not only to stop him, but to save these children from the effects of his experiments before it's too late. I need to get back to my lab and these kids need to get off this property before it all goes to hell. . ."

"Look," Mouser said. He was back at the computer. The fight was right outside Zaki's window, so he had switched the security monitors to the inside of the arena and turned up the volume. The large flat screen on the wall of the office showed a scene of massive destruction coupled with the eerie stillness that often accompanies the end of a massacre. The lizards were gone, but a few new predators had arrived to sample the spoils including a flock of Gargoyles busily picking through the dead looking for the choicest bits.

One predator, however, stood alone, surveying the collateral damage left behind by the triumph of science over morality with supreme indifference. He had won, the rest was not his concern.

Zaki Kiriyenko absently brushed an invisible speck of debris off the lapel of his impeccable suit jacket, turned on his expensive designer heel, and stepped back into the floating Skybox. The glass door closed behind him with an inaudible snap and the box began to rise into the air.

Cassius stared at the screen. His lips had drawn away from his teeth and the skin of his face had gone grey and tight against his skull. The room went silent.

"Pull up the blueprints to the arena," he said. "I want to know the fastest way to that Skybox." He held up the thumb drive. "You take these kids and get this back to the Deeps any way you have to do it. Swear you'll make it happen."

"You can't go after Zaki on your own, C.T. He won't be alone and look at the damage a few demons with medieval weapons have already managed to do. You'd never make it. And even if you did, he'd kill you without a second thought."

"I'll take it," Mouser said, reaching for the thumb drive. "Me, Starr and the Lab Rats---we can get everyone to the train."

"I'm going after Zaki," Cassius said. "He killed my wife. He kidnapped my son. He took what I was creating for the good of mankind and turned it into a perverted weapon that demons are going to use for their own evil purposes. He's here and I'm going to kill him if it's the last thing I do."

"I can't believe I'm saying this," Bishop told him. "But I'm either coming with you or I'm going to knock you unconscious, tie you up and drag you to the train."

"Look. Angels."

"What?" All eyes turned toward Suzee. She was standing at the window, her forehead pressed to the glass.

"The angels. They came to save us kids, just like they said they would. They're beautiful."

Susan Elizabeth Morgan was absolutely right. Backlit against a rising harvest moon, the sky outside the window was full of winged figures, both dark and light."

"Holy shit!" Mouser said. "Those are Raptors and the guys in white look like the statues on the corners of the Angel Tower on the Guardian Building. Holy shit!"

"Mouser! They're angels. They'll hear you." Suzee said.

When Bishop turned around, Cassius was gone.

"Damnation!"

"You! Bodyguard, what the hell?"

"Mr. Kale took George and Sean with him. I have orders to get y'all to the train and that's what I'm going to do. So, listen up! Anything that isn't a weapon and doesn't fit in your pocket, drop it. Anyone old enough for a driver's license, up front. The rest of you Lab Rats, grab a kid. If they need a bear, grab it now. We will not be coming back."

Mouser scooped the maps he'd just printed out of the copier. Bishop handed Mouser the thumb drive. Mouser gave Bishop a quirky smile. He'd been responsible for getting this data, so it was his to protect and deliver because it was going to save the world. It was a hacker's dream come true.

"Take a map, dude," he said to Bishop. "Better hurry. He's got a head start."

"Stay safe kid," Bishop said.

Mouser hung the cord connected to the thumb drive around his neck and dropped the device inside his shirt. "Neither rain, nor snow, nor demon might . . ."

But Bishop was already out the door.

27

Lena, Queen of The Cage was waiting for Zaki inside the Skybox. She was dressed in a black pantsuit and high heeled boots. Two large metal suitcases stood next to her feet, packed and ready to go, just as Mr. Kiriyenko had requested.

Nicolai Tesslovich was pacing a nervous groove in the carpet by the windows. Ten steps one way, ten steps back.

"It's absolute pandemonium out there." He said to Zaki as soon as the outer doors had shut behind him. The Skybox started to rise. "I don't understand why the Houses are trying to chase down two Raptors when we have important business to conduct. This is simply unacceptable! This building is falling down around our ears. We need to leave."

"My business here is done, Nicolai. I am leaving. Lena, bring the cases, the submersible is waiting."

"A submarine? What are you talking about? Where's the helicopter you promised?"

"Plans have changed. I have a small underwater craft that will take Lena and myself to the other side of the lake. I'm afraid there's only room for two, and my prototypes of course."

"You bastard!" Tesslovich said. "We're partners! After all I've done for you. All I've been through! Did you forget I'm a lawyer and we have a contract? You can't get away with cheating me out of my share! I'll sue you. I'll take what you're doing to the courts, to the media, to the Houses. I'll ruin you!"

The Skybox stopped its ascent. The door to the private elevator opened in the back wall. Lena picked up the cases, her face was without expression. She did whatever Mr. Kiriyenko wanted. She could crush Tesslovich like a bug. Zaki had only to ask.

Tesslovich looked around frantically for something to use to stop them from leaving. There was still one Angel Slayer on the table, almost hidden by the rumpled demon skins. He grabbed it by the hilt. Although it was corroded with poison, he knew it was still very sharp. One cut would do the job, or at least disable Zaki to the point that he could be persuaded to take Tesslovich with him instead of the demon girl. Didn't all the legal manipulations, betrayals and vicious business deals Tesslovich had done for Zaki and his company over the years mean anything? He'd been promised billions in return. He wouldn't be turned away like a beggar at the door.

Zaki reached into his suit coat pocket. It was a casual gesture, without haste despite Tesslovich's weapon. He pulled out a small device about the size of a cell phone and pointed it at the lawyer.

"Is that tiny thing a weapon?" Tesslovich asked contemptuously. "I survived a decapitation. Your devices have made me immune to death. You should hope that they've done the same for you, you half-breed coward."

Zaki pushed a button. Tesslovich took one step forward, dropped the sword and clutched at his face. Green goo began to stream from his nose, ears and eyes. His body heaved and shuddered, then seemed to collapse in on itself, losing fluids, deflating, becoming virtually boneless until it was little more than a sack of skin lying on the floor. There was a final scrabble of fingernails against the carpet and it was still.

"You forget, Nicolai. I invented those little devices. I control them. What saved you also has the power to kill you. It's a lesson my patron will someday learn for himself." He dropped the device back into his pocket, picked up a leather satchel, put the strap over his shoulder and turned toward the open elevator.

"I see no reason to linger further, my dear," he said. "Let's be off."

The map Mouser had given Bishop was confusing. Maybe, Bishop conceded, running after C.T. Kale on his own had been a bad idea. Zaki was more than dangerous, he probably had body guards, and what was Bishop? One guy with a sword and a gun full of demon loads.

He took another look at the map. There was no YOU ARE HERE arrow of course, but it looked like the quickest way to the Skyboxes was a service passage that ran behind the arena wall. They seemed to be served by both a freight elevator and five private elevators that ran to each of the boxes. Bishop headed for the freight elevator. He met no one the entire trip and stepped out into a deserted corridor when the elevator stopped. Everything was extremely quiet, as if the walls had been soundproofed against the raucous noise produced by the arena. After the cacophony of last few hours the silence made him feel like he might be the last man left on earth. That post-apocalyptic scenario hit him a little too close to home and Bishop found himself hurrying to catch up with Cassius.

Luckily each box had a back door as well as an elevator. The one to Skybox One had been pried open and stood slightly ajar. He heard a familiar voice inside and called out "Don't shoot me" before he pulled the door wide enough to slip through. Inside, C.T. Kale's bodyguards had their guns ready and pointing at him anyway when he entered the Skybox. Cassius himself was down on his haunches poking at something on the floor with a chopstick. It was vaguely man-shaped, and the chopstick was covered in green goo.

"What is that?" Bishop asked him.

"I think it's the remains of Nicolai Tesslovich."

"Looks like somebody turned the counselor into a rug."

"That's more accurate than you might think. His bones and internal organs seem to have totally dissolved. All that's left is his skin and clothing."

"Is that a demon thing?"

"Nope. I think this body was attacked and destroyed by its own nanobots."

"Spontaneously?"

Cassius shook his head. "More likely they were programmed to do this if given the right trigger."

Bishop glanced around. "No Zaki, huh?"

Cassius got to his feet. "Already gone," he said. He bent over and picked up a sword that lay only a few inches from Tesslovich's left hand. "I think this is one of those Angel Slayers things I keep hearing about. Let's wrap it up and take it with us. If I can analyze the poison maybe I can determine how to counteract its effects." He handed the sword to one of the bodyguards, who wrapped it in a scarlet demon skin, which unfortunately seemed the least risky way to carry the weapon.

There was the sound of a muffled explosion, and then another. The Skybox swayed on its supports. Bottles on the buffet table fell over and loose decorative items crashed to the floor.

"What was that?"

"My guess would be the lab," Cassius said. "We need to get to the train before this building goes up as well."

Bishop looked out the Skybox window. The screens in the arena were faltering but most were still broadcasting the battle outside. Even though the outside lights were on and a nearly full moon had finally escaped the clouds gathering over the lake, it remained impossible to tell one Raptor in combat from another. As he watched, a male Raptor plummeted through the opening in the roof to the floor below. His body didn't move. The air began to fill with smoke.

"Ariel," Bishop began, making a vague gesture toward the screens.

C.T. put his hand on Bishop's shoulder. "She's out there with her own kind, Frank. She was trained for this so odds are she'll make it. We can't wait here to find out. You need to come with us."

Bishop nodded. Frankly, there was nothing else he could think of to do.

Ariel crooked her finger at the yellow demon. Her leg had started to throb again, reminding her that putting weight on it was a bad idea. All around her the battle raged on. The wolves, Deepers and released adolescents were mopping up the ground with the lesser demons. They were surrounded and could neither fly, hide or run away.

The angels, or knights, or whatever they were, were battling flying lizards and armored demons who were attacking in groups. The lizards had become both numerous and enormous. The House demons were wily and vicious, but the knights appeared to be a match for both. Ariel had even gotten a glimpse of the Guardian. The old bastard had taken on a couple of armored house demons and seemed to actually be enjoying himself.

Raptors were everywhere, in the air, on the ground, fighting, going to the aid of Deepers, pulling wounded out of the fray. Zaki's prisoners fought right along with their rescuers. They had a lot of scores to settle. The Gargoyles seemed to have wisely disappeared.

To give the yellow demon credit, she'd come to the party expecting an easy win and instead she was fighting for her life. Even with the tide of battle turning, her arrogance was still in place. Ariel could tell that by the disdain with which she killed. She'd wanted to do battle with Archangels and the ones that had come to the fight weren't even flesh and blood.

If Ariel had the yellow demon in her sights, the demon obviously had the same thought about her. Things had been going according to plan for the demons until the mob of Raptors and all their friends arrived. Zaki had orchestrated a show for the other demon houses but he had already struck a deal with the House of Eight. The families of the Eight would have the real technology, the other houses would be given bots programmed to respond to certain outside commands including the destruction of their hosts. In addition, there were bots that could control the will of whole armies of humans or demons. The House of Eight would rule the world as they had done for thousands of years before angels and humans drove them underground. And now look!

The demon looked around for the female Raptor. She wasn't the only female Raptor, but she was the one Zoven hated the most. If the House of Eight was going down to defeat this night, Zoven would make sure this Raptor didn't live to see it.

- 28 -

There was blood on the white tiles of the subway steps and walls. Some of it was red, but most of it wasn't. When Bishop, Cassius and the two guards stepped out onto the platform, the guns on top of the train cars tracked their progress. They put their hands over their heads. It seemed the wisest thing to do.

"Walk forward sir," a voice called. "Keep your hands where we can see them. Are you alone? Is there anyone behind you? What's that you're holding Mr. Kale?"

"We're alone, Jason. I have a demon sword with me. I can lay it on the platform if you want to examine it."

"They're clear," another voice said. "Sorry sir. Just being cautious. Please proceed to the train."

A door slid open and hands helped them inside.

"What's going on here?" Bishop asked.

"We had a demon attack. They used some of our soldiers as shields to get close to the train. We lost people, but so did they. We're not taking any chances no matter who shows up."

"Good idea." Cassius said.

"We sent some kids on ahead of us. Did they . . .?"

"They made it Mr. Bishop. The young ones are over there. The others are helping out with the wounded in the next car. Pitched right in like they'd done it before."

Cassius handed the wrapped sword to one of the guards. "Put this somewhere safe," he said. "Somewhere no one can touch it."

The second and third train cars were full of wounded. The Lab Rats were doing what they could to help, carrying water, passing bandages, holding instruments. Starr was helping stitch someone up. She seemed to know what she was doing.

"She's good," Mouser's voice said as he came up behind Bishop. "The Rats got torn up a lot when they fought. They took care of each other."

Bishop swung around. Mouser was okay! He'd made it! He had an irrational impulse to hug the kid which he suppressed by putting his hands in his pockets.

"So, Starr?" he said to Mouser. "Seems like a keeper, huh?"

Mouser actually blushed. "I need to give the thumb drive to Mr. Kale," he mumbled.

Bishop jerked a thumb toward the first train car and Mouser made a beeline toward the connecting door.

Bishop looked around. Wounded were everywhere. So, were the dead, covered in sheets, waiting for who knew what? The Rapture seemed a long way off.

He spotted Sister Mary Catherine. She'd put an apron over her jeans and sweatshirt and wrapped her hair in a piece of white rag to keep it out of the way. The apron had a considerable amount of blood on it, her face was drawn and there were deep circles under her eyes. She'd come for more bandages and was going back to the last car with them.

Bishop threaded his way through the makeshift stretchers and pallets. "Cate?"

"Frank!" she said. "You're still alive. Thank God for that. I'd toss a few more prayers for you in His direction, but at the moment I'm too busy asking Him to cut the wounded a break."

One of Cassius' men stuck his head through the connecting door. "We're getting ready to move this train out. A larger infirmary has been set up in the Hauptmann garages. Medical staff are standing by. We have ambulances to take the worst cases to a better equipped site where we can operate if necessary. We'll offload these wounded and come back for more. If you have bodies to move into Zaki's train, please do it now. Anybody staying at this end, detrain."

"I'll stay," Sister Catherine called out. "They'll be more wounded before this train comes back." Other Deepers, armed and not, volunteered to stay as well. Mouser, Starr and a couple other Lab Rats got off the train. Bishop found himself reluctantly putting his feet back on the platform. Cassius was standing there.

"I'm going back to my lab for a few things, Frank. We'll send more medical supplies, water, and a fresh team back with the train. You sure you want to stay?"

Bishop looked over at Mouser and Starr and Sister Catherine. "If they're staying I'm staying."

Sister Catherine climbed into the temporary morgue car on Zaki's train followed by Bishop, Mouser and Starr. She had a bowl of clean water in her hands and she'd pulled her rosary out from under her shirt. She began to bless the dead. Bishop waved Starr, Mouser and the other Rats out of the car. This wasn't a job for kids.

"Take five," he told them. "Get some water. Have a sit. There'll be plenty more to do in a little while. And guys? Stay frosty. The demons came in this way, and more may try to leave this way."

Bishop was glad to see Deepers with automatic weapons crawling onto the top of Zaki's fancy train. No one was taking any chances on being surprised.

- 29 -

Bodies were laid out side by side in the makeshift morgue car. Most were uncovered only because the sheets were needed for the wounded. Some bodies were demons from the earlier attack. Sister Catherine drew the sign of the cross on their foreheads and said a prayer over them the same as if they were human. After a few bodies, the bowl of water had a dirty pink tinge and was starting to tremble in her hand. Bishop stepped forward to take it from her, so she'd have both hands free to do her work. She was almost finished when she got to a large body covered by a ragged piece of tarp. As she leaned over it, a gnarled hand shot out and grabbed her by the throat. The demon started to sit up. Bishop dropped the bowl of water and grabbed for his Glock. He shot the demon twice, then a third time just to be sure. He had to pry the creature's fingers off Sister Catherine's neck, breaking a couple in the process. The nun was unconscious.

"Help!" he yelled. "Need a little help in here!"

Mouser, Starr and a Deeper helped him move Sister Catherine to the next car. It was one of the plush ones with upholstered benches and overstuffed chairs. The bar had already been raided for alcohol and water for the infirmary.

"Frank?"

"Right here Catie. You're okay. He just knocked you out. You need to rest.

"But . . ."

"If you haven't been formally introduced, this is Mouser, and this is his friend Starr. They're going to sit with you while me and a couple of my pals make sure there are no more surprises in the morgue."

Just as he stepped out of the car he heard another shot. Two Deepers jumped out of the morgue car.

"Just makin' sure," one of them said. "I guess if we get more demons down here we'll need to assign a watch dog to guard their dead."

There was another explosion overhead. A huge cloud of smoke, dirt and dust blew down the subway stairs onto the platform. The lights over the tracks blinked and swayed. Tiles fell out of the ceiling and broke when they hit the ground. People were coughing and pulling their shirts over their mouths and noses until the worst of it settled.

"Whoa!" somebody said.

"Zaki has officially left the building," Bishop announced. "He must have planted a few bombs as a farewell present."

"What about our people upstairs?"

"This stairway's blocked," somebody yelled. "We might be able to get a couple people through the rubble if we have to, hard to tell."

"The fight is pretty much outside now. Do you know if there's another way out of this tunnel besides up the stairs or back the way we came?"

"The plans say the tracks dead end up ahead." Mouser offered.

"Let's hope the plans are wrong. I'll need flashlights and a couple of guys."

The light and the track ended a scant ten feet from the engine of Zaki's train. The tunnel beyond looked like a gaping black hole in space, one that promised to suck you into its darkest heart and never let go.

Bishop and the two-armed Deepers pulled Infra-red goggles into place. Mouser and Starr and the other Rats seemed to have no problem negotiating the dark. Bishop had given up on trying to keep Mouser or the Rats out of danger; they were probably better equipped to deal with what was going on than he was.

Bishop adjusted the strap on his goggles. All they seemed to do was show him a dim green hole instead of a totally black one. The platform seemed to continue into it, hopefully right to the end. He much preferred to be three feet above the track than down on the cinders where god-knew-what was waiting. Behind him he heard one of the Deepers trip over something and curse.

"I see something up ahead," Mouser called over his shoulder.

The tunnel ended at some sort of iron scaffold. Bishop was trying to puzzle out its use when he was blinded by a sudden explosion of light.

"Aaagh!"

"Sorry." When all the flashing purple spots cleared Bishop could see Mouser standing next to a panel of buttons mounted to the wall. "I think it's an elevator," he said. He pushed another button and a flat platform with a railing on two sides began to rise to the level of the train platform where it stopped.

Bishop stepped onto it. It was solid, and its surface was gouged and scratched as if heavy objects had been rolled over it. He looked up and could see metal doors set in a stone ceiling about twenty feet in the air.

"Is there a button labeled doors?" he asked. "Don't push it until . . ."

The doors in the ceiling started to open.

". . . I tell you to. Turn off the lights!"

The tunnel went dark. The group stood and watched as the night sky appeared overhead.

"Where do you think this comes out?" Mouser asked.

One of the Deepers shrugged. "Near the parking lot? If they move things in and out this way they'd need a hard surface for the trucks."

Bishop motioned everyone onto the platform. "Might as well take a look," he said. "Let's hope nobody noticed the doors opening."

The first thing Bishop saw was that the fighting had stopped. There were still Raptors in the air, but most of the bodies on the ground weren't moving. Off to one side, a pyre was blazing with blue-white flames. There was no smoke, no crackling of wood or flight of ash and no matter how high the flames reached, they were unaffected by the breeze that was starting to come up off the water.

There was very little sound. The large stone knights seemed focused on gathering up dead demons and the occasional lizard and adding them to the pyre. Raptors were flying to and fro above the rolling lawn and woods. They were searching out and bringing in their own wounded and dead.

"It's over." A familiar voice said behind Bishop. Bishop turned to see Cassius standing behind him.

"I thought you had things to do."

"I did," he answered. "And I guess this was one of them."

The small group moved forward. They received a few glances, but no one really paid them much attention.

"Get our medics up here with stretchers," Cassius said to one of the Rats. "We'll take the living first and then our dead."

A group of Raptors and two or three wolves were moving from body to body, separating the wounded from the dead. Dead demons were being toted to the pyre and tossed in. Dead humans and wolves were moved to one side and laid carefully on their backs with eyes closed. Raptors were being laid out side by side, arms crossed on their chests, their bodies carefully wrapped in their wings creating a chrysalis from which no butterfly would ever emerge.

Mouser broke into a run. He didn't want to look at the dead. He wanted to find Ariel. A living, breathing Ariel. Hurt, unconscious, he didn't care. But alive.

He darted over and around the yet unsorted bodies covering the ground yelling "El!" "El!" A wounded demon grabbed for his foot. Mouser kicked it away.

Bishop found himself right behind Mouser. He was looking for any familiar face, Ez, Dingo, Juke, Old Bill. A figure stepped out from a crowd of Raptors and Deepers gathered around something in the middle of the battle field. It was Dingo. Bishop headed straight for him. Dingo was upright, but still furry. He tried to catch Bishop's arm, but Bishop spun away from him. He followed Mouser who burrowed through the arms and legs to see what was being blocked from view.

"El!" Mouser screamed. His voice had a note of anguish that turned Bishop's blood cold.

"Stop, boy!" A furry arm grabbed Mouser around the waist and held him until he stopped struggling.

Tomas was on his knees on the ground. He'd dropped his sword and the bottoms of his wings were dragging in the dirt. He was torn and battered but not nearly to the degree of the fallen Raptor he was holding in his arms.

Ariel had spiraled to the ground as she fell. Her legs were twisted together, arms splayed out on her open, bloody wings. Her face was still as death, bruised and swollen in some places, tight and pale blue as fine porcelain in others. Her body was bleeding from multiple wounds. Twenty feet away from her lay an unmoving yellow demon dressed in House of Eight armor. Ariel's sword was buried to the hilt in her chest.

The Guardian stood at the edge of the circle. His face had no expression.

"Get Ham," Tomas pleaded. "He'll know what to do!" He put his fingers on the artery at Ariel's throat.

Dingo literally tossed Mouser to Bishop and took off at a run.

"She's still alive!" Tomas yelled.

"It's too late, Tomas," The Guardian said. Brother Gregory dressed in his usual brown robe and carrying a canvas satchel over one shoulder scuttled up to The Guardian and said something in a whisper. The Guardian shook his head. Gregory said something again, but more insistently. The Guardian waved him off.

Ham arrived. He took one look, knelt down and started pulling boxes and packets out of his medic bag. He lifted one eye lid, then the other. He ripped Ariel's bloody pant leg up to her waist with a large knife, tore open her shirt and started packing the wounds with white powder. He yelled for water and a stretcher.

Mouser's body relaxed. "You can let go of me now," he said. Bishop's fingers felt cramped and numb when he relaxed his hands. He'd had no idea how tightly he'd been hanging on to the boy.

"We're taking her back to the train," Cassius announced. In the confusion, and the transfer of a winged Ariel from ground to stretcher, Bishop might have been the only one to see Brother Gregory slip something from his bag into Ham's furry paw.

Cassius took one handle of the stretcher, Tomas took the other. A Deeper and Dingo took the other end. Tomas wasn't looking very good himself. He stumbled once but refused to relinquish his hold on the stretcher.

"You okay, son?" Cassius asked him.

"We can't let her die," Tomas said. "You have all that stuff in your lab. You can give her something, right?"

"I swear I'll do everything in my power to keep you and your friend alive and safe." Cassius said. "Everything."

The trains were loaded as quickly as possible. The Deepers took their wounded and the worst of the wounded Raptors. They took the freed prisoners, including the Rats and the young demon who'd been stuck with knives. On the last trip they took their dead.

The Guardian had offered to burn their dead, but Cassius said no. There were goodbyes to be said and they had their own ways in the Deeps.

Cassius left Ariel with Sister Catherine and returned to the lift and rode it to the top to find Bishop. The knights had set flame to the arena and the lab building. The structures burned white hot with no noise or smoke until they were nothing but ash.

"What will the police think happened here?" Bishop asked him.

Cassius shrugged. "A devastating lab accident? Science is so weird and dangerous to most people, it could have been anything, especially with no traces left behind."

The remaining Raptors rose into the air. It was time to get wherever they were going before dawn. Brother Gregory stopped by to tell Cassius that The Guardian would be interested in speaking with him after all this inconvenience was over and done with. Cassius waved him off. Bishop gave the monk a nod. Brother Gregory just tucked his head and scurried away.

The two men stood and watched the stone knights lift the corners of a golden net. Its contents flopped and heaved like caught fish. The knights rose in unison carrying a net full of live demons out over the lake until they were a mere speck on the horizon.

"Let's go," Cassius said. "I think we're through here."

"It's not over is it?" Bishop asked.

"Not even close."

The sound of birds and the rays of early morning light woke the little man. He was lying on sand, half-in, half-out of the water in a patch of reeds on a deserted beach. He was wet, and his suit was burned black in some places and torn in others. He was missing a shoe and half the hair on one side of his head. Both eyebrows had been burned totally away. He managed to crawl onto his knees and staggered from there to his feet. The last thing he remembered was being in a boat going really fast, running for his life, then nothing. He looked around. There was no one else in the water or on the beach, alive or dead, but he could hear the sound of cars so there must be a road nearby. He felt his inner vest pocket. His knives were safe. But the most important thing was he was alive and everyone else in the boat was obviously dead.

His survival could be nothing less than a sign, an omen. Unlike his stupid brothers, he had always been lucky. He had always been the one destined by fate to be rich and famous. Otherwise he would be dead too. He started to walk toward the road. He would hitchhike into town, he decided. He would get money and buy new clothes. He would sharpen his knives and he would practice until he was better than he'd ever been. Then he would find the man Bishop who was responsible for all the things that had happened to him and he would finally take what was his. He would take his revenge.

*Thank you for reading **Raptor**. I hope you enjoyed it. If you did, I would really appreciate it if you posted a review.*

Raptor is the first book in a trilogy.

Below is a preview of Book Two that will be published Winter of 2018.

BITERS

– 1 –

Ariel could feel the poison on the blade of the yellow demon's sword spreading its venom throughout her body. She had managed to block a killing blow and use the last remnant of her strength to drive her sword through the demon's heart, pinning her to the ground. She took one final step, wavered for a moment, then collapsed within an arm's length of her dead enemy. Ariel, Raptor of her City, took one final breath, and floated into a sea of impenetrable darkness.

– 2 –

Bishop leaned back in his squeaky wooden desk chair, lifted his feet onto his desk and crossed his ankles. If he'd owned a fedora he would have tilted it down over his eyes for a brief nap. If it had been the 1930s and he was Sam Spade, this would have been the cue for a tall, blonde bombshell to walk into his office and beg him for help. When he heard the office door open he raised one eyelid hoping to see the babe of his dreams, but all he got was his old partner, Vice Detective First Class Ray (Rain) Mann, and the smell of takeout Chinese.

Rain gave Bishop's office the once-over. Bishop couldn't blame him. The last time Rain had been inside his office it had just been trashed by a homicidal, knife throwing circus gypsy whose calling card was a severed goat head stuffed with a curse. Bishop had to replace everything except his desk, which was solid oak and must have weighed over two-hundred pounds, making it hard to destroy.

"I'd say you redecorated the place, except it looks exactly the same as it always has." Rain dropped a newspaper and a brown paper bag on Bishop's desk. The newspaper covered a deep, triangular knife hole in the surface of the desk that Bishop had never bothered to fix. The knife had held the goat head upright so it's dead, yellow eyes could stare balefully at the office door.

"Do you still have the Maltese Falcon in your bottom drawer?"

"You never learn," Bishop said. "The Maltese Falcon goes in the file cabinet. I have a fifth of cheap whiskey in the bottom drawer of my desk."

"You got a laptop too. Isn't modern technology against the rules of the Ancient Gumshoe Brotherhood?"

"I'm charmingly retro, but not a fanatic." Bishop pulled the newspaper toward him with one finger. The headline read 'Dumpster Killer Strikes Again'. He minimized the solitaire game he'd been playing and closed the lid of the computer. It had cost six-hundred dollars, plus tax and software, and he had no idea how to use most of its functions, but it was a lot easier to type reports on than his desktop or his 1940's manual Underwood that now sat in a place of honor on his bookcase. His old, faithful PC had been tossed out his office window during the trashing. Luckily, he'd been insured.

Bishop swung his feet off the desk as Rain pulled up a chair. His old partner was elegantly dressed as usual: his pale blue shirt and Navy pinstripe suit set off his mocha skin and unusual blue eyes. Bishop eyed the white cartons Rain began to set out on the one section of the newspaper. He inhaled the odor of exotic, stir-fried grease and spices.

"My momma always told me I should beware of policemen bearing gifts, especially Chinese food from Kung Foo Garden and Laundry Emporium, which just happens to be one of my personal favorites." Bishop said.

"Your momma had wisdom."

"She was the terror of our neighborhood and you know it. The parish priest crossed to the other side of the street when she was out on the porch. What's up?"

"Well, first off, I've been promoted."

"Out of the Seventeenth?" Bishop was shocked. The 17th Precinct was a rat hole, but it had been home to both of them until Bishop was fired for insubordination and refusal to be on the take.

"Naw, I'm not that lucky. Out of Vice into Robbery Homicide."

"Congratulations?" It was more of a question than a statement.

"Yeah. Thanks." Rain was rubbing his disposable wooden chopsticks together to get rid of the splinters before he attacked his carton of Pineapple Prawn Chow Fun. Bishop had always found that particular dish too sweet for his taste, plus, he had a hard time keeping the slippery noodles from falling off his chopsticks into his lap, which was embarrassing. "But I think the Captain's happier to have me counting dead bodies and chasing down stick-up artists than having my Vice snitches telling me who's paying off what to whom and how much."

Bishop pushed his laptop to the side of the desk to make room for the food. He began to help himself to rice and the Garden's Special Kung Foo Pork with Szechwan pepper sauce and walnuts.

"The Captain's still on the take? What a surprise."

"Other than being a weasely coward and backstabbing son-of-a-bitch . . ." Rain delicately fished a prawn, a wide Chow Fun noodle and piece of pineapple from the carton with his chop sticks and moved them into his mouth without difficulty. He chewed and swallowed. ". . . the Captain also has a serious gambling problem and a lot of bad luck. The big boys have him firmly in their pocket. He does whatever they tell him. In just two months, three of my Vice busts have just evaporated into thin air like piss on a griddle, and they smelled just as bad. Evidence disappeared, witnesses recanted, the District Attorney refused to file charges. Screw it, I'm much happier in Homicide . . . up 'til lately that is."

Bishop used his chopsticks to pull over the third carton of food. "Red Snapper in Lobster sauce." He was impressed. "You must want something."

"Hey, you owe me one."

"More than one bro, so stop beating around the twice cooked pork and tell me what you need."

"Okay, just to catch up on recent events so we're both on the same page. You were involved in whatever happened with Zaki Kiriyenko, right? Dude dopes his race horse and starts running the fight club from hell on his estate, then he just totally disappears along with most of the buildings on the property. Only thing left by the time the police and CFD got there is a big pile of ash. And two days later, you show up like the Pied Piper of the Apocalypse with a bunch of missin' kids that Zaki allegedly kidnapped for evil purposes."

"Just doing what I was hired to do by the families, returning their kids."

"Before that, you got cursed by a midget circus freak, and one of my snitches feels compelled to give you a charm against demons."

"He was a short gypsy knife thrower, and you were the one who dragged me to Madam Zebella's Good Fortune Con Shop to get rid of the curse," Bishop said.

"Then there's your 'martial arts teacher'. Smokin' hot but scary, like she might be some kind of secret CIA assassin."

"Actually, she's a winged super hero who fights the forces of darkness to save humanity." Bishop stabbed a piece of Snapper in Lobster sauce with one chopstick and stuck it into his mouth. He figured he'd better eat it now. If Rain was going to arrest him for the alleged body in his alleged rental car, the cops probably wouldn't let him take leftovers into the jail.

"Very funny." Rain obviously didn't believe in super heroes.

Bishop sighed. It was time to get Rain to the point. "Are you asking me for my help or trying to make a case against me for associating with hotties and weirdoes?"

"I'm just sayin' if something freaky is goin' on in this town you probably know a lot more about it than I do. Or you know somebody who does."

Bishop turned the bag the food had come in upside down. Two fortune cookies rolled out onto the desk, one landed right in front of him. He tore open the cellophane, cracked the cookie and pulled out a thin strip of paper. It had a lucky lottery number on one side, Bishop had never had much luck playing one of those, so he turned it over to read the fortune. The words were in red ink. Probably some kind of edible food coloring in case you were idiot enough to eat the cookie. The fortune said: 'You are about to start a dangerous adventure.'

He dropped the slip of paper and looked at Rain who said, "You really got a bottle of rye in your desk?"

"Why don't you start at the beginning," Bishop told him as he leaned over to pull open the bottom drawer.

– 3 –

"Billy Goat Gruff Malt Whiskey?" Rain read off the bottle. "That's got to be swill." Rain didn't drink or smoke, he gambled, and he was convinced that alcohol and cigarettes would interfere with his ability to calculate the odds.

"Actually, it's more like irony," Bishop said. He hadn't forgotten the cursed goat head the little man had left on his desk during the hunt for the kidnapped children. He put one elbow on his desk and propped his chin in the palm of his hand. "So, let me get this straight," he poured himself a shot. "You've just discovered a forth adult male, killed in exactly the same way as three others: he was robbed, drained of blood and thrown in a city dumpster. You don't know precisely where any of the victims were killed because there was no blood at the scene and no one knew they were in the dumpsters until the garbage trucks delivered their load to the landfill in Westport.

"Right."

Bishop tapped the newspaper. "You obviously have either a serial killer, or some kind of drug war execution thing on your hands. I can't see why homicide would need my help on that."

"Yeah, but see, what we're tryin' to keep quiet is that all the bodies were covered with bites."

"This city is full of rats, dude. They chew on what's thrown in dumpsters all the time, including dead bodies."

"The bites weren't caused by rats, Frank. The coroner said they were made by a whole different kind of teeth. The bites were also in places where the arterial blood supply was closest to the surface of the skin."

Bishop felt a creepy feeling crawl up his spine. He poured himself another shot. "So," he said, "Four bodies. Most of Homicide is thinking 'crazed serial killer'. But you came here to ask me about this because you think, based on my sordid history, I must know somebody who might know something about, let me guess, some sort of mutant creature with a craving for blood?"

Rain looked uncomfortable. "Well, you seem to attract some pretty strange cases, and I have a responsibility to look at all the possibilities, even if one is pretty far out there. Call it a hunch."

"You don't play hunches, Rain. You play the odds. There must be more you're not telling me, and I can't help if you won't tell me all of it."

"Okay then, here's the kicker, but this is absolutely confidential. The teeth marks? They indicate there's probably more than one biter involved. Based on the size of the bites," Rain continued, "the bites were made by an animal the size of a Labrador Receiver or humans the size of four to five-year-old children."

– 4 –

Bishop made the turn through the bent and broken gates that marked the entrance to The Gates of Eden, Zaki Kirienko's estate. They gaped wide open on torn hinges. The two metal figures on the gate were still reaching out toward the apple and the snake. The tall stone pillars that had supported the gates were still wrapped in yellow police tape. Bishop was happy to see that Gargoyles no longer perched on top of them, and he hoped they never would again. The guardhouse was a melted mass of steel and plastic, and Cassius Kale had an armed guard on duty, just in case rubberneckers or a stray demon showed up. Bishop rolled down his window.

"Mr. Bishop?" The guard asked, looking at his clip board. "Mr. Kale is waiting for you at the house. Just follow the driveway . . ."

Bishop raised a hand. "I know where it is," he said.

The house was virtually untouched by the battle that had happened on the estate a little more than a month ago. Everything but the house had been laid to waste. The lab, office buildings, the arena, the Zoo and Golarium were gone. Even the sub-basements had been reduced to holes in the ground.

Bishop got out of his car and knocked on the half open door. Cassius himself pulled it open and invited him inside. The entry hall was spacious, its floor was set in alternating squares of black and white marble. An oval, Louis XIV table sat in the exact center of the hall and still held a large, blue and white Chinese vase filled with dead flowers. A double staircase wound upward from either side of the room to join a wide balcony that jutted out over the double doors to a large living room. The furniture was dusty, but expensive. Bishop was no expert, but even he could see there must be tens of thousands of dollars of antiques in the house.

"You must think it strange that I came back here," Cassius said as he led Bishop through the living room toward the back of the house. "I'm afraid I can't offer you anything in the way of refreshment, the lease on the house was just signed yesterday and I haven't had a chance to stock it."

"You're renting Zaki's estate?" Bishop was dumbfounded.

"Well, one of my companies is. It's a shell corporation, many times removed from anything directly connected to me. It seemed like a good idea considering that there's a tunnel connecting the property to the Tesslovich mansion and the Hauptmann Department Store." Cassius waved a hand, his gesture seeming to encompass the house and all its contents. "It came furnished. I have an option to buy it and Tesslovich's house as soon as all the legal bits are worked out. Zaki Enterprises has declared bankruptcy in the United States and is liquidating its assets."

"I thought you sealed the tunnel after we took out the wounded."

Bishop and Cassius were moving quickly through a large dining room containing an enormous Chippendale dining table, twelve chairs and sideboard. "It was a quick job," Cassius said, "and mostly cosmetic so the police wouldn't track the tunnel back to the closed subway stations and the Deeps. Let's go through the kitchen, it will be faster."

"Where are you taking me?" Bishop asked uneasily.

"Outside." Cassius grabbed a leather satchel sitting on the kitchen counter near the backdoor. "I need to collect a few more samples before the next storm hits."

Bishop frowned, stuck his hands in his trouser pockets and followed.

It was a long walk from the house to the site of the lab and arena complex. Bishop could see that great drifts of ash covered the ground and filled the holes left by the building's sub basements. The ash was deeper on the sloping lawn where the bodies of demons and Raptors had been set alight by cold, blue Angel Fire. The white ash puffed around their feet like clouds of fine dust. It didn't cling to their shoes or trousers like Bishop would have expected. Instead, it fell back into place as soon as they'd passed. Cassius reached into his satchel and brought out a glass jar. He removed the lid and stooped to fill it with two inches of ash. He held the jar up for Bishop's inspection.

"Weightless," he said. "Odorless, tasteless, inert. It has no trace of what was burned, nor does it have any other discernible properties, animal, vegetable, mineral or synthetic." He removed another jar filled with a colorless liquid and poured that into the jar with the ash. The ash immediately dissolved, leaving the liquid at the same original volume. "It dissolves in water, leaving the water the same volume as it was before the ash was added." Cassius looked down the lawn at the sky. A dark, pregnant mass of clouds was moving in from across the lake. "A good deal of it is already gone, this storm should just about finish it off. It will vanish into the earth like it was never here."

Bishop looked around. So much death had happened in this place; so many lost, before and after. And in the end, the head monster got clean away. "Is this why you asked me to come here? To watch the last bit of evidence, disappear?"

"No," Cassius straightened up, put the last few bottles of ash into his satchel and looped the strap over his shoulder. "I asked you here to tell you that Ariel has disappeared."

"What?!"

"She disappeared from the infirmary in the middle of the night. No one saw her go. There's no word on the street about where she might have gone or been taken."

"You think she may have been kidnapped?"

"By whom? The Guardian has no reason to believe she's still alive, otherwise he wouldn't have just appointed Tomas the new Raptor of the City. She won't take that very well when she finds out you know."

"Understatement of the year, but if The Guardian found out Brother Gregory slipped her the antidote, God only knows what the consequences might be."

"Well, obviously we can't report her as a missing person. But I thought, you being a private detective, maybe you could try and find her before she does something . . . impulsive."

Bishop massaged his temples. An angry and impulsive Ariel on the loose was a migraine in the making. "And you had to tell me this in the middle of the killing fields because . . ."

"You never know who might be listening." Cassius started back toward the house.

"Are you going to live here?" Bishop asked.

Cassius looked around. The first rain drops were hitting the ash creating small holes in its perfect surface causing more and more of it to dissolve. "No, I don't think that would be wise. But I plan to put this place to good use."

– 5 –

Bishop couldn't help but think about Ariel on the drive back to the city. He had to admit to himself that she was important to him. Not romantically he told himself, but because she was fierce and brave and reckless and took no shit from anyone. And she had wings, what could be more awesome than that? He'd accepted what she was and the world she lived in, although that world had sometimes scared the shit out of him. It had been three days since he'd stopped by the infirmary to see her. She had still been in the coma, but her fingers had moved when he touched her hand. It had given him hope. Now she had disappeared. Whatever he had to do he was going to get her back.

Bishop's first stop was the Caf'. The Caf' was in a half-underground basement that catered to hackers and homeless street kids. Its shabby appointments hadn't changed since Bishop had been taken there by Ariel and introduced to the adolescents that called it home. He walked down its steps and pushed the door open. Ez, the old werewolf who kept an eye on everything that happened in the Caf', raised his head from the book he was reading, pulled a mug from under the counter and started to fill it with coffee. Mouser and Starr, who had been joined at the hip ever since both were rescued from Zaki's lab, were sitting head to head over Mouser's laptop. Bishop would have to break the spell they were under before they noticed him. He acknowledged Ez and the coffee and walked over to Mouser's favorite table and put a hand on his shoulder. The young hacker jumped at his touch and knocked heads with Starr, who punched him in the arm.

"Ow and Ow!" Mouser said, rubbing both places. "Don't sneak up on a guy like that, Bish." He looked at Starr. "That's going to leave a bruise y' know."

"Pussy." Starr said. But she said it with a trace of affection. Letting your boyfriend know you really like him is so 1970s.

Young love, Bishop thought. Giving them this information is going to be hard. "Can we go over to the counter?" Bishop asked. "I have to talk to you two and Ez about something."

"Is Ariel . . ." Mouser's eyes were wide with alarm.

"No. I'll tell you what happened.," Bishop said. "Go take a stool."

Ez pushed the coffee cup toward Bishop, who took a grateful sip before beginning to talk.

"Ariel has disappeared from the infirmary. She either woke up last night and left under her own power, although that seems unlikely after a month in a coma, or she was taken away."

"No!" Mouser said.

Ez was more practical. "Who would take her? Only a few of us know where she was. Raptors are pretty resilient. She could be awake and okay, or she could be wandering the streets, alone and confused. Maybe she went home."

"That's my next stop," Bishop said. "But I wanted to let you to know. I thought you guys could maybe put a posse together. They'd need to be sworn to secrecy. A blood oath might not be too extreme under the circumstances. But let me check a few more places before you notify the troops. If I can find her first, our secret can stay safe."

Mouser looked like he might tear up. Bishop knew this was much too close to his own abduction to be a lab rat at Zaki Enterprises. He gulped the rest of his coffee and took Mouser by the shoulders. "We'll find her," he said. "Whether it's easy or hard. I promise."

Snapping his fingers, Mouser suddenly said, "Cameras! I can hack any camera in the city. There will be cameras near the infirmary and ones all over the place for traffic control or security purposes. Some of them are bound to pick up her trail."

"Good man." Bishop told him. "I'm going to check with the Bad Dogs and look at her apartment. I'll stay in touch."

ABOUT THE AUTHOR

B.A. Bostick is an enthusiastic fan and author of urban fantasy. Her stories have appeared in anthologies and the first episode of her new Vampire novel *Take My Breath Away* and her fractured fairytale *Reptyle Dysfunction* are available on Amazon.

Bostick lives in Northern New Mexico, the Land of Enchantment

Visit the author online

Website: www.babostick.com

Facebook page: https://www.facebook.com/baBostickAuthor/